THE K

20TH CENTURY
HUNGARIAN SHORT STORIES

THE KISS

20TH CENTURY
HUNGARIAN SHORT STORIES

CORVINA

Published by Corvina Books Ltd.
Budapest V, Vörösmarty tér 1, Hungary 1051

Selected by István Bart

Translated from the Hungarian
by László T. András, Patricia Bozsó, Paula Balo, Martha Cowan,
G. F. Cushing, Thomas J. DeKornfeld, István Farkas, Zsuzsanna Horn,
László Jakabfy, Jascha Kessler, Susan Kun, Etelka Láczay, Edna Lénárt,
Zsuzsa Madarassy-Beck, Eszter Molnár, Charlotte Rogers, Ivan Sanders,
Judith Sollosy, Peter Szente, Paul Tábori, Albert Tezla,
Christopher C. Wilson, Katharina M. Wilson.

© Corvina Books, 1995
Péter Nádas, "Family Portrait against a Purple Sunset",
courtesy Rowohlt. Berlin Verlag
ISBN 963 13 4099 6

CONTENTS

THE KISS

FROM THE TALES OF AN AGEING JOURNALIST

by ENDRE ADY

Inscribed on a tombstone you can read, *"Here dwells Rozália Mihályi. She lived twenty-six years. Peace be to her ashes. 'I will go and be with Christ, for that is best beyond all things.'"*

Rozália Mihályi—may the good earth be kind to her—she was an insignificant lass of the theatre while she lived. She dyed her red hair, as I have since learned, but her lips were naturally ruddy. She laughed loudly and merrily, though not with a light heart; the gentlemen of the theatrical board liked their chorus girls to be gay. She was the disinherited daughter of a Lutheran minister, and Death terrified her only because she would not get to play in the operetta *Touch Me Not*. For five years running she had been promised the part by managers, directors, even critics. *Touch Me Not* cost her more kisses than love, money, and her *toilette* combined. Yet she died, poor thing, with her great ambition unfulfilled, and she flooded her death bed at the hospital with tears.

The other paraphernalia of Death did not concern Rozália Mihályi, for she was a reckless woman. Now she lies at Arad or Kassa, I will not say where, or since when. I never met Rozália Mihályi, yet no woman looms larger in my life; the story, too, that I am about to relate is a story about her, small yet deep as any mountain lake. The real heroine of this story, then, is Rozália Mihályi, who is now with Christ, for that is best beyond all things.

*

I had already asked Marcella Kun eight times to kiss me and to say that she held me dear. Being an aspiring second primadonna, she could turn it to her advantage. After all, I wrote the reviews.

She was a dark-haired girl, clever and open-minded; moreover, she probably did not find me repulsive. At most, my embraces would not overjoy her; and then, too, she saw the trouble ahead.

I was a most virile lad at the time and made no bones about the fact that I was a veritable madman in my lovemaking. Let her whom I chose for myself also go mad and scream with joy, and let her boast of it afterwards.

Marcella Kun was right to fear this, she who had contrived to keep her porcelain complexion white till then, during and in spite of all embraces. There were times when I told her what I had dreamt about her, and that I considered her the most desirable cushion in Creation, the resting place, the haven, the harbour where a man should rest, and where he would willingly rest for ever.

In short, Marcella Kun was afraid of me, and because she was afraid of me, I had free access to the hotel room where she lived. She admitted me into her presence even when she was taming her wild, coarse black hair with a variety of combs. By degrees I won the right to hold this strong, black hair, which mocked her delicate frame, up to my cheek. If, however, the proximity of Marcella Kun's neck, shoulders, and indeed her entire little body intoxicated me unduly, I received a chiding.

"Would it satisfy you, Sir, to ravish me, body and soul, and hear me call you a rogue? Would you have such plundered success, such loveless love? Well, would you?"

At such times I trembled and wept; and above all, I wept because I was such a foolish, weak man. A woman like her occasions different treatment. But I craved another kind of woman in her, better, generous, and infatuated, whereas her eyes, dark Marcella Kun's eyes, were blue, cold unfeeling bad blue eyes. They had never turned up in their sockets, I felt, they had never been stunned with love. "Just you wait, you bad, blue eyes, just you wait! I am after your fire."

I promised myself I'd end this farce. After all, I am no male Marcella Kun. I did not learn the ways of love so I would know what love was, but so I could consume it, and burn myself with it, as is only right. And so, one fine day I said to Marcella Kun, "Marcie,"—that was my petname for her,—"tomorrow afternoon you will admit no one but me. I will have exclusive entry. You will receive no one but me tomorrow afternoon."

Such mighty preparations and preprogrammed bravery,

though, I recommend only to men with fine, barbaric constitutions. My own mighty prearrangements and pretended courage resulted in a cursed, demented night. I was a most weary fellow the next day, and in the afternoon, knocked on Marcella Kun's door only to save face.

She wept. No matter. Her bad blue eyes grew soft and moist, and so blue, they were almost brown. When I entered she grew faint and was unable to stand, and—there could be no doubt about it—at that moment, she even hated me. I would have liked to cradle the diminutive, pale-black, foolish little thing in my lap and rock her gently like a baby, to sing to her in a melancholy voice so she could sleep, so I could sleep, for the night had been a bad one. I would have liked to sing a lullaby something like this, *"Marcie, little Marcie, let us not kiss. What's the use of kissing? Marcie, little Marcie, I will tuck you in, and we will touch cheeks and feel our tears mingle like two silly infants. Marcie, little Marcie, all I want is to cry with you today, to howl with all my might."*

But man is a pitiful creature who must love even when he feels no real inclination. So I sat down by Marcella Kun's side and with great, pretended passion, proceeded to bite her lip. Her sole response was to insist on the advisability of pressing a perfectly clean white linen handkerchief to where it bled. Feeble and sad, she stood up, and when she had found the handkerchief, came back, but as if she had just received a fatal wound and were heading for Calvary.

I unpinned her hair, she suffered it, but all the while she spoke in the devout manner of old women telling their rosaries.

"I know you men. I know how futile it is to talk, cry, or plead. So be it. But I do not want this thing. It brings me no joy. It is painful. However, you are all of a feather. Dearly have I paid every time I have had anything to do with a man, especially one whom I loathed, but I had to, the one who wrecked my body, too."

I heard yet heard not what she was saying, for I was kissing her slippers by then. For man is a pitiful creature who is capable of love even if a moment before he had no appetite for it. I felt compelled to seek out her eyes, to gaze up at her face—and thought I had surely gone mad. For Marcella Kun's eyes were no longer blue but nearly black, her hair was red, her lips were like rubies.

She was other than herself, and for a moment or two, we were both clearly bewitched.

(Of course, today I know that Rozália Mihályi had come to work this witchcraft. I recognize her perfectly from the descriptions of those whom I had encountered and interviewed since, those who knew her very well, this, the grandest, the mightiest woman in my life.)

I did not have my fill of Marcella Kun that afternoon, but I did not yet crave the memory of her kisses, fine as they were, I still say so today, I dare say so. Of course, they were mournful and sad, too, whereas men of my disposition go in pursuit of the kiss expressly to be delivered of sadness. I nevertheless saw her again when in my blood our kiss had already become like a goblet that remembered too late to overflow. My blood sprouted roses, blazing, wrathful, abundant roses of love.

(Horrible! Horrible! I can see it again; again, Marcella Kun was like the descriptions of Rozália Mihályi. Again, we embraced, but now I loved a chimera, not her, a red haired, full-lipped, dark eyed Other. Marcella Kun was there, too, but Rozália Mihályi was far more substantially there. And someone else seemed to have joined us as well, someone all three of us loathed...)

Marcella Kun bowed her head, kissed me and said, "It is all the same now. You asked for it. I warned you!"

I asked her whom she had in mind that time when her talk fell on my deaf ears.

"I was in Győr at the time, and he was a journalist," she said, "and the manager's friend. He said I must, he'll have me thrown out otherwise, and there would be no place for me anywhere in the country."

Marcella Kun even told me the name of the man, and I was overjoyed, as you can imagine! A zero, a non-entity, oh! It was well worth receiving the souvenir of one of his amorous adventures into my blood!

I thought of ways not to take it too much to heart; it was all so singular, so fascinating, after all. But malignant and spiteful, my health, like Job's health by now, raged with resentment. ("Whose kiss has come between us, pernicious and noxious, between myself and Marcella Kun? There is someone here I must go in search of, there is someone I have yet to find. Great secrets lie hidden here. After much exertion I manage to obtain a kiss, and what happens? Someone who has beaten me to the mark goes and poisons my kisses.")

Marcella Kun did not lament overmuch with me. On the contrary, she seemed gratified. What is more, at this moment I wanted her so desperately, had they brought me the purest vestals of Aphrodite, I could not have cared less. In thought I craved just one thing, to be outrageously wicked.

"Well, my virginal angel, will you reveal the whereabouts of your lover, the man so worthy of you?"

She was not shocked. She was not furious. She just told me where he was to be found.

("I'm off. I'm off in pursuit of the scoundrel," I thought. "After all, what should a man keep a track of if not his own kisses? Let me learn who had sent him to Marcella Kun, so Marcella Kun should later tell me that she had already exchanged a fatal kiss.")

I had heard about him. He was a journalist, a Hungarian from Pest, ignorant, mean, and Jewish. He talked big at first, but a couple of good slaps in the face, and he turned meek as a lamb.

"You knew Marcella Kun. But who came before her, you impudent scoundrel, you cur?"

A submissive confession followed. He beat his breast and presently divulged a name: Rose Mihályi.

"Rose Mihályi?" I said. "Red hair? Ruby lips? Dark eyes?"

"Yes, yes, in Arad, once. But you're a man, just like me. Try to understand."

"So it is the chorus girl Rozália Mihályi, is it? Good bye, and may you be damned!" ("I know this woman, I have seen her many times while I embraced that other. Just you wait, Rozália Mihályi, you will be called to account when we meet!")

And so, I set out for the town where Rose Mihályi reputedly lived. A kiss is no trifling matter, after all, and if a man's kiss has proven unlucky, he should at least find out with whom and by whom he'd come into such a mighty, melancholy, yet ultimately just brotherhood.

I would be lying if I did not hasten to add that during this painful phase of my life, when I played her tormentor, I loved Marcella

Kun more than ever. I should also mention, perhaps, that precisely at this juncture, Marcella Kun's bad blue eyes were beginning to turn into the loveliest of doe-like eyes for the benefit of someone else. But I was preoccupied. I had to find Rose Mihályi. I had to find Rozália. For man is a pitiful creature who does not always get from a kiss what he had bargained for. (Perhaps this is the great inducement to the human kiss, I philosophised on the way. Still, it is not right, not right at all... Yet, strange as it may seem, at this time I regarded women with red hair, bright red lips and dark eyes with special attention, even on the train.)

I won't reveal whether it was Arad or Kassa, but arrive I did, and mightily pleased with myself in this curious hunt for the viper of my embraces, I made inquiries after Rozália Mihályi.

"Let me see. It is March, so she must have died at the beginning of February," said the old cashier at the theatre. He winked slyly and added that there are far prettier girls that she in the chorus.

I felt like a child deprived of its party favour.

"But it is her I want, it is red hair I want. I want Rozália Mihályi."

The old man sent for the porter, who told me in which row of the graveyard Rozália lay. And to put my mind at ease, he whispered in my ear, "She was a good girl, mind you, and pretty. But poor child, she died of a nasty disease."

("It is no use continuing the search for the one who has sent me a message by way of a bad kiss," I thought. "I cannot talk with Rozália Mihályi, I cannot extort a confession from her. I can do but one thing: I can turn Rozália Mihályi into the Muse of Life, into the Muse of Love. She was unfamiliar enough to me for that, but burst into my life with sufficient force. Besides, there is no telling how long I would have to look for the person who had sent me a sad message about love through Marcella Kun, as a reward for my male animality.")

The next morning, which proved to be bright and sunny, I took a beautiful wreath to the graveyard for Rozália Mihályi's tomb. That is where I read, *"Here dwells Rozália Mihályi. She lived twenty-six years. Peace be to her ashes. 'I will go and be with Christ, for that is best beyond all things.'"*

Oh, Lord, and so it is! But what about those who cannot go?

They must proceed to live as long as they can with the thing that had killed Rozália Mihályi. Red hair, ruby lips, dark eyes. I see them now, I shall continue to see them all the days of my life. And I shall continue to kiss, too, though now I know that the human kiss is merely a way of sending a message, and that at times this message is very, very sad.

Translated by Judith Sollosy

THE CHICKEN AND THE WOMAN
by SÁNDOR BRÓDY

1

Once upon a time, there was a parrot who owned a woman. The bird was well-satisfied with her; she provided food and drink regularly and did not torment him by trying to make him learn useless words. He'd known three, anyhow, ever since his fledgling days. One was an uncomplimentary definition of a female, beginning with *wh* and ending with *e*; the other two were magic: "Give me money!"

The parrot neither maltreated his human servant, nor made her work too hard; all she had to do was collect the small change that rewarded his daily artistic performances on the street corners of three different boroughs of Budapest. This green emissary from tropical climes picked horoscopes from a rack, told fortunes, bestowed blessings and even boosted the state lottery. He couldn't quite remember himself when he had hired his assistant or where his own genius had developed; the date and the various circumstances were somewhat confused. The woman, over thirty but not yet forty, recalled her own past with a slight shiver of horror, especially the moment when her husband, whose profession was the cleaning and mending of clothes, had told her, "Take that cage and your bird. It's all you brought into my house—and that tawdry dress you're wearing. The rest, all of it, down to the last wooden spoon, is mine. Get out of here!"

He kicked her once but didn't raise a finger to hurt her. He was furious for she'd been fooling around with some very young boys who'd boasted about this to each other and to outsiders. The tailor kept their child with recourse to the argument that it was the product of *his* honest toil. It had been weaned and would even eat bacon rind. It didn't cry for its mother—but she kept on bawling outside the door and in front of the house; all in vain, for the tailor was a stubborn man and she, who had come to town from the countryside, would turn neither to the police nor the courts, not even a priest, for she felt that she wasn't "clean". She was ashamed that those with whom she had played her games had been barely adolescents—and she'd gone pretty far with them. Still, she couldn't spend the rest of her life in grieving; nor could she make a living by carrying round the cage or selling the parrot. The first day she took the bird to the Town Park to join its companions; they spent the night there, among the melodious birds and the whistling, loitering men and women. The second day she had met an old crone who accosted her for a different purpose; but seeing that she was too thin for it, recommended another business—selling horoscopes. She even helped the woman to obtain the rack and the green and white printed bits of paper. For the greatest luck may be built on misfortune; the old crone had had a lodger who had followed in her footsteps but had left this planet for Other Worlds. She died owing six crowns in rent and had left her equipment in lieu of payment.

So Willy, a native of Ceylon, took up his post with the woman on the street corners of Budapest and picked out horoscopes whenever there were customers. He never mistook male for female and whenever a stubbled face appeared in company with a smooth one, he wouldn't dream of pronouncing the bad word starting with *wh* but only mentioned money. The parrot made a living and so did the woman at his side. Both of them became less frivolous; nobody seemed to want the woman, and the bird with the colourful plumage gradually grew old. They both became sad as it befitted those who serve fate and fortune and the simple-minded. When war came, it profited them, too, at first; later the bird suffered because of a shortage of his usual seeds. A new plague of fleas infested him—these came from Norway and he couldn't fight them, though he made his servant give him frequent baths. He was bored with living in the streets, anyhow. All those marching companies, bound for the front! He was irritated by the soldiers, they were much too noisy and tawdry in their uniforms, one or two even plucked at his feathers, departing with green or red loot, festooned in flowers, and feather in cap, the band playing. The woman bawled for all she was worth as they marched away, walking alongside for a few yards. Meanwhile, boys left without their fathers, pushed cigar butts into the bird's bony beak. The woman had turned sentimental because of all the pomp and circumstance, because of all the men, and when she returned to their stand, she shouted into the bird's ear, "Willy, my husband's gone off with this one..."

Silly woman and wise bird! The parrot did not wish to wait for the end of the war; he left. He died on the job while picking a horoscope for a Service Corps officer; a horoscope that forecast the arrival of an unpleasant letter and added: "You have envious enemies, especially among your best friends." (A badly-paid clerk or even a puisne judge would have been glad to be given the deceased bird; not, of course, for making any attempt to revive it. Food, food, food, meat, fish or fowl!)

There was no question of getting another parrot because of the economic jealousy of bleak Britain. How long since a wise bird of fine plumage had been imported from overseas! And they wouldn't fly in just by themselves. Surely, God will punish England in the fullness of time!

2

There was a chance of obtaining a cockatoo—but it would have to be stolen. The shop in which exotic birds were sold and where the horoscope woman looked around recommended a humming bird—but only for a weekly rent. Finally she had to give up such dreams and bought a common siskin. However, it did not impress the people—and it was undisciplined. In an unguarded moment it messed up all the precious bits of paper and winged it across the Danube, probably making for the slopes it had left, rashly, in its young days to come and work in Pest. The poor woman was getting poorer and poorer; she had every reason to fear that the streetcorner public would forget her.

So she bought a chicken. The old crone with whom she lodged—with all her hard work she now had her own room and even a cooking-stove in it—offered her a starved, skinny chicken. As a Hungarian chicken (it came from the Tisza district), it was by no means remarkable, just ordinary black-and-white; it had lived isolated, without friends or food, around the railway station of a poor district. No dog teased, no child harmed it; blinking, scratching, chirping modestly, it probably had no other thought in its head but to survive—*Vivere!* as the Italians would say. It was certainly not bothered by the fact that its body wasn't fit for the lordly gullet of Death. Obviously it felt no duties to fulfil. Politics were far from it, but it did not lack brains; after a lesson or two, it started to pick out the horoscopes—even better than its former green-plumed colleague. The woman hid a grain of maize in every bit of paper, and the chicken, though its sort made the worst artist, obeyed. The people were delighted that instead of a foreign bird it was a domestic one that delivered the bits and pieces of fate; the starving servant girls and the soldiers—who had fought on alien soil for a vague cause and had survived only to roam the city aimlessly—lined up with confidence in front of the chicken, and before long, the poor woman became rich. Because of this, and also because she couldn't resist the currents of the times on her street corner, she decided she would buy a military uniform for her little boy, who must be about eight now. A few more years and he would be conscripted. She groaned at the thought but she hadn't actually seen her child for eight years; she had tried during the first years but it always ended in blows. So she suspended her maternal feelings; but now, being rich, she wanted to surprise her baby with a rich present. She spruced herself up. Her figure, though spare, had never been bad; only her face showed the traces of the skull underneath—the skull that is the end of men and women alike, the ugly bones of which survive our death. "She isn't bad, but she's a death's head!" people used to say about such women—and usually, they were unlucky creatures. Still, this woman was beset by men, especially in the evenings.

They were terribly ragged heroes with everything, not just their clothes, crumpled and dirty about them. For two years they had led lives little in keeping with human dignity, and this showed. But they liked to talk to her, not incidentally because she was from the countryside. Usually they asked her, when would it end? "Maybe the chicken will tell!" she replied in an encouraging tone. "Tell us, Babs!"

The chicken, who'd been baptized Babs in a shameless ceremony, picked at a white piece of paper—or rather the grain of
maize in it. The soldier, reading, absorbed greedily the printed
contents—which he took to be true just because they were in print.
They read: "You are lucky, sir! (My hero!) The emperors will
make peace; after all, they're kinsmen, before you could be struck
down by a hero's death. Their Majesties have realized that the war
which they and their servants and the great rich men have started
might turn out badly, regardless of which way it goes, left or right.
They have started to correspond. You, too, will receive a
letter—however, it won't contain money, for our money's gone to
hell. It's as plentiful as chaff. You need a big blue banknote even
to fill your belly with a slice of fried pumpkin. Don't worry about
your wife (sweetheart) being untrue to you. Not with these *mu-
jiks!*"

This slangy, informal piece of writing, circulated by some hack
printer, made a great impression on the soldiers. Some even took
it home to their wives (sweethearts). Some even believed it—for
you cannot live without faith, especially today, when even faith is
of little help.

3

It was after sunset that real life began around the horoscope woman. The soldiers bound for battle came and so did the maimed,
limbless, half-crazed beggars who had returned from the war.
Once there was one who had been wounded in the head and could
only make the same sounds that Babs did, tweet, tweet, cheep-
cheep... Otherwise he was a fine, good-looking Hungarian lad. It
must be admitted that the majority of the warriors did not loiter
on the street corner because of the woman and the fortune-telling,
but for other women—or sluts. Along the boulevard and from the
side streets they poured out in swarms; the more tawdry, the sad-
der they looked; most of them had become what they were during
the war—wives, mistresses, girls left without fathers; but some
of them might have been servant girls who tried to bridge the difference between the low wages and the high price of food. And

then, too, the utter misery that cast its shadow over the whole continent made itself felt in the more secret organs of these frail women, and not just their empty stomachs. Centuries before, the plague had performed the same function in this part of the world that the raging sickness called politics carried out now. Demure blondes lusted for life and surrendered to love, except that money had mattered less in those days than now.

The sluts bargained with the one-armed and one-legged warriors on the dark corners of dead alleys with little regard for heroism; bread and compassion were both in short supply. Still, there was no grumbling, not yet, not even now. The lenient policemen had nothing to do—it happened only once that they had to intervene in a quarrel between two women over a soldier with a silver medal who had brought back, under his tunic, souvenirs from the battlefield, or when a lecherous militiaman, in search of love, came upon his only daughter. Roaring, he drew his bayonet—but then he sheathed it again. The girl ran like a hare through the jungle of the streets—to sell herself again. Others found a tree in the Town Park—and used a branch as a vertical bed on which to swing forever.

Babs and her mistress gathered much experience as sociologists, too. Under the influence of events, Babs would even leave her imprint upon the horoscopes. This, at least, provided a true mark of the times on literature. The woman remained calm and chased away those (mostly drunken) soldiers who instead of mercenary love sought a gentle, domesticated mate—even if her lips were unpainted. Through such adversity and even more in her prosperity, the woman became very much more sober, and whenever she thought of a man, it was her husband and no one else. Before, she had slept with the parrot; now she shared her bed with Babs, whose legs were tied—though it was well known that fowls were the worst of bed-fellows. But she, too, had her dreams. Of her husband, her child—or another man and another child. There were some soldiers to whom she gave a sideways glance, and did not charge for their horoscope.

4

One day there came a one-armed, tired, not very tall soldier. She stared at him and he stared back. Suddenly she drew her kerchief over her eyes. The soldier bent down and looked under it.

"So it's you, is it?" he demanded angrily.

"No... yes, it's me," the woman said with a sigh. She felt like leaving the horoscopes, the magic chicken, all her wealth, and running away. But her feet were rooted to the ground. It was her husband facing her, the tailor who'd never again pick up a needle with his right hand, for his whole arm was missing. "Where did you leave it?" she asked with profound sadness.

"Just threw it away!" replied the soldier, almost gaily. "It's nobody's business," he added proudly. "It was my king and my country that claimed it!" he continued, suddenly depressed.

"And what did they give you for it?"

The tailor, being a soldier, did not reply. He began to tease the chicken, and giving the woman another searching look, he said, "I can still get a business like yours. Was this what you wanted?"

He raised his voice as if it all had happened only yesterday. The old wounds were reopened, his eyes flashed and once again, distracted, the woman could only think of flight. Luckily, both the crippled and the still unscathed soldiers had struck their bargains, disappearing into the squalid tenement houses; only flighty servant-girls and old women, trudging homewards, were still about. (Why did these poor old women keep dragging themselves along, why didn't they stop when it was mysterious enough how the young ones could continue on their way?) The kerosene lamp burned above the horoscope rack. Babs herself had called it a day and was dozing.

"I must go home," said the woman and began to gather up her things.

"So you've got a home, a new one? Maybe a husband, too?"

"I have my own room. No husband, though. One was enough."

"Maybe you still think you've the right to be uppity, maybe you still..."

She caressed her former husband's armless shoulder and said, gently, "God forbid. I wish you'd broken my bones. That's the least that was coming to me. You were right..."

"I wasn't. I wasn't right at all. The business went to the dogs, too. And I was always sick. To feed at an eating house! Never had a decent meal. I ached for you long enough..."

"There you are!" she said and blushed.

"Whatever I felt, whatever I believed, whatever I saw—it's nobody's business. It wasn't important. I went crazy, that's why I made such a fuss. Now I've seen all the dirty killing in the world. So you slept with somebody—and if it wasn't just one, well, what harm did it do? Who died of it? You've learnt it from your mother... I should've turned a blind eye to it—for my own mother's sake. What did I want? What did we want? No one should put another's nose out of joint... One's filthy, the other's a snotnose... Why, I could blast it all to hell!"

The crippled soldier invoked the saints and the Holy Virgin, spicing his speech with rude words and ancient, potent oaths—which was, truth to tell, a judgement of morals, in the manner of a tailor and a maimed soldier, a confused or maybe sobered soldier, passing judgement.

"And the whole thing wasn't true, anyhow!" said the woman and pushed her scarf back from her forehead. "Where are you going now, home?" she asked suddenly in a tremulous voice, for all the time while they were talking, she was thinking of the child but hadn't dared to ask; it was only now that she plucked up enough courage to do so. "Where is he?"

"In a good place!" and the soldier pointed to the ground—or rather, underground.

With one hand the bereaved mother embraced Babs, with the other she covered her eyes.

"Woe and woe is me!" she cried, unable to stop. "It's God's punishment... I always tried to see him, only to catch a glimpse... I even picked a uniform and a little sword out for him... Oh, my God!"

The soldier helped her to load her pack on her back and swinging his stick in the air, he tried to comfort her.

"Don't wail like that. You ought to be glad he's dead. What's the good of a boy? To learn a trade and then be driven at the guns that have been cast from bells? Down below, he can't be harmed. Who would harm him? Though somebody might invent a way.

They'll wire up the bones of the young 'uns in their coffins. Make them stand at attention. Face the gunfire! Bullets in front, bullets at the back. Whether dead or alive, it won't make any difference..."

The jocular and probably slightly touched tailor laughed crudely. The woman listened with her mouth open, trying to interrupt with questions. "How old was he when it happened? Did you call a doctor? Did he catch cold, or was it something bad he ate? Where's he buried?" But the soldier was laughing so hard that he couldn't hear, nor could he answer the questions.

The women put out her flickering lamp and started off.

"Well, good-bye," said the man. "I'm going to the convalescent home."

It turned out that they were going the same way, far out of town. By the time they got to the gasworks, it was he who carried Babs and their talk was sweet. During the second half of the walk, she was already reproaching him for frequenting that part of town where all the sluts swarmed. Was he looking for a particular one? Pooh! He denied it–though she had hit upon the truth.

Along the dark streets they kept close together, the woman clinging to the man's stick, and when they reached the crucial spot, her lodgings, they entered it together, in silent agreement. And they lay down in the same bed. They soon put out the candle and instead found the light of supreme, eternal happiness. Neither of them saw the other's crippled, bedraggled, imperfect being; nor did they see the sad state of the human race. He had no right arm, she had no morals; they clung to blind and all-powerful love as all of humanity was doing, increasing its numbers as if in a daze... These two, long separated, embraced and clung together in ecstasy, crying, caressing, kissing as if to raise each other from the dead. She put her arm in the place of his missing one and thus they woke, late in the day and not of their own accord: the autumn sun shone through the uncurtained window, straight into their eyes.

"Look at it–I've grown an arm! he said. "No... not mine but yours! No matter," he added, smiling. "I'm hungry," this was his second discovery.

5

She jumped up, more briskly this time than eight years before.

"What would you fancy? What shall I cook for you?" she asked and the next moment she had on her apron, and was standing in the kitchen. She looked around—there was nothing fit for her husband. The old crone, too, had nothing. Outside the two shops there were two thousand people queueing up. The poultry-baskets were empty in the little market. In vain she clinked the money under her apron.

She went home, depressed, and as she sat down in the kitchen for a moment, Babs began to peck at her leg—probably to tell her it was time to go and pick out horoscopes, and eat maize. She caught up Babs, twisted its neck without a moment's hesitation, then blew at the feathers of the creature that had now achieved complete wisdom. She decided that it was plump enough to be fried in its own fat, so she made short shrift of it. And when the clock struck noon in the neighbouring church, the tailor was tackling the learned fowl at the neatly laid table from the plate before him.

The woman watched him with a smile and ate a morsel or two herself. The crone, the landlady, brought black coffee in a mug and stole from her other lodger a cigar for the soldier. It was warm; their stomachs were settled, and now, reunited, neither of them felt the pain any longer—the pain of yesterday or the pain of tomorrow.

Translated by Zsuzsanna Horn and Paul Tabori

SULLEN HORSE
A LEGEND OF THE HORTOBÁGY

by ZSIGMOND MÓRICZ

1

Dawn is breaking. The thirty-thousand acre back of the Hortobágy gives a great shudder. There are gentle creaking sounds, as when a horse yawns and the bones crack in its face. Soft wisps of mist float upwards and disperse in all directions. The horses in the herd raise their heads from the ground and neigh at the fading stars.

The young horseherds had all collapsed on the ground where they lay like clods of mud, one here, another there; they had dropped to the ground after the horses and now, tucked up in their sheepskin coats, they are snoring gently. They had been grazing the horses all night long and did not notice the dawn.

One human figure stands immobile, an old man on the verge of senility, the oldest head herdsman, András Erszény. The Sullen Horse, that is what they call him on the puszta. His two hands are clasped round a long straight stick. He leans on it, while his richly-ornamented whip, thrown round his neck and draped over his shoulders, is merely for decoration. He stares towards the east; his eyes, screwed up, gaze into infinity.

For thirty-four years, since he has been here on the puszta, not a morning has passed without him staring the sun in the face. On 4 April the herd is driven outside, at the end of October it is dispersed. While the herd is in the open he stands guard over it night after night. Not once has he slept through the night and the dawn. When they disperse the herds and drive them towards the town, he still stays out on the puszta. He is not attracted to his birthplace, he does not want to see his house and his wife. He has no wish to see his wife. He is a hard man, and has been for thirty-four years.

2

Behind the sheep-pen the young herdsman is tinkering away at something in the brightening morning light. Just look! It is a bicycle. It has a bent pedal, and he is repairing it. He has turned out the contents of his tool-box on to the grass —a hundred varieties of odds and ends neatly laid out as in a workshop. He picks out a small pair of pincers and works with them, then hammers away with gentle tappings. He is so absorbed in his work, listening to the drumming noise, that he fails to notice that his father, the head horseherd, Sárkány, is there behind him on his horse.

"And what the devil's this?"

The boy starts up in fright. He had wanted to repair it yesterday, but he had been sent off to help the watchman and there had been a lot of spring-cleaning work to do. He had not got down to it. By the time the evening meal was ready darkness had fallen. He could scarcely wait for morning to come and got up, turned out of the tool-shed, and cautiously set to work.

Now he gives his father a scared look. He stands up like a mother hen protecting her chickens with her body. He had even put the radio out on the grass with all its parts neatly set out in order. He wanted to repair this too; it only required a little time, but on the puszta a young herdsman has no time to spare for his own affairs.

"Damn you!" Sárkány the head horseherd shouts haughtily and neatly spins him round. His face turns red. "Haven't I told you?"

He had told him. The boy knows all too well that he had been told that if ever he dared touch that infernal bicycle again, his father would smash it to bits. But he did not believe that the old man would do that, whatever he had said.

But herdsman Sárkány was suddenly seized with a fit of blind rage. He dashed at the bicycle on his horse and trampled on it, out of his mind.

"Devil take you! Would you try to pull a fast one on me?"

The boy trembles as he watches the horse's great shoes pounding to pieces the delicate network of spokes in the bicycle-wheel and kicking the tools and odds and ends in all directions. And that was the end of the radio, crushed to pieces in the dawn beneath the horseshoes.

"Either you're a horseherd or a double-dyed idiot!" roars the old man, seizing his son and shaking him. Then he tosses him away like an old rag among the bits and pieces.

"I'm not having you make a filthy mess of the Hortobágy!" he pants and puffs, then leaves his son.

The boy stands dumbfounded, his face in flames; he's no longer a little boy to swallow such insults, he is sixteen.

The watchman crawls out from beside the reeds surrounding the sheep-pen. He is old, unmarried and somewhat weak in the head. He looks with horror at what has happened. He crawls on his belly and picks up one of the tools that has been kicked away, then weaves his way to the bicycle, bends over it and pats it as if it were a girl who has had a beating. He pats it, fondles it and blinks at the boy, "Rock-a-bye, rock-a-bye..."

The father's voice comes from a distance. "Hey, you..."

The boy gives a start. He holds his head between his hands. He waits, not having any desire to move. He waits for the shout to be repeated two or three times, then sets off in a rage, his head hung down and his big hat pulled over his eyes, towards the voice as if going to meet a murderer.

The idiot remains there and gives the poor dead bicycle-frame a stream of kisses.

3

The village comes awake too. The tiny houses stand in the white light of dawn.

The horses are let out. They run between the houses, their numbers gradually growing, without a single human being to accompany them. They all know their own route. They are off to the puszta.

Children watch them go. And even from the windows it is only the children who watch them. The adults go off to harvest, and the village is left to the children.

By morning the puszta is a miraculous world. The morning belongs to the animals. Cows move over the flat ground singly and in groups, then merge into immense herds. Lambs come along, so do sheep, suddenly raising their heads on the bank of the little ditch and bleat to the sky. A cow on the top of a six-foot high mound looks as if it is about to take off into the firmaments.

Hungarian ewes surge forward; their horns are sharp and their long woolly fleece droops low. They cannot find space for themselves on the vast puszta and nudge and bump into each other. Geese fly off cackling and cover the pasture. Pigs grunt. They dig at the soil. The puszta comes to life.

Herdsman Sárkány nods to his son who cracks his long whip. The herd of horses circles round at a gallop, rejoicing in its freedom. The boy once again pulls his hat down over his eyes.

"You've got what it takes to be a horseherd!" his father rebukes him. "You've got Sárkány blood in you. Your father's a Sárkány, your grandfather was a Sárkány, and all your ancestors were Sárkánys... They're ploughing up the Hortobágy and there are fewer horseherds... Their glory's coming to an end. But there'll always be a place for a Sárkány on the Hortobágy..."

The boy stares grimly into space. The other young herdsman, Pista, a round-faced, oafish lad, comes into sight.

"Am I to leave the herd to him? To that Pista Czibere? When I've got you here? He's no horseherd, just a swineherd among horses..."

But the boy refuses to be consoled. In his heart there is no relief. A kind of wild and bitter anger seethes in him.

Father and son stand side by side, like two statues. Around them grazes the herd of horses. The herd makes a sudden move, and they jump on horseback. They round them up from their horses. The puszta glitters and the clouds sparkle with sharp specks of purple and gold light.

They meet once again on their horses. The father swerves to join his son.

"Jancsi, my lad, doesn't your heart leap with joy? You're my own beloved son... I'll find a husband for Juliska. I've had my eye on Péter Bundi's son for her. I'll make a farmer's wife out of her... But I'll keep you alongside me to enjoy the glory of the horseherd's life. Come on, lad, don't pull such a long face or I'll crack this whip about your neck..."

The boy refuses to calm down. His eyes flash, but he turns away so that his father cannot see.

"And all you want is a bicycle, you miserable little worm! It isn't even dawn and there he rides off on his bicycle... I told you so, but you wouldn't leave good enough alone."

The boy gallops away, round the herd of horses. All of a sudden he appears beside his father again.

"Today's the day of the Bridge Fair. Today your mother's coming out. They're bringing out the food. And farmer Bundi'll be there too; we'll get the girl's engagement settled. Then there'll be just the two of us, lad. We're of horseherd stock... Hold your head up!"

A horse interrupts him with a yawn. It yawns like a man, opening its mouth long and wide.

Once more the father on his horse catches up with his son.

"Listen! Don't you dare play me up! Or I'll talk to you as I do to a foal. I'll take you to the Sullen Horse, he'll take you in hand. You'll soon learn what's what..."

4

Morning has fully arrived.

Herds of cattle get to their feet. Cows stretch themselves. At the well the shepherd wakes and begins to draw water. The sun shines on the well, its rays breaking on the sweep. The shepherd drinks water from the bucket.

The village is deserted now. All the animals have gone out to pasture, except for a young calf still at home. And a three-year-old boy. The child has a long whip in his hand. He frightens the calf, which jumps and frightens the child, who runs off barefoot and dressed only in a shirt, dropping the whip.

Sárkány leaves the herd of horses to the care of the young herdsmen. He nods to his son and they gallop together over the empty plain. They leave herds of sheep and cattle behind them. And pigs. They reach the Sullen Horse.

They greet each other without dismounting. They shake hands.

"Father, I've brought my boy to you."

The Sullen Horse nods. He gazes at the boy. He in turn looks down. He is not going to parley with him.

"He's gone to the bad. He wants to go around on a bicycle. He's not ashamed of himself, though he's the son of a herdsman. I'd like you to take him on and cure him of it for me... He's no respect for his father."

The Sullen Horse nods.

A young herdsman gallops up.

"Sir, the sorrel's dropping her foal."

The Sullen Horse nods towards the boy.

"Take him along with you." With these words they set off and arrive at a gallop where the mare is giving birth. Shepherds are already on the scene, helping.

The little foal is now lying on the grass. The puszta produces its own fruit. New life begins to stir beneath the sun.

The horseherd releases the feet of the newborn foal from the caul. A horse looks over at the mare as she gives birth. The mare lies panting on the grass. Sárkány calls to his son.

"Herdsman, show what you're made of!"

Another lad gallops up.

"Another one's just had a foal."

They gallop over in that direction.

The second mare has herself completed nature's divine work. She is lying on the grass with the foal beside her just like a corpse in the caul, like a fish in a net.

The little foal makes a movement and tears open the caul. The mare looks after her offspring. Two horses come and sniff at the foal. Such is the life of the puszta.

5

Peasant carts are crossing the puszta, with horses tied alongside. They are off to the Bridge Fair.

A horseherd gallops along with horses; he too is off to the fair. Here comes the cart with food on it, bearing the wife and her daughter.

Jancsi rests with the young horseherds lying on their cloaks. He is as sullen as a young bullock.

A young horseherd arrives at a gallop, jumps from his horse and strides over to them.

"It's a great day."

If anyone utters a word, it is like the tolling of a bell. On the puszta people do not speak. Here they only keep silent. Words are rare.

"What's the matter?"

"The woman is coming!"

"Which woman?"

"Mrs András Erszény. The Sullen Horse's wife."

They are all struck dumb. It is incredible.

"She's coming?"

"Yes."

"She's not been out here for thirty years."

"Thirty-four. But she's coming now. She's at death's door and says she wants to make her peace with her husband."

"Make her peace?"

"Because they had a terrible quarrel once."

Even Jancsi pricks up his ears.

"What about?"

"The Sullen Horse was still young in those days, and he owned his own herd... He married a herd-owner's daughter. She was dreadfully ugly but dreadfully rich. And at the wedding-feast he had them play, *"For it wasn't her beauty I loved, poor lad that I was, but her wealth."* Then the young wife turned up her nose and the next moment deceived her husband."

They laugh. Beneath the open sky they laugh as if they were in the bottomless depths. The clouds echo their laughter.

"That was what made the old man so angry. He came out to the puszta, and for thirty-four years hasn't set foot in Debrecen."

They laugh again. The ground reverberates with laughter.

"And she's coming today?"

"Yes."

Jancsi does not laugh. He pulls a face as long as a fiddle. They have a dig at him.

"What's the matter with him?"

They try to put the newly-arrived lad in the picture.

"He's crying over his bicycle."

"I'm not going to be a horseherd."

"Then what are you going to be?"

"A chauffeur."

Silence. Everyone is silent. A shadow falls across them. The shadow races right across the puszta. Something makes the horses go wild and they break into a gallop. There is a great noise of galloping feet on the puszta. The young herdsmen leap on their horses and chase them, then get in front of them and turn them towards the big well, where they draw water. The long troughs fill up. The horses crowd the troughs and drink. The buckets are drawn up, the water in the troughs rises and falls, and the horses are like schoolchildren—good schoolchildren.

"Where's Jancsi?"

They look around, trying to find him. Jancsi has disappeared.

"After him! The Sullen Horse will kill him."

The puszta is full of dashing figures. Everything moves and gallops.

The children are going to school on the puszta. Even the school is in the open air, with the desks set out beneath the sky. There is a teacher at work there, a skinny teacher. He makes them sing.

Jancsi arrives.

"Sir!"

"What do you want, lad?"

"I want to be a chauffeur."

"A chauffeur?"

The teacher looks at the son of the puszta in astonishment.

"That's a fine decision."

The young horseherd hangs his head.

"My father will beat me to death."

"He'll be glad to hear it."

"No. He's smashed my bicycle to pieces—and there wasn't anything wrong with it except that its pedal had been twisted... And my radio was almost finished too. The mechanic's son gave me one of those little crystal sets..."

And he goes into an explanation. And he astonishes the teacher with the technical terms he uses.

6

Wives on the puszta.

In the sacred days of old, women were forbidden to go out to the Hortobágy. All thirty thousand acres of pasture were owned by some hundred men who lived on it. A hundred hard-bitten herdsmen. They went their rounds there, living side by side, their lands measured by eye. There was not even a tree or a mound thrown up to divide the pusztas of Máta and Zám from each other. Only the shepherd knew where Pentezug was, yet for centuries there was hardly a quarrel; he recognized his own land by the place where the thyme grew best.

Today, however, it is the wives who bring out the food in carts. They get on to their carts in Debrecen or Nádudvar or Újváros, and there in the bottom of it is enough food for a month. They come out for a single day with the two horses sent for the purpose by the owner, but they do not sleep there; when the sun goes down they have to return. Or at the very latest when Orion comes up. Till then, till round about midnight, they may flirt as they like out there, but then they must go. The puszta may not be disturbed by women's skirts. For the wind on the puszta is dangerous too, but all the same, a turmoil greater than any storm can be stirred up by the starched underskirts of womenfolk, though scarcely visible fluttering above their boots. But all the same...

Why, even little Juliska causes a great stir in the hard hearts of the young horseherds. Pista, the chief of them, who stands by the flowing mane of the horses like a mobile grave-post over a tomb, utters not a word but just gazes at Juliska who stands beside him while he plaits his whip. The heavy ornamental whip is made of thirty-two strips of hide. They smile at each other and Pista does not look up again; it is as if nothing has happened; his fingers work away and he has no other care in the world... Or perhaps it is as if everything were already arranged, and the brown fingers can get on with their work; they smile once more at each other, and that is an end to all Sárkány's dreams. One or two little smiles seal Juliska's fate, and the decision has been made: her life is now bound to the stars of the puszta, for here there is nothing to bind anything to, even the rope of a tent.

Meanwhile their father listens in the hut to his wife's rapid talk and with a nod or two of his head decides that this must be done and so must that. This affair of Juliska's will not be like this, but like that... But though Mr. Bundi may have twenty-seven horses on the splendid puszta, all Juliska can see is the horseherd Pista smiling, whether she is awake or asleep. She would even go and pick flowers if there were any on the Hortobágy, on the parched grasslands, on St. Peter and Paul's day. There are thistle stalks, and since there is nothing else, Pista gives her one. They may chop her in two, to her this thistle is more beautiful than any cultivated garden-flower. She runs off, carrying the flame of love in her heart, with only her mother to guess the secret of that little heart...

"Where's Jancsi, father?"

Sárkány's expression grows stern.

"There's something wrong with him."

"What?"

"He's been bewitched."

"How do you mean? He's still young. The rose of love hasn't budded for him yet."

"Love?... Not a bit of it! A bicycle—that's what he's in love with... He doesn't want to be a horseherd."

The woman knows this well enough. She waits trembling to see what more problems are going to make life difficult.

"But I smashed it into pieces... You can see it, it's behind the hut."

The mother runs over and looks at the wreckage of the miracle. She wrings her hands.

A young herdsman approaches at a gallop and shouts down from his horse, "Has Jancsi come home?"

"What for?"

"He's escaped from the Sullen Horse. We don't know what's happened..."

The head horseherd snarls. "I'll kill him!" He hurls himself on to his horse and dashes off. The two riders leave a trail of dust on the puszta.

His mother clasps her hands and watches them go with mounting fear. One brings up children, and look what happens. Tears trickle from her maternal eyes. She stumbles off to look for her daughter, and finds her beside the lad who is plaiting his whip. Terrified, she calls to her, "Come here, will you?"

The girl pulls herself together and darts over to her mother. "Mother!" and she falls on her neck.

"Well, now, lass."

"Mother, I could die for him."

"Has he spoken?"

"No, he hasn't but I'll die for him."

"Do you love him?"

"Yes, I do."

"Your father will kill you."

"Never mind."

The mother is at a loss.

"Is that why you wanted to come out to the Hortobágy?" she whispers in a reproachful voice.

"No, I didn't know then, mother."

"Then how did it happen? Tell me."

"I don't know. I only know that it did happen."

A stork circles round in the air. It settles on its mate. A stallion circles round a mare; their heads meet and they neigh together, biting at each other.

Love on the puszta is swift as lightning.

"Has it only just happened?"

"Yes, just now."

The mother looks dismayed. There is nothing she can do now. She knows that well from her own experience. A young horse-herd has only to look once at the girl he wants to marry. It is very rare indeed if he has to look at her twice or three times before making up his mind... A young horseherd does not go courting. When the time comes, he gets married, and that is that.

7

The boy gallops along on horseback. The puszta is not big enough to bear all his misery. Suddenly he sees something that makes him stop. A car. He looks up into the sky. Storm clouds are gathering. He looks down into the car. There is no sign of anyone near it.

"It's going to get soaked."

He dismounts and gazes at it. The car has soft leather upholstery. It would be a pity if it were to fill up with water. But he does not know what to do about it. He does not know how to put up the hood because he does not know how the mechanism works.

In the car he finds a book which describes how to handle it. He looks at it.

"Damn it, it's in German."

He shakes his head, but looks at the diagrams and identifies the various pieces of the frame one by one.

The storm approaches with increasing speed, and he hurries more and more.

At last he sets to work, and one by one undoes the buckles, the struts, the gleaming nickel parts, and by the time the storm arrives the car is completely fixed up and he stands there beside it like a sentry. His horse takes fright at the storm and gallops away.

The gentlemen, the passengers in the car arrive as the rain is bucketing down. They are two gentlemen and are delighted to see that the car is all right. They ask the young horseherd why he did not sit inside the car. He does not understand German, but he knows what they are asking and pats the car lovingly.

"It won't do me any harm, but it would be a pity for *her* to be drenched with water."

"Do you want to be a chauffeur?" ask the gentlemen.

"A chauffeur? That's just what I want to be."

They seat him in the car and take him away with them.

The boy sits beside the gentleman who is driving, his eyes following his every movement.

8

Sárkány is once again with the Sullen Horse.

"Where's the lad?"

They look around. He is nowhere to be seen. A young horseherd reports that he has gone off.

"Where to?"

"That way, towards the west."

Sárkány the head herdsman goes in pursuit.

"Perhaps he's with the fuel-makers."

He rides that way. On the way he leaves behind the wild puszta and arrives at the young men who make "Hortobágy fuel". They collect cow-dung from the puszta in carts and turn it over with forks. They make a fuel-store out of it, and stick it together to withstand rain and wind.

"Have you seen my boy?"

"He didn't come this way."

"Where can the villain be? I'll kill him, I'll kill him!"

"Perhaps he's with the sheep-shearers—the young shepherd is a good friend of his."

He rides off that way.

The sheep are rounded up into a pen, a great crowd of them. They are sent into the shearers and shorn of their fleece. The sheep, shorn thin, leap briskly from beneath the shears and run off nimbly as if they were newly-born.

"Is my son here?"

"No, he's not."

"Then where can he be?"

"Who can tell on the puszta if someone gets lost?"

In the distance a fire breaks out. They catch sight of the glow from it.

"Something's alight over there... Perhaps that's where the boy is. Children love to watch fires."

Sárkány continues his progress on horseback towards the fire.

It is a haystack that is burning. Shortly afterwards the little house nearby catches fire too. This is right on the edge of the Hortobágy, and they can see it in the village, and ring the bell madly. Firemen rush to the store and drag out the hoses. They go at a gallop out to the puszta. The straw is burning. The horses are restless in the summer stables. The little house is burning. The straw crackles as it flies from the roof. The wind stirs up the burning straw.

"Hey, is my son here?"

"We've not seen your boy."

A storm breaks. The fire draws the storm as if the one could not exist without the other. In the sky the clouds whirl past and the black herds of heaven thunder along. The swineherd, lying beside his pigs, gets up and gazes at the sky, shading his eyes with his hand. A black cloud moves across the sun. The swineherd hustles the pigs into a shed. Two horses gallop towards the village, having got loose from one of the herds. With the black clouds, the horses have gone wild and gallop in all directions over the puszta. A horseherd rides through the rain. A stud thunders past with the horseherds in pursuit. The cowherds pursue restless cattle with their big sticks.

Sárkány can be heard shouting now here, now there.

"Have you seen my son?"

"Nobody's seen him at all."

A herd of cattle dashes over the puszta. The huge beasts are like primeval wild animals in a flood.

A shepherd takes a walk with his dog in the rain.

Herdsman Sárkány gallops through the storm and arrives home. He comes across a horse struck dead by lightning.

The sky clears and the remaining clouds gleam bright. The earth is damp and the grass sparkles more gaily. But the horse has met its doom.

"Is the boy at home?"

The woman waits impatiently for her husband.

"Come along now, come in, lunch is ready."

The watchman is grilling fish on a stick. Sárkány has no appetite. He is gloomy.

Nevertheless his appetite comes with the fish, and he settles down to enjoy his food.

His wife speaks up.

"I've something to tell you."

"Well?"

"We've got a problem with that girl... I've got to tell you today, because I'm only out here with you for this one day."

Sárkány looks hard at his wife. What problem could there be? Is there nothing but trouble today?

"What are you making a fuss about?"

"She doesn't want to marry the herd-owner's son, that's the problem."

"I haven't asked her. It's nothing to do with her. That's my affair..."

"But that's not how it is."

"Then how is it? Are you against me too?"

"I'm not, but you can't give the girl orders. That's not the sort of world we're living in now... *She's* going to live with him..."

"She's going to live with him? Why, who does she intend to live with?"

The woman grasps her husband's hand and leads him out behind the hut and into the open air. Pista the horseherd is standing there on the threshing-floor, tough and stern. He has a pipe clenched between his teeth. He scrapes at the pipe with his finger and merely says to the girl, "Are you listening?"

"Yes, Pista."

The lad works at his pipe unconcernedly.

"I'd like to marry you."

"Truly?"

"I would indeed..."

But by now the horseherd is upon him.

"You would indeed, if I'd brought up the girl for the sake of such a beggarly bastard as you."

The two men glare at each other. The woman wrings her hands.

The lad's eyes flash.

"How do you mean, sir?"

"How, you cur? Like this..."

And from the side of the hut he pulls out a stick and brings it down on the back of the lad's neck. He stands up to it. He too bends down to the ground and picks up another stick.

"This'll do too."

With this the two fall on each other. They do not watch to see where the end of the stick lands, but give each other a good beating. Like two bulls in the meadow. A bull grazes in the meadow, raises its head and gives a bellow. The scuffle comes to an end. The great sooty-necked bull goes on grazing.

These are men, they are ashamed of the weals they have received. They pant and regain their breath.

The woman whimpers, "Perhaps the boy has gone to the fair."

The horseherd does not speak. He fetches out his horse and hoists himself on it. He goes off towards the fair. He gallops madly, then slows to a jog. He pulls his hat down over his eyes. His whole life and all his dreams have dissolved in smoke. His son wants to live on a bicycle; his daughter does not want to be a herd-owner's wife. And that means the end of life on the puszta... And he had already made plans for his daughter to go into the village... He would have made a big herd-owner's wife out of her... Ah well...

They are driving cattle towards the fair. Horses are being led along in fives and tens.

They are driving a herd of cows over the stone bridge. The Hortobágy Inn comes into sight.

The fair is a huge whirl. Cymbals, accordions, barrel-organs and all kinds of noise in confusion.

9

After the storm the Sullen Horse is busy settling his stud when they come and tell him that he is wanted back home in the hut because a woman is looking for him. The aged man is astounded. A woman? For him? For thirty-four years no woman has ever looked for him.

He does not move. He stands there and gazes into the distance. The puszta wind brings music to his ears. He can clearly hear the band at the wedding-feast. He closes his eyes. His grey, tanned skin quivers. His face twitches. As if in a dream he sees the wedding-dance where he ordered them to play, *"No, it wasn't her beauty I loved, poor lad that I was, but her wealth..."*

He sees his little wife as she suddenly stiffens and draws herself up. She is not beautiful, but she is young and his own. He opens his eyes. There is nothing here but the bleak puszta.

"Can she come here?" asks the young horseherd.

"Who?"

"The old woman."

"As far as I'm concerned she can come."

He does not look at him. He just stands and waits, like a stone statue.

The old woman approaches slowly, giddily, with her head-scarf pulled down over her eyes. When she arrives, she stops and says simply, humbly, with the grief of old age, "András."

"Who's that?"

"It's me... Me... If it's true..."

He looks at her. And a great flame leaps in his eyes. It is his wife...

"Eszti?"

The woman just nods and weeps. She wipes the streaming tears with the corner of her kerchief.

"It's me, András."

"I don't know you."

"I'm your wife."

"I haven't got a wife."

"I'm still alive... for a while yet... And you're alive too."

"I've not been alive for a long time."

But the woman just stands there. Now that she has come out here, she is not going to leave him.

"András!"

"What do you want? Whoring mare! You deceived me!"

"No, that wasn't true... That's all I want to explain, while I'm alive... It wasn't true... I only did it to frighten you... I've put up with it for thirty-four years. But now I'm old and I can't bear it... I can't die, András, with the knowledge that you believe it to be true..."

The man suddenly relents.

"It wasn't true?"

"No."

"You say that before God?"

"In God's presence, András."

"Because He sees us here... With His own eyes, Eszti... He's up there in heaven... He'll strike you with his thunderbolt if you're lying..."

"I'm not lying... Thirty-four years have been enough for me... Have you heard anything about me during that time?"

András Erszény, head horseherd, thinks hard. No, indeed he has not heard anything—nor, for that matter, has he asked about her. But bad news travels fast, and no news of any kind about the woman had ever reached the puszta.

Suppose this were possible? That his sternness for all these thirty-four years had been in vain? Oh what an accursed life, accursed honour...

"I'm going to die, András... I've not got much time left..."

"Then what did it?"

"A song... It was that song, the one you had played at the wedding-feast."

Both of them shut their eyes. Both of them can hear once again that old song, *"Poor lad that I was... I sought wealth..."*

"I wanted to show you that it wasn't just for wealth. So that you'd come to your senses... and there'd be someone who loves me too. But that's a long time ago. Perhaps that wasn't true either.

A wind blows the woman's black skirt... A wind flutters the wings of the horseherd's shabby ancient sheepskin coat. The Hortobágy wind plays with them, laughing at these children who have grown old.

The man stretches out his hand.

"I believe you, Eszti. Go and sin no more."

The woman stoops over his hand and kisses it, firm as it is. The man pulls it away, feeling the tears on the back of his hand. He looks at his hand.

"That's all right then... Well, Eszti... My dear little Eszti... Now we're going to the fair."

He lays his hand on the woman's shoulder and his eyes gaze into the distance. Into the clouds, and he seeks the truth, the distant light of something impossible, the Sullen Horse...

10

The Bridge Fair is a mad whirl. A roundabout. Wooden horses, young horseherds riding on them. Brass instruments. Fair-goers bargain with each other and come to terms. The sheep that have been sold are branded. Shepherds with shabby boots bargain with buyers in good boots. The horns of the cattle are branded. Smoke rises from the horns. Children whirl round on the roundabout. A flock of sheep is driven over the stone bridge. A brass band. A peasant cart with horses tied to it. A trumpeter blows as if to burst his lungs. They drive cows across the bridge. Cymbals clash. Carts and horses are driven across the bridge. The bridge is the central point in the incomprehensible infinity of the Hortobágy. A big drum and a drummer. They drive vast numbers of cattle over the bridge. One trumpeter, two trumpeters, a brass band. Carts and horses.

A car; in the seat the boy Jancsi puts on the chauffeur's coat. He has been left to guard the car. He puts on the chauffeur's cap. He is proud.

Sárkány is at the bar in the barn, drinking. Drinking fearsomely. Around him there is a swirl of herdsmen and buyers. Now everything in him is ringing loud in his ears. He drinks and sings. He sits with some herdsmen and drinks and sings in a horrible voice. He goes out and looks round. By chance he comes alongside the car, and his son is terrified. He curls up as he approaches and suddenly recognizes him. He recognizes him, his only son in the chauffeur's fur coat and cap. He gives him a long look. His eyes grow cloudy. Beads of moisture cover his eyes and bubble out in huge drops from beneath his eyelashes.

"You're off then?"

"Yes."

He is no longer angry. He shrugs his shoulders and turns away. The boy calls.

"Dad!"

He looks back. The boy leans out of the car.

"They're good people. Gentlemen. I'm going to be a chauffeur."

He opens his arms wide. He embraces his son, who leans out of the car and kisses his father's cheek. Then he pushes him back into the seat.

"Just look after yourself... There too they can make a man of you... So long as you don't forget the honour of a horseherd..."

He stumbles back to the bar.

"Play up, damn you!" he yells at the gypsy.

He begins to dance. The little lad and the idiot watchman join him. He does not know how this one managed to slip out after him. And he dances. He dances with a fearful splendour. He slaps the side of his boots. The grazing herd comes to view. The grazing cattle. The sheep on the pasture. The storks in flight.

He tries to mount his horse. That lad, Pista. He slips off the horse. At this he begins dancing again. Beside him there dance an old couple. András Erszény and his wife. The Sullen Horse...

Everyone stands round them watching. And he begins to dance once more. He threatens the world with his fist. But he is in a very good mood. His face is a mixture of tears and laughter. He is revenging himself on the whole world.

The Sullen Horse dances majestically. The little old woman stumbles. He takes her in his arms and leads her to a bench. Then the two of them dance by themselves, Sárkány the herdsman whose life has come to an end today, and the Sullen Horse whose life has come to new birth today. The Hortobágy laughs as dusk falls. The Hortobágy laughs with the delight of a thousand, a million years, at the frailty of the human race.

Translated by George F. Cushing

LITTLE EMMA

by GÉZA CSÁTH

I found this story in a diary. The boy who wrote it was a remote relation, and did away with himself at twenty. His mother recently died and the diary came into my hands. I had for a while no opportunity to examine it, but last week I began reading it, and was surprised by its casual and simple directness. I found some interesting items in the third notebook, and transcribe them here, offering them a little condensed, and with a few corrections in punctuation.

Little Emma was the prettiest of my kid sister Irma's friends. Her sweet little face with its gray eyes and her blonde hair seemed lovely to me from the first. I was in my second year, she and Irma first graders. Other boys liked her too, but never said so because they were ashamed to admit noticing a girl and a first grader too. But I knew right away that I loved little Emma and would always love her, and would marry her too one day, though I was ashamed of it.

Little Emma often came over to play with my two kid sisters and my brother Gábor. Sometimes there were other girls, like Ani and Juli, our nieces, whom we used to kiss in the cellar, in the attic, the garden and woodshed.

September was lovely and warm, and the balmy weather was even more enjoyable than summertime because I was back at school from two to four and eight to eleven in the morning, and playing ball outside was so much fun. We never tired: we'd run home for a snack, come right out and play till supper.

School was also more fun—more interesting. The new teacher, Michael Sladek—tall with a red face and a thick voice—used a cane.

Our house was in the fifth district, and so our school was on the edge of town. Most of the boys were peasants. Some went barefoot and wore checked calico shirts; others had boots and velveteen trousers. I envied them because I felt them to be different, tougher and braver than I. There was one called Zöldi, four or five years older than anyone else: he carried a jackknife in the cuff of his boot. He showed it to me once, saying, even God can't scare me!

I told my brother, who didn't believe me.

Our new teacher didn't give us reading or let us do handwriting the way our nice first-grade teacher had. Instead he lectured at us, and then called us up to the blackboard to report. If someone talked or fooled around, he'd warn him just once; the next time, he called him up and said, slowly, Lie down, boy! And he'd turn to the class and say, He gets three. Who wants to give them?

This was exciting. Ten or fifteen boys usually stood. The teacher would review the volunteers, call one forward, and hand him the cane.

"If you don't give it to him as hard as you can, you're next!"

The class would watch the beating and hear the howling in dead silence. We all admired the ones who didn't yell or weep; but I felt we hated them a bit, too. I've thought about this, but can't explain it.

As for me, punishment didn't scare me. I was perfectly aware that the teacher would think twice about it, my father being a Major and carrying a saber—he wouldn't have the guts to cane me, no sir!

The teacher found out soon enough that Zöldi was best at it, and from then on he did the punishing and did it well. His way of holding the cane differed from the others'. Hardly an hour passed without at least one or two "strokes". And then there were those warm, golden afternoons when we were all so restless—then, the whole of our second hour was taken up from three to four by canings. A boy huddled weeping in every other row.

One of those times I had a nosebleed and was allowed down to the janitor for water to wash it off. The bleeding stopped and I was going up again when I saw little Emma in the girls' corridor on the ground floor. She stood at her classroom door, her back to me, but she noticed me just the same. Obviously she was there being punished. I went to her, wanting to kiss her and sympathize, but she didn't seem at all unhappy. We said nothing, we only looked at each other. She was sweet and proud, as though she meant to make me realize my father was a mere Major, whereas hers was a Lieutenant-Colonel. She took her braid, untied its pink ribbon, and made a new bow. I watched her at my leisure. Each time she glanced up at me my heart beat.

She came to see us the next afternoon and asked me to keep it a secret—she'd been punished and had had to stand outside the door. I said nothing about it. But that evening I asked Irma why.

"None of your business," was her answer.

Disgusting Irma! I'd have loved hitting her right then, kicking her everywhere. She was jealous, she didn't want me loving Emma, and she didn't want Emma to love me.

She wouldn't let her play hide-and-seek with me, but stayed beside her, coddling and kissing and hugging her. She even stopped me from talking to Emma by calling her away, linking her arm in hers and strolling down at the far end of the yard. It made me bitter every time.

However, their close friendship soon turned to hatred. I noticed one day that they left school with different girls. Emma didn't come to visit after that. I asked my sister why they'd broken up, but she turned and ran off. For spite I told Father at table. Irma refused to answer his questions, so she had to go kneel in the corner, and she didn't get an apple either!

Weeks have passed. Uselessly I tried to talk my sister into making up with Emma, but she's stubborn and silent. Her eyes are misty with tears though, and she cries in bed for no reason.

Towards the middle of October, a terrible thing happened at school. For a change the teacher wanted Zöldi to be the first one caned. He called him, "Come here nicely now!"

Zöldi said nothing, but stood there.

The order came, "Drag him here!"

A dozen boys surrounded him, even some from the last rows. Many of us were scared of Zöldi, and sore at him too. Even I hated him and at first, no use lying, wanted to help drag him out. But it crossed my mind my father would be contemptuous of me if he ever heard I had ganged up with a crowd against one kid. So I stayed in my seat, choked up, my knees shaking. The boys were puffing and panting, trying to shove Zöldi out of his row; a few were grabbing at his legs where he held to the footboard; others were working to force his fingers from their fierce grip on the bench. It took them at least five minutes to budge him out of there and get him down on the floor, where he pinned himself tight again. He didn't dare strike any of them though, because he must have realized that the teacher, who stood on a chair watching the scuffling, would have interfered. Sladek's face was brick-red with rage.

Finally they all latched on to Zöldi by his arms and legs. They dragged him up to the desk, scraping his back along the floor.

"Don't let him get away! the teacher shouted. Turn him on his face and hold his hands and feet down good!"

With all their strength, exhilarant, the boys followed his orders. Zöldi could get hold of nothing, and they kneeled on his arms, four squatting on his legs, two of them leaning on his head. This was the moment the teacher was waiting for. Calmly he crouched beside them, disposed the boys so none of them would be in the way of the cane, and went to work then, dealing Zöldi half a dozen strokes. They sounded awful. Thick, sharp whistles. I burst into a chilled sweating, yet as if held in a magnetic field, stood on my toes on the footboard so as to miss nothing of the sight. The teacher stopped. Zöldi has taken them all without a peep.

"Will you stop being so *stubborn,* Sladek said quietly. And after waiting, dizzy with rage, he hollered: Answer!"

But Zöldi didn't answer.

"All right, my boy, the teacher hissed, it makes no difference to me if you don't answer now—because you will later!"

And furiously, faster and faster he went on with the caning. I couldn't even count the blows anymore. Despite all the strength in that big man, he was panting with exhaustion. Finally he stopped, worn out, and hoarsely demanded again, "Will you *stop* being so *stubborn!"*

Still no response from Zöldi.

The teacher mopped his brow and went on with his "strok-ings," slower now, pausing after each one and repeating, *Will you stop being so stubborn!*

This went on for another dozen "strokings." Then a terrible howl: "Nooo!"

The teacher laid the cane down and sent the boys to their seats. Zöldi got to his feet, fixing up his ripped clothes as best as he could—they had been torn in the scuffling—and returned to his place. His face was smudged from the floor, tears fell on his jacket, and he spat blood.

The teacher, however, called him back.

"Who said you could sit down! Get back here!"

Zöldi staggered up front again, his head hanging. Sladek rubbed his palms together as though he'd just finished a neat bit of work, and said gently, with an unctuous, charitable voice, "My dear fellow, you must realize I gave you that as a warning for the next time. It's most ungrateful in you to disobey your teacher. I discern in you an unfortunate tendency, so I think I shall have to slap your face too."

The slap, however, became a few slaps, and he went on and on slapping Zöldi's face until the boy sank dazed against the blackboard. But he pulled himself away and ran out the door. The teacher cursed and slammed it after him, and then seated himself at his desk again. You could have heard a pin drop.

I got home, ran a temperature, and became delirious. I was put to bed. My father came and questioned me in the evening. I had to tell him what had gone on at school. My parents execrated Sladek, and the next week I went to another school in the best part of town.

I couldn't see Emma every day then. My heart bled.

I read in the paper of October 25th that some coachman had been hanged for robbing and killing one of his fares. A long description of his behavior on death row and in the morning under the gallows. That night my parents discussed it at dinner, and my father described a hanging he'd witnessed when he was twenty.

"How I'd like to have seen it," I cried.

"Be grateful you haven't," he said. "And don't you ever go to one, because you'll dream about it for seven years as I did."

After school next day, I suggested to my brother Gábor that we might build ourselves a gallows, and string up a dog or cat. Gábor liked the plan, and we worked on one in the attic. We stole a clothesline and made a noose. We quit work on the gallows because we hadn't a handy beam for it, and also worried that our parents would stop us if we arranged hangings out in the yard.

Gábor wasn't too keen on torturing animals, though once he got started he came up with great ideas. The year before, for instance, he'd sliced a cat alive with the carving knife. That was in the garden. Ani and Juli trapped the cat, all of us held him down on his back, and Gábor slashed him down his belly.

We got the rope up over a rafter in the attic. A dachshund had strayed in from the road that afternoon, and we shut the gate, caught him, and lugged him up. The girls were jubilant as Gábor and I calmly prepared.

"You're Judge," Gábor pronounced "and I'm the Hangman. And I'm reporting: Your Honor, everything's in readiness for the execution!"

"Excellent," I said. "Hangman, you may do your job!"

And I lifted the dog as Gábor tugged at the rope. Then when he commanded, I suddenly let go. The dachshund whimpered distressfully, kicking his yellow-spotted black feet. But he soon went limp and still. We looked at him awhile and then went for our snack, leaving him dangling there. Afterwards the girls hung around the gate and lured another dog in with a lump of sugar. Lugging it in their skirts, they brought it to Gábor for another execution, but he refused, saying one hanging a day was enough. Juli opened the gate and let him out.

For a few days we forgot all about it because we had a new ball and Gábor and I played catch steadily.

Later on we were talking about Emma. Gábor said he hated her because she was a showoff; he said Irma was stupid for having been so crazy about her.

"I hope they never make up; otherwise she'll be back here boasting and all," Gábor said angrily.

Gábor didn't get his wish, because the very next afternoon Irma brought Emma in with her.

"She's repulsive," Gábor whispered.

"She's a sweet darling," I said to myself, though I was sore at Irma, too, because Irma was flooded with pleasure and while we were playing kept calling her aside to hug her and practically choke her with kisses. Yet they quarreled later anyhow.

"So you won't promise not to talk to Rosie anymore?" Irma said, almost in tears.

"I certainly shan't," Emma said firmly, with a grin.

Juli and Ani whispered to one another. Irma, Gábor, and I were all looking at little Emma—God, how beautiful she was!

Those sunny autumn afternoons were growing to a close. The yard was ours alone: Father and Mother went riding, the cook gave us our cocoa and went back to work in the kitchen.

"Have you ever seen a hanging?" my sister asked Emma afterward.

"No!" said Emma, with a shake of the head, her hair brushing her cheeks.

"But you've heard about it from your father, haven't you?"

"Yes. He said a murderer was hanged," she replied coldly, uninterested.

"You know something? We've got a scaffold all our own," Juli declared.

And we got Emma up in our attic to see an execution. Gábor and I had buried the dachshund in a dump a few days earlier. The noose dangled there emptily.

"Now we can play hanging," Irma said. Emma must be convicted, and we must hang her.

"We should do it to *you,*" Emma laughed.

"Hangman, do your job," said Gábor, giving himself the order. Little Emma paled, but still smiled.

"Don't move!" Irma said.

And I looped the noose about Emma's neck.

"Not me, I don't want to be hanged," the little girl whimpered.

"The murderer begs our mercy," Gábor intoned flushing, but the Hangman's assistants seize the condemned! Ani and Juli took her arms.

"No, I won't let you!" little Emma screamed, and started crying.

"Mercy is with the Most High," Gábor recited. And Irma lifted her friend up by her thighs.

She couldn't manage it and staggered. I went to her and helped. It was the first chance I'd ever had to hold Emma in my arms. My brother yanked at the line, wrapped his end around the rafter and tied it. Little Emma swung there. At first, she flailed her arms about, and kicked her short, thin, white-stockinged legs. Her movements seemed very odd. I couldn't see her face because the attic was quite dark by then. Suddenly the movements ceased. Her body stretched, as though it were seeking something to stand on. And then she moved no more. A ghastly fright took us all. We dashed recklessly down from the attic, scattering and hiding in the garden. Ani and Juli ran home.

Half an hour later, the cook, fetching something from up in the attic, found her body. She called Emma's father over, before our parents had even come home...

The notes recording this incident stop there. The diary's author, whose misfortune it had been to have become a participant in this terrible thing, never mentions it again. All I know about the later history of the family is that the father retired as a Colonel, Irma is a widow today, and Gábor an officer in the Army.

Translated by Charlotte Rogers and Jascha Kessler

THE LAST CIGAR AT THE GREY ARAB
by GYULA KRÚDY

The colonel had to shoot a man that day on assignment from the Casino, for the gentlemen in the English Room (named in honour of a visit from the Prince of Wales) had so decided.

The duel was to be held that afternoon in the barracks, and the man who had insulted the Casino was not to leave the premises alive. The colonel shrugged his shoulders. "Very well, I will shoot the journalist," he had said indifferently. But meanwhile he had grown hungry. This was the only sign of nervousness he felt on the day of the fatal duel. A horrid, unprecedented hunger descended on him. His stomach was hungry, his mouth was hungry; still groggy with sleep he licked his lips, savouring foods he had never tasted nor desired before. They had told him that the reporter sentenced in the English Room of the Casino to death at his hands—he being the best shot in the country—was so dreadfully poor that his evening meal consisted of cracklings eaten out of a piece of paper with his ten fingers; and that he kept the salt in his waistcoat pocket and had radishes and onions waiting in his desk drawer until he had eaten the cracklings. He could not possibly afford a good wine and, therefore, went far out of his way to get to some cheap inn where he would pour the cold wine into his burning stomach.

The colonel, who gave as much thought to the game of life and death as does a rook in a game of chess, if not less, became unbelievably hungry and was obsessed with such cravings as women are wont to have in a certain condition.

"I'll be longing for quicklime before this is over!" the colonel brooded.

He wore a rain cape over civilian clothes, his canary-yellow shoes squeaked, he carried an umbrella-cane, and from time to time he glanced into the closed hackneys, feeling that no one would recognize him in this disguise, as he strolled quietly through the rainy city before the duel. He was never going to speak of this hour to anyone, so after some hesitation and a few suspicious glances in all directions, he made up his mind and stepped into a butcher's shop on the outskirts of the city. The butcher's wife greeted his greying moustache indifferently—an ubiquitous butcher's wife in her greasy dress, her white apron, sleeves rolled up to her elbows, and chafed arms. The wedding ring on her finger had long since cut deeply into the flesh, marking her as an experienced housewife, just as the rings of the years cut into the trunks of trees. Cracklings had been freshly fried. Their stimulating aroma was rising before the tiny nose of the butcher's wife, and the colonel motioned towards the plate they were in.

"A pound," said the colonel.

"That will be too much, sir," the woman spoke up in such an intelligent tone that the colonel was startled. "A few ounces of these cracklings are enough for a snack. Otherwise I couldn't take the responsibility for your stomach. It's not a light food."

"Well then, give me twenty kreutzers' worth," growled the colonel; he did not enjoy having clever people about. The butcher's wife took out a book of poems and tore a few pages from it to form a cone. The colonel thought of the journalist. It was said that he too wrote poems.

"What sort of poetry is this?" he asked, as if he hoped to disguise not only himself but his occupation from the butcher's wife.

"An old man with whiskers used to come around here, and he brought me poetry. Maybe you know him. His name is Vajda... János Vajda."

"I know him," replied the colonel, turning red; but he was not telling the truth. It would have been unthinkable to conduct a lengthy discussion with a butcher's wife in Üllői utca.

The butcher's wife selected a few stout green peppers from a basket and cut off a thick hunk of brown bread. "Take these along," said the good soul, handing the colonel the package wrapped in paper, so that he could tuck it under his rain cape. The colonel could not understand why he was submitting to the will of a woman he had never seen before.

"What sort of tavern could I eat this in?" he asked rather condescendingly.

"There's a tavern called the Grey Arab hereabouts. It has a sign with a gypsy painted on it. Go there—they'll give you salt, and wine too," said the butcher's wife, and in a preoccupied manner she gazed through the open door, as if looking out for the next customer.

The colonel raised two fingers to his hunting cap, left the butcher's shop twirling his umbrella cane, and hardly noticed how he came to be seated in the tavern known as the Grey Arab. A man need take but one step along the road to ruin, the second follows hard upon. The colonel, the member of the Casino, would never have dreamed that he might be a customer of the Grey Arab one day. He had, it is true, occasionally heard in the club room of the Casino, that solemn hall where not only the decorations over the fire-place but even the leather chairs looked as if they had been cast in bronze, that there had been several instances when some of the younger barons and their hired drivers caroused in taverns on the outskirts of the city, dancing with the kitchen maids to the music of a barrel organ; but as to himself, never in his life had he expected to be a guest in such a hostelry. And now, here he sat at a table with a red cloth, manipulating a black-handled knife and fork over a coarse plate that had been placed before him by a young man with rolled-up sleeves, whose sole aim in life was apparently to show how he could lift the beer barrel with one hand when the tavern was filled with customers.

"What is your name, son?" asked the colonel in a fatherly tone.

"They call me János," the young man answered, as if it made no difference.

"Well, János, my son, I want you to know that I am going to shoot a man today whom I have never seen, whom I do not know, and who will be stood up in front of me like a dummy on a drill-yard."

Possibly the young man called János failed to comprehend the colonel's words, as he had been waiting for the attendants from the clinic to come, so that he could start tapping a fresh barrel of beer. The arrival of these people in their white hospital coats was his signal that it was time to put the new barrel on tap, with all the customary ceremonies. The horse-traders who were playing cards at a corner table, with the stout innkeeper presiding, drank wine and soda in any case, because they could put the sturdy glasses down beside them on the chairs and easily fish the cigar and pipe ashes out of them. The few customers who came in on the run—coach-drivers transporting freight, hearse-drivers, official messengers, postmen, horse-drawn tram-drivers who happened to have business down that way—they never drank anything but wine either, because there is more value in wine than in beer. Only the attendants from the clinic could be counted on as serious beer drinkers, for only they had enough time to drink the beer and listen to the conversations that usually accompany the drinking; the day's dissections had been concluded over there and the world-weary professor had given his hands a final wash and labelled the corpses that were at last ready for burial, although there might still be a need for others next day, worse luck to them. As I say, the attendants from the clinic promised to be unwearying customers once their work was over. So János never answered the colonel.

But the colonel may not even have expected an answer, for without a word he set out the paper with the cracklings on it, put the cool green peppers before him, sliced the brown bread with great enjoyment, and was just about to start eating when János stepped out from behind the bar.

"Beer or wine?" he demanded boldly.

"A good mug of beer," replied the colonel, although the army doctor had forbidden him to drink beer, because of his heart. János nodded; he knew there must be enough for one more mug in yesterday's barrel. He started in the direction of the tap, then stopped short. No, he could not give that stale beer to the colonel because he had reserved it for a porter in the neighbourhood who had stolen a girl from him, but who was still sending his small son over every evening for beer.

"Have wine instead," János called back to the colonel.

The colonel flared up.

"Weren't you ever a soldier? Is that what they teach you in the army nowadays? I asked you for beer because I felt like beer."

The hearse-drivers and the other transients glanced toward the colonel's table, since in the cheapest of places just as in the most refined drawing-rooms everyone listens eagerly to a raised voice. No one who dares speak loudly can be an ordinary person.

"Let him have it, János," said the owner, who was deeply engrossed in a card game. "Let him have it!" he shouted, and he slapped down the cards he had in his hand on top of another card which had accidentally fallen on the blue cloth that covered the table. Then he glanced guardedly at the man who had dared to speak loudly in his tavern. The proprietor had once been a cabdriver; he knew the human race well, but not even his eye distinguished a member of the Casino in the gentleman with the yellow shoes. Therefore, by persistently tipping the stale barrel, János tapped the last mug of beer and then, with a show of strength, tore the barrel away from tap, letting the remains drip through the hole into a dish, so as to save something for the enemy porter. After that he kicked the barrel away, as if there would be no further need for it in his lifetime. The new barrel was already waiting beside the bar; the attendants from the clinic would be sure to rejoice seeing it, and they would keep the promise they had made János in regard to his sisters-in-law in the village, who wanted an old wart healed. They would see that she was looked after.

Meanwhile the colonel was eating the cracklings with his fingers. One piece had become hard from frying, but the next melted in his mouth. Like life itself, thought the colonel, and memories of his youth came back to him. When he was serving in country garrisons he used to send his orderly to the butcher's shop in secret for cracklings towards the end of the month, while he stayed in his quarters as if he were already preparing for his examinations to become a staff officer instead of following the example of his fellow-lieutenants who went to grand restaurants and ordered plenty of champagne to run up their already unpaid supper bill, rather than suffer the ignominy of owing only a modest sum. No one could be expected to take umbrage at a bill embellished with champagne. He even learned to shave himself, so he said, rather than permit a strange hand to approach his face. He drove the boot-trees into his boots himself, because the orderly was clumsy. And he locked up his container of fine moustache wax in the closet because he once noticed a queer expression in the eyes of the orderly as he looked at it. Ha, those old-fashioned orderlies; they'd swallow their officer's castor-oil for them if necessary, but they couldn't resist the desire for a container of moustache wax.

As he ate, the colonel lifted the mug of beer and suspiciously held it up to the window.

"No doubt that chap I am about to send to the other world drinks this sort of thing because he can't afford better!" thought the colonel, and he tipped the mug with his eyes closed, as if he were drinking to the young man's salvation.

And the beer tasted good to the colonel. God alone knew what that taste was in the stale beer. It was as if the hopes were flowering inside it; as if it soothed, relieved, and filled one up with its flavour. There are those who like stale beer just as there are those who like it freshly tapped. Why, in certain regions do they drink beer out of "boots", since no one can drink that much at once? And why don't the regular beer drinkers, the decent people, eagerly gulp down their freshly tapped beer instead of patiently waiting, as they gaze about with reflective eyes, for it to settle? There is some mystery about beer, some mystery that no son of man can ever fathom.

Such were the thoughts that passed through the colonel's mind as he sipped his bitter beer, collected the remaining morsels of his cracklings, and continuously discovered tiny new meaty bits around the stem of the green pepper. It was no small pleasure to cut them from their nests. And the brown bread was almost as sensational as the bread he had once eaten during some military action, a bread to which the aroma of the saddles and other horsy accoutrements still clung. Now he looked about the little tavern in Üllői utca in a more friendly way; there was time enough before the execution of that scribbler.

"Life is strange," thought the colonel of the Casino as he noticed the innkeeper's wife, who must just have risen from her afternoon nap. She minced fatly into the tap-room so as to have a quick look at her husband before doing anything else. Would she manage to catch him at some crime that she could scold him about in the evening in their own room?

"My little chick-pea!" the stout innkeeper shouted, upon noting his wife's stealthy approach in those everlasting felt slippers of hers. He pulled off the cap with the red tassel which he never lifted to anyone, and waved it in the air.

"My little chick-pea!" he cried out again, and slammed down the cards in his hand on the table in the style of a winner. In all likelihood he meant this slam to set to rights the afternoon dreams of his wife, since women's afternoon dreams can be dangerous. Sometimes they dream the truth, and then you can never again, not with all the kisses in the world, restore the old spirit in them. Jealousy was apt to torture those publicans' wives who slept in the afternoon, and who would jump up and into the high shoes they had only pulled off half-way, in the belief that they were going to catch their husbands making love to the maid. The innkeeper may have had the most honourable and presentable past, he may have been able to point with pride to a blameless father and mother who bequeathed him their family morals; all the same there has never been an innkeeper in the world whose wife was not righteously jealous. Yet anyone can see how difficult it would be for an innkeeper to escape from his own premises to give vent to unrighteous passions. It is scarcely possible, is it, to mistake one's own tavern for another, where one can carouse on credit anyway, as a member of the trade? So what use is it for his wife to take away his wallet in the evening? It borders on the impossible—does it not?—for a tavern-keeper whom everyone knows to get mixed up with women in his own district, as this would have an adverse effect on his business. Nevertheless the wives of innkeepers since the beginning of time have always laid down their heads for the afternoon nap with anxiety. That is why the owner of the tavern known as the Grey Arab slammed his cards hard on the table when he looked up from among his friends and noticed his wife.

The colonel also sized up the innkeeper's wife.

She was a part of the establishment, and every customer had the right to look her over, whether with pure or impure thoughts. The colonel thought as follows about the innkeeper's wife:

"She's not an absolutely worthless woman, although of course she could not be compared with Countess Denise or any of my other acquaintances. It would be good if the common people and the middle class produced more women of that type..."

Every now and then the colonel would swell with pride as he thought of his own calling. After all, that afternoon he was to kill a man who had insulted the Casino in his newspaper... Then some nerve moved under his waistcoat button, a nerve he hardly knew existed until that time; and that nerve announced that he was filled with insatiable hunger again. If the colonel were a superstitious man he might have been apprehensive of some special warning. But as he was not superstitious he followed the movements of the innkeeper's wife with homage in his eyes. These movements had become springier once she found her husband only in the company of his card cronies and not among the kitchen maids. There is no greater shame for a woman than when her husband deceives her with her own maid. So the innkeeper's wife, in a mood of tolerance, condescended to notice that the unknown guest was nodding and motioning to her with his head.

"What can I do for you?" asked the innkeeper's wife after the colonel had nodded to her for perhaps the tenth time. Then as if speaking in a dream here under the vaulted ceiling of the Grey Arab, the colonel replied as follows:

"You need not believe, madam, that I am really what I seem in my strange disguise. I have a very respectable position in society, and only momentary circumstances force me to appear in the dress of a common citizen. I repeat, madam, my sole purpose is not to be recognized prematurely, before I complete my business with a certain gentleman at a certain place in this neighbourhood."

The colonel pointed in a direction which his hostess could hardly be expected to understand, namely towards the barracks in Üllői utca. The innkeeper's wife put her hand into her apron pocket and impatiently rattled her keys.

"Perhaps you would speak to my husband if you want anything out of the way," she replied robustly, and was already moving off in her felt slippers. But the colonel became more animated.

"Only my lady could solve this particular problem," he said with sudden decision. "I would like to eat something which I could consider an exclusive speciality of the Grey Arab."

"And what might that be?"

"I beg you not to think me ridiculous for my strange request. I was thinking for example, of some sort of stew left over from the midday meal, just the remains at the bottom of the pot that have got all cooked together in their own juice. I shan't mind if they're a bit burned, too. You see, I believe it's the leftovers of any food that taste best, for it's cooked the longest. I can pay, you know."

"Our guests like their stew in the early morning," said the innkeeper's wife, pronouncing the word as "stee-ew."

"The *stew...*"

"The stee-ew," answered the innkeeper's wife. "I will see if there is any left in the kitchen. There was some beef stee-ew at noon."

The colonel's eyes sparkled, although his eyebrows had long since become unused to this. After a while the innkeeper's wife called out from the kitchen. "János! Give this to the gentleman!" and slammed the window shut.

Well, this really was the remains of stew that János brought, with his clumsy finger in the plate. The juice was as thick as a cooked tomato, the meat was charred; most of it was so bony that the innkeeper's wife would not have offered it to any of her guests. But the chances were that she would never see this peculiar gentleman again anyway.

The colonel inspected the pieces of meat with delicacy. He turned over one piece, then another with his fork, giving special attention to the charred pieces, as if he were particularly fond of these. The tap boy stood beside him for a time with a certain air of superiority. This was a type of food that would not even please hansom-cab-drivers who just happened to drop in here, for hansom-cab-drivers liked their food fresh. The colonel, after selecting a tidbit that appealed to him (from among the bony pieces), played with the meat in his mouth and for the sake of style picked the bones from between his teeth with his finger. It appeared that he wished to pursue the road to ruin at all costs...

"Do you know, János," he remarked as he sucked on a bone, "I like oysters, too, but today I have a whim—I want to eat the same sort of food that a certain someone generally eats somewhere or other so as to imagine myself in his place. Yes, I want to feel just like that miserable pauper who is now writing his will somewhere, if he has any sense. I am eating this stew as an act of penance. I ask for pardon in advance, I announce my intentions beforehand, because I do not wish to take anyone unawares. A gentleman, before slapping someone in the face, knows it is proper to warn the person in advance that sooner or later that slap is coming to him. Only a highwayman strikes treacherously from behind. I am warning the gentleman in advance that this affair will end badly for him.

But now, on the threshold of his death, I lower myself to him, I make my peace with him, I do penance with him, although I myself am entirely innocent..."

The tap boy picked at his ear with a match, as if he had not understood a word of his guest's speech.

"I wouldn't fight here. The master is a pretty strong man."

The colonel smiled beneath his moustache, as if to imply that his disguise had really succeeded; no one would recognize in him a member of the Casino. He scattered the remaining bread into the gravy and speared it with his fork.

"I see they know how to handle the remains of stew here. I even suspect there were tomatoes in the gravy although that is not usual everywhere. The charred green pepper and potato speak for themselves. But the most interesting part of all is that the whole dish had a special flavour as if it had been prepared long ago for carriage-drivers and other customers who for some reason couldn't return. They had to wait about under the eaves of houses and stare into the faces of passers-by and for their own private amusement conjecture which of them might have become a fare if by some chance the carriage were not already occupied. Fortunately, however, the carriage is occupied and the fare is courting a pretty young lady upstairs; it wouldn't be usual to tell the driver just where. It would appear that carriage-drivers don't come here any more?" the colonel inquired.

The tap boy did not know himself why he answered the stranger, who could not possibly hold his own with the regular customers. One could not even suppose he came from the police and was investigating something here, for the police soon gave themselves away, if not through their demeanour, then through their voices.

So in answering the question the tap boy had to condescend still further to the level of the customer who had drunk the porter's beer.

"Maybe the gentleman wishes to sell a horse? The carriage-owners generally come this way about six o'clock, from Ferenciek tere, Gizella tér and the other places where the trade takes them."

The colonel almost burst out laughing. It really did no harm to disguise oneself occasionally and act as if one was acquainted with the "people". Prince Rudolf had been frequently reproved in the

Casino for not behaving in conformity with his rank, but he was now proving that the prince was right when he went among the "people" in disguise. All he needed now was for Lucziánovics, Wampetics, Müller, or any of the Casino's other cab-drivers to find him here in the Grey Arab. He really would get a ribbing in the Casino next day! He laughed, but wiped the red gravy cleanly off his plate, even using his bread crust for the purpose.

"They say that aristocrats eat a lot." He turned now and winked his eye at the tap boy. "I don't know if it would be permissible for me to go out to Madame in the kitchen; I am not familiar with her disposition. But I would just like to inquire if there aren't by any chance some trifling leftovers of roast pork? I am thinking of cold pork, of course, just the stump at the end of it, the "keel", as they say. I would just like a taste, which couldn't be sold as a proper portion anyway, but which my type of afternoon customer might be glad to get."

"I'm sure that chap who is sentenced to death also eats this sort of thing when he wakes up after his evening debauchery in some tenement or flophouse or wherever that type of people live. I am convinced he has heartburn, that his head aches, that he's in a daze. Perhaps at this very moment he is in a pawnshop, trying to get hold of some friend's jacket."

It cannot be denied that the guest of the Grey Arab was lucky in everything his capricious stomach fancied that day. The colonel's stomach, which had the same gourd shape as the majority of stomachs, did not feel well that day for some reason; it manifested symptoms of nervousness which even affected the colonel's disciplined mind. Why did his stomach crave all sorts of edibles that he would never even have been aware of, except on this particular day when, just out of pity for his unfortunate opponent, out of his kind, sympathetic heart, out of pure chivalry, the colonel wanted to descend to the point of imitating his poor way of life? Let no one claim that the fellow had been shot dead by someone who looked down upon the pit from a plush box; he also had a heart for the tribulations of the poor. The tap boy actually returned with a piece of pork, and moreover it was the part of the ribs that was best roasted; some of the ashes from the kitchen were still on it, and the bones might have been pickaxes for the trial the teeth were given. Some people prefer for the tender, smooth, even section of the chop, but the colonel wanted to resemble his miserable opponent in every particular, and he doubted that the journalist could afford the better cuts. He asked only for radishes and onions as a side-dish, although he generally avoided those pungent vegetables.

"I might quite well have lunched at the Casino, possibly on lobster, which is said to be at its best during these months," the colonel explained to the tap boy, on whom his singularity was beginning to cast a spell. "I know Miss Finkelstein quite well, too, who delivers the lobsters to the kitchen of the Casino, and when I stroll through the market before dinner she tells me what sort of lobsters were delivered that day. Recently the young lady informed me that among the small lobsters fished from the Tisza, which are only good for soup and stuffing, a particularly large lobster had been sent to the Casino. It had only one scissorlike claw, and its tail was like a cat-o'-nine-tails. She advised me to follow the trail of that lobster and find out what the Casino had planned for it. I immediately rushed to the Casino, and announced my claim to the lobster with the one scissor-claw. It made a very nice little portion after three smaller lobsters were added to it. The three smaller lobsters were a family in themselves—they were rare specimens too. But none of them could compete with the old one. A man must be on the alert if he wants to bag something tasty, eh, János?"

More important people than the barman at the Grey Arab might have been disquieted by the colonel's words. The colonel pared the bones clean and then chewed them in order to match in every possible way that miserable creature who might have been eating just like at some other inn, provided he had the money. The colonel was a good man and would willingly have invited the poor creature to be his guest, before sending him to the other world at six o'clock that afternoon, by decision of the Casino; but the fellow would have had to sit at another table, of course, since not even the kindest heart could offend against the knightly code of etiquette. How many times had he been forced to sit under the same roof with deadly enemies, simply because they were gentlemen of his own rank! It would have been improper to make a scandal out of every chance meeting. The leftover pork was truly well roasted, and the colonel made a sort of promise to János as he ate that if he ever had business in this neighbourhood again (he gestured over his shoulder with his hand) he would not fail to visit the Grey Arab.

"I'm sorry I cannot specify the date beforehand," the colonel said, cutting the radish which had found its way into his hand and studying its white flesh carefully. The radishes testified that discerning people patronized the Grey Arab; each radish proved faultless when sliced. Their snow-white stomach perspired delicately, but there was no sign, for example, of that brown worm which finds its nasty way into the heart of the radish, nor was there any sign of that rot which so utterly saddens the lover of radishes when he discovers it, the sort of thing that might make him think that nothing honest, neither radishes nor people, could be found in this world any longer—the outside deceives, the inside may be hollow, even in the most honest of vegetables. The colonel's radishes did not deceive. Their inside offered what their outside promised—health. He crunched the radish, food of the poor, whose consumption had given rise to so many teasing remarks, both in the Grey Arab and at more elegant hostelries.

"I like oysters very much too," the colonel announced in the midst of these radish rites, thereby causing János to look at his guest really suspiciously; was this queer chap playing him for a fool? "But today I am interested only in this type of fare, this abstainer's fare, this fare of penance, because a man must think of his conscience too, somehow. If I were to shoot that poor devil on a full stomach and in a French champagne mood, I migh reproach myself afterwards that our contest had been unequal—I was light-hearted and brave and so I had to win, because luck is always with the brave. I like oysters very much, but I have never eaten more than two dozen. As a matter of fact, a friend of mine died because he ate twenty-eight oysters at one sitting. Yes, indeed, twenty-eight, but the smaller sort. The octopus is another story again. Fishermen generally kill them with an axe. Tentacles of octopus in a sour sauce with a generous quantity of red onions, pepper and spices make a delicacy as pure as eel. Do you have a wee end of salami?" asked the colonel with sudden nervousness, as if he had detected the smell of it somewhere. "A scrap which has already been put aside as being too small to slice from any longer? Just the end of the salami, where the string is: not everyone can chew it, but I have good teeth, I could probably bite tight through a copper kreutzer."

By this time the tap boy was completely at the colonel's service. There was some sort of magic in the stranger's words which could make one listen day and night. One had only to look in the icebox. Such salami ends can frequently be found in the iceboxes of small taverns; they sometimes wait for weeks until a connoisseur claims them; at other times they very soon find an owner in the form of a hurried cab-driver, who will take the scrap out of the pocket of his cloak some time or other, while waiting.

In this way the colonel's singular appetite finally led him to a special sharp cottage cheese with a penetrating odour which could be spread thin on a salted roll; other cheeses were generally hard. He was just about to complete his meal when a hired carriage pulled up abruptly in front of the Grey Arab, and a tall, pale young man stepped out.

If the colonel had had any sensitivity to civilian clothing, he would have noticed the studied care of the young man's dress. His cloak had a collar and was black, like those that the heroes of novels wore in the last century. He had a Byronic shirt collar and laced cuffs, a loosely knotted blue cravat with white dots, and a white, embroidered waistcoat; it was as if all the items of his wardrobe had been borrowed from a theatre. But it is equally possible that they had been given to him. His legs were as thin as those of a comedian, and this was accentuated by tight black pants. He wore high-heeled feminine shoes.

His face very pale, the young man stepped in at the door, as if asking for help. The agitation in his face suggested some unconquerable fear, as if he had happened in this place while fleeing. His hair was long and fell about his forehead and ears. The face was smooth, passionate, languishing.

"Maybe he's a musician," thought the colonel, whose attention was instantly aroused when the young man jumped from the cab, although he generally paid little attention to his fellow men. He felt some sort of attraction to this peculiar young man; he would probably not even have minded if for want of any other table the young man had sat down with him. The young man looked neither to right nor left, however, but stepped directly to the bar, as if to the counter of a chemist's shop for first-aid. With trembling fingers he took out a coin, and with the avidity of an alcoholic he pounded it on the metal top of the counter. The tap boy turned from the colonel to survey the newcomer.

"Give me a glass of strong slivovitz," demanded the young man in an other-worldly voice. "Plum spirits," he added with a bitter laugh, as if to make fun of himself for getting into a position where he had to drink that type of liquor.

The colonel, whose second glass of wine and soda was being measured out (so that he could resemble the drunken journalist in this too), shook his head sadly and wondered what would become of a man like that, who at such an early age was already loafing about in taverns.

But the young man was still completely disregarding the silent imprecations of the colonel who was watching him challengingly. He stared into the tap boy's face, as if entreating him for mercy at a time of great crisis. The tap boy callously handed him the glass of slivovitz. The young man clapped the glass to his mouth, and was just about to give himself up to drinking, when his eyes found themselves unexpectedly on the sardonic, supercilious, haughty face of the colonel. Although in all probability the colonel did not intend it, the expression on his face was quite insulting, as it usually was. In the life of the great world such a facial expression was most important, although it was no more than a mask. The true faces of many people can be seen only when death moulds them.

The young man's face, when his glance fell on the colonel, was so transformed by horror that one might have thought he had seen the devil or death itself. The glass slipped from his fingers and broke with a crash on the uneven floor, although it was of the thick and hardy sort. Then the young man raised his hand suddenly and covered his eyes, as if he could no longer bear to gaze upon the frightful apparition before him. Blindly, dazedly, he turned around and flitted through the door like a ghost. "Head for the barracks!" he roared in the ear of the driver, who cracked his whip between the horses like a death shot. (Subsequent conversations established the fact that no one in the neighbourhood knew the cabby, although every cab that was worth anything stopped at the Arab, even if it meant making a detour.)

"Hey, what about paying?" yelled János, while even the proprietor jumped up from his quiet card-playing, for nothing like this had happened at his tavern in a long time, and it could not be forgiven, even though it was only a matter of a few kreutzers. The tavernkeeper was about to order János to run after the cab even if he had to go all the way to the barracks, when the other stranger, the colonel, motioned to him and said with a quiet, grave face:

"I'll pay for that glass."

The words of the colonel, although he had spoken them very quietly, created a sensation at the inn. What possible connection could there be between the two strangers, the young one and the old one? What kind of secret was hidden here? Finally a wise cabdriver (retired) solved the problem with his native common sense.

"Most likely his uncle!" he said at the cardtable, motioning towards the colonel with his thumb; and the game went on, since the clinic attendants had not arrived yet. On some days there was more dissection than on others.

The colonel sat very still in his seat, as if a melancholy presentiment had come over him since the appearance of the young man in the tavern. Although he could not have been described as having an adventurous mind, the strange thought nevertheless flashed through him that this young man might be the journalist with whom he was to conduct the fatal duel that day. The colonel had never seen the journalist, he was simply acting on an assignment from the Casino, and its motive could have been termed revenge, even though it might end in death. János, the tap boy, still excited over what had just happened, stood where he was and complained to the colonel, since the innkeeper was deeply engrossed in his card-playing again.

"We'd be in a fine mess if all our customers were like that, throwing his glass on the floor and then running away without paying!"

The colonel only nodded to the youth; he was repeatedly taking his watch out of his pocket. He still had about a quarter of an hour before the duel, and he wanted to arrive exactly on the dot. (The barracks were about a two-minute walk from here.) The fact is, the colonel felt it was quite superfluous to have a long meeting with civilians, the seconds and the doctor, before the duel, which in any case could not be dispensed with. The seconds and the colonel's doctor, Emil Kosztka, were certain to be in their places. And no one was dimply likely to imagine that he, a retired Mounted Colonel, would arrive late as a result of cowardice. He simply wished to avoid superfluous conversation. He would shoot on signal and then wait with his hands in his pockets. Would his opponent be in a position to return the shot? More than likely he would not. There is a saying, "With his last strength he fired his pistol and aimed true." Nonsense. It might happen once in a hundred years.

And if he were actually to find that eccentric-looking young man before him in the riding rink inside the barracks, with his Byronic white collar and long white cuffs making perfect targets for a pistol—if his adversary were actually that miserable, irresponsible young man—it would make things quite unpleasant, but it would not change his position in the least. When you came right down to it, the colonel had no connection with the chap, nor with any of his relations, with any mistress he might have had, nor with his father, nor mother. The Casino had made a certain decision and there was no appeal to a decision by the Casino...

"Give me some of those spirits too," the colonel now spoke up, almost against his will, for he had grown somewhat ashamed of trying to identify himself so closely with an adversary who after all was nothing but a journalist dressed up in a white embroidered waistcoat for a duel with pistols.

János failed to grasp his words immediately, since he was no mind-reader and could not follow the colonel's thinking. But he gradually understood, and poured the slivovitz into a glass—perhaps just the same kind of glass the young man had dropped a few minutes earlier. The colonel, after sniffing it briefly, poured the stuff down his throat with a steady hand. It was truly a powerful drink, no doubt a favourite of coachmen who arrived here at this end of the city after spending entire days in the winter snowstorms driving good-for-nothing passengers about. Or perhaps the coachmen who transported corpses all their lives to the dissecting lab next door liked these spirits. There was no question about it, everyone in the neighbourhood was fond of the Grey Arab's famous slivovitz; so why shouldn't the colonel like the taste?

"I will be leaving now," said the colonel after suppressing a couple of coughs, as it would never have done to let them know that this cabbies' brew had overpowered him slightly. But at any rate he had drunk it down in place of the miserable scribbler.

When he asked for the bill, much to the colonel's amusement the woman came out of the kitchen with a slate and chalk, if you please. He thought what a wonderful joke it would be if Stettner, the head waiter at the Casino, were ever to add up the bill on a slate and produce the change out of a skirt pocket instead of on a silver tray. Out of gratitude that his business was with the woman, the colonel took his crispest note out of his wallet, and it crackled as proudly as if it was unspent money from last month's pension. The woman counted, her neck bent in honour of the money, and worked eagerly, naively, as if undertaking the most important assignment she had ever received in her life.

"I hope everything was satisfactory?" she asked, returning the change and making the note crackle once more before placing it in her masculine wallet. "Maybe the stee-ew...?"

"The *stew* was very fine," he answered impatiently, for he had begun to suspect that her curious intonation as she said the word was for his benefit only.

Then he looked into his cigar case and eyed his treasures one after the other, various types of cigars, some of which he might carry about for weeks, so as to light up the proper one at the proper moment. He quickly found the short cigar that would be suitable for the tap boy, but for himself he was undecided. Finally he selected a fine Havana, a species of cigar which no one had ever lit in the Grey Arab since it was built.

No, under no circumstances did he wish to resemble that pauper now, once he believed he had seen him. He was sure this must be the reason the man had dropped the liquor glass after catching sight of him; the colonel was convinced that the whole town recognized him. Especially his enemies. No, such inhuman fear would have been improper in any face other than that of his adversary.

The colonel lit his little cigar seriously and ceremoniously, after tearing off the gold and red band. How silly of him to have thought he could forget even for a single afternoon his rank and social position, his circle of friends and the mode of life he was accustomed to, just to "lower" himself to the level of an unknown man and his possible habits, and all this by way of asking pardon for shooting him that evening—liberating him from the torments of life. "Anyone who ever asks for forgiveness"—he was lighting his little club cigar—"is the biggest fool in the world, because there can be no question of real forgiveness anyway. If a man is afraid of death, he ought to watch his step..." And the colonel blew out the first cloud of smoke, blew it all about himself, as if to blow away once and for all what had happened to him that afternoon.

The Havana did, in fact, have a fine flavour, as is proper for a last cigar.

With this incident of the cigar we have just about finished with the Grey Arab and with those various gentlemen who would be arriving there from all over the city, for they presumably had homing instincts. The attendants from the clinic certainly arrived at long last, because dissecting, even in the clinic, cannot go on day and night. The hearse-drivers arrived from all parts of the city, as hearse-driving is also relieved by periods of rest. And towards evening cabmen loitered in front of the tavern, the ones whose stables were somewhere in the neighbourhood. There was work to be done around the bar, and the aroma of "stee-ew" floated out through the open door of the kitchen. János, the innkeeper's wife and the others had had time enough to forget the colonel whose awe-inspiring eyes had roved about the room that afternoon, but who had really been a friendly chap, even willing to speak with a tap boy. At this point in the evening, a belated hearse-driver appeared at the bar and stood about grimly like a man who is dissatisfied with his occupation, scratching one leg with the foot of the other, and not speaking a word until he had consumed two glasses of the powerful spirits.

"I had to dispatch some colonel in civilian clothes," he remarked, after wiping his moustache with a dirty handkerchief. János, too, found time to listen.

"These gentlemen wear fancy uniforms all their lives and we never have any business with them, because the army takes care of it, provided they die in uniform. But my load dressed in civilian clothes before his death, to make more work for us. They say he was shot in a duel in the barracks, and they were at a loss over what to do with him. But then that's what we're here for. So he's at the morgue now."

The tap boy did not reply to the hearse-driver, for at that moment a coachman from the centre of town arrived, a man who had many friends here; one had to watch carefully what he ordered because he was prone to make a row at the slightest provocation.

At about midnight, as the guests were beginning to thin out, János the tap boy leaned his back against the cupboard and reflected on the peculiarities of his afternoon customer. It never even occurred to him that the corpse which had just been transported might have been the customer in question—the one who had dropped the fancy cigar band that was still lying there in the corner.

Translated by Patricia Bozsó

ABDOMINAL OPERATION

by FRIGYES KARINTHY

"To hell with him!" exploded the first assistant surgeon Vajda. He was as crimson as a schoolboy after a ticking off. Savagely he tore off his rubber gloves. "To hell with him! I wish he wouldn't shout at me. I'm not a school boy."

Telekes, the second assistant, slowly peeled off his gloves and held his hands under the faucet. He was smiling.

"Don't be silly," he said soothingly. "After all these years you start taking offence...? He's been shouting for six years at you, at me, and he hasn't eaten us yet. Besides, as you know very well, he's especially fond of you...."

"I couldn't care less. He can keep his fondness for his grand-mother...."

"Now, now, keep your shirt on. Besides, he was right this time.... I hope you won't mind my saying so, but you were really absent-minded today.... I meant to tell you myself that you kept holding the lamp under his nose instead of beaming it straight into the abdomen."

"So what? Couldn't he say so? Or just make a sign? Must he shout at me as if I were a servant? In front of all those old hens? And over a local-anaesthetic case, who could hear every word? There's prestige for you! I've had it. I'm fed to the teeth.... If this is your idea of a thrill, carry on with him for a thousand years.... I'm not married to this clinic. I could have been running my own sana-torium long ago... I don't give a damn for the great honour of be-ing assistant to the celebrated surgeon. I'll tell you where you can put the honour! It's all very well for him. He's not going to shout at me any more, because if he does—"

He broke off; Telekes had dug him in the ribs. For several min-utes more he could not speak, wondering in dismay if the old man might not have overheard his last few words. The professor had entered quite soundlessly. Vajda stole a glance at the familiar, pleasantly rugged, gnarled face as it bent over the basin. The professor looked rather morose; apart from that, he showed no emotion. Nevertheless Vajda winced as he noticed that the old man was about to speak.

"Well, boys, we can call it a day."

The sound of that rough gravelly voice at once quietened Vajda, and he was relieved by a curious soothing combination of reassurance and cockiness. So he hadn't overheard anything, thank heaven. Good.... He'd better stop shouting at me, or I'll—

"I am looking forward to these six days, you know," the professor went on. "Not because of the congress itself.... having to look at all those stuffed shirts.... I suppose I'll manage to stomach it somehow.... But at least I'll get a chance to laze around in bed in the mornings.... and read a decent book for once...."

He leaned forward to wash his face, which was spattered with blood. At the same time he gave a grunt of pain. Both assistants turned to him.

"Goddamn!" he swore. "This thing's not going to give me any peace, I can see that. I'll just have to go through with it."

They looked at him inquiringly, but the old man barked:

"What are you gaping at? As if you didn't know I've got a hernia. You think I can't see how you fellows snigger every time I grit my teeth while we work?"

They were flabbergasted; but the professor, paying no attention to them, continued.

"You won't snigger any more, my bonny boys! I've had enough."

For a second he seemed lost in thought; then, as if he had just made up his mind at that moment:

"I say! Won't these six days come in useful!... The honourable Congress will do very well without my presence.... At least I won't be wasting time. I'll be able to read in bed all day. Why, it'll be a wonderful chance to rest, too. On the fifth day, properly strapped, I'll be dancing a tango."

He became animated.

"And furthermore I'll lie right here, in one of the private rooms. If anything goes really wrong Professor Stuffed-Shirt can always come in for a consultation.... Whew! By George, what a treat! Get Room Seven ready for me."

His animation spread to his assistants. Telekes beamed.

"Whom do you have in mind, sir?" he said. "Professor Horkay, perhaps? He'd be the man, I should think. We could ring him up right away. He'd be at home now...."

The professor looked up abruptly. He made a ferocious grimace as if he really were going to slap one of their heads off.

"You must be daft! For me? Another professor?" he thundered. "That's all I need! No honourable colleague is going to shove his paw into *my* belly! Not likely! I won't give 'em *that* chance, not I. You're mad, son."

Telekes forgot to shut his mouth.

"But—in that case...."

"What case? What do you mean, case? Don't keep wagging your head back and forth like a duck's arse.... The creatures I'm surrounded with! Immediately start wagging this way and that! For the love of God! I certainly was blessed with you.... Believe me, I'd rather do it myself. I'll have to put up with a couple of miserable chiropodists like you! But I'll be keeping an eye on you, never fear."

They stood transfixed, unable to say a word. Already the professor was issuing orders.

"Get cracking! Prepare the big operating room. Operating table in the centre. Call Hilda for injections."

"I beg your pardon, Professor. But right now? Us two?"

"When then, for Christ's sake? After dinner, when I have my belly full? I happened to skip breakfast this morning—so no purgative is needed.... Now listen, butcherboys. In half an hour I'll be shaved, changed into pyjamas, and over in the blue room.... Meanwhile you'll have a thorough wash and get the full hernia set sterilized.... Have Hilda mix fresh novocaine, since it's a local job. Got it?.... Oh! I nearly forgot to tell you.... You're not getting off too cheap.... I want a mirror, a big one. See? You're to have it hung above the lamp, tilting it so as to bring it parallel with the headrest, where my mug will be. I'll be watching the show in that mirror. I'm not going to have you butchers loafing on the job—you can give up hope of that.... Here's your chance to show what you know.... Get cracking! It was nice meeting you. See you later, at the slaughter-house."

And everything happened as in a strange dream.

When the professor showed up at the door of the operating-room half an hour later, wearing heliotrope pyjamas, the table stood at the centre of the room, with the mirror suspended above it. Dr. Hilda, the anaesthetist, was blithely filling up the hypodermic syringe; the two assistant surgeons, pale and agitated under white masks, were laying out the instruments without a word. They all but sprang to attention when the professor entered. Telekes was about to say something, but was promptly silenced by the old man.

"What! You call this lighting? Lower Number Three, confound it! You want to blind me so I can't see a thing, eh!"

All three assistants began jumping about like soldiers. The professor threw off his dressing-gown. "Put up that head-rest! That's right. Lower the legs.... Where do you expect me to park my behind? Can't you see? Don't touch me, or I'll bite you!"

This last was addressed to Dr. Hilda, who had wanted to give him a hand as he clambered on to the imposing operating table. For a while he fidgeted on the table, chiefly concerned about the position of his head; then he launched forth once more.

"All right now. Let's have the cloths. You will leave a space the width of two palms below the navel. Right there, chump! Don't goggle. I marked the spot out for you! Did you think I'd leave that for you to do? I did it in the bathroom.... You're not going to make a bigger cicatrix on me than is absolutely necessary.... You're to make the incision precisely where the line starts. You will move all along it and make a cut right down to the scrotum. Come on, now, let's have the iodine.... No, no, I want Hilda to do that."

The syringe was shaking in Dr. Hilda's hand. A roar brought her round.

"Lower, for God's sake! You call that a stab? Plunge it deeper, you fool! How many times have I got to tell you to hold the needle straight? You're supposed to plunge it into the weal, not next to it. Do you want to make me howl the way that old hag was doing yesterday? I can see very well you're holding it over the wrong place!"

The two surgeons chuckled, but their teeth were chattering.

"You two had better stop laughing. I'll see shortly whether you're the tough lads you pretend to be.... That'll do, Hilda, dear. I didn't feel that fourth one.... Now for the iodine and the scalpel. Or rather.... Wait a minute. I want Vajda to do the iodizing.... Or no. Let Feri do the iodizing. Mr. Vajda will do the carving."

Assistant surgeon Vajda started at the scornful overtone the word "mister" carried. But a curious sort of pride spread through him, and his face flushed.

"Yes, yes, Mr. Vajda. It's you I am curious about, since you have a tendency to make light of these minor hernia cases. Now I'd like to feel on my own belly just how steady your hands are.... All right, Feri, that'll do. Even iodine palls after a while. Look at Mr. Vajda. Isn't he impatient! He just itches to start carving me up. This is the great day of reckoning he's waited for so long! Right, eh?"

And the professor flashed a sidelong glance at the stunned surgeon. Holding the sterilized knife ready, Vajda approached the operating table.

"Well, I'm going to shut up for a while. I want to watch the mirror.... Now listen. Adhesive, cloth, a dozen frogs.... Second, weal, third iodine.... knife.... (Slanted incision).... Tampon before applying ligature. No dabbling with your finger as you usually do. Lift funiculus with your index. Understand? I'll be seeing the rest. Ready? One, two, three, go!"

The knife ran swiftly along the abdominal wall. Already Telekes was mopping up blood; Hilda was getting the tweezers handy. For two minutes dead silence prevailed. There was hardly any fat beneath the professor's swarthy, soldierly skin; the gleaming, silvery lobe surged into view through the gaping wound. It was odd, though, that the flabby fascia should have failed to be revealed behind it. It would have to be lifted out before being tied up. H'mm. Odd that this fascia should fail to appear....

"Aha," the patient sneered. "Aha!"

The surgeon's hand twitched.

"Oh, you tumbled to it at last? Or did you? I was wondering.... Spring a little surprise on us and we go off in a swoon, eh? Well, perhaps you'd better go on searching for it. It must be somewhere about, mustn't it? Well! Thank Heaven!.... Now we'll have a little butchering, shall we. Resection can wait. Meantime, shred of gauze slips out of wound, and I get a haematoma the size of a water-melon...."

The surgeon turned purple.

"Well?.... Well?.... Whatever is to be done now, one wonders. Good gracious! Just what *ought* one to do? It would be nice if I told you. What? But you see, a surgeon who is such a stickler for his professional reputation—he ought to know.... And what if I don't say a word? Eh? I am now a helpless patient. Can't possibly prompt you, you know.... You just have to work out your own salvation!"

Beads stood on Vajda's brow. He was straining to remember. Suddenly, it all came back to him. The fourth finger! He seized the prepared, ligatured stump with a forceps, lanced it, and tied it up. He sutured the muscle with a thick thread. The last stitch!

"Thank Heaven!" the patient nodded, with disdain.

Telekes took the threaded needles—three of them—from Dr. Hilda, and passed them on to Vajda. The latter placed two threads on the cloth and introduced the third into the wound.

"Right-hand side!" the professor bellowed. Vajda was puzzled; he got flustered and yanked the needle out.

"Jesus Christ! Now he's yanked it out! I didn't mean *that,* you fool. I meant the other ones! I've told you a thousand times over that you should place them *on your right*.... if you want them within easy reach for your left hand.... Why don't you put them on top of your head? Or press them in your prayer-book? For Christ's.... I certainly was blessed with you!"

Fortunately, the two sutures had now been completed; Telekes was handing Vajda the clasps, one by one. The ordeal would soon be over. Before it was ended, they had to endure one more outburst.

"Easy, damn you! You should do that slacker! What d'you mean, thrusting your paw into an abdominal wall that's just been slit open, as if you were grabbing your gal? I certainly was blessed with you.... Are you finished? Thank you very much! You call that fifteen minutes? Of course, you boys thought I wouldn't find time to look at the clock while this was going on.... Well, you might like to know it's taken eighteen and a half minutes. Shame! What a disgrace! Come on, give us a sponge-down! Where's János? They ought to have rolled up the stretcher by now. How long do you expect me to keep my legs raised? Apply some collodion, that's all."

Vajda, his face flushed, bustled about as the patient was transferred to the wheeled stretcher. He pushed the door open and rushed ahead.

Wrong again!

"You stay here, doctor," said the professor, covered up to his chin. "I want Dr. Hilda to see me down to my room. I've seen enough of you two for the time being. You will be good enough to drop in on me just before inspection."

But at the door, as the stretcher was wheeled past the stupefied first assistant, the professor turned his head to the side and stretched out his right hand from beneath the cover. As he spoke there was in his muffled voice a hidden smile, charged with the self-satisfied peace of a dressing-down successfully administered.

"Humph.... Now give us your paw.... I never fancied for a moment that I could entrust this to any Horkay. I'd sooner see it done by someone who's at least learned the job from me.... You've done quite a good job. And that eighteen minutes—that's not so bad, either.... Humph.... And if I let out a yell now and then.... why, you don't want to take that seriously. After all, one's got to use one's lungs, hasn't one? No one's ever heard me bawl out anyone but people I'm fond of. Well, see you later."

The assistant surgeon still felt the warmth of the old, bony hand in his palm, after the stretcher had disappeared around the corner of the corridor.

He turned around as if in a dream. Telekes was cheerfully pulling off his gloves. He was laughing heartily and shouting from across the room.

"What d'you say to that? Magnificent! Grand! A capital fellow, the old man. What! Has absolutely no equal in the world. I swear, my final exams at medical school were nothing to this for cold feet!"

Vajda stood by the instrument table, lost in thought; he was rummaging among the forceps. Telekes jabbered on excitedly.

"Well! And you? The ordeal he's put you through! I could see the blue funk you were in. I saw that for two pins you'd have tossed the whole scrap-can in his face! He just caught you in the right mood! And the best of it is—I hope you realize that the operation wasn't even indicated? He could have coasted along with that hernia without dressing for another ten years, couldn't he? Did you ever suspect he had that? I didn't. It's just that the fit was on the old boy—I tell you, he's got a screw loose, the old bastard. It's fantastic! When all is said and done, though, I think we might be proud of this. It's a unique case, I should think... What's the matter? Have you gone dumb? Absent-minded again?"

Vajda was standing in the middle of the room, staring at his empty palm as if he were seeing it for the first time.

"Tell me," he said suddenly, speaking in an odd, alien voice, and continuing to stare at his palm. "Wasn't Capernaum the name of that town?"

"What town? Have you cracking up?"

"Where the Master.... appeared to His disciples and made Thomas, doubting Thomas, reach his finger into His side which had been pierced with a spear as a punishment for not believing that genius is a law unto itself?"

Translated by István Farkas

OMELETTE À WOBURN

by DEZSŐ KOSZTOLÁNYI

Kornél Esti was heading homewards from Paris after a year of study. When he entered the third-class compartment in the "Hungarian coach" and his nose was assailed by the familiar stale smell of his poor country's misery, he felt that he was at home.

Towards evening legs and heads were strewn about the dirty floor, as on a battlefield. Groping his way to the lavatory, he carefully avoided the scattered legs and stray heads whose owners were flopped over with fatigue and snoring. He had to take care not to step on a mouth or a nose.

At times the sleepers fidgeted, reassembling their lost limbs from beneath the wooden seat or elsewhere, as on the Day of Judgement; they would start to sit up, rub their eyes, and then fall back into the exhaustion they had brought with them from abroad. Most of them were returning emigrants, wrapped in gaudy rags, with sacks, pillows and eiderdown quilts. A poor woman in a kerchief, coming from Brazil, held her little girl asleep on her lap.

In the semi-darkness of sundown the student was saddened at the prospect of having to spend a night and then another day among this stinking menagerie before reaching Budapest. He had been standing throughout the trip. His legs were trembling. He was nauseated by the reek of clothing and acrid smoke.

At eight in the evening, the train pulled into the station at Zurich.

Leaning out of the window, he was fascinated by the sight of the town straggling over the hills, the villas looking like toy houses with idyllic little lights glimmering in the windows. It had rained in the afternoon. The air was pure, vapourless and translucent as glass. Suddenly he was seized by an irresistible longing to get off and continue his journey next morning.

Originally he had intended to make the trip in one go, chiefly to save money. He delved into his pocket and found eleven Swiss francs in it, all his wealth, which he had exhanged at the border. He quickly grasped his bag and sprang down from the train. He had his ticket stamped, left his thin, battered case in the railway check-room, and wandered into the city. He did not regret it. It was truly wonderful to roam about unknown streets, to which no memory bound him, to peep in at a window for the first, perhaps the last time, to watch the people with their closed umbrellas walking calmly and contentedly about. He could not say why, but their slightest gestures enchanted him. He yearned for all of it. Hotels lured him looking, as they did, like ancient and splendid mansions.

Soon he found a students' hostel and a little back room for three francs. He washed and hurried down to the lake. In a frame of embankments and houses on stilts, the lake looked like a china inkstand with light blue ink undulating in it. A single boat with its romantic lantern was rocking near the opposite shore. For a while he mused over it. Then he realized that he was hungry.

He was very hungry. He was desperately hungry. No wonder. He had eaten nothing all day but two apples. He thought he might get a bite at a milkbar before going back to the hostel. He wandered from one street to another, searching with increasing ill-temper for a dairy. But the diligent, sober Swiss had already gone to bed. He glimpsed a light amidst the foliage. It seemed to be a tidy little garden restaurant. He went in.

Unsuspecting, he walked between two rows of blue hydrangeas towards a table in a corner. By the time he got there he was surrounded by four waiters in tails as promptly as a burglar by the secret police. He looked at them a little startled, perhaps somewhat reproachfully, for descending four strong on a defenceless man. He clearly found them too many.

The waiters discharged their duties deliberately and mechanically. Each had his own function. One took his hat, another helped him get out of his shabby, weather-beaten old raincoat, the third hung it on an iron coat-rack, and the fourth and tallest, an ice-cold, indifferent gentleman with sparse black hair parted in the middle, as stiff and dignified as a major-domo, ceremoniously handed him a thin, leather-bound book decorated with gold tooling, which one might have taken for some incunabulum, one of those early printed books of which only a single specimen exists. But this book lay on every table. It was the bill of fare.

Suspiciously, irresolutely, Kornél sat down and opened the resplendent volume. He saw on stiff paper the name of the restaurant, the date of its foundation—1739—, a red coat of arms, and underneath an endless list of dishes in faultless typescript. He turned the leaves absent-mindedly, trying to find his way about in it. The four waiters stood at easy attention, without the slightest sign of impatience, but rather like young beaux at a ball filled with pleasant anticipation. Undeniably, there was a certain solemnity about this scene.

Now the major-domo, with his head slightly tilted, asked in an exquisite exhalation of French whether he wished to dine. The guest nodded. He ordered three scrambled eggs.

In repeating the order with all due respect, the major-domo emphasized his guest's desire for scrambled eggs as a first course; yet he remained standing at the table and a dreamy smile flitted across his face, as if he had not quite understood the order. It was a matter of common knowledge that there were three kinds of omelette: Omelette à Napoléon, Omelette alla Zingarella, and Omelette à Woburn. The question was which one the guest was pleased to prefer.

He had to make a decision.

He felt an aversion to Napoléon on account of his ambition to conquer the world; Zingarella did not appeal to him either. As for Woburn he had no idea who or what it might be. Well, it was immaterial; the main thing was that it should be brought as soon as possible, the more and the cheaper the better because he was famished. But he could not simply blurt this out. He heard the waiters speaking Italian among themselves, so he changed over to Italian. The major-domo coolly replied in German, as if declining such familiarity. A gentleman ought to speak but one language.

Embarrassed, he decided in favour of Omelette à Woburn.

The major-domo acknowledged the order with a nod of his head and danced away; then the other waiters placed various wine lists before him, eager to bring him an assortment of champagnes in pails of ice, sweet French, dry English, or sack, or bottled light wine. The guest asked for water. Soda-water? No, ordinary water, well-water, tap-water. Yes; yes.

Finally he was left alone.

At first his attention was arrested by a buffet in the centre of the restaurant, with a violet flame flickering on it for some unknown purpose. Later he saw the waiters warming plates over this strange perpetual light, to prevent their cooling by the time they were placed before the guests. At this late hour there were only a few people in the restaurant. At some distance from him there was a fair-haired dandy in a tail-coat who looked like a diplomat; opposite the latter sat two well-to-do young ladies with their grey-haired father, who seemed to be an industrialist, an old Swiss patrician; near them sat a party of eight or ten ladies and gentlemen, all dressed in evening clothes. These must have been about halfway through a long supper. They were drinking champagne with red wine. At a glance from the major-domo the waiters successively brought various glasses and goblets; the silver dishes with their silver covers were taken round, and the guests helped themselves unhurriedly, as if absorbed by the turns in the conversation. They took a slice of fish, a claw of lobster; or they tasted the glamorous flesh-coloured meat which at such restaurants is sometimes tinted like the faces of women; more than one of the ladies merely glanced at a dish and motioned it away.

Kornél gazed about him mistrustfully. Cut-glass glittered on every table, the crystal chandelier in the centre cast a magical, subdued light on the shirtfronts and on the ladies' diamonds and tiaras. Frankly speaking, it would have been all the same to him if the restaurant had not been quite so glittering. He soon made new discoveries. The waters of the lake sounded with even strokes directly below his feet. This delightful pavilion had been built to jut out over the lake. On the platform gypsies with beards and spectacles were playing stricty classical music, from printed sheets.

All this looked extremely ominous and impelled him to study the bill of fare thoroughly. The average prices varied between fifteen and thirty-five Swiss francs. There were, however, dishes without any indication except question marks, as if the distinguished proprietor, ensconced in the self-assurance of centuries of wealth, was shrugging his shoulders in scorn of petty details. As a rule, neither the waiters nor the guests ever talked about such matters, carefully avoiding any allusion to money, that despicable, filthy, ignominious article which everybody, of course, had so much of.

At this point he knitted his eyebrows and grew sober, like someone who suddenly finds himself in a trap. He looked up Omelette à Woburn, with which he had established a liaison in an unguarded moment. He found it, but only among the entrées, mentioned as an item in a group, without a fixed price. He began to multiply and divide, to calculate what the eleven Swiss francs in his pocket were worth in various other European currencies; but these arithmetical operations did not add to their value. He rubbed his stubbly chin with a perspiring palm. He felt very bad indeed. If anyone had offered to release him at the price of cutting off the little finger of his left hand, he would have agreed to the bargain without an argument. He glanced more and more often at the exit.

Since he had waited for half an hour to be served, and it looked as if they had forgotten him entirely, he decided to beat a retreat. He rang.

In a second the waiters were at his table. They were so numerous that each guest had two or three apiece.

Apologizing volubly, they assured him that his food would be ready in a minute or two. In the meantime he ordered some bread to sedate his hungerpangs.

A waiter brought it in a pretty little cut-glass dish. It was toast, tissue thin, a wafer, like the host at Holy Communion to nourish the soul and prepare it for eternal life. He crunched it slowly.

About a quarter of an hour later a mysterious coming and going commenced around the buffet. The whole staff marched up to it, as to an altar. A waiter brought a huge dish covered with a silver lid; for a few moments he fussed about the violet flame and then actually came towards Kornél. A warmed plate was put before him on the table and, with the aid of the other waiters, the operation of serving was begun under the major-domo's personal supervision. When the lid was removed from the dish, Kornél dared not look at it immediately, only later. After such preliminaries he would not have been surprised to find that a diamond the size of a walnut had been baked into the omelette with a ruby on one side and a sapphire on the other; so he was disappointed to find that the Omelette à Woburn looked exactly like the scrambled eggs his mother used to make. There it rested in the middle of the silver platter, as if lost in infinite space, fried in the shape of a fish. The waiter seized it with a knife and fork, but before putting it on his plate, perhaps in conformity with the restaurant's traditions or actuated by the exterior resemblance of the Omelette à Woburn to a fish, he snipped off the two ends with lightning speed, like the inedible head and tail of a fish, and nonchalantly threw those yellow, exceedingly appetizing pieces on another silver dish held by an assistant waiter, thereby undoubtedly making the portion smaller. Kornél absolutely disapproved. He looked after them with wistful, longing eyes.

In a flash he had gobbled up the omelette. It was even smaller than he suspected, scarcely a mouthful. He had already eaten up his bread. He did not have the courage to order more. So he drank two glasses of water instead.

The waves on the lake were murmuring, the orchestra was playing the Meistersänger, the nearby party were still meandering through their dinner, but all this held little interest for him. He was worrying about what was going to happen next. Ready for the worst, he asked for his bill. He closed his eyes while the majordomo totted it up with a fountain pen. He was imagining all sorts of scandals, embarrassing scenes, amazed faces at first, then suppressed, agitated altercations, in the course of which he would be shown the door, a scuffle, policemen, the demand for his papers. His heart was in his throat. At last he opened his eyes. The bill was already lying before him on a tray. It was for a total of four francs. He took out his wallet and fingered it slowly, with volumptuous enjoyment, as if it were difficult for him to find that ten franc note in his wad. He threw it on the table with a lordly air. He got six francs change. He jingled it in his hands, like winnings, and in his elation put a franc into the hand of every waiter, giving two to the major-domo.

Having been grossly over-tipped the waiters exchanged glances, bowed, and left him to himself.

He put on his raincoat unassisted.

On the way out he passed the major-domo, who, with one arm raised, was apparently engaged in guiding some extremely important operation. Kornél stared him in the eye, trying to force a greeting out of him. But the major-domo was so occupied that he failed to react. So Kornél raised his hat.

That was wrong too.

Blushing, and with a feeling of sick shame that made his very nose itch, he reached the street. He drew a deep breath and broke into a run. He ran all the way to the statue of Zwingli. Here he took rough stock of his situation. He could not go back to the hostel; all he had was enough money to redeem his case in the morning and travel on. Nevertheless, he felt happy, as if he had escaped death after some terrible adventure. He roamed about bare-headed in the starlit summer night. Again and again in the course of his aimless promenade, he found himself in front of the restaurant, which was darkened by now. He sat down on a bench at the lakeside. He thought of all sorts of foolish things. The diplomat-dandy rose to his mind, and the heavy industrialist with his two well-behaved daughters, the party which mixed champagne with red wine, the major-domo who did not return his greeting, and the Omelette à Woburn, too, whose ends the waiter had so heartlessly cut off and thrown on a silver platter.

All of a sudden, as if heavy with sleep, he bent his head down to the arm of the bench. But he did not sleep. He was sobbing with soft, quick gasps.

Translated by Zsuzsanna Horn

ADVENTURE IN UNIFORM
by SÁNDOR HUNYADY

When the war broke out, I joined up as a second-line reservist in the Fifty-first Regiment with the grey facings. True, I had not been given the volunteer's braid, but none the less I was very nicely off. My unit was stationed in Kolozsvár, where I had been born, and I knew half the town. I was a journalist and had joined the regiment almost straight from the editorial office. My sergeant called me "Mr. Editor". My military service consisted of getting into my uniform twice a week in order to present myself for appearances' sake at company headquarters. Otherwise my life went on as usual. I wore civilian clothes most of the time, and through the windows of the café I would watch companies marching to the station on their way to the front.

I am not saying all this just to boast. The older I get, the more ashamed I am of having cheated myself out of my share of suffering when everyone else was suffering. But it is part of the picture that the reader should know what an irresponsible puppy and how far from being a fine soldier I was on that summer's Sunday afternoon when this story began.

Yet I had a fine martial air at that moment. I was wearing typical private's uniform, with heavy laced boots and tight-fitting blue trousers. Round my waist was the regulation belt, with the double-headed eagle on its brass buckle. I had just left the barracks; my day's service was done. I was hurrying home to my rooms to change back into civvies and to go to the theatre, where I was courting the second *soubrette*.

As I said, it was a Sunday afternoon. The street was crowded with promenading servant-girls in their best clothes. Kolozsvár is a veritable catchment area for all the folk currents of the neighbourhood. And the small groups of Székely, Rumanian and Hungarian girls sauntering along arm in arm gave the servants' parade the iridescence of a peacock's tail. Each village was represented by its own characteristic dress, by the characteristic colour of the hair, figure and temperament, by its ribbons, skirts and kerchiefs. What gaily swarming crowds! How brightly the clean-washed, eager faces shone! Everybody was in a hurry to cram as much happiness as possible into an afternoon that was passing far too quickly.

Many of the girls looked at me invitingly, some of them smiled at me, a few even accosted me. Indeed, why shouldn't they? I was twenty-two years old, and in my private's uniform and iron-heeled boots I must have looked exactly like any other peasant boy from one of the neighbouring counties. I found it all very amusing. I felt like a prince in disguise. I winked back at the girls and even pulled their pigtails. I behaved just as a private should who is out for a bit of a Sunday adventure. I scored victories and suffered setbacks. The girls joggled me, trod on my feet, pinched my arms. The wide-rolling river carried me gaily along amidst its little eddies.

Suddenly the tide swept me up to a tall girl from Kalotaszeg. We bumped into each other. I looked at her. She was a lovely creature. Clean as fresh linen and slender as a birch sapling.

I caught her arm.

"Where are you off to?"

"I'm off to find a sweetheart," she answered flippantly.

I drew her towards me.

"Then you can stop right now, because I'm doing the same."

The girl looked at me. It was an honest, serious, scrutinizing look, as if I were a chicken or cabbage she considered buying at the market place. Finally she nodded.

"All right. Let's go together."

A wave of pride rushed over me. Deep within me I felt a strange warmth spreading, the legacy of a million years. The spark in her touched off an answering glow in me. I was filled with a sense of triumph, and at the same time of tenderness, of melting devotion. And I knew that she felt the same about me. We walked on silently through the jostling crowd. Our mood was touched with a new gravity. My hand was scorched by the touch of her strong elbow as I cupped it in my palm to prevent her being whirled away from me.

She really was a lovely girl. Chestnut hair, grey eyes. Her soft light-brown skin seemed to be too taut for her full face. It stretched tightly over her nose, her lips, her chin. I was inclined to think that she could hardly shut her eyes, the little muscles round them were so elastically resistant under that clear complexion.

When I first accosted her I had been perhaps a bit familiar. But after a few minutes of silent walking, I involuntarily spoke to her more tenderly, with greater respect. And I saw with surpise that this serene young peasant girl responded at once to my new approach. She too dropped her flippant tone and asked me with simple directness where I came from. Was I from Kolozsvár?

I told her I came from Szilágy County. I even invented a name for the village: Pokozd.

"And you, I see, come from Kalotaszeg," I said to her. "What's your name?"

"Vilma Jakab. And yours?"

"Sándor Nagy," I lied, for I was in no doubt that the girl would leave me flat and run off angrily if I told her I was not of her own class.

As we strolled on she told me that the place where she worked was in Bocskai tér, and that her master was some kind of civil servant. It seemed to be a decent family. Still, she didn't know the place very well yet... She had only come up to Kolozsvár from her village two weeks ago.

"I'm free till eight," she told me, "but then I have to go home. They will be having supper at home tonight. Not that they couldn't manage without me. It's just a cold supper. Sausages."

Each Sunday this peasant promenade follows the same precise course, reminiscent of the march of ants along the ground. The colourful stream flows first through Honvéd utca, then up the right-hand side of Fő tér; from there it continues through Union and Bartha Miklós utca towards the Szamos river and turns again along the right-hand side of the avenue. The right-hand side is crowded, thick with dust, loud with noise, and one is bumped and pushed along continuously under the ancient trees; the other side is almost completely empty. Only a few people stroll there in the shadow of the trees opposite. I thought this was just a matter of custom, so I said to the girl:

"Let's cross over to the other side. What's the use of getting squashed in this crowd?"

The girl stared at me.

"Sándor! Don't you know that we are not allowed to go over there? The policeman would chase us back. That side is reserved for the gentry."

Of course I didn't know. Gentleman idler that I was, how should I have known the extent of the stupidity and insolence reflected in such police orders?

The blood rushed to my head. Without thinking I mumbled to myself furiously.

"What a damned shame. I'll have to write something about it."

"What did you say?" the girl asked fearfully.

I evaded a direct answer.

"Damn them, it's a dirty trick, not to let one walk where one wants to! Why are those people over there better than we are?"

The girl did not have the slightest notion of socialist ideas. She simply shrugged her shoulders.

"I don't know why you should get so angry about it. We can go down there if you like, where the geese and ducks are, we won't find many people there."

But I was furious. It suddenly occurred to me that I couldn't take her to the Kiosk, a "first-class" restaurant either. The waiters would promptly inform us that it was no place for privates and servant girls. Impudent swine! For the first time I was feeling on my own hide what the arrogant measures taken for the convenience of my kind of people meant to others.

There was a little amusement park along the avenue, so we went there for want of a better place. We rode on the swings. We weighed ourselves. We looked at the Tattooed Lady. We took turns hitting the test-your-strength machine. When I paid, I changed a five forint piece.

The girl stared at me and the coin.

"Where did you get so much money?"

"My father has quite a bit of land and we are also part-owners of a threshing-machine." I lied to her, quite fluent by this time. "Five forints are nothing to me."

But the girl did not let the matter go at that. "We also have land and a house. But my father would kill my brother if he threw away good money the way you do..."

By now I had completely forgotten that I was due at the theatre. I had forgotten the *soubrette* and my own position in civil life. Deep down in my heart I was wishing that the Szilágy County background I had invented was true and I myself really a peasant boy who that Sunday afternoon had found the one true love of his life realized in this fresh, lovely, natural young girl.

It was an afternoon of perfect bliss. There was only one dangerous moment in it. A bow-legged, pockmarked old cavalry corporal tried to take the girl away from me. First he walked up and down before us like a dog in heat. Then he picked a quarrel with me, claiming I hadn't saluted him properly. He made me stand at attention and gave me a thorough dressing-down in front of the girl. He had the authority, for he was a corporal and I was a mere recruit. I tried to put up with his insults patiently, but felt my face turning pale and the muscles of my right arm quivering with a desire to pull out my bayonet and plunge it into this yellow-toothed, tobacco-smelling vile rat.

The tension between us was growing more dangerous every moment. By now our eyes were flashing out something quite different from what we were saying. I don't know what would have happened if the girl had not intervened, if she had not drawn her arm through mine in a gesture of profound solidarity and turned humbly, yet very firmly to the corporal:

"I know quite well why the honoured corporal is badgering this young man. Please leave him alone, sir. In any case you won't be able to separate us anyway, because you see we are from the same village..."

And she squeezed my arm to her side.

The corporal stood quite still for a few seconds, staring at us very hard as if calculating inwardly whether it was worth his while to risk a row. Then, perhaps a spark of humanity sprang to life in him, or he saw something hard and determined written on both our faces; he put his sword firmly under his arm, turned on his heel and went off in search of new conquests, venting his anger in a single sentence:

"Damn both of you and your village as well!"

When the danger had passed, we walked on quietly side by side for a while. It was she who at last broke the silence. Quietly, tenderly, wisely she spoke her mind:

"You see, Sándor, that is why you ought to try and get a promotion. If you had had even a single star on your uniform that corporal wouldn't have dared to be so insolent towards you. Because people only dare to be as mean as that with those who have nothing and nobody in the world. One doesn't need to have much, just a few pitchforks of hay, and people will immediately overlook this and that, and be nice to one, for they'll reckon"who knows when we'll need a bit of his hay...' "

Plenty of my girl friends had tried to inspire me to greater ambition in the past. But I had always resisted their attempts. Yet there was so much selflessness and tact in this girl's attitude, such wisdom in what she said, that I felt like kissing her hands.

Our arms round each other's waist, we walked on in silence —private and servant-girl—amidst the gradually dispersing crowd, as dusk began to envelop us.

When the church clock struck half past seven, and the girl began to talk of having to go home soon, I said to her with a heavy heart:

"It won't be easy to part from you, Vilma..."

She considered a while, then looked up at me and said:

"We don't have to part. You can come up to my room. You will have to wait while I serve supper. Then you can stay with me. But only come if you don't have to go back to your barracks before morning, I wouldn't want the porter opening the door for you in the night and asking you whom you'd been visiting."

Plain talk indeed! A frank invitation to a night of love. But it was not said lightly. She spoke simply and without beating about the bush, as of something natural and human, a part of life as simple as breathing.

"Thank you very much," I answered gratefully. "Luckily, I can stay out all night, the sergeant is a pal of mine."

We started off quietly towards Bocskai tér.

On the way the girl told me that her employer's name was Ferenc Bodrogi, she did not know where he worked except that it was in some kind of an office. He had a wife, a son and a daughter. His son was away at present in the army. They lived at number four on the third floor.

Her explanation first startled me, then I very nearly burst out laughing. I knew the family extremely well. Bodrogi was an engineer at the gasworks, I had gone to school with the son and had even flirted with the daughter. I had been to their home quite often. It was strange for me to have to enter the familiar gate and go up the dark, and narrow backstairs, only lighted on the second floor by a very small gas lamp.

When we reached the third floor the girl searched in her skirt for the key to the kitchen and unlocked the door. I knew the kitchen quite well too. Sometimes, when the bell was not functioning at the main entrance, I had knocked at the back door and come in that way. There had been a little Rumanian servant girl in the house before. She had been rather pretty too, and I remembered pinching her cheeks.

Vilma now turned the light on and took off her shawl. I stood on the threshold of the open door and wanted to go in after her.

She turned towards me.

"Stay outside on the balcony for a bit, Sándor, till the family has gone out or gone to bed. One of them might come into the kitchen. There's no need for them to see you. They might not even like your being here."

"They certainly would not," I thought to myself as I stepped out on the narrow open balcony. It was quite dark by now. Lamps shone brightly in the doors and windows looking out to the balconies which ran round the inside courtyard of the huge block of flats on each floor, and you could see shadowy figures moving about in the kitchens. Somewhere a servant-girl was singing. Another soldier, presumably on the same errand as myself, loitered on the first floor balcony, leaning against the iron railing.

It was a hot summer evening. "The smell from the courtyards of houses like this is certainly pretty awful at this time of year," I thought to myself as I sat down on a dustbin, between a cold flat-iron and a paper-sack containing charcoal.

Vilma was busying herself in the kitchen. She got the plates, forks and knives ready, sliced the bread and put a clean napkin in the bread-basket. She peeled five pairs of sausages, and sliced onions to go with them. From the cupboard she took out some cherry-strudel—obviusly left over from lunch. She called to me through the open door of the kitchen:

"Will you have some, Sándor?"

I would have liked to, but Vilma was unable to bring me anything for in the door leading to the flat appeared the daughter of her employers. There was a time when I had found little Piri attractive. I had particularly admired her skin and her hair. Now I no longer liked her face. It was much too hard. I was annoyed, too, at her not returning Vilma's friendly "good evening" when she came into the kitchen. From the dark balcony I noted the boredom with which she went up to the table and idly picked a cherry out of the strudel.

My blood boiled to hear her talk to my Vilma as if to her slave.

"Hurry up that supper, Vilma. We're going to the cinema. When we're gone, you can put the table in order, do the beds, and then you can go to bed yourself, we won't need you any more to-night. Only don't forget to wake me tomorrow at seven, and clean my tennis shoes."

When the young lady had flitted back into the flat, Vilma came out into the passage for a moment and said:

"Isn't she pretty? Her name's Piri."

The bell in the kitchen rang impatiently. Vilma carried the sausages and onions out and left the kitchen empty.

I could follow every step of the girl in my thoughts. I could visualize the dining-room, the dinner-table, the settee, the clock, the pictures on the wall.

She went on hurrying to and fro between kitchen and dining-room. They rang for water. They rang for salt. I heard her turn on the tap. When, at long last they were through, Vilma came out to the railing and shook the crumbs from the tablecloth. Then Piri appeared once more. This time she had her hat and coat on. She measured out sugar and coffee for the next day's breakfast from the cupboard. Then she left without saying goodnight.

The main door slammed and I saw the family I knew so well go down the stairs.

At last the girl called me in.

"Go into my place while I put the kitchen in order, will you?"

What she'd called "my place" was a tiny room, or rather a cubby hole, ventilated through the kitchen. There was barely enough space for the iron bed and the single chair, on which stood a tin wash-basin. The girl's coloured skirts and cheap blouses hung from two nails in the wall. At the head of the bed stood a small painted wooden box, the kind peasant boys take with them when they go to do their military service. On that wooden box lay a Roman Catholic prayer book, which had been stuck full of holy pictures with paper-lace edges. The Holy Virgin wore forget-me-not blue veils, the pictures of Christ were pale and waxen, with blood dripping from under the crown of thorns.

I sat down on the bed and silently watched Vilma putting the kitchen in order. Outside the heavy summer smell from the yard had appalled me. But in that windowless little chamber I thought I was breathing in the light smell of village soil. The smell of a peasant house with an earthen floor. Perhaps it was not just a fancy, perhaps she had brought that far away fragrance with her clothes.

I grew impatient.

"Aren't you coming?"

"Right away. Just let me wash my hands properly," she replied, "I've been slicing onions, you know..." And she went to the tap by the wall, where she washed her hands thoroughly with a big cake of crude laundry soap.

At long last she came into her tiny cubby hole.

"Get up, so that I can make the bed."

I rose, took her by the waist, and drew her to me... I have had plenty of adventures with women. But never before, or since, have I felt such purity, such dramatic strength in any embrace. My own strength was as nothing compared to hers as she put her muscular arms round my neck. She took my head in her hands and looked straight into my eyes.

Softly she said:

"It's all because of your eyes. That's why you're here. I loved your eyes the moment you first spoke to me..."

Well, this adventure turned into a genuine love affair. We met on three consecutive Sundays and there was a holiday in between when we were together too. Four times in succession, and each time I put on my private's uniform and played the peasant boy. Or rather I didn't even play the role. I simply behaved naturally, in harmony with my happy mood. I only had to take care not to talk about things that might awaken the girl's suspicions. And in fact our conversation was much more interesting than is usual on such occasions. And that by no means because of my intelligence; it was due to the wealth of her emotions, her utter sincerity, her remarkably expressive and colourful language.

On the fifth Sunday afternoon I did not go to our usual meeting-place in front of Hintz, the chemist's, on Fő tér. Why did I stay away? I can't remember. Perhaps I had something to do, perhaps I simply overslept. The fact remains that I did not go, but kept my civilian clothes on all day and at about seven o'clock that evening I chanced to pass the chemist's shop.

She was still standing in the doorway of the Hintz house, motionless, a shawl round her head and shoulders, waiting. One could see by the way she stood that she had been there for hours. Her face was earnest and sad. There she stood, looking out into the rain from the entrance. For it was raining and growing dark. So she did not recognize me in my suit and rubber raincoat. Indeed, she hardly looked at me. She was expecting somebody quite different—a young soldier in a blue coat with belt and boots.

As I walked past, my heart gave a leap. But I did not want her to see me in my elegant clothes. Besides, I wasn't alone. A colleague of mine hung on my arm, for we had only one umbrella between us. We were discussing the war, and were walking fast because of the rain.

But when we were about three blocks away, my throat grew suddenly dry. I thought of Kipling's native girl who waited for forty years at the crossroads for her unfaithful British soldier. I ran all the way back to the chemist's shop. But she was no longer standing in the doorway. Poor girl, she must have just left. It was half past seven by that time, and she had to go home to lay the table, serve the supper.

I cursed myself. My heart ached. I loved that girl.

On the following Sunday it all came right again. We met as usual. I lied to her about having served a day's detention in barracks. We walked together, we rowed on the tiny lake by the avenue, and fed the swans with breadcrumbs. And at night we again lay together in her little room, in the narrow iron bed, clasping each other closely in the earth-scented dark. Suddenly the girl laid her head on my breast and whispered:

"How long can we be like this? One of these days you'll be put into field-grey uniform like the others and I'll see you marching to the station with flowers in your cap. And when that happens, I'll drown myself in the Szamos..."

I very nearly gave myself away at that moment. I should only have had to turn on the light and show her my hands: "Look how soft my hands are. Open your eyes at last: do peasant boys have hands like mine?"

But I did not have the courage to do it. I was afraid of making her unhappy. I felt she would not take what had happened between us as a joke. But I also knew that the truth was bound to come out. I simply could not go on cheating this pure, kind-hearted creature who had given herself to me so completely, without any thought of what people would say if they found out, without fearing shame or unhappiness. Once she had said to me very simply: "If I have a baby I can never go home again. My mother would shut the door in my face."

I don't know exactly how I conceived the miserable idea that it was much better to let her find out about me by herself, without my telling her. Just let her see me in my true light and draw her own conclusions, so avoiding a big scene. I could always add further explanations later.

It was a stupid idea. Today I can find no excuse for my accepting old Bodrogi's invitation to supper. Why did I have to do such a thing? Perhaps it wasn't I that did it, but the devil, who sometimes gets the upper hand in us.

The old gentleman found me at the café.

"Come and dine with us tomorrow night, young man. My son's back on three days' leave from his unit."

I dressed with meticulous care for that supper. I had a fine beige summer suit, and that is what I put on. I looked at myself in the mirror and saw an exquisite dandy.

I rang the front door bell. Piri opened the door to me.

"Well, here you are at last! Nearly half an hour late."

We had a quick nip of rose brandy. Then we sat down to table. I was placed next to Piri. I had a vague idea that they might not be disinclined to offer me her hand in marriage. Only, of course, I would have to pull myself together, take the bar exams or get a teacher's diploma.

The hostess called through the door:

"You can serve now, Vilma."

Everybody was jabbering away around me. My friend was telling me about artillery training, the hostess was complaining about market prices and the engineer was analysing the situation at the front.

Piri put her hand on my arm.

"What's the matter with you? Why are you so nervous?"

It was at this moment that the girl came in. She was carrying a big platter of stuffed eggs. She was standing quite close to the table by the time she saw and recognized me. Her face first turned as white as a sheet, then it changed to a flaming red. She did not say a word, she even looked quite composed. But I sensed her deep pain as her arm and elbow trembled when she offered us the eggs.

I could not look at her as she carried the platter round the table. I just stared in front of me. There was complete silence. When she reached my side and offered me the food, I whispered:

"Good evening, Vilma."

"Good evening," she answered dully, an empty look in her eyes. And again I sensed that she had to summon all her peasant strength to keep from fainting there beside the table, with the dish in her hand.

Miss Piri began to giggle:

"So you know each other, do you?"

And with ingenious feminine intuition she added:

"Perhaps from some soldiers' ball?"

Everybody broke into laughter, amused at the incongruity of such a ridiculous supposition. The girl herself, her expression set and cold as stone, walked mechanically round the table offering the food. When nobody took any more, she went quietly out of the room. Her hands were full of dishes, and she pushed down the door handle with her elbow. Then she closed the door again very softly from the outside.

We ate and ate. They spoke to me, but I did not answer. I did not even understand what they were talking about. With all my heart, with all my mind, I was in the kitchen, seeing the insect powder strewn in the corners, the entrance to Vilma's tiny room with the narrow iron bed, the nails in the wall, and the gay clothes hanging from them. At the table my hosts scolded me for being so absent-minded. In my confusion I muttered something about a sudden toothache, and Mr. Bodrogi advised me to apply some rum. His wife rang the bell hanging above the table for the next course. She rang once. She rang twice. She rang a third time. Nobody came. Finally, with a look of annoyance on her face, she got up from the table and went out into the kitchen herself.

There was a long, painful pause. I felt my heart throbbing in my throat, but I lacked the courage to dash out into the kitchen and find out what was happening there. What could have happened? From out there one could hear a low, subdued discussion, followed by ominous silence. Finally the door opened and the hostess reappeared, holding the second course in her own well-manicured hands. She sat down in her chair, her face red with anger.

"That girl," she said "has gone mad. She says she won't stay another minute. She's given back her pay. She put it down on the table and declared she'd rather throw herself out of the window than come back into this room. Have you done anything to this girl, Sándor?"

They all stared at me.

"Me? I didn't do a thing," came my cowardly denial.

Nobody was laughing now. The dining-room was charged with a sense of calamity. We ate in silence. Everyone could feel that something serious had happened. Suddenly Piri jumped up and, on the pretext of going for the mustard, ran into the kitchen, as if unable to control her excitement and eager to satisfy her curiosity. But she was back again in a minute.

"The silly girl has already packed all her things. She's given me back the key to the kitchen. Here it is."

And she put down on the table the little key I knew so well.

"Has she really gone?" I asked in a low voice.

"She is just leaving," Piri answered sharply, lookig straight into my face with malevolent curiosity. Suddenly all the restraints of patience, good manners and friendship which bound me to these people snapped. I threw my napkin on the table and jumped up. Without even an apology, I ran out like a lunatic. I raced along the passage and down the stairs, taking the steps three at a time. I caught up with her just as she was stepping out into the street. She had her shawl on and was carrying her heavy wooden box in her right hand. Her shoulder sagged under its weight. I sprang in front of her, all out of breath. She stopped. She looked at me with a warm gentleness, without reproach, as though she were saying good-bye with her eyes.

"Vilma, my darling," I stammered and tried to take her left hand in mine.

She put it behind her.

"Let me go, sir," she said softly, but with such indescribable firmness that I had to step aside. Once more she looked at me. Then she turned her head away and stepped out into the dark street carrying her green wooden box. I never saw her again.

Translated by Zsuzsa Madarassy-Beck

AMBITION AND HILARITY
by TIBOR DÉRY

It was a cold night in winter. The full moon, perched on a factory chimney, tossed gentle shafts of light into the room whose only window gave on to the railway lines crossing Ferdinand Bridge. The night's stillness would have been complete but for the noise of an engine being shunted; it snorted, coughed and cleared its throat; then, whistling lustily, it jolted past the house. Its moonlit smoke lingered outside the window for a moment.

Évi drew her hand from under the blanket and dipped it into the silver haze that hovered, vibrating, above her bed and instantly coated the hand with a flimsy, glittering, silver glove. The little girl gazed at her hand with delight: her five fingernails were shining like five tiny moons. She moved one leg from under the blanket to stretch it too up into the moonlight, but by now the smoke outside the window had cleared and the tiny leg looked piebald, like a map of Hungary. For a time she looked at it with disappointment, angrily wriggling her uncomprehending toes. Suddenly she laughed and jumped out of bed. She put on her stockings and shoes hurriedly and tumbled into her coat, then tiptoed slowly towards the door.

Six people slept in the room: a jobless barber, a one-eyed teamster and his wife, a student, a Polish woman refugee, and a master shoemaker. Évi's older sister worked at night, shovelling snow in the Great Boulevard, and would get home at six in the morning—her hands ruby-coloured, her teeth sparkling, her stomach frozen—and without speaking a word would go to bed, curving, body and soul, into a living question-mark, one that never had an answer. The six other occupants of the room would keep on snoring, while Évi wiped the mist from her sister's hair with her hand and melted the ice in her eyebrows with her breath. The six fellow lodgers snored in six different ways; one of them made fine bagpipe music.

The moon was still up. The leg of the table cast a shadow so thick that Évi involuntarily lifted her legs over it. Realizing what she had done, she laughed inside her coat, which she had pulled up over her head. Out in the night, the shunted engine shrieked, and the window-pane, patched together in a hundred places, instantly began to grumble and complain.

"And where are you off to?" the old shoemaker mumbled behind her the moment she laid her hand on the door knob. She turned around and tossed her head. She was just waist-high to the old man. She could put her teeth into his stomach.

"Why don't you answer my question?"

She said nothing. Pursing her lips, she almost stamped her little foot, wobbling in its brown man's shoe. The blue-painted table was silent, and so was the blue-painted bed and the silver moonlight; only this old devil had to go and open his mouth.

"Where are you going?" he growled for the third time.

She opened her eyes wide.

"Me? Going out!"

"And you are taking your doll with you?"

She looked down. The blond head of her doll showed under her arm.

"That's to bring me luck," she said and, turning her back on the old man, left the room.

She had to clamber down three flights of stairs to reach the house door, where two waiters returning from work at midnight always rang the bell about this time. She was lucky, for, after about a quarter of an hour of hanging about, she was able, using the first waiter as a cover, to scuttle out into the street like a little lizard. The concierge said nothing.

The cold immediately bit into her ears. She laughed and broke into a run, holding the doll tightly under her arm lest it should catch cold. An arc lamp hung above the railway tracks, shedding light up and down the street, but after she had turned the corner she waded through moonlight and nothing else. One half of the street was black, the other pure silver, and both were deserted; there was not a living soul, not even a stray dog, to be seen down its length. In the silvery half of the street stood a wrecked four-storey building. It was just possible that it was inhabited by some lions, but at this moment no lion could be seen sitting outside the partially collapsed door and combing its mane in the moonlit night because, evidently, they disliked cold weather. Not a single window was lit up all down that row.

She could have walked more slowly, for her appointment was for a quarter to one, outside the arrivals side of West Station. The cold was so bitter that frost closed her nostrils and the snow-laden trees lining the pavement seemed to growl nervously from time to time. "My," she thought, "how *they* must be shivering, standing on the same spot all through the winter!"

A man smoking a cigarette was standing by one of the trees; he stopped her.

"Where are you going?" he asked.

The little girl, hopping from leg to leg, took in the situation with her eyes and ears. Since they were alone in the street and neither motor-cars nor trams could be heard, she switched on a well-mannered smile and looked at the man with round-eyed innocence. He wore a good topcoat and a red silk scarf—hardly the type to strip a child of her clothes.

"Why don't you answer me?" he said. "Where are you going at this time of night?"

"Go to hell!" she thought.

A small cloud sailed below the moon, smudging the shadows on the white snow.

"Have you lost your way?" the man asked. "Maybe you can't find your way home?"

Évi blinked her eyes but did not speak.

"Why don't you talk?" the gentleman asked, throwing away his cigarette. "Something wrong with you?"

She continued to smile innocently and silently shook her head. "If he asks me another," she thought, "I'll spit on him." Luckily for her, two men came round the corner of the next side street and were now walking briskly towards them.

"Come, tell me where you're going," the gentleman asked.

Across the street, a shop-window was oozing light, and it was in that direction that she now nodded her head.

"There," she said in a ringing voice; she turned slowly and sauntered off. In the middle of the road she shot a mali-

ciously gleeful glance back and saw that the man was not following her.

The window was bright with sheer, chestnut-coloured silk
stockings; on a side shelf lay a few pale-blue petticoats with lace
trimmings; further inside the shop, a man was stacking white
boxes. Was that man the shopkeeper, she wondered, or was he
stealing something? She pressed her nose against the glass and
took a good look at the man who was working with such calm
movements. He had a thin black moustache and fine dark eyes;
never once did he look in the direction of the display window. Évi
watched him attentively and calmed down when she saw that he
put a box or two back on the shelves. Back in the far corner of the
shop stood a small iron stove red-hot with a roaring fire; those
short, snapping sounds could not be heard, only seen, out in the
street, but the colder the blast of the wind from the Danube, the
more obvious was the crackling of wood and, after it, the puff of
heat from the stove—it was as though the senses had changed their
functions. "Nice, that stove," she thought as she moved on again.

The little band Évi joined outside the arrival platform of West
Station at a quarter to one sharp was made up from four different
districts of Budapest. One member had come from Angels' Field,
one from Zugló, another from Ferencváros, and a fourth from an
ill-reputed district called "Chicago". Évi was the youngest member of the set and the only girl. They didn't even say hello to her.

"What've you brought your doll with you for?" asked Lajos
Hikker, a boy who had a fatty growth near his right ear. He wasn't
much taller than Évi, and she didn't answer his question.

"Is she deaf?"

She pressed close to Totyó.

"Well?" Totyó asked her.

"It's to bring us luck," she said.

A mixed Hungarian-Russian patrol was striding along in the
thick snow that had not yet been cleared away across the street;
their shadows reached as far as the opposite side of the square.
The five youngsters flattened themselves against the wall. Feri
Rácz, the one from Zugló, gnashed his teeth in anger, while the
other Feri Rácz, the one from Ferencváros, stood silently with his
chin pressed against his chest. Totyó was whistling softly.

"Why don't we get going?" one of the boys asked when the patrol was swallowed up in the thick, dusty shadow of the side street. The vast moonlit square in front of them was empty; now and then gusts of wind drove fistfuls of snow across it. Further ahead, somewhere near the crossing of the Boulevard, a blowlamp was sparking, throwing off tiny blue stars. The five little ragamuffins listened to the silence.

"Maybe the ocean is like this," Zugló Rácz said, holding his breath. The wind tugged at his military tunic, which reached down to his knees and was tied about his waist with a thick rope; the pointed top of his hood drooped. "Maybe it's like this."

"Shut up!"

Totyó also hurried him up. "Can we get going?" asked the same boy as before, and he did get going. "Take it easy!" Totyó growled and shoved him back with his elbow. "Don't get excited!" He went forward, in front of the gang, his clenched fists in his bottomless trouser-pockets, elbows turned outwards; a lock of raven-black hair hung over his forehead, under a red beret. His small snub nose was pink, the colour of early cherries. The girl strode on his right, half a step behind him; then followed the other three boys, single file, each with their feet tied up in rags.

"The password's Ambition and Hilarity," Totyó informed his followers, acknowledging with a quarter-turn of his head the distance of three steps that separated him from them. "If anybody stops us, keep dead silent. I'll do the talking. We've come up from Komárom, going to my aunt's at Aggteleki utca, and she's waiting for us with eyes red from weeping."

"And if they think they'll run us in anyway, then what?" Lajos Hikker called from the rear.

"Ain't finished yet," Totyó stopped him. "In case of extreme danger, at the signal the party disperses in five directions. Reassemble half an hour later at the same spot."

After they had left the Great Boulevard, streetlights no longer lit up their cheeks. In a narrow lane the moon shed light only on the top storeys of the houses, and down below a gaping abyss seemed to divide the darkness, its direction hinted by the snow and by an occasional gleaming window-pane. Here and there crows flew up from the pavement—out of litter with a stink of

greens—and alighted on the white snowfield of a window-sill. The
streets were sinister with danger.

After half an hour of silent marching, Totyó stopped. "This is
the place," he announced, twisting his fists out of his trouser-
pockets. He examined a narrow cellar window with a missing bro-
ken-out pane. "Zugló Rácz, go across the street and stand guard!"

"Me?" the boy said, making a face as if about to cry.

"What! Already?"

"You're leaving me out?" the child muttered, and his small
face, hardly showing under his pointed hood, paled to the colour
of cheese with the sudden onrush of anger.

"You'll wait until we're all inside," Totyó explained patiently.
"Then you'll signal to say if you can see the light through the shutter."

Zugló Rácz cleared his throat.

"Just be careful," he hissed. "I'm not the kind you can double-
cross."

Totyó stepped up to him and grabbed his coat at the stomach.
"Listen. I don't like dirty words," he said, and swung his narrow
shoulders slowly, like a prize-fighter. "But I can give you a clout
right now that'll slide you home on your own damn snout!"

The smallest member of the gang, Évi, was lifted through the
broken hole in the window-pane first. Her tiny bottom disappeared into the sooty darkness behind the opening. In its place, after a bit, her strawberry-flushed face popped up. The lids over her
blue eyes flickered with fear.

"Trouble," she whispered.

"What's up?"

"I can hear rats."

"All right. Let's go on in!" Totyó ordered. "Hikker!"

"Wait!" Évi cried. "Gimme my doll first!"

Next they heaved the chap with the wen through the window;
he was followed by Ferencváros Rácz, and finally the chief was
pulled in. They had to lower themselves to the stone floor of the
cellar from the inner window-sill, a distance of about two metres.
They listened for rats since, judging by the smell of the place, Évi
might be right. There was silence. Évi flung herself into the darkness without making the slightest sound, as if she were jumping

into a barrel of tar, Totyó as if into a bowlful of cream; and as for the other two boys, they could have whistled with sheer joy while they leapt. In the cellar, a number of turret steps led to the wooden door that they had to force open.

Upstairs, in the pastry-shop, they switched the lights on. In no time the thick yellow light had rolled all over the long shop like warm honey. The pastries were laid out on silver plates on a long glass counter and protected by cheese-cloth; the walls were lined with shelves upon shelves of potbellied glass jars filled with sweets. From the cellar below came the sound of excited steps as Zugló Rácz hurried upstairs. Totyó gathered his gang around him.

"Now listen, you gang of runts," he said, burying both fists in his pockets. "Situation evaluated. It's like this. Martial law don't apply to us, since none of us is fifteen yet. We're orphans. That's an extenuating circumstance. 'Cept for Hikker, none of us has been picked up yet—touch wood—and that means there's no case of second offence. If we get nabbed, every bloody bloke's to turn on the waterworks and say he done it 'cause he's been starving. Right?"

"Right," the four thin voices chimed.

"Then... Ambition and Hilarity," Totyó muttered, paling.

Each of the five patrons sat down at a different, round, marble-topped table. The lights—for no known reason—went out, but luckily Hikker got hold of a thick, gilded votive candle. In the flickering shadowy light of this candle, the glass jars lining the walls threw sparks, the red marble tables flared, and the smooth, shining top of the long counter suddenly leaned out—like happiness itself—and, in all its light, shook hands with the children.

Nineteen pieces of confectionery, including cream buns, fell to each one's share. Totyó had twenty-two. A piece of chocolate-coated pastry that Ferencváros Rácz had somehow snatched during the division of spoils had to be retrieved out of his mouth. Severely and promptly punished in the form of a clout over the ear, he narrowly escaped losing a tooth in the whipped cream that was squeezed out of his mouth. With the help of a bottle of vermouth, a glass of ambition and hilarity could be dealt out to each table. Totyó was in the act of filling the fifth glass when suddenly the curtained door at the back of the room flew open, and there entered a very tall, thin man in long white underwear, with a red silk scarf tied about his head. Speechless with sleep, he stared at Totyó; then, licking his lips, he examined each member of the stupefied company.

"Well, well!" he said in surprise, raising the forefinger of his right hand. "What's that you're drinking?"

He shook his head in disapproval, and his big yellow jug-ears grew stiff with shock. "Well, what is it?... Cinzano!" he muttered, casting an outraged look at the revellers. "The only genuine bottle..."

He was silent and, shuddering, drew his coat more tightly together.

Évi pressed her doll against her chest. "God," she thought, "please help me. I wish I could give him a kick in the belly so he would faint." The four boys by her side still said nothing. The pale blue eyes of the leggy confectioner then shifted to her.

"You bring your doll with you?" he asked and, as though he couldn't believe what he saw, he rubbed his cheeks with the backs of his hands. "How did you all get in here?" His face reddened with anger. "Can't you boys speak? I asked you, why didn't you switch on the lights? Are they out of order?"

"Please don't get excited," said Totyó. "We've done nothing to put the light out of order. Maybe the fuse is blown."

"Blown, blown," the man in the underwear muttered. "That's not the point. The point is, this burning candle here constitutes a serious fire hazard. Didn't it occur to you that you might set the whole place on fire?"

"Oh," Zugló Rácz, suddenly finding his voice, exclaimed, "we've been taking good care not to do that. We really have."

It was only at this point, it seemed, that the man realized what was going on in his shop. With two quick strides he reached the marble-topped tables and, leaning forward, began counting in a faltering voice.

"You were going to eat up all this lot?" he cried, stupefied. The draught now flattened the flame of the candle, and the long shop grew dark; only the white patch of the protruding seat of the shop-owner's drawers stood out. "Two... four... seven..." he counted. "Why, there are twenty pieces!"

"Only nineteen," insisted Hikker, on whose table the inspection was taking place.

"What d'you mean, nineteen?" the man burst out. "I've counted twenty."

"There's only nineteen," Hikker repeated. "There are nineteen pieces for each of us. Count them again, please."

The tall lean man flared up. "Me? Count 'em over again?" he shouted, and his voice suddenly rose to an absurdly high pitch. "What! Me? Count 'em... Now I call that a bit too much!" In his sudden temper he grew to such a height that his head almost hit the ceiling and the five patrons jumped backwards in alarm. "Nineteen for each of you, eh?" he sneered. "Not twenty, only nineteen? All right now. You come along with me to the police, all of you!"

"Please, sir, don't!" Totyó said.

"Did you come by way of the cellar?"

Évi nodded assent.

"Fathead," Hikker whispered to her.

The confectioner ran to the cellar-door. "Stop whispering, damn you!" he mumbled as he ran. "Why, of course. Where do you think they could come from? Here! They've forced the door open! Now you come along to the police!"

The five children exchanged smiles. Ferencváros Rácz gave Hikker a dig in the ribs; Zugló Rácz heaved a sigh of relief. The four children watched Totyó's face tensely. He winked at Évi.

"Please forgive us, sir," she piped up instantly, sniffling as though choked with tears.

"What!" the confectioner said, taken aback.

"Will you please forgive us, sir!" Évi repeated. "We've had no food for three days."

"Three days, my foot," the confectioner muttered. "Sure." His eyes alighted on the doll, which Évi now held out imploringly towards him. "They go and ruin the lock... They go and set my shop on fire! Where did you pinch that candle?"

"Someone gave it to me as a gift," Totyó replied in a sorrowful voice that nearly made Zugló Rácz's eyes fill with tears. "Please, sir, no food for three days! Honest! None, really, except for some frozen potatoes yesterday that the mice had been at and fouled."

"I puked it up," said Hikker.

"I couldn't swallow either," said one of the Ráczes.

"They made me sick, too," said the other.

In an imploring gesture Évi again swung her doll before the confectioner's nose. "Please forgive us, sir," she whimpered, and her little snub nose suddenly turned green with anger. "And please permit us to eat these cakes!"

The lights, for some mysterious reason, went on, and at the same moment the draft put out the suddenly unnecessary candle. The stronger light at once made the air in the room feel colder.

"Come, come," the tall confectioner said, casting a reproachful glance toward the chandelier. "Now get a move on!" he growled the next moment and threw the cellar door open with irritation. "D' you think I've got money to throw away?"

"Please, sir," Totyó cried, "please let us have some pastry first!"

"It's old stuff anyway!" Ferencváros Rácz called out.

"It'll be dry as dust by tomorrow morning!"

"God will repay you for them," Hikker shouted.

"We haven't had no food for three days," moaned Zugló Rácz and with both hands he began to pull savagely at the rope that belted his ragged tunic.

"You'd better put on your clothes, sir," Totyó said, "so you don't catch cold."

"My father died of pneumonia," Hikker muttered, his eyes flashing angrily, and jumped so close to the confectioner's hollow belly that he almost hit it with his nose.

For the third time, Évi swung her doll.

"We will pay you for those cakes, sir," she said in a sing-song voice, and two heavy tear-drops ran down her cheeks. "Tomorrow we'll bring the money and pay the price. Word of honour!"

"Please give at least two cakes to each of us!" cried the Ferencváros boy.

"Two!" Hikker echoed disdainfully. "Of this lousy old stuff? Five!"

A truck then passed the shop; it must have been a heavy one, for the glass door behind the shutter began to clatter.

The confectioner leaned forward, grasped Hikker's shoulder and turned him round. "What's that you have behind your ear?" he asked with curiosity.

"It's a wen, sir," Totyó answered.

"That's none of your business," Hikker growled, twitching his shoulder. His face paled. Behind his back, one of the Ráczes gave a burst of angry laughter and the rest began to shout. Totyó was hissing excitedly. Évi pressed both her hands tightly against her belly as if she were about to throw up.

"I've never seen anything like it," said the confectioner. "Let me see your ear and I'll give you a chocolate bun."

"One bun!" Hikker's voice trembled with rage. He reached into his pocket, drew out a small black gun and fired it at the confectioner. The lanky man sawed the air with both arms, his knees gave way, and he came down, falling face forward near the outermost marble table.

When, after half an hour, they could at last sit down, one to a table, another lorry rumbled past the house and the glass door gave an even sharper rattle than before. Totyó winced and became pale and, lifting up his nose, listened for noises in the street. He then shrugged his shoulders, spat, and with head bowed, made for his table. Before the table, on which twenty-two pastries—including six cream buns and three "moor's heads"—were waiting for him to eat them, stood Lajos Hikker, with the fatty growth behind his ear, his hands thrust into his pockets.

Suddenly there was silence in the room. Totyó lifted up his head: his forehead looked white beneath his red beret. Hikker stood completely still. They were facing each other and so close that their noses almost met; their brows were covered with beads of perspiration. Apart from Évi's agitated breathing from the next table, no sound was heard in the harshly lit pastryshop.

"Well!" growled Hikker.

Totyó returned his opponent's steady stare, gazing into his eyes so hard that his scalp grew stiff and his belly began to quiver. He had brown eyes; Hikker's were blue. The gold-framed mirror on the wall behind Hikker's back reflected quite distinctly the large fatty growth behind his ear. Totyó began to blink — those blue eyes were the colder and more ruthless ones. He lowered his gaze to Hikker's nose.

Suddenly he let his head hang down and stepped back.

"All right," he said hoarsely, and he spat again. His face was now even whiter than when the confectioner's body had flopped at his feet.

"Hand over your cap!" Hikker commanded.

Totyó took off his cap. "All right, stand down!" Hikker said as he put on the emblem of chieftainship and stole a quick glance in the mirror. He drew himself up, ran to a corner of the shop and, triumphantly whistling like a blithe song-thrush, urinated into the spittoon. "Ráczes!"

The two Ráczes jumped to their feet.

"The Zugló chap will switch off the light," Hikker commanded. "Ferencváros Rácz will light the candle, because it's safer. And now," he announced in a solemn tone after the lighting had been changed and the gold-spattered semi-darkness had engulfed the corpse that lay in front of the cellar-door, "and now let the thing start. The password?... But say it softly!"

"Ambition and hilarity," breathed the group of customers.

Évi was eating her seventh cake when she noticed that she was lagging way behind her companions. On Ferencváros Rácz's table there remained but a few little cones, some pink, some white, among the paper trays. The little girl broke into loud laughter. "My, what frightful diarrhoea we'll all have tomorrow!" she said, and shoved a whole "moor's head" into her mouth. The whipped cream trickled down both sides of her chin and made a thin white moustache under her nose. She laughed again while licking up the cream from her chin with her pink tongue. Hikker's face was smeared all over with yellow cream, some of which was splashed even on his forehead; his nose was dark with chocolate. Zugló Rácz, his eyes closed, was eating rapidly, shielding with his left arm, as with a sort of protective hedge, a collection of two caramel-topped cakes, three cream buns and four walnut-cream cakes that he had left to the end. Totyó was sitting with his back to them.

"Why should we have diarrhoea?" Hikker said. "I'm sure I could eat a hundred pieces of this stuff."

"The hell you could," said the little girl. "That many would be too much food even for the lion to gobble up."

"What lion?" asked Ferencváros Rácz, groaning; pressing his back against the back of his chair, he took a brief rest. By now there remained before him only two little pink cones; the glazing of one was full of blisters, while the point of the other was missing.

"The one that lives in Vág utca," she replied. "You know, in that big wrecked building. I've told you about it before."

"It's no good saying you've told me about it before," the Ferencváros boy mumbled. "How would a lion get to be in Budapest?"

"Maybe he's a refugee from Transylvania," the Zugló boy declared.

"There are three lions, not one!" Évi cried. "I'm sure they've fled here from Transylvania. At night, when there are no people in the street, they come out and crouch down by the street door and comb their manes."

Hikker too stopped eating; his eyes were shining.

"I'll go and see for myself if that's true," he announced. "If they *are* there, I'm going to kill'em."

"All by yourself?" Évi asked in awe.

"You can join me if you want to, any of you," Hikker said. "You don't have to, though. I'm told hunting lions is a rather dangerous job. I heard that from a guy who used to work at the Zoo, you see. He had his right arm snapped off by a lion."

"I say, Hikker, do you like cream buns?" Évi asked.

The new chief screwed up his eyes and looked searchingly at the girl.

"Maybe, I do," he said.

"I'll give you one cream bun and a little pink one for one of those whipped cream things," she offered.

Hikker shook his head gravely.

"That's not enough," he said.

"I'll give you two cream buns," she said; she fixed her innocent blue eyes on the chief's face and smiled coquettishly. However, Hikker wagged his head as vigorously as if he were holding out for at least five cakes in exchange for his one whipped cream pastry. She lost her temper. "Nothing doing," she snapped and, grabbing her glass, downed the remainder of the vermouth.

Ferencváros Rácz, having finished his cakes, got up and shuffled out to the kitchen. He returned in a few minutes with a huge paper bag under each arm. The sight made Hikker jump to his feet.

"There's at least five more bags like these in the kitchen cabinet," the boy from Ferencváros reported. "Walnuts, and sugar, and a hundred eggs, and black raisins. I also found a ten-forint note by the sofa he slept on, and also a silver pocketwatch."

As on their way to the kitchen they had to pass the corpse, Hikker ordered the blood-stained face of the confectioner to be covered up with newspapers. Meanwhile the candle had burnt itself out and so they had to switch on the light once more. The strong electric light—like the white hand of a doctor—brought them round from their intoxicated trance; all of a sudden the air in the room was filled with the sharp ether smell of danger.

Zugló Rácz stumbled in his nervousness. "Don't you fellows think it's time to quit," he asked in a trembling voice, and once more tightened the rope he had loosened over his bulging tummy.

The other Rácz turned pale too. "Why?"

"I have an idea," said Totyó, "that the car that drove by a little while ago was carrying a police raiding party."

"So what?" the boy from Ferencváros whispered. "It must be an hour since it drove away."

Zugló Rácz was unable to budge: the very soles of his feet were itching with suspicion, his knees were weak from fear. "You can't eat dinner with a corpse in the room," he whispered.

All eyes turned towards Hikker, who was standing over the body, holding a bottle of rum under his arm and stuffing raisins into his mouth. "Who said you couldn't?" he said disdainfully. "For three days during the siege I slept side by side with a corpse like this."

"Oh!" Évi was enraptured.

"Whose body was that?" the boy from Ferencváros asked.

"My dad's," said Hikker. "We couldn't bury him—mother just wouldn't let us."

"My dad was killed during the siege too," Évi said. "But I wasn't at home at the time."

On one of the shelves in the kitchen stood a potbellied white porcelain mortar. They poured into it half a bottle of rum, a paper bagful of pounded sugar, walnuts and raisins, and, following the advice of Ferencváros Rácz, mixed with it twenty egg yolks. As there were no chairs in the kitchen, the mortar was placed on the floor and they sat down cross-legged in a circle around it, each with an ice-cream spoon in his hand.

"Not so bad," was the expert opinion of Hikker, who was first to dip his spoon into the mortar. "Could do with a pinch of cinnamon though."

"And a bit of jam too," whispered the boy from Zugló.

"Ah, drop dead!" Évi said. "What d'you want to put jam into this for? Why, it's as thick as asphalt as it is."

After three spoonfuls of the stuff, her hand grew leaden and suddenly she was overcome with such terrible fatigue that she was hardly able to keep her eyes open. She edged closer to Hikker and laid her head on his shoulder. The boys were still smacking their lips but the shadow of hopelessness already showed in their faces too. A spider was running across the opposite wall. Suddenly, the little girl burst into tears.

"What's the idea?" Totyó asked her.

She did not stop sobbing.

"What's the matter with you?" Hikker muttered. "What're you crying your eyes out for?"

"I always cry when I see a spider," she said sobbing. Suddenly, she threw her skinny arms around Hikker's neck. "Oh, please look at it so it'll drop from the wall!" she implored him. "And where'll I go when we've finished and leave this place?"

"Where?" repeated Hikker, astonished. "What d'you mean, where? Why, back to your sister's, of course."

"The bed belongs to her by day," she explained, swallowing her tears. "She only lets me lie there till I've breathed the ice out of her hair. You take me with you."

"Me?" said the chief, his jaw dropping. "I got no place."

Ferencváros Rácz broke into ringing laughter. He was as tight as an owl. "Let's go to a café," he shouted. "You know, one of those places with bands where you can get some sleep. It's on me."

Évi stared into the fellow's face with tears in her eyes.

"Where do you get the money?" Totyó asked, with chattering teeth. The Ferencváros boy drew from his pocket a real, green ten-forint note. He moistened it with spit and stuck it on his forehead. "That should be enough even to tip the gypsies,", he said firmly, while, swaying a little and with some difficulty, he scrambled to his feet. Zugló Rácz, hanging onto the other Rácz's legs, hoisted himself to his feet too. Totyó was the third to get up. The Lady and the Chief remained seated for a bit.

Down below, a bit of morning light was already trickling into the cellar, and they were able to find their way without a candle. Totyó being the tallest member of the party, the others clambered on his shoulders up to the cellar window and, through it, into the snow-covered street, from which night had already withdrawn its ambiguous dark lights. Évi scooped up some snow and washed the cheeks of her doll.

"When you die," she said to Ferencváros Rácz as the party, having at last been rounded up, started off in the direction of the Great Boulevard in an unexpectedly heavy snowfall, "when you die, I don't think it'll be in a horizontal position. Get that money off your forehead!"

"If you don't like it that way," the Ferencváros boy retorted, "you can go and sleep with your lions."

Translated by István Farkas

"HOHEM" AND "FREIER"

by JÓZSEF LENGYEL

The word "hohem" or "hohem-boy" means a kind of professional thief and criminal, both in Hungarian and in international slang. The opposite of "hohem" is "freier", a simpleton who works to make a living and is not a lawbreaker. The original meaning of "hohem" is clever; "freier" means free. The "freiers" never realize they are "freiers", but a "hohem" would not dream of referring to them by any other description, even though the time came when thousands and even hundreds of thousands and millions of so-called "freiers" were imprisoned in various parts of the world.

How did this discrimination in nomenclature come about? The following description, which has more in common with natural history than with literature and whose proper place might be in a supplementary volume to the great Brehm's *Life of Animals,* may serve to illuminate the subject.

The newly arrived transport of prisoners first encountered the "hohems" in the "distribution centre". The "freiers" had not yet begun to settle in the windowless makeshift barracks of plywood when the "hohems" were already milling about them like vultures. Pockets were soon emptied of their contents. Hands reached down from the upper bunks and lifted hats from the heads of people crowding into the place.

A "freier" just transferred from prison and hauling heavy bags was among the last to arrive in the camp with his two suitcases and his sack. He met a few people in the yard who had already been plucked and had managed to get away from the barrack-room. He was unable to understand what was going on. Standing on the door-step, his eyes still blinded by the sunshine, he tried to distinguish something inside the dark barrack-room. He heard shouts and the noise of a brawl. With all his bags Freier made an about-turn. He looked in the yard for a spot of fresh grass near the high wooden watch-tower that had not yet been trampled down by the spring transports. There he spent the day sitting on the heap he had built of his treasures, the two suitcases and the sack. He never even went to fetch his food from the kitchen. ⁻

It was the end of May, with a benign warm sun. The air turned chilly only after sunset. Freier tugged a warm fur coat out of his huge sack; he evidently meant to spend the night in the yard.

From the door of the barrack-room Hohem watched Freier putting on the fur coat, making up a bunk with his two suitcases, buttoning up his fur coat carefully, lying down on the two suitcases, and adjusting the sack, bulky even without the coat, as a pillow under his head.

Inside the barrack-room it was dark, jammed and turbulent, like in a tram when a short circuit makes the lights go out. In the yard there was fresh air and best of all—that was why Freier chose this spot—almost above his head on the high wooden watch-tower, one of the eight towers surrounding the camp, a sentry was standing, even though it was on the other side of the double barbed-wire fence. Unceasingly the sentry kept his eye on what was going on inside the barbed-wire enclosure; he had to see that nothing went wrong in the "no man's land" between the two barbed-wire fences. The sentry's proximity had a soothing effect on Freier.

Days are long at the end of May. It was still light when Freier fell asleep. He was fed up and exhausted from endless journeys in hot, stinking and stuffy freight cars; no wonder the fresh air full of a scent of grass lulled him at once into a deep dream.

Clouds were still glowing with the red reflection of the setting sun, but the searchlights from the watch-towers had already begun sweeping over the camp and the barbed-wire fences. Lights-out had not yet sounded when the short, skinny Hohem with his greenish complexion ambled over to the sleeping Freier without the slightest haste. After taking a good look round, he stretched out on the edge of the narrow bunk Freier had built of the two suitcases.

There was little room left for him beside the stout Freier. He supported himself by resting one foot on the ground; but he did not shove Freier. He lay on his side, as thin as a blade, next to the huge, podgy body of Freier, even plumper in his fur coat. Nestling close to the sleeping man he remained motionless for about half an hour. Knife and homebaked bread, beast of prey and victim warmed one another with their bodies.

At last Hohem stirred. He fingered his man Freier all over with a light, nervous touch, until at last he felt the wallet in the sleeper's right trouser pocket.

Freier must have realized that he always slept on his right side, and that was why he put his valuables into his right-hand trouser pocket. This was a frequent and very clumsy dodge, in Hohem's opinion. Even clumsier than that of the beetle which pretends to be dead when it sees the enemy approach.

He pulled a pin out of his lapel. A "hohem" is never without a pin, just like a glazier, who always has his cutting diamond handy. Only a most careful and thorough search could deprive him of this tool—and then not for more than half an hour. The first tiny nail or piece of wire Hohem picked up from the ground and hastily sharpened on a piece of brick or on the concrete floor of a cell would replace the lost pin at once. If no steel or iron object could be found, a piece of sharpened wood or a splinter wrenched off a board in the bunk would do well enough. But now, as in most cases, he had a real pin to remove any obstacle that such a bug-brain like Freier could think up.

Very precisely, yet effortlessly, just as a flea bites, he pricked the sleeping Freier's back.

The sleeping man reached round to his back and began scratching it with a ludicrously slow movement. This may even have made the sentry smile.

Hohem gave him another flea bite with his pin. The sleeper started scratching again, shrugged his shoulders, rubbed his back, and—without awakening — mechanically turned over to his other side.

The pin's work was accomplished. The pocket with the money in it was no longer under the sleeping man's body, but on the upper side, within Hohem's reach. But Hohem did not stir. For another good half hour he lay stiff beside Freier, waiting for the man who had been disturbed in his sleep to sink back into the deep ooze of his dreams.

Only after they had warmed up to one another again did another tool come to light, this time from the sole of Hohem's shoe—a thin razor blade. With one single calculated movement Hohem slit the fur coat. A second movement and he had cut out the pocket. The result of the third was that the wallet landed in Hohem's hands.

The next operation took rather longer and required considerable skill. The precaution may well have been unnecessary here in the prison camp. The sentry could quite well distinguish the glitter of the tiny blade in the glare of the searchlights, but it never occured to him to disturb Hohem's work. He had only one responsibility, to make sure no one approached either the outer or the inner barbed-wire fence; the 'no man's land' between the two was twelve yards wide. Not even grass was supposed to grow in this prohibited area. It was nothing but black mud that prisoners, under the eye of a special sentry, hoed and raked every week to keep it flat and smooth, unmarked by a single footprint on the raked lines. After heavy rains the enclosure was raked again. And that was all the sentry had to do: watch the prohibited zone. Events taking place beyond the fence, in the camp, concerned him only if they affected this area; and then strictly on the side where he was standing, and only for as long as he was on duty. That was what he was ordered to stand on the watch-tower for. Other things attracted his attention no more than a fish swimming in the river attracts the attention of a child crossing the bridge. Less even—for children are living, they aren't waiting on sentry duty so as to be able to live afterwards...

Hohem had a thorough knowledge of sentries. Still, a real expert couldn't work rashly, carelessly. It may be that he was thinking it wouldn't do to get out of practice...

Railway-robbery was the line he worked in, a refined and actually rather jolly profession. By the time the victim with his dopey surprised mug starts hollering, the swag has long since been deposited safely with a colleague three cars back. The passengers in the compartment, and presently the whole car, start discussing the affair. They all try to guess, occasionally telling one another off—did it happen just now, or was it during the night? Who was the thief? What station could he have got off at? What will they do now? What kind of telegram to send? The thief himself, making his face look stern and giving profound nods with his head, takes part in the general discussion.

"Nowadays, you know..." he says, and makes a gesture of resignation... "Oh, well, that's how it is." The passengers who agree whole-heartedly, act as if they understood the deep social and moral truth expressed in that wave of the hand...

The blade now ran lightly down the side of the sack. The hardest part of the job was about to begin. The things in the sack were to be brought to light one by one from beneath the sleeping man's head, so that not the slightest tug or jerk should disturb his dream. Slowly Hohem penetrated the sack with his left hand, at the same time sliding his right palm under the sleeping man's head. No sick-nurse, no nanny, could have held and sheltered a helpless head entrusted to her with more tender care than this right hand. The left hand meanwhile pulled one item after another out of the sack.

After the first pieces of clothing had been removed, a figure stepped out of the dark doorway of an adjacent barrack-room into the yard, which was clearly illuminated by the sentry's searchlights; it was Hohem's confederate. He strolled up to the two men lying side by side and began taking away the loot.

The work proceeded without a sound. The rule was: Never get flustered, never act in a panic. At last Hohem made a kind of pillow out of the sack and rags—the latter, being completely worthless, had immediately been flung aside by the confederate—and stuffed it under the sleeping man's head. Only then did he pull away his right hand.

This done, Hohem slowly withdrew from the body that had been a source of warmth for both of them. He got up from the bunk of suitcases and mustered them as if he wished he could see through their sides. Not yet, not tonight, but tomorrow this would all be his booty. Wearily and rather reluctantly he started for the barrack-room at a leisurely pace. In the glare of the searchlights the narrow, black, raked furrows cast shadows between the two barbed-wire fences.

It would be fine, thought Hohem, to play the gentleman at the bar of some railway restaurant, to pour a glass of brandy into a mug of beer, give it a good stir and gulp it down, then cross the rails without staggering, just clearing his throat and hemming, with nothing but the good warmth of the drink in his body, and jump on to the steps of a train that has already started.

"Ah," he sighed, and looked at the sentry. "Ah, one day I'll be free..." In the morning, he thinks, the boys will smuggle the things out, under their clothes. Then in the evening they'll bring back the drink in a chemist's ice-bag... It may be midnight now, half past twelve, half past one at the most. His hands, which had been as firm and steady while he was working as those of a surgeon at the operating table, were shaking now. His fingers were trembling.

Sullenly Hohem stepped into the barrack-room. His buddy reported, "The swag's all right". He did not reply. He was sombre and quite inaccessible, once more a professor. He climbed into his bunk and tried to sleep, to make time pass more quickly. At present he was not even living. He was waiting...

When Freier awoke next morning he gaped at his sack, utterly at a loss. He grabbed at his pocket; nothing was left of it. He ran up to the barbed-wire fence, under the watch-tower.

"I've been robbed," he shouted to the sentry. "Didn't you notice anyone?"

"I came on at six this morning," the man responded reluctantly. "Don't go near that fence," he added sternly, for he saw that Freier was about to touch the wire.

If Freier is not a fool, he won't go and complain to anyone. But of course he is not sufficiently experienced, he has not gathered enough prison-camp lore to realize what a lot of trouble Hohem saved him last night. And he doesn't know that only when he has lost both of his suitcases (not tonight, tonight he is going to keep awake) will his perfect freedom be restored...

A small bundle—a pillow-case containing a shirt, a mess-tin, a spoon and tobacco—this much Freier will always have, even if the worst comes to the worst and he is robbed a hundred times in the next ten years.

On the other hand, if Hohem is released or only taken from one place of work to another, he will always travel with nothing on him. Before he will be escorted to the gate of the camp he will have abandoned his spoon and his mess-tin. The spoon must be left behind, for according to Hohem superstitions spoons taken away bring disaster. Anyone who takes his spoon away returns to the camp. The mess-tin is harmless. But take the tin without a spoon? One can always get another.

Facts do not justify this superstition. On the contrary, in most cases they prove something else. Freier, with his spoon on him, does not come back to the camp, for the simple reason that it is very rare for him to get out alive at all. But Hohem, who sometimes escapes and sometimes is set free, often returns in spite of having thrown away his spoon.

Translated by Edna Lénárt

THE ORGAN
by KÁROLY PAP

"Ten p.m.," the clergyman announced. He smiled and said, "Drink, gentlemen, while you can. Mother! Bring our artist friends another bottle!"

The clergyman's stout wife rose from her seat with difficulty and headed for the kitchen. Large moths flew in a frenzy about the enormous lantern above the arbour. Red apples and yellow pears were piled high in the two baskets standing on the octagonal table, and the clergyman's guests, worn-out wandering actors, sat crowded together beneath the dark-green wild grapevines of the arbour.

"Honestly, Reverend," declared the director of the troupe, "you're the only person in the whole village who unselfishly supports the arts."

"Go ahead and eat, gentlemen," the clergyman replied, "I'm glad to have you here."

He listened with forced attention to the actors while they grumbled about their hard lives, interrupting one another, stammering and stumbling over their words.

"Help yourselves to some apples for later," the vicar offered, and one after another they stuffed their pockets with fruit.

From the farmyard came the wailing of the threshing machine. Around the arbour and in the yard where it had begun to grow dark, the vicar's daughter was playing hide-and-seek with the youngster from next door. Her voice was drowned in peals of laughter.

The actors ate greedily. They always drank their glasses to the bottom, at the same time making sure that their talk did not cease for a moment, as if they were afraid that silence might cause the vicar to rise from the table. One after another they related their life stories and their dreams. They lied about everything; they told of schools they had never attended, theatres they had never performed at, luxurious wardrobes and magnificent roles of which their own recklessness had deprived them from the beginning. Only the women kept silent. Their eyes fluttered greedily from the apples to the pears and back. Occasionally they shyly dipped their withered lips into their wine glasses, and when they thought themselves unobserved, stretched out their hands and swiftly crammed their baskets and hats with fruit. Then they sat blinking in silence, trying to ward off sleep.

The clergyman sat heavily in his chair, fussing with his pincenez and wiping his forehead. All this interminable talk affected him like the continuous gurgling of some distant spring. It merged with the stormy noise of the threshing machine.

"Yes," he said absent-mindedly, "there's a lot of misery in this poor country... Come, gentlemen, help yourselves to cigarettes," and he placed his huge cigarette box in the centre of the table.

The clergyman caught sight of the the coachman passing by the arbour. "János," he called out, "you can water the horses. It's ten o'clock already. I've just looked at my watch."

"I'll water them when necessary," the coachman answered sullenly, and disappeared into the darkness.

Out in the yard the children had tired of their game and were saying good-bye. The girl came in to her mother. Both took leave with a quiet "good night" and went into the house to make the beds. Everywhere there was silence, only the pigs were fidgeting in their sty, some dogs were restless in the village, and from somewhere on the horizon came the sound of the marsh, like a vast, barely audible rattle. The women sighed. A child had already stretched out in sleep on the lap of one of them. Gradually, the discussion under the arbour faded away after all. The faces of the comedians relaxed as they gazed past one another with impenetrable expressions of sad emptiness, all listening to the distant sound of the marsh without understanding that everlasting monotonous music made by frogs which, more poignantly than any other noise, reminds the weary of the endless monotony of wandering.

At this point, the conductor spoke. He wore a wry smile as he talked as if in a dream. "How lucky frogs are," he said. "I wonder which of them is the conductor?"

"He's our conductor, you know," the director whispered in the clergyman's ear. "He's a very intelligent man; he was even an attorney and an army officer once."

"I see," replied the clergyman with no conviction whatever. "I can see that you are all intelligent gentlemen. It's very unfortunate," he added. He looked around, stopped for a moment, and suddenly lowered his voice. "Of course," he whispered, "what you really came for is the organ." He put on his glasses again and his eyes wandered from face to face. This remark instilled new life into the actors. They all wanted to talk at once but seemed to be the victim of some sort of confusion.

"I was afraid," the director whispered at last, "that Your Reverence had forgotten all about it..."

"I didn't want to mention it in front of my wife," the clergyman replied. "You see, gentlemen, she is not as modern in this respect as I am."

"Oh, of course, yes, yes, certainly," the actors exclaimed.

The clergyman continued. "I hope you didn't mention this to anyone in the village. I'm very willing to lend you the organ from our church, but if any of my congregation were to find out about it, it would be extremely unpleasant for me."

"Of course, of course, naturally!" The comedians smiled, and insisted in turn, with words, heads and hands that they had said nothing to anyone and would never breathe a word.

"Mum's the word," said the conductor, who was the last to speak.

"That's right," answered the clergyman. "I'm acting on my own responsibility, but my congregation would never understand how the vicar could have lent the organ to a group of comedians."

"That is completely understandable," said the director. "They would be quite incapable of such noble thoughts."

"I, on the other hand," continued the clergyman, "understand your position perfectly. If you are simply unable to obtain music anywhere at all, to whom else could you turn if not to the minister?"

"If you will permit me to say so," the conductor replied, "Your Reverence will surely understand that just as there is no true religious service without music, so there can be no theatre without music. Who knows," he added with a tired smile, "which is the real God: the one in the church or the one in the theatre?"

The conductor gave the actors a searching glance, then turned his eyes to the clergyman again. Blushing slightly, he said, "You, at any rate can understand me." Since he was unable to guess anything from the clergyman's expression, he attempted nonchalantly to explain his words. "I was an organist once myself, and now I'm on the road and make music with these strolling actors. What must be, must be."

"Because of a lady," the director whispered to the clergyman.

"Well, yes," said the clergyman, "you have to make a living after all. But you also have to know how to keep quiet... You mustn't say anything about the fact that the same organ with whose assistance I sing along with my congregation..."

"As pants the heart for cooling streams..." the conductor sang softly, *"when heated in the chase..."*

"As I was saying, the same organ," the clergyman continued, "will be used to accompany your singing of a foxtrot or... *My lips seal your lips with a kiss..."*

The director nodded. "What an excellent memory!"

"And just where is it that you will be performing?" the vicar inquired.

"At the Mermaid Inn," replied the director, promptly adding, "there is a moth on Your Reverence's ear."

"At the Mermaid Inn?" repeated the clergyman, and carefully squashed the poor creature. "I hope that you are as aware of my position now as I am of yours."

"Oh, oh," protested the comedians, wilting with exhaustion.

"Because I, too have performed on the stage..." the clergyman continued, trying to impress them. "When I was a student—gentlemen, did you know this?—we performed the Gypsy Baron, and I can still remember it! *To be a musician..."*

"I fed 'em," shouted the coachman from outside, and the entire group became silent and waited for the coachman to disappear into the darkness again.

Now the whinnying of the drinking horses could be heard from the yard; the threshing machine droned as exruciatingly as if it were hungering for human beings rather than mere sheaves.

"Hey there!" came the curses of the coachman. "Damn you!...
I'll break your back!"

"Today is Monday," the clergyman continued after a pause,
and took a couple of sips of wine, "so you gentlemen can use the
organ for six days without being disturbed. But by Sunday, of
course, it must be back here for the choir."

"I was thinking, Reverend," mused the conductor, "that the
Lord created the world in six days, and on the seventh he rested.
The organ will perform with us for six days and on the seventh it
will rest in the church."

The clergyman continued his stream of thought. "And I would
appreciate it if you gentlemen would somehow cover up the organ
a little, perhaps with canvas or something, so that my congregation should not recognize it."

"I'll go out in the forest," suggested the conductor, "and collect
nice big branches to decorate it—then nobody will recognize it."

"That will be better still," answered the clergyman, slowly
rising.

"We'll camouflage it," said the conductor, "like the cannons
during the war."

"He was an officer," explained the director. Following the clergyman's example they all slowly dragged themselves to their feet.

"All my men are busy with the threshing," the clergyman said,
"so you gentlemen have nothing to fear. But to be on the safe side,
go across the yard one at a time and wait for me on the church
porch. I'll be along right away, I just want to get the key and my
lantern."

The actors nodded approvingly.

"The ladies are sleepy," continued the clergyman, "and since
they can't help us anyway, it would be best if they went home."

The women were already getting ready to leave. "Watch it,
children," said the eldest, who had a child in her arms. They
strolled away from the arbour, whispering as they disappeared
through the garden.

"Do you gentlemen have anything to light your way?" asked
the clergyman as he reached the door. The director and the conductor pulled a candle and matches out of their pockets.

"You think can handle it?" asked the clergyman.

"We think so," the actors replied. "There are seven of us."

The clergyman disappeared into the kitchen.

"What a fine man," the actors said to each other. They pocketed some more fruit, divided up the remainder of the wine, and started out one after another towards the church, which lay still at the end of the estate like a white giraffe sunk in the ground up to its breast.

The clergyman had already entered the inner room where his wife was preparing for bed.

"What is this?" she asked in a whisper, so that her daughter lying on the couch should not wake up. The poor child was timid and given to epileptic fits as it was. "You intend giving the organ to those actors?"

"I have already promised to," he answered.

"Are you crazy?" his wife cried excitedly, "It's all very well to give them apples and wine, but the church organ? To that kind of people? You want them to announce it to the whole village?"

Her breasts quivering the minister's wife stood with her back to the mirror, combing the dandruff out of her hair with rough, angry strokes.

"Quiet," answered the clergyman. "You don't understand. These people have to live also. They can't help it if it happens to be the church that has an instrument and they happen to need what the church has."

The clergyman put the church keys into his pocket. "Anyway," be continued, "rest assured, the poor fellows won't be able to carry the organ down anyway. Seven men with no sort of tools can't possibly manage in the middle of the night..."

"But if you promised them the organ," his wife said, "then you'll have to provide them with rope."

"I can't," answered the clergyman, and he lit a cigarette and looked about for his little flashlight. "I haven't got any." He turned to his wife. "I promised them the organ because I felt sorry for the poor fellows. They're tired, hungry wanderers. They're married and have children. But I can't give them ropes or men."

"Then why did you start up with them?" his wife whispered. "It would have been better if you had told them the truth right from the beginning."

"The truth?..." replied the clergyman. "I wanted them to see that my intentions were good, so they wouldn't be able to say. "The minister was this, that and the other." Instead, they'll say, "He did what he could." The rest is in the hands of God. I give them hope, and then..." He continued thoughtfully, hugging his wife. "Actually rope wouldn't be enough, they'd need a pulley. As a matter of fact, even if I provided them with one they'd only be able to lower the organ with it but they'd never be able to pull it back up to its place by Sunday. As far as the staircase is concerned, that's far too narrow. Even you know that, you little goose. We used pulleys ourselves to pull it up when we got it. But I just haven't the heart to refuse the poor devils. I don't want them to curse the Lord on account of me. You must understand that!"

"I wouldn't have bothered at all if I were you," said his wife.

"Just leave it to me." He winked and raised his head.

On the couch the little girl was moaning in her sleep; she threw off the red blanket as if snakes had covered it with their poisonous spittle. She lay uncovered like that for a few seconds, then her naked arms and legs began to quiver and she mumbled unintelligible words. Her mother's hairbrush stopped in mid-air, she went over to the couch and covered her daughter again.

"They're always chasing her in her dreams," she said bitterly.

"You shouldn't give her so much to eat," the clergyman replied. He took his huge watch out of his pocket, looked at it but did not put it back. Instead, he set it down on the table. That was where he usually left it for the night. Immediately its noisy ticking could be heard.

"Big birds and animals keep chasing the poor thing," the mother continued, "she told me so yesterday." She bent down to her daughter. "My little darling," she whispered, smoothing the covers over and over again.

The clergyman removed his soft collar and with his neck uncovered, walked slowly out of the room. The actors were smoking as they waited on the church porch. Bored, they browsed among the old inscriptions carved on the walls.

"Gergely Tyuki helped to erect this church to the glory of God and his wife's memory," one of them read.

"He must have been a great lord," remarked the director, "to build a whole church for his wife."

"Oh!" exclaimed the conductor, who had the wound of a great love on his lips. "If I could just once see a church with the inscription "Built by Mr. X. in memory of the unforgettable nights spent with his mistress, Y.!" Anyway," he continued, "this is a pretty big tombstone for one woman. I once read somewhere that every church is a tombstone which man places above his greatest desire, the ashes of his belief... What is the value of resurrection?" he sighed. "Life is all that counts, life..."

"Well, just watch out," said the director anxiously, "that somewhere in all this darkness you don't get stuck as a cantor again."

Disregarding him, the conductor said, "How many homes the son of God has to sleep in and how bare and few are the lodgings of man here on earth! I, for example, haven't the vaguest idea where I shall sleep tonight, since I couldn't even pay the peasant for the bed yesterday."

"Ask the priest," suggested one of the strolling players, "to let you sleep on the spot where the organ usually sits."

At that moment the clergyman approached.

"Well, gentlemen, let's go," he said, opening the door that led to the choir section. The comedians slowly climbed the stairs, holding candles and lanterns and following the minister with his keys and his flashlight. Whispering, panting, coughing and clearing their throats, they bumped against one another and the wall. The smoke choked them and the air got stuffier and stuffier. But the conductor had the hardest time of all catching his breath. Full of bitterness, he carried the remains of a bullet in his lung, the ruins of a face in his heart, and a broken-down church in his memory—the church where he used to be an organist when he was still a servant of God and not of the theatre.

"Tsk, tsk," he said, "I used to play in a place like this."

Finally they reached the top of the steep staircase and went over to the organ. The director was standing at the edge of the staircase, measuring the distance between the walls.

"Won't this staircase be rather narrow, Your Reverence?" he asked anxiously, and scratched his ear-lobe.

"Heave ho!" shouted one of the young actors and with bravado took hold of one corner of the organ, which did not budge. While the clergyman and the conductor removed the music stand and the ornamental figurines standing on the cover, the rest carelessly tested their strength with the organ. The clergyman raised his flashlight high, the director was measuring the space at the foot of the stairs, and the conductor was leaning against the rails of the choir section and thoughtfully gazing down at the nave of the church. The organ, however, did not budge. Exhausted, the comedians stared at it stupidly, and one after another they began to look as though they had no faith in their own strength. Finally their eyes turned to the clergyman, who was strong and fat and two heads taller than any of them. He encouraged them, standing still with the organ keys and the candelabrum in his hands.

"Gentlemen, perhaps you should all try it together at once," he said, and yawned broadly.

"Well, come on, come on," the director prompted the troupe, "or we won't have anything in our pockets tomorrow. I'll give you the signal!"

At this they all tried to find a good place for their hands to grasp the organ.

"I can't get a decent grip on it," one of them grumbled. "If it only had a handle. After all it's made of stone," another said. "It's as heavy as a dead ox," said a young actor, and spat into the palms of his hands. Now the director himself stepped over to them and braced himself against the organ. Only the conductor stood alone, apart from them, beside the rails of the choir section. From below, the gulf of the four painted walls gaped up at him nakedly, with the altar at the back like some mysterious, huge gate, and the pews like an army of deep ditches.

For a few moments the minister played with the idea of lending these men a hand, but his belly was very full, for he had probably eaten too much dinner; and besides, the whole thing was futile to begin with.

"I never thought," he said, "that it could be this heavy. It's an old instrument. Since it was brought up here, nobody has ever thought of moving it. It's cumbersome, and tone shows its age too," he added, and as if to comfort the actors for the eventual failure of their efforts he continued, "I don't even know if you'll be able to use it because of its tone. Perhaps it would better if the conductor tried it out first."

The conductor, however, stayed where he was, and as the others stared at him reproachfully, he said impatiently, in a low voice, "Whatever it's like, that's what it's like. It'll be good enough for us." He thought to himself how wise it would be if at this very moment he were to throw himself down from the railing right into the ditches of pews. His skull would burst apart and that would be the most appropriate and the most worthy music ever made by man.

"I think," said the young actor, hoarse from exertion, "the reason we can't budge this thing is because we didn't put enough into our stomachs. If His Reverence would feed us on turkey for just a week I bet we could lift it like a feather."

The clergyman smiled.

"Come, come now, you gentlemen aren't that starved."

The conductor alone took no interest whatever in the whole affair, just as if he did not even notice what was going on. In a dream of melancholy he stared down at the church from whence the ghost of his past was rising in the full vestments of faith. "No matter what happens," he thought to himself, "I was not hired as a porter." Whatever may have attracted him about being a strolling musician, he had not joined the actors in order to sweat; and anyway, everything that happened to him as he wandered from village to village with this troupe was so disgraceful that nothing new made any difference. He fidgeted with his hat and his cane.

The comedians tried over and over again to budge the organ.

"If only it would move once," the director said, "the rest would come easy."

He looked meekly at the clergyman who was arranging the white signboards on the hymn indicator.

"Would you be so kind," the director finally appealed to the conductor, "and give us a hand?"

"My strength wouldn't be much use," the condutor replied with a hopeless gesture.

"Why not?" asked the clergyman absent-mindedly.

With a sad smile, the conductor looked the fat clergyman over from head to foot, and on his lips were the words, "Your Reverence, you, on the other hand, might be some help," but he held his peace and just said, "I am a musician because that is what I was born to be. Have a look at my hands and face. Weak and fragile. I can't help it. Why should those who are hungry and thin like you, weak and fragile like myself, undertake such jobs?"

The director grew more and more exasperated.

"You must admit," he said, bridling up gradually in protest, "that in a spot like this, no musician is thin or fragile. We're all poor devils on the road who want to eat and sleep and feed and clothe our wives and children. In these circumstances everyone is the same."

The actors were getting nowhere. They grumbled and tried again. They hated the conductor; what did he have to be so fussy for? It they had nothing, he would have nothing either. He would die of hunger along with them. What did he want? It was like this everywhere today. Didn't he know that? Well, he'd find out!

They started to blame one another. "Mr. Tömb isn't even lifting, of course," said a scrawny, ill-looking actor.

"Me?" returned Mr. Tömb. "You're the one that isn't lifting!"

The conductor crossed his arms. He had expected this all along. Nothing was any use. New villages would follow, fresh miseries, other immovable organs, more kind-hearted, fat clergymen, more thefts in the middle of the night from strange manor houses, endless, useless resurrections of a past that had been thrown away for ever. He would have been perfectly willing to call on the entire company, the vicar included, to join him in a leap into the stone arms of God that reached up so invitingly from below. But it was best not to mention this to them. His colleagues had gone hungry so often as a result of their so-called art and the clergyman had dined well so often through his alleged faith that they would be stubborn and hardheaded. To them death was not peace but a struggle.

But the bickering of the actors was getting more and more heated, and even the clergyman was beginning to tire of his spirit of good-will. What was the use? The comedians were nothing but comedians after all. The poor did not know how to behave with those who only wanted their good. They did not know how to endure, suffer or stick together when need be, they had no piety in them at all. Probably there was some way they could carry the organ down.

Now the director snarled angrily at the conductor. "You just stand there watching while we break our backs, eh? What do you think you're doing, anyway?"

Made haughty by his sorrow, the conductor replied, "I have already said what I had to say. You're the kind who always think your happiness depends on just one person... Leave me alone!

"And you think," the director began to shout "that all we lack for complete happiness is for you to sit down and pound the piano every night? That's nothing," he yelled, "to make music! Why do you whine just because you have to grab hold of something?! Who do you think you are?"

"I'm the same person," answered the conductor quietly, "that I always was. I know that what you people need is the kind of musician who will sleep in a ditch if necessary, or be a porter or a comedian or whatever you want! As a matter of fact, he ought to carry an organ around in his waistcoat pocket, and if he can't do that he shouldn't be ashamed to make music for you on a willow whistle or even a comb."

"Yes," the actors declared unanimously at this point, "if we had known what sort of person you were we certainly would never have hired you as conductor."

"Whatever I got for myself through you," replied the conductor, "was little enough for life, but more than enough for death."

The clergyman had had enough of these people and was more than ready for bed. Besides, the threshing was still going on outside; he ought to go out and have a look, and his wife was probably waiting for him impatiently.

"Gentlemen," he interrupted, "just remember that you're in the house of the Lord. Don't shout so, your voices carry out into the fields."

"All right," said the conductor with quiet emotion, "it can be heard out in the fields but it can't be with you. I'd have been better off if I had stayed by myself from the beginning. I'd rather play on an ice-floe all alone or whistle with the wind, but with you people I wouldn't even want to play the organ in St. Peter's. I'd rather be my own ghost than your accompanist." His sorrow seemed to magnify the pride in his heavy heart, and he shouted, "You riff-raff! I'm proud and I'm glad of it!"

"Riff-raff?" the indignant comedians shouted. "What an insult! You organ-grinder! You with your dishonourable discharge from the army!"

The clergyman did not know whom to be angry with, the conductor or the actors. It was really outrageous how much time he had to spend over this business. The threshing, the horses, his wife, this whole ugly affair would be found out in the end. He wiped his forehead with mounting nervousness.

"You might as well know," the conductor continued, his pale face flushing, "that I always felt my situation to be most humiliating—to have to torment music for your cheap theatricals. Believe me, it wasn't love for your way of life and it wasn't even hunger which brought me among you, but my own bitterness. You deserve everything you're getting here—the village, the clergyman, the organ, and me!..."

"Rubbish!" shouted the actors in chorus.

The conductor strode swiftly to the staircase, stopped there and shouted emotionally, while very near to fainting. "Kill and destroy each other, but not me!" He turned to the clergyman. "This house shall yet be a manger and from another manger shall be a new church where a new Saviour is born! Just get along until then, but without me!"

"I won't be spoken to like this!" the clergyman protested. "How dare you say such things here? You're not as clever as you think. Only jailbirds talk that way!"

The conductor already had one foot on the stairs. Agitatedly, he hung his cane on his arm. "You keep quiet," he shouted at the clergyman. "Just let your stomach talk!"

He swallowed his last thought, and the staircase swallowed him. The outraged actors cursed. The clergyman wanted to follow him to make him pay for his words, but instead he wiped his neck with a handkerchief.

"What an uncouth man," he exclaimed. "How could he ever have been an organist or an army officer?"

"That's what that rotter always told us," answered the director, "but I'm going to report him to the police; he still owes me his travelling expenses. That good-for-nothing isn't going to get away!"

Slowly the actors returned to the organ. The clergyman, however, nervously replaced the candelabrum muttering as he did so, "If I had known this, gentlemen, I would not have gone so far. I wanted to help you, but all this is really not worth the trouble."

"But Your Reverence," cried the director, bowing, "excuse me, but he and we are two different things! I'd like to have belted him!"

"It would have done a fellow like that some good," grumbled the clergyman, and his agitation made him sweat.

"We would have beaten him up," the actors declared, "but we had too much respect for this holy place."

The clergyman waved his hand. "This whole business must come to an end."

"What do you mean?" asked the weary actors.

"The way I see it, if you have no conductor you can't use the organ anyhow."

"Can I smoke here?" asked one of the actors. Exhausted, the others sat down on the choir benches and quietly berated the conductor.

"I think," the clergyman suggested, "that we might as well go now."

"Excuse me," the director insisted. "Just because the conductor has left the group stranded in this disgraceful way doesn't mean we're finished. Mr. Tömb can play a little bit."

"That's right," answered Mr. Tömb feebly. He took an apple from his pocket and began nibbling at it, an example the other actors followed.

"I can play well enough for our purposes."

"Actually," the director explained to the clergyman, "it's not so important to have an artist play the organ. What counts is just to have some sort of music so we don't have to accompany the play by whistling."

Meanwhille, the young actor had written on the wall, *I was here in 1926. Imre Tolna, actor.'*

"Just let's try it," begged the director, thinking to himself: 'Don't worry, you're not going to fool us any more, my friend!'"

"You gentlemen are rather aggressive," said the clergyman.

"It's the spot we're in, you know," the director temporized slyly, "just try to be a little more patient with us."

But the clergyman was thinking of something else. "This conductor," he said, "is likely to arouse the entire village."

"We'll beat him to death!" one of the actors said.

The clergyman, however, was growing more and more anxious. "At any rate, I'm going to see what he's up to. You gentlemen can make one more try. But do be careful, because neither the organ nor the church belongs to me. I'll be back soon." And having said this, the clergyman disappeared down the staircase.

"Boys," the director said, "get a good grip on yourselves, if you don't want the same thing to happen here that happened in Ötvös and Pinnye. Here there's some hope! This afternoon I was talking with the intelligentsia. They'll come, they just don't want to hear any prose. There's going to be a fair tomorrow. I promise we'll take a million."

"If we could only take this infernal organ apart," one of the actors said.

"There are still six of us!" the director said excitedly. "We've got to manage it. The conductor doesn't count, he was a weakling anyhow. It's a good thing he's gone. Mr. Tömb will play and there'll be that much more in everybody's pocket. Come on, boys, while the minister isn't around to make difficulties!"

The actors rose slowly from the benches, removed their jackets in silence, rolled up their shirt-sleeves and unbuttoned their collars, exposing thin and sallow chests. They sealed their candles to the benches, spat into their palms, put aside the hymn-book racks and got to work for one last try.

In the meantime, the clergyman had gone out into the road. There was a heavy silence in which the occasional whine of the threshing machine in the distance could be heard. They were working until dawn in many places in order to make up for the next day, which would be spent at the fair. The clergyman set out to see what his labourers were doing. However, when he passed the arbour he thought of his daughter and went into the house first. On entering the room he was greeted by snoring and the ticking of his old watch. He found the wine, and drank a glassful. He looked to see whether his daughter was properly covered-up... His wife was sound asleep... Everything was all right...

He went out silently and walked toward the field.

The huge motor was shaking and quivering in a swelling cloud of chaff lit by the red light of lanterns. The threshing machine, like a thirsty elephant, lifted its black trunk to the sky.

There were many stars out. Hoarse from dust and fatigue, the half-naked farmhands and the girls with their skirts hitched up were feeding and tending the machine. From inside the thresher could be heard the quivering rhythm of the sieves, like a monotonous, powerful sobbing.

"Well," the clergyman addressed the mechanic, "how goes it?"

"There'll be a hundred-pound yield," said the man, black from soot, as he climbed out from under the machine.

"Did you see anybody walking around here?" the clergyman asked.

"Anybody?"

"I gave the actors some wine," the clergyman explained, "and I think the conductor got drunk. I thought perhaps one of them had passed this way."

"No," replied the mechanic, and walked about the thresher with his oil-can, checking the various parts. The clergyman sat down on the gear-box. The girls began to sing quietly as they worked, *'Kindly, kindly do I hover / As love blooms on the lips of my lover.'*

The machine droned into the melody and swallowed up the song. The clergyman reckoned the yield.

There was a good harvest this year; he would be able to enlarge the stable and have a big shed built on to the back of the manorhouse. The singing and droning enchanted him. This is the real church, he thought, and looked about him. The threshing machine was like the organ. He went over to it and held his hand above the opening of one of the sacks. He took the grain over to a lantern and blew into it gently. The kernels were good and heavy. This is the real hymn, he thought. He too would have liked to dress as a servant of the earth, but instead he returned the grain to the sack. Carefully, he poured it back to the last kernel and gazed silently at the labourers, their shadows bent in the chaff dust.

"Mr. Dél," he called to the mechanic as he was about to leave, "tell everyone that this late work is just for today."

"Yes, sir," replied Mr. Dél, standing beside the machine.

The clergyman slowly started towards the church.

"Ridiculous," he thought, "this is what happens when you try to be good. Lucky thing the staircase is so narrow." Suddenly he came to a halt. Suppose someone were following him...

"Your Honour, Your Honour..."

The clergyman turned round in alarm. An old farmhand was standing submissively behind him. A soft breeze was blowing.

"Your Honour," said the old man, "please don't be angry. I only came to ask Your Reverence if... considering this late work, whether a little drink would be possible... not only for me... I ask in the name of the others..."

"Why didn't you mention this at the machine?" the clergyman rebuked him. "It's a wonder you don't creep into the house after me!"

The old man apologized.

"All right... all right," the clergyman said. "Just go back. To-morrow."

"May the Lord reward Your Honour," the old man said, and turned away.

The minister cut through the barn with rapid steps. He reached the church, went up the porch, and was on the staircase leading up to the choir when he saw a light through the large door which led to the nave of the church. He approached in surprise, but before he realized what was happening, he opened the door to the nave of the church. Holy Saviour!

With ropes around its girth, the organ was swinging heavily and slowly in mid-air below the choir, like a cube on edge.

Down in the nave some of the actors were waiting open-mouthed for the descending instrument. Others, leaning far out over the balustrade with beads of sweat on their foreheads and bare necks, and their eyes bulging, were lowering the instrument, which had been tied up with traces, harnesses, and ropes.

When they noticed the clergyman, the organ stopped in mid-air. The director approached, stammering, "Forgive us, Your Reverence, the staircase really was too narrow. It'll be down in a moment; we collected a few ropes without asking your permission..."

The clergyman was nearly speechless.

"Who said you could do this?" he roared. "What is the meaning of this?"

"But, but..." stammered the director.

Up in the gallery the thin, exhausted comedians could no longer either hold on to or lower the organ. They ground their teeth, bit their lips, made hissing sounds, and then suddenly cried out. "Ha-a-a-a, ha-a-a!"

The organ slipped from their hands and fell out of the ropes like a black cube, as if some unknown hand had hurled down its enormous, dark slabs from the darkness of the steeple.

The clergyman and the comedians leaped aside at the same instant. With a monstrous rumble the organ shattered into smithereens before their eyes. There was a tense silence. The hum of the threshing machine could be heard again from outside. The clergyman shuddered, while up above in the choir section the actors pulled on their jackets and scurried out of the door to the meadow like terrified rats. But two of them were still standing confused and frightened beside the clergyman, who was shouting, "I'll have you arrested, you robbers, you thieves! I'll have you taken to the police! Get out of the village immediately!"

"Y-yes," stammered the director. "It was an accident... The spot we were in..."

"To hell with you!" bawled the clergyman, and the last actor brushed past the director on his way out of the door to the meadow.

The clergyman could barely control himself.

"You miserable wretches!" he turned on the director. "Why didn't you wait for me? Couldn't you wait?"

"We were afraid Your Reverence had changed his mind," the pale director stammered.

"Now who am I supposed to ask to return the organ?" the clergyman raged. "This organ cost at least three million!" He needed to let out at least one violent oath, but habit and practice forbade this.

"Excuse me, Your Reverence," the director mumbled nervously, "I really have nothing else but this gold watch here... my gold watch," and trembling, he searched about for the watch in his waistcoat.

"Oh, go to the devil," fumed the clergyman, "gold watch indeed!"

"This is all there is," faltered the director. "This is all... really!"

And with his hand shaking, the poor man did take out the watch, but it flipped from his fingers, and, as a round golden fish fleeing the net springs lithely into the lake, the watch fell on the wreckage of the organ.

Both men leaped after the watch at the same time, and their fingers touched.

"Well," said the clergyman, more calmly, "that's the end of yours now, too."

The director could not speak for agitation. He knelt down and searched for his watch among the debris.

"Paupers, and they don't even take care of the little they've got," the clergyman went on, still more tranquilly.

"That's the end of my watch," stammered the director. "The end... I saved for five years..." He put what was left of his watch back into his pocket and stood up.

"Go, go," said the clergyman, and he started for the door. "Get out of this village as fast as possible, all of you, and never say a word about any of this. There's nothing else you can do anyhow."

"I saved for five years!" the director lamented.

"Hurry," said the clergyman. Once again he took a cautious look about, and left the porch and the director.

One after another the comedians emerged from the darkness.

"Well, what happened? What are we going to do?"

"Run wherever your feet will carry you," the director told them briefly. "That's what the minister said."

"The minister?" asked the men.

"You can all go to hell as far as I'm concerned too," the director finished. "That was the end of my gold watch!"

"Did that bloody minister take it?" the young actor inquired.

"Idiot," raved the director, "it fell on the stone floor."

"And what about our travelling expenses? Who's going to pay for that?"

"The Lord, who punished me for coming here!" answered the director, and with that he walked out on his troupe.

"The police will pay!" laughed the young actor. "Come on, let's go scrounging!"

The others agreed, and after they had divided up the places where they could scrounge best, they slowly headed for their night's lodgings.

Translated by Susan Kun

ROOM 212

by ENDRE ILLÉS

On weekdays the professor had lunch at the hospital, in his study, at a low, round table with a glass top. This day they put his favourite meal before him, an omelette of four eggs with pieces of green pepper fried with it, on which he sprinkled finely ground red pepper. Afterwards he asked for an orange salad. With it he drank a glass of dry wine.

He had a lovely room. One wall was pierced by an enormous window; from there he saw the snow-covered garden in winter, in spring the trees bending in the whistling winds. A giant Persian rug hung on another wall, a bookshelf behind his desk. Sometimes he even stayed overnight, sleeping on the couch.

The plates were taken away, and he had just opened an English medical journal when his secretary came in.

"Someone to see you, sir."

The professor glanced at his watch. Two thirty. He never could manage lunch much earlier.

"Did you tell him I don't see out-patients at the hospital?"

"I did. Neither at the hospital, nor at home."

The professor folded the journal.

"Is some relation of his a patient here?"

"I asked him. He said no."

"His name?"

"He wouldn't give it?"

"What does he want then?"

"To speak to you, sir." And she added as though this had some significance, "His wife is with him too."

"Has he been to see me before? Do you remember?"

"I don't think we've ever seen him before."

"Ask him for his name once again."

The secretary returned. "He'll only give it to you, sir."

The professor sat down near his desk.

"What can we do? Send him in."

The stranger appeared. He wore a navy-blue suit with a yellow turtle-neck sweater. His hair was turning a dirty grey; his narrow, pointed beard and the thin moustache above the bloodless lips were the same colour. His wife stood behind him, tired, broken, in dark grey.

The professor looked the man over, his hollow chest, the baggy suit on the thin body, and he could already hear his heavy breathing.

"I was told you'd like to speak to me."

The other two came forward, all the way up to the desk. Then the man spoke his name.

He spoke very softly.

The professor asked him to repeat it. He had been watching him all along, but only then did he take a real look.

The dreaded man stood before him. That dreaded man who only a few years before had held the lives of others on the palm of his hand like the severed leg of a frog, which will still twitch convulsively if hit by an electric current. The man who could know the heart throbs of a bird tight in the grip of his hand.

"You are...," the professor faltered.

The stranger stared at him. "Yes, I am."

The professor reached for the ballpoint on his desk and toyed with it.

"What is it you want me to do?"

"I am a sick man. I should like you to have a look at me."

"I think my secretary has already told you, I don't engage in private practice."

The man's eyes grew more rigid still. They were beginning to resemble marbles. He wanted to soften his voice to a pleasing tone but it remained flat and dry, it cracked like dry reed—this voice could not accept any foreign material, any softer overtones.

"Yes," he said. "But I trust only you, professor. I can only trust you."

The professor held the ballpoint tight.

"Why me, exactly?"

The man in the navy suit drew a big breath.

"I thought it over carefully, for weeks on end. Because I thought it out... I thought about it before it all became clear." He spoke crudely. "I never had you investigated, neither you, nor any member of your family. None of them, ever!... Although I could have done so, once..."

He stopped—as though he could not exhale the few cubic centimetres of air which he had just breathed in so deeply a moment before.

The second, third, fourth moment too passed, and the man remained silent locked in a stiff cramp. In this heavy silence the professor asked, "What could you have done to harm me?"

The spasm finally relaxed.

"I was informed that when a colleague of yours issued a press statement that the recovery rate is better during the winter in the less heated, in fact in the cold wards, than in the well heated ones, you issued orders to keep up the heat! Keep the wards as warm as they had been. Stoke up the fires. I should have had that investigated. What was behind those orders of yours. But I did not..."

The professor clicked the ballpoint and doddled his name on a white sheet, once, twice, five times—this is how I would have signed my evidence then, he thought.

He looked up.

"May I ask, why you did not pursue the matter?"

The man in the navy blue suit relaxed a little.

"Because I am prejudiced. I like the cold better than well-heated rooms. Those who are prejudiced should maintain their objectivity." He continued in the cracked, splintery voice of the broken reed. "I am ill, professor. As ill as the others at your hospital here... Take me as your patient, you have got to help me."

The professor stood up.

"If you really are ill and, as far as I can tell by the looks of you, you no doubt are... I'll arrange for you to be admitted."

"But will I get a private room?"

"Naturally."

"And you will examine me? Just you alone?"

"Naturally. Me too."

"I don't trust anybody else."

"If you want to stay at this hospital, you will have to trust everyone here. Incidentally, where are you employed now?"

There was a moment's pause.

"Are you working anywhere?"

"I am assistant manager at the Costume Hire Company."

"So you are insured." The professor doodled his name on the white sheet for the sixth time, then made his decision. "You will be placed in Katalin Ivándy's care. She will be in charge of the preliminary tests. She's my assistant."

"And I'll get a private room?"

"I've already promised that."

"And my wife..."

"Your wife cannot stay here." He picked up the housephone and called his secretary.

"Please take the patient to Dr. Ivándy's. I'll ring her right away."

When the man, his wife, and his own secretary left the room, the professor smiled. But this smile could only have been caught by those who knew him very well. "I might as well have said, take him away," he thought.

Late in the afternoon Katalin Ivándy reported, "Advanced cardiac asthma. I have prescribed Cedilanide and Diaphyllin, and Noxyron for the night."

"Right," said the professor.

Dr. Ivándy continued. "His ECG would even justify Prednisolon."

"Let's wait with that. I'll have a look at him myself first."

"He's afraid of waking at dawn. He says that's when it's worst. He gasps for breath."

"If he can't breathe, give him extra Diaphyllin."

"He asked his name should not be on his chart."

The professor smiled again.

"Open the telephone book, and take the first name that catches your eye."

Katalin Ivándy still had something to say.

"He's a difficult patient, he won't undress. Just sits on a chair... Complains that his window faces the courtyard."

The professor knew how his patient felt.

"Have an armchair placed in his room, with a cushion, and get him to sit in that. With his back to the window. That way he won't see the courtyard."

Before he went home, the nurse on duty came to see the professor.

"They brought something to eat for number 212. The person who brought it said it was from home. Shall I give it to him?"

The professor took the lid off the two-tiered container: pork cutlet with rice and stewed apples, pink sponge-cake on the bottom plate.

"He got the same here. We took it to his room, but he wouldn't touch it," said the nurse indignantly.

"He trusts them more at home," the professor assured the nurse. "For now—take him this 'home-made'... Eventually he'll grow to like us."

The next morning, however, even before the consultant's round, the professor went to room 212 in a state of exasperation, Dr. Ivándy and the matron trailing behind him.

The patient was standing by the window, and hearing them enter, turned around.

"Don't do that again!" said the professor in a sharp, raised tone of voice.

"What, professor?"

"Giving ten forints to the boy in the next ward to take your tablets. Haven't you ever heard of adult dosage and children's dosage, and that the latter is considerably less? Haven't you got scruples? You could have poisoned that boy!"

Number 212 looked at the professor for a while, as one who does not wish to answer. Nonetheless, after some time he spoke, very quietly.

"Did the boy tell on me?"

"He did not. You were caught."

The voice of number 212 now took on a bit more colour.

"A strange custom this is, professor, that there are three pills prepared for me in a small cup to go with my breakfast. I have to swallow them, and I don't even know what I'm swallowing."

"That is not a strange custom, these are the hospital regulations!" The professor was becoming more and more exasperated.

"You are at this hospital now and not somewhere else! Did you think we wanted to poison you? We usually give treatment here."

Number 212 defended himself humbly, underhandedly.

"I beg your pardon... I meant no harm. I beg all of your pardons.. But a professor must also consider his patient's peace of mind as a condition for recovery."

"Naturally."

"Then let me ask you please to give me a presciption. My wife will pick up the drugs, and the doctor or nurse can pick out each time what I should take. That would make me much calmer."

Before the professor could answer, Dr. Ivándy's face flushed. She asked indignantly, "So you really are afraid we'll poison you?"

"Yes."

"Are you afraid of me? Your doctor?"

Number 212 did not look up at them. He was examining the linoleum-covered floor.

"I have enemies. I'm protecting myself." He only lifted his head when the professor spoke.

"If you keep this up, I'll have you thrown out of the hospital," the professor said. He turned and walked out. Dr. Ivándy and the matron followed him.

In the corridor Dr. Ivándy added, "This morning I had him scheduled for routine tests, X-ray and laboratory, but he didn't go to any of them. We haven't a single report on him yet."

The professor leant on the banisters.

"Let's leave him alone for a day or two. Let him make up his own mind what he wants," he said finally.

On the third day, in the early afternoon, the professor's secretary announced number 212's wife.

"We will leave, professor."

"If that is your decision, no one will stop you."

"Please don't be angry."

"Why should I be?"

"Please believe me... He didn't want to offend anyone. It's not in his nature."

"If you say so, I have to believe you." When she was already at the door, he decided to ask, "Why exactly are you leaving? You do know, don't you, that your husband is ill. His illness, will soon become worse. What will you do then?"

The woman turned in gratitude, in pain, at the kind words.

"I don't know, professor... I don't know... The problem here was that he got a room facing the courtyard... He began to be afraid then, right in the first half hour... Afraid of the courtyard... Perhaps if you had put him in a room facing the street... then... perhaps..."

But she couldn't finish and left.

Translated by Etelka Láczay

ONE-MINUTE STORIES
by ISTVÁN ÖRKÉNY

MEMOIRS OF A PUDDLE

On March 22nd, 1972, it rained all day and I collected myself in a very pleasant place. I might as well give the exact location: in front of No. 7 Dráva utca, Budapest, 13th district, where there is a pothole in the pavement.

It was my home. Many a man stepped into me, then looking back they cursed me, swore at me, and used harsh words which I am loath to repeat. I was a puddle for two days, taking the insults lying down. It is common knowledge that the sun shone again on the 24th. Oh, the paradoxes of life! I dried up just when the weather turned fine!

What else shall I say! Did I do all right? Did I make a fool of myself? Did I perhaps fall short of the expectations of the people at 7 Dráva utca? Not that it makes any difference, really, but all the same it would be nice to know, if only because after me new puddles will go on collecting there. We live fast, our days are numbered, and while I was spending my days down there, a new generation sprang up, vigorous and ready for action, all of them ambitious potential puddles and they bombarded me with importunate questions as to what they might expect in that promising pothole.

But all in all I "puddled" for a bare two days and all that this allows me to say is that the tone of life is abusive; that Dráva utca is damned windy; and that the sun is forever shining when it has no business to, but at least you don't have to trickle down the drain pipe. Oh boys, what holes, what depressions! Bursting pipes! Sagging roads! These are great things nowadays! All you young people, listen to me, forward to Dráva utca!

Translated by László T. András

The Right To Remain Standing

If the conductor, who had already looked me up and down a couple of times, though without showing any real interest, should happen to say, would passengers please move to the front of the bus, then—and you can bet your life on this—not a word would pass my lips though I would not budge either, I'd stay put, rooted to the spot. There are sound reasons why I must remain standing right here. To begin with, my brief-case is down on the floor, propped against my ankle, and in it five bottles of beer, ten pairs of frank-furters, mustard, bread, butter, cheese, and a bottle of three-star brandy, weighing some 15 to 20 lb. between them, and I've got no intention whatever of moving it; I am in fact happy that the case is not upset either when the driver puts the brakes on, or starts. All this has to be since there are unpredictable, impossible and hyste-rical people in this world, like my best friends, who have to let you know right at the last minute they are coming over to eat. I can't very well explain all that without looking a fool in front of all the other passengers; so I keep mum and stay unbudgeable right where I am.

Now if the conductor should choose to speak to me personally, and this possibility cannot be completely excluded, saying, would that gentleman there in the grey raincoat please allow passengers to get on the bus, then I should be forced to say, politely but firmly, 'My dear woman, I would advise you to keep your mouth shut.'

If the conductor should happen to reply, and this possibility cannot be lightly dismissed, that she objected to such an offensive tone of voice, then I would say, still politely, or if not politely, then at least with calm restraint, 'My good woman, turn blue, go bald, and above all, go dumb! All you do is lecture, annoy and insult the passengers.' If she should then answer, and this sort of thing has happened before. 'One more word from you, Sir, in that tone of voice and I'll call a policeman.' I should make a come-back telling her to call out the whole police force, the army, the fire service, the armoured units if she liked, but I won't budge from this spot which I have as much right to occupy as any other passenger in the world.

Now then, if she dared call a policeman, and the policeman were able to scramble on to the crowded bus and had the nerve to call me to account, then I should tell him, without a trace of irritation, yet determined, 'My dear fellow, drop dead.' Should he reply, which is not at all impossible, 'My dear Sir, if you use that language, I'll be forced to take you to the station,' at this point, there being a limit to my patience as well, I would say, 'My dear fellow, you won't take me anywhere, if you don't stop I shall take you to a place where you won't like it at all. I'll jump up and down on your belly until I squeeze out your last breath and you lose any desire to make further threats.'

After this—and this is not only conceivable but very likely too—the police inspector, in front of whom I'd meanwhile find myself, would read me the riot act. 'Look, you seem to be such an educated, well-bred person,' he'd say, 'your bearing and dress suggest a well-balanced mature man, how could you have said such a thing to a policeman who only did his duty when he came to the assistance of a working woman who, in her turn, did nothing but carry out her duty, doing so with the utmost civility?' I wouldn't even answer, disliking arguments as I do, but would step back, open my fly and piss on the carpet that had enough oil and ink stains on it anyway, and having finished and buttoned up my fly, I might, at most, say, 'Look, Inspector, you can take that for an answer.'

If after all this, which still lies well within the realm of possibility, the senior psychiatrist of the mental hospital should ask me with strained suavity to close my eyes, stretch my arms and start walking in an imaginary straight line towards him, I would not, to be sure, close my eyes or stretch my arms, but would be off in that imaginary straight line towards him all right, taking a kick right at his crotch that would send him somersaulting backwards behind his desk.

And this is not all. For if after all this the hefty male nurse, standing behind me, threw himself at me and tried to hold me down, I, whom luckily all this would not take by surprise, would kick him in the shin with such force that he'd fall flat on the floor and I'd be on top of him so that he couldn't move. Then I would gouge out his eyes, using my two thumbs on the corners, pressing them deep into the sockets, which operation would make the two eyeballs jump from their holes with a soft popping sound. After this, to make doubly sure, I would toss out his brain for good measure, and the passage being free, I'd pick up my brief-case, go down to the street, hail a cab to get home in time, ready to receive my dear friends, hospitable as ever.

Translated by László T. András

PORTRAIT OF A MAN

To say that I'm well off would be an exaggeration, but I have nothing to complain about either. When I was released I was taken on at once as a watchman. Not much money in it but not much work either. Five thousand containers full of sulphuric acid and a few hundred iron barrels of industrial alcohol. My job is to see that nothing is stolen. This is a paying proposition only if you stop others from doing what you get away with yourself. It's not my line, unfortunately, especially as I only got out thanks to an amnesty. Still, I had to keep an eye open for something on the side which, considering my state of mind, is not easy, after the way I was let down in connection with that trouble I had. I took a vow not to trust anyone in future and to do everything on my own. If it means having to starve, I'll starve but I'll rely strictly on myself alone.

I had a stroke of luck right at the start. I saw a notice and I went straight to the Institute of Immunology in Timár utca. They asked if I wanted to give blood. Yes, I said, blood. Since then I have not only learned the routine but, even if I say so myself, this connection has grown more and more fruitful over the years.

I can't give precise figures, though I keep a diary; one day the notebook got soaked in my pocket. However, allowing for a small margin of error I can safely say that from 1951 to the present day I have sold 68 litres of blood to the Institute. It is well known that prices have fluctuated a lot in the meantime. They paid 30 forint for 1/10 litre at the start, you can't look down on that considering conditions at the time. I bought this hat then, socks, suspenders, this and that. Later, when they had a big drive for voluntary donors, the price went down to 25 forints, as a result even the old regular donors left the Institute high and dry. It is well known that on January 1st, 1956 the price of blood went up to 50 forints and this rate is still valid today.

I shouldn't like to use the expression that it was a smart dodge on my part that I went on giving blood in the 25 forint times without a word of complaint, after all that's the kind of man I am. I have some reason to think that they had taken a liking to me even then. A young doctor came up to me one day and asked if I didn't fancy switching over to bone marrow. I asked him if marrow excluded blood, but he reassured me that there was no reason why I should not go on giving blood. Bone marrow would mean a little extra money, which, I must say, I could use then. I don't like a badly dressed man and the underclothes I had were pretty badly worn.

As far as I know they need bone marrow because radioactive rays used in the latest kind of physical research attack bone marrow and you can cure that only by transplantation. As far as I was concerned, I didn't lose by the deal. They give you an injection, all you feel is a sting on your chest and the same needle which is stuck through your bone immediately sucks out the marrow. They usually take 5 cubic centimetres a time, the price of which is 150 forints. Nothing much really, strictly speaking, but all the same I don't think it too little. Money for jam, as far as I'm concerned. After all, in three or four months your stock of bone marrow is thoroughly replenished.

I was pleased with my success, but I didn't believe myself that my career at the Institute would develop futher. But it did! Some three years ago the same doctor to whom I owed the bone marrow came to see me again. Thanks only to his good will I was among the first who received blood contaminated with isotopes. I venture to say that in this field I also stood the test. To tell the truth these research institutes for understandable reasons lack practical common sense, as a result confidence men and other shady characters perpetrated the most impudent frauds.

This is what happened at first with the isotopes-contaminated blood. In this examination, as is well known, they take 20 ccs of blood from your veins on the first day and then they immediately contaminate it with isotopes, then reinject it back into your blood stream. The price is 150 forints. But this is not all. After an hour they check on the effects with some kind of counting apparatus and they take 5 ccs of blood, for which they pay 50 forints, as a control. This means that right on the first day you lay your hands on 200 forints. All you have to do afterwards is come in once a week when they take 5 ccs of blood and pay 50 forints on each occasion. It is sad, but I can't hide the fact that there are people who take the 200 forints and never again even look at the Institute. Many experiments were wasted because of them.

Learning from experience the Institute took counter-measures. The situation now is that they only pay out 50 forints on the first day and everybody goes through with the weekly control examinations. They only lay their hands on the 200 forints after the last examination proves negative, in other words, when the contamination is over. I'm not saying this because I want to give myself a halo but I'd like to emphasize that it was not my behaviour which compelled them to take these counter-measures.

I won't say that when I calculate my yearly income and add all this together it comes to an astronomical figure. True, I haven't mentioned smaller sums which mightn't seem significant but which nevertheless play a role in my modest budget. Thus on each occasion, even when I only give blood in the ordinary way, I get a free snack consisting of bread, a piece of cheese, a small tin of pig's liver, two chocolate biscuits and a bottle of fruit-juice. I also get travelling expenses, two tram tickets each time.

My state of health is good. I'm also lucky because I am an optimist by nature, though I don't look at the future through rose-tinted spectacles. In other words, I'm honest with others, and also with myself, both in a positive and a negative way. If I can continue giving both blood and bone marrow at the same time for a few more years, which I have no reason to doubt, then I think I can safely say that when it comes to essentials I will lack for nothing.

I owe all this to my own resources. I've never asked anybody to help me. That's why I haven't had disappointments, as I did in the past. Not having harmful habits or passions has also helped. I don't even smoke. I like a walk, I enjoy fresh air, I like the even-

ing crowds in a city, and colourful shopwindows. I like rain and
snow too. I don't mind the heat either. I always go about bare-
headed. Summer or winter I always wash myself in cold water.

Translated by László T. András

THE LAST CHERRY PIT

There were just four Hungarians left now. (In Hungary, that is;
there were still quite a number scattered around the globe.) They
dwelled under a cherry tree. It was a very fine cherry tree; it afford-
ed both cherries and shade, though the former only in season. But
even of the four Hungarians, one was hard of hearing, while two
stood under police inspection. Why this was so neither of them
could recall any more, though from time to time they'd sigh,
"We're under police inspection."

Only one of the four had a name—i.e., only he could remember
it. (His name was Sipos.) The others had forgotten theirs along
with so much else. With four people it is not essential that each
should have a name.

Then one day, Sipos said, "We ought to leave something
behind to remember us by."

"What on earth for?" asked one of the two men who stood
under police inspection.

"So that when we're gone, something should remain for pos-
terity."

"Who's going to care about us then?" asked the fourth Hungarian who was neither Sipos nor one of the two men under police
inspection.

But Sipos stuck to his guns and the other two backed him. Only
he, the fourth, insisted that the world had never seen a sillier idea.
The others were highly offended. "What do you mean?" they said
indignantly, "how can you say such a thing? You're probably not
even a true Hungarian!"

"Why?" he countered, "maybe it's such a godsent being a Hungarian these days?"

He had a point there. And so, they stopped bickering. They

racked their brains about what they could leave to be remembered by. To carve a stone would have required a chisel. If only one of them had a stickpin! With it, Sipos reasoned, they could etch a message into the bark of the tree. It would stay in the bark for ever, like a lattoo on a man's skin.

"Why don't we throw a big stone into the air," suggested one of the two who stood under police inspection.

"Don't be a fool, it'd fall back down," they told him. He didn't argue. Poor man, he knew he was short on brains.

"All right," he said to the others after a while. "Why don't you come up with something better if you can. What is it that would last?"

They put their heads together. At long last they agreed to hide a cherry pit between two stones (so the rain wouldn't wash it away). It wouldn't be much of a memorial to be sure, but for want of anything better, it would have to do.

However, they were faced with a problem. While the cherry season lasted they had lived on cherries, and afterwards had gathered up all the pits, crushed them into a fine powder, and consumed them. Consequently, there wasn't a single pit to be had for love or money.

Just then, one of the Hungarians who was neither Sipos nor one of the men who stood under police inspection remembered THE CHERRY. (He was no longer contrary, but was, in fact, with them heart and soul, and couldn't wait to help.) But the cherry grew so high up on top of the highest branch of the tree that they couldn't pick it back then. And so it had stayed where it was, shrivelled down to the pit.

They concluded that if they stood on each other's shoulder they could bring down the solitary cherry after all. They mapped everything out in fine detail. At the bottom stood one of the two men who were under police inspection, the one short on brains but long on brawn. On his shoulder stood the man who was neither Sipos nor was under police inspection, and last came Sipos, the flat chested weakling.

With a great deal of effort he climbed to the top of the column made up of his three companions, and once there, stretched out to his full height. But by the time he had reached the top, he had forgotten why he had bothered to climb up in the first place. It went straight out of his head. The others shouted to him to bring down the shrivelled cherry, but it was no use, because he was the one who was hard of hearing.

And so, things came to an impasse. From time to time, all four would shout in unison, but even so, the problem persisted, and they stayed just as they were, one Hungarian on top of the other.

Translated by Judith Sollosy

NOTHING'S LOST
by GÉZA OTTLIK

1

Jacobi arrived in the famous European city where he had spent his childhood and which now, on his fiftieth birthday, was to honour him with a golden violin. He arrived at the beginning of March, hence two weeks earlier than was absolutely necessary. He prowled about the streets for days in the mornings, in the after-noons, at night, looking for something, but though he traversed all the districts he had once known, there was nothing that he truly recognized, everything had become unfamiliar.

He looked restless. He was thin. He had lost a lot of weight lately. He was a tall, thin, restless man when left to himself in a strange hotel room. Whenever he saw anyone looking at him he screwed his face into a smile, to give his wrinkled countenance a pleasant, serene appearance. But on the plane, when arriving, he became silent. From the windows of the plane he watched the indistinguish-able outlines of the city unfold beneath them. He was wearing light summer clothes. The stewardess, all maternal solicitude, cautioned him to put on something warmer as it was still almost winter here, not more than ten degrees centigrade above zero.

Jacobi looked at the map in his guide-book and tried to com-pare it with the scene below. Only the ribbon of the river could be clearly seen. Beyond the river a triangular patch glistened in the sunshine; he would have liked to know what it was. When the stewardess had passed him Jacobi threw the guide-book on top of his pile of newspapers. He had not left her unanswered out of im-politeness; it was not emotion that had made him tongue-tied. The first wave of exhaustion was accompanied by a slight giddi-ness, the familiar, fleeting spell of feeling faint. With his forefinger he wiped two tiny beads of perspiration from his brow. He took a magazine from the bundle of papers and gave it to his neighbour. Then he took his bottle of pills out of his pocket and swallowed one unobserved.

There was a page-long article about him in the weekly paper. "After an absence of forty years we may once again greet Péter Jacobi in the town of his birth. In those forty years he has conquered the world with his violin." The article was mostly made up of photographs; the text was short. Jacobi in tails, Jacobi in swimming trunks in the company of Einstein. The Duke and Duchess of Windsor minus Jacobi. Pictures of the city forty years ago. The chief burgomaster who was to present him with the golden violin. The façade of the city College of Music, a modern playground in a new residential district. He laughed at the article, and turning to the beautiful, thirty-year-old woman with the tense neck sitting beside him, said something to her quietly in a foreing language, keeping the smile fixed on his face. It was thirty years since he had last seen the city—they had in fact moved when he was eleven, but he had spent another eighteen months here later. It was not his native town; he had spent his childhood here from the age of two, but had been born in a smaller town that lay in the hills. And as for the conquest of the world, two of his concerts overseas had been cancelled one after the other, which was why he had been able to come here two weeks earlier than planned.

From the map in the guide-book, by tracing the railway lines there, he managed to find Budapest South, but in fact the railway could not be found whichever way he juggled the map. He put it down beside him and closed his eyes. The pressure in his head increased and the mild attack of giddiness did not subside. It would pass. It would pass but first it would enclose him, it would immure him in a vacuum where he would flounder helplessly. For the present the vacuum loomed, threatening to engulf him, but he could still see his way out of it, out this weakness, if only dimly. He had left the city thirty years ago, early in the morning. He remembered the forecourt of Budapest South. The girl whom he had not married strolled up and down beside him underneath the glass dome. She had torned up unexpectedly to see him off. They had parted for a good long time before that morning. Jacobi had told her that he did not love her. How had she learned the time of his departure? Jacobi was agonizingly embarrassed. The girl did not make a scene but perhaps expected something from him. A kind word at least. Jacobi was on tenterhooks; he mumbled a few clumsy, ungracious words, not exactly hostile, but at any rate without compassion. Not long after, someone wrote to him that the girl had had an accident on the street.

Had she been knocked down by a car? Run over by a tram? Had she lost a leg? Or had she perhaps wanted to commit suicide? Had she recovered? Jacobi never knew for certain what had happened to her and what became of her. "She had an accident on the street." The picture of the girl's broken or mangled body, the body he had known, haunted him for years, for decades. It assailed him so often in his waking hours and in his dreams, now openly, now taking him unawares, that he grew accustomed to it, so bored with it that he thrust it aside irritably together with the foolish thought that he had been in some way responsible. Lately however, since his own death had become an impending possibility, he would have somehow liked to put that terrible conversation at the railway station right. It simply would not do. He should have said something after all. "Listen, who the hell asked you to come here, for God's sake, get lost," or, "Come with me, let us live together and love each other till death do us part." Or at least, "Listen, let's wait till the train starts and throw ourselves under instead of standing here snivelling."

Instead of standing here snivelling. Listen, let's not stand here snivelling. He shook his head and wiped his brow. The beautiful woman sitting beside him had just asked him something. She spoke quietly, in a foreign language, the hum of the plane muffling her words still further: and suddenly Jacobi could not tell whether they had been speaking in English, Portuguese or Spanish. He stood up, at last able to breathe freely. He stood up, put on a knitted cardigan and took the proffered magazine from his neighbour. Unesco, Beethoven. These were the only two words the woman had understood and Jacobi translated the short, incorrect little article for her. "Péter Jacobi, whose name has been repeatedly mentioned in connection with an important Unesco delegation. The significance of his visit is augmented by the fact that we wish to improve commercial and cultural relations with the overseas country of which he has been a citizen for the last twenty years. Last year he won the international grand prize for his series of recordings of Beethoven's ten sonatas for piano and violin, none of which will unfortunately be heard at the single concert he will be giving in Hungary, as he has lately had to part company with his permanent accompanist..." Jacobi did not translate this last half-sentence, but his neighbour nevertheless glanced at the top photograph of Jacobi in tails, standing on a platform, beside him on his right, her back half-turned to the audience, the bent head of a girl with long hair could be seen.

On the bottom photograph of the page a lot of children were running about. They were not using the swings and other brand new paraphernalia on the playground, but were apparently engrossed in an old-fashioned game of puss-in-the-corner, their back against the trees. One of the tiny girls had left the safety of her tree-trunk "home" and was running with her hands raised high, her fingers crossed, as if her life depended on it, crying: pax! At least that is what it looked like to Jacobi. Beneath another, less clear photograph, the caption read: "The former Széna Market–the present-day Delano-Schweitzer tér–in 1915." They used to live on the left bank, in Újvilág utca. The long, wide street, flanked on both sides by large houses five or six stories high, led into the Széna Market. He ransacked his memory to ascertain which of the old trams on the photograph had run in their street. The 171? Or was it the one marked NB or MI? What was that steep little street called that wound up to the top of the hill from beside the cinema? And what was the name of that coffee-house opposite with the plate-glass windows? Metropol? Municipal? He thought he could just make out a letter on the photograph: Café M...

Beyond the Széna Market they had a playground. A large, sloping field beneath the villas. He remembered a little girl, who, whenever it seemed certain she would be overtaken or caught, always shook her pigtails, raised her hands high and cried, very unsportsmanlike, pax, pax, pax!

"Go home then," Jacobi, aged nine, had once angrily replied.

2

In the sudden silence the woman sitting beside him asked, "What brought you back finally?" The rest of the passengers were unfastening their safety-belts; a bald-headed man had wormed his way beside him and was pumping his hand, speaking rapidly in the same foreign language; his tense-necked neighbour was putting fresh lipstick on. Jacobi remembered that the concert agency had notified him that the television and the press would be there to greet him at the airport. He bent towards the window. There were indeed quite a number of people bustling about around the plane, press photographers, newsreel photographers, journalists. He jammed his straw hat down on his head, then took it off again and asked his neighbour for her pocket mirror, unembarrassed. He had to arrange his features. He sat down for a moment with the mirror. He tried a serene, worldly, yet grave smile. He could not step in front of the cameras looking as he did. From the window he saw a young man, probably sent by the concert agency, waving a bunch of flowers at him. This reassured him a little. If he had managed to recognize him from his photograph there could not be anything seriously wrong with his face. He tucked the violin-case under his arm and emerged from the plane smiling a practised smile. He waved his hat at them, all of them, and began to descend carefully, but with absolute assurance, looking at the cameras, not the steps. Jacobi's smile was pleasant and unaffected, deriving from an inner serenity and permeated by the radiance of his profound seriousness. But it was not he they were photographing. He noticed it too late.

The reporters and photographers had surrounded a plump, fortyish man. The young man from the concert agency tore his hair and rushed off after a member of the television crew, still carrying his bunch of flowers. For a moment they both turned back towards Jacobi, the television man's face beaming with joy. He made some sort of sign, then was off again as his companions and the film people had dragged the plump statesman back to the plane and had persuaded him to descend the steps once again. The young man from the concert agency trotted after him, the flowers tucked under his arm. Jacobi soon lost sight of them, because following the fervent leave-taking of three or four of his travelling companions, conducted in various languages—*Au revoir, cher Maestro, à bientôt!* It was terribly nice, really, dear Mr Jacobi...—he began to feel dizzy again. He strolled slowly into one of the buildings and sat down on the first bench he saw. He took another pill.

He sat motionless. He may have sat for a long time but it may in fact have taken only a few minutes. His mind was empty of all thought, incapable of concentration. The drone of the plane's humming in his ears was accompanied by a buzz of voices, snatches of conversation, fragments of sentences spoken in foreign languages which seemed to spin irrationally back and forth, back and forth in his head. He paid no attention to their buzzing but let his mind relax completely, and the incoherent, jumbled tape continued to spin inside his brain, as though it had an existence entirely independent of him. *(Par exemple, mon cher Maestro! En effet, c'était précisément pour ne pas manquer votre récital que j'ai fait un détour...* I see, Mr. Jacobi, but if you have never been back home for thirty years... I mean, that's quite a long time, isn't it? Putting it at forty years doesn't seem such a terrible inaccuracy...) He awoke to find a policeman politely shepherding him further into the building. (Awfully nice of you, my dear Maestro. *Bien sûr, cher ami, mercredi prochain. Quelle idée, que je ne l'oublie pas...!)* They steered him hither and thither until he finally found himself in a bare little room off a corridor. The sign on the door said "Foreign passports". There was a man in plain clothes sitting at the desk who motioned him to move across the room and take a seat at the other desk by the window. (*Par exemple, Monsieur Jacobi,* it may be a terrible inaccuracy, *cependant c'est précisément pour que* your compatriots of *quarante* years ago should get a chance, *une bonne chance, de ne pas manquer votre récital,* even if the town doesn't happen to be *exactement votre* birthplace...)

"By the window," he said. He got up and walked across to the other desk where Jacobi had sat down. And, as though out of politeness, he began to ask questions. What was his name? How long did he plan to stay in the country? What was the purpose of his visit? Why exactly until next Wednesday? For a consideration?

Which burgomaster? Could he prove this in any way? Has he a labour permit? What guarantee can he give that he will leave
the country at the appointed time?

Jacobi's replies lacked assurance. The man recommenced his
volley of questions, then lifted the phone and dictated the first two
questions, and the replies of the violinist to the stenographer who
instantaneously appeared. For a while the dictation continued,
then the official raised his head to look at Jacobi.

"I cannot consent to your admittance into this country."

Jacobi made no reply so there was a long silence. The male stenographer leaned back in his chair and timidly picked at his nails.
But the violinist was not afraid. He did not really understand what
it was all about. It was here, in this bleak little office, that his
mother tongue assailed, overwhelmed, intoxicated him.

Paralysis had struck the blood-stream of familiar foreign words
as soon as he had descended from the plane. His mother tongue
had besieged him as an enemy is besieged. Notices, placards, the
loud voices of doormen, film-people, parents, children and policemen, coming from telephones, through the loudspeakers, indifferently, incidentally, impudently, offhandedly; everyone
spoke the language here. It was a bold, hair-raising conspiracy
against him. Hearing them all speak his mother tongue to him,
seeing his replies taken down in the same language dulled his
senses, lulled him into a stupor. He would gladly have repeated
his round with the man in plain clothes for the third time.

Exit. Entrance. "Passengers are kindly requested..." Imagine,
darling, Oh forget it. Damn it! The king of all razor-blades. Entrance forbidden. In this room with the "Entrance forbidden" sign
on the door Jacobi had given the reply he had learnt at the age of
three to the first question put to him: "What is your name?"—"My
name is Péter Jacobi, I live at 27, Újvilág utca, second floor, flat
three." It was the formula to be repeated to strangers if he ever got
lost. He recited the words in a singsong voice and in his pride at remembering them so well he repeated them twice. The man sitting
at the desk did not interrupt him: he had grown used to
all sorts of strange things. But he questioned him exhaustively
upon the business of the golden violin, and bid him state his permanent address twice. "I have no permanent address," Jacobi

said. "You have no permanent address?" "No." "But it says here in your passport..." "That used to be my permanent address. It is no longer." "No?" "No longer." Jacobi corrected himself quickly, confusedly: "Not any more." "You mean that it is no longer your permanent address?" "I mean I don't live there any more."

Window, window, Jacobi thought. *Finestra,* window, *fenêtre.* Open the window, Péter. Don't sit at the window. Don't break the window. Jacobi was thinking of real windows. Bedroom windows, the windows of Otto's flat. Kitchen windows. Windows open in spring. The window of his room, closed against the rain. Window, window, window. Window. This worthy man in plain clothes had said window to him. Jacobi, as if he had forgotten to wipe off the smile intended to be televised, looked at the official, his face unaffectedly grave, lit up by his inner serenity.

"So you are receiving a golden violin—about this size, you said?"

"No, no."

"Well then what size?"

"A little one," Jacobi replied. "A miniature one. A small one. A tiny one. A minuscule one. A diminutive little violin. An itsy-bitsy little golden violin. A small tiny minuscule diminutive little..."

This time, a trifle irritatedly, the man in plain clothes interrupted him: "And this is the purpose of your visit?" "No," said Jacobi truthfully. "You perhaps intend to resettle permanently in this country?" "I have not thought about it yet." "You have not thought of staying here?" "Perhaps I have. Perhaps I have thought of it."

Perhaps, perhaps it was the wrong thing to have said, Jacobi thought. Though perhaps he had replied in this way so that he could use the word "perhaps". But in reality Jacobi was no longer thinking about his last reply. The man in plain clothes seemed to have lost patience with him, who cares, his gestures seemed to imply; he dictated two statements and demanded some sort of guarantee from Jacobi. Because of this word Jacobi was in fact thinking that he must have been able to read at the time the new word in the long three-sided log that had been in the dyer's window for as long as he could remember had aroused his curiosity. The shop was on a street corner a couple of houses further down from where they lived. It was not a particularly interesting shop.

But in the centre of the window in front a three-sided, varnished log had been placed and it said: *H. Millner and Sons—Dyeing Cleaning with Guarantee.*

Perhaps, perhaps he had heard the expression "guarantee" before then, but he had not known what it meant. Even later, when he came across the word in writing for the second and third time and tried to synthesize its surmised meanings, its diverse associations, its signification still remained vague, indefinite. Once he saw an advertisement in the paper for raincoats and tarpaulin, guaranteed impermeable. Guarantee might then mean some sort of obscure manufacturing process used by curriers or weavers: tanning, steeping, soaking with a special dye or perhaps with grease or wax? Or could it be a form of carding, combing, or weaving? These conjectures were contradicted by a sewing-machine which he had come across on one of the boulevards on the other side of the river. There was a price-tag on it which also said, guaranteed for two years. He had to dismiss the possibility of the gleaming machine having been guaranteed in a tanner's tub, on a spinning-wheel or power-loom or even in a kiln. But as the different meanings of the word multiplied, the nuances settled layer upon layer on the first meaning he had known, and were all in some way connected with H. Millner and Sons. There was a picture in one of his story-books of a prairie, a waterfall in the distance, the characters standing on a crag and the caption read: "I guarantee the safety of the lady, the brave Indian said." The unusual combination of words, though obviously the result of a mistranslation not uncommon in children's books, potently evoked that remote and alien world and filled it with magic. From there, from elsewhere, various other meanings were steeped, soaked, drenched and woven into the guarantee of the dyer, meanings that bore a nuance of adventure, of valour, such as *salvus conductus,* security, endurance, perseverance, word of honour, plighted faith, or, more tangibly, flight across the Cordilleras, a rumbling express above the precipice, the discovery of a long-lost father shipwrecked on a desert island.

The brave Indian could no longer be separated from H. Millner and Sons and Jacobi had grown accustomed, whenever his friend and he stopped for a moment in front of the dyer's window, though this rarely happened, because almost anything was more interesting than the dyer's shop—but if and when they stopped, out of pure absentmindedness, engrossed in the conversation, he had grown accustomed to placing his right foot, mechanically, on the step below the shop window, assuming the posture of the Indian in the picture, his bronzed torso bare, his foot on the crag, placed there with careless, disarming elegance.

"The export of precious metals is restricted."

"You must obtain a work permit," said the man in plain clothes. "Sign here."

Jacobi stood up. He looked at his watch. Still looking at his watch he moved the chair aside and placed his right foot upon its seat. He signed the papers bending forward, with his right foot up on the chair.

3

He was a tall, thin, restless man when left to himself in a strange hotel room. The telephone had begun to ring for the third time when he finally turned over, raised himself and reached out for the receiver. He had been lying on the bed, fully clothed, motionless, his face to the wall for a long time. The room was spacious, elegant, and unpleasant. He thought it empty. He scattered his belongings so there would be something of his everywhere but the room remained empty. "Oh, no, not at all," he said over the phone. "We must have missed each other at the airport. Oh, no, it doesn't matter. Not today. I can't make it today. Not by any means. Tomorrow, yes, tomorrow. You're welcome." He dropped the receiver carefully back in its place and stood up. This room hasn't even got a window, he thought, only a wall made of glass.

He put on a scarf, a coat. He began to hurry, as though he really had something to do. The porter handed him some letters, *le courrier, Monsieur.* The other called him Senhor, or Signor Giacobi. He opened two of his letters, the third, which had a handwritten address, he thrust into his pocket. With firm steps he walked out into the street and turned right.

He walked across a bridge, stopping for a moment in the middle to look down into the water. He took the handwritten letter out of his pocket, tore it into shreds unread and threw the pieces into the river. Having reached the other side he continued his journey by underground. Then on foot. A lot of things had changed but he had no difficulty in finding the little square. True, you had only to walk straight ahead along the big boulevard.

There was the equestrian statue, there the Wagner coffee-house. The billiard-tables should be there, on the back street side. A parade of some sort caught up with Jacobi as he was about to cross the street. The members of the procession were carrying placards and it all seemed fairly quiet and orderly, but many of the passers-by flocked after them and as they passed the square and reached the next intersection of the boulevard one block further, there was a sudden uproar, police cars arrived, and almost seconds later the square, the streets, the boulevard were silent and empty. The scanty traffic stopped altogether, members of the procession, passers-by and police had all disappeared without a trace. There had been no sound of shooting.

The windows were all empty too, and the big new apartment buildings, all were empty inside. The restaurants, the schools, the buses were all empty of people. Nobody lived in those flats. It was in such a deserted city, here, in an empty street at dawn, that that girl had once run away from him. He had caught up with her, they had tussled with each other. She had run away again. He had caught up with her at the foot of the statue, they had argued fiercely, he had entreated her, but she had turned away. It was summer. What had happened later, what had happened then? They had breakfasted happily in the Wagner coffee-house many times. They had also breakfasted unhappily in the Wagner coffee-house. One New Year's Eve the Wagner band had played the Siboney rumba. They had thrown snowballs at each other by the statue early in the morning, each dancing the rumba alone in the snow.

The billiard-tables were no longer there. This corner of the coffee-house had been converted into a café with a private entrance. Jacobi turned into the side street and entered one of the houses, walked up to the second floor, but when he saw a strange name on the door he did not ring. He did not linger either. He turned back, walked to the underground and took a tram as far as the bridge the way he had come. From there he walked back to the Széna Market.

In Újvilág utca there was a brand new office building where nos. 27 and 29 had once stood. The dyer's was still there on the corner but the shop window in no way resembled the old, discreetly tasteful, modern shop window that it was now, dressed according to the latest fashion, in the *fin de siecle* style, reminding Jacobi of the way his grandmother's dining-room had once looked. But he could not find Otto's house. He stopped hesitantly in front of two or three doorways but did not recognize any of them. Of course even if he had found the house there would have been no trace of Otto; he had died young and Jacobi knew that Otto's parents were also no longer alive. He was not looking for them. He was not even looking for their house, he had noted the tall building that had taken its place with relief. Perhaps it was of this that he had wished to be assured; that there was no trace of their old flat, that there was not a particle of it remaining. He mused upon a young girl's gentle face and childlike brow, a face that the Siboney had brought to his mind. Her name was Flora. Or was it Fanny? Dora? Bianca? No, it was Flora after all. She was fifteen, he twenty. Or were they both ten? No, no. Flora was a piano graduate. What became of her, he wondered. Never mind, he thought. He was looking for the Széna Market and the big coffeehouse.

The square was unfamiliar, as unfamiliar as its new name, which he thought absurd. He would have been hard put to recognize the big coffee-house because a supermarket had been set up in its place. Jacobi went into the store and strolled through it, spending some time leafing through the maps in the book department on the first floor; in the end he found an architectural book on the city which he bought because of the old photographs. From one of the pictures he recognized the corner on the river bank, lined with trees and kiosks, where his twenty-two-storey hotel had been erected. The book brought back memories of the small hillside park at the foot of the church because he was able to make it out on two of the old photographs presenting a bird's-eye view of the city.

The little park lay above the Széna Market, higher than the sloping field where he had once admonished the little girl for her unsportsmanlike behaviour. Pax, pax! Go home then. The little girl had taken offence, had begun to cry and ran off. Jacobi had wavered, called after her, turned back, but had finally started after the child. He soon caught up with her, gathered her up in his arms and carried her back to the others. The little girl cried even harder. "If they catch you, don't say pax." "But they always catch me!" "Because you're little." "Pax!" "If you say pax you can't play any more." But it was no use, the little girl ran off again, crying, shouting: "Pax, pax, pax!" "Leave her," the others told Jacobi. They watched the little one rushing desperately down the hillside, crying, wildly flourishing her arms toward the heavens.

But the next day the little girl had been there in the field again. And on the third day Jacobi, though disheartened at not being able to recognize anything, and because even familiar things seemed to remain completely alien to him, nevertheless left the morning rehearsal and went up to the little park on the hillside. He did not like the pianist who had been assigned to accompany him: a young girl who wore frieze trousers. She had undoubtedly not been chosen with any intention of offending Jacobi; you could tell she was held in high esteem. She evidently thought a lot of herself. She was a cold, hard, self-confident young woman and to cap it all she was always late for rehearsal as she had other business to attend to in the mornings. So on the third morning Jacobi left her after an hour. He excused himself, called a taxi, and crossed over to the Széna Market.

Perhaps they had not given him this cold, frieze-trousered woman out of undisguised contempt, perhaps she was indeed the great promise of the future, but the violinist found her manner of playing unbearably sentimental. He walked up the hillside. The field had disappeared; it had been covered by buildings. But the little esplanade, the terraced park at the foot of the church was unexpectedly identical with its photographs, just the way it used to be. Nothing had changed here in the past forty years. He even found a bench on the upper terrace where they had often left their things, and perhaps even the pebbles, the grass and the flowers were the same. But Jacobi still could not recognize anything, anyone. He suddenly felt utterly alien, a stranger. He escaped almost at a run.

4

He had not come for this. He had come to discover his ship-wrecked father on the desert island. He had come to guarantee the safety of the lady, brave Indian that he was. He should have taken a girl across the precipices of the Cordilleras. He had come to get to the bottom of an age-old mystery. He took the golden violin from the burgomaster, people clapped, he bowed, his pleasant, unaffected smile permeated by the radiance of his profound seriousness. He survived the ceremonial dinner, and the attack of giddiness was mild and passed quickly, and in his hotel room, a tall, thin, restless man, he removed his tails, laid down his golden violin and turned to the wall. The next day, luckily, the woman in the frieze trousers called off the rehearsal.

He had not come for this. It was not for this that he had learned to walk, it was not for this that he had learned to speak the language of men. He was a spy among them, the agent of foreign powers. His papers were good. He travelled hither and thither with his Amati. But only on commission: he was a spy of the angels in the world of humans. And yet, for a long time now, something was wrong. The emptiness he felt when the attack of faintness overcame him was himself. It was not a symptom of his illness but of the way he played. No one noticed, because he had learned to play his violin so that humans could understand, so they should not notice that something was wrong. But it was not for this that he had learned to play.

And the more he felt that his playing had become empty, the more exasperated he became with the woman in frieze trousers filling the C minor sonata with her own emotions. His resistance was physical. It almost made him puke. But luckily the next day they greeted him in the city College of Music with the happy news that the woman had called off the rehearsal. An old college professor would replace her as a special favour.

He was a bespectacled man about sixty, sixty-five years old.

He held his head in a strange manner. When he made a mistake Jacobi glanced at him out of the corner of his eye, surprised, because he was an incomparably better player than the woman; and when he saw the nape of the old man's neck, his boyish neck, he kept glancing back at him involuntarily from behind his violin. The back of his neck seemed to draw his gaze. It was good to look upon the nape of his old compatriot's neck, it was the only familiar thing he had encountered in the entire city.

Estella. Her name blazed in the pitch-black sky like a star, like love itself. Her name was Estella. Not Flora. It was here, in the corridors and at the entrance of the city College of Music that he had lain in wait for her childlike brow, her infinitely tender little face to appear. Estella. Come on, Estella. Jacobi was in love with someone else. He knew he was in love with someone else. Not with Estella. With her he was friends. They went together everywhere they could. He always waited for her and dragged her along with him to the students' canteen, home to his parents, to concerts, and considered her face, her childlike face, her innocent brow his own property.

The old pianist made another mistake. Strangely, this put Jacobi in the true mood for playing. He not only liked him for the boyish nape of his neck, but also for hitting the wrong note twice. He had not felt music to be so genuine for months, perhaps for years. When the sonata was over the old man remained seated at the piano, motionless. He sighed, lifted his hands and dropped them helplessly back on the keyboard. He did not say anything. At last he moved, extending his right hand toward the violinist to touch him. It was only then that Jacobi noticed that there was something wrong with his eyes. He could barely see, was perhaps blind. His spectacles were not misted over, but were made of thick grey glass. Jacobi took the delicate old hand between his own.

They agreed. The old pianist consented to accompany him at the concert without demur. Jacobi took him by the arm and led him down the corridor, which was really unnecessary as the old man managed to find his way about with amazing assurance, especially here in the familiar building. But even in the street he was capable of masking his blindness perfectly. His stick was not white, just a finely carved cane. "Can you recall anyone by the name of Otto Grynaeus?" the violinist asked. The old man stopped, visibly reflecting over the name, but did not reply.

"He was a *Wunderkind,*" Jacobi said, "forty years ago. He used to play a lot here at the college."

"All of them were *Wunderkind,*" the old teacher replied.

I wasn't, Jacobi thought. He had once told a journalist, and henceforth often repeated the story, of how he had begun to learn to play the violin for his friend's sake at the age of five. Though in reality it probably happened later. It was Otto's parents who first remarked on their son's remarkable sense of sound. He could not quite reach up to the piano when he first began to tap at the keys above his head, and once a guest had heard him reproduce a sound coming from outside note for note on the piano, striking the keys with both hands, rapidly, one after the other as was his wont. The blare of a horn, the squeal of tram brakes, a cry or the ringing of a bell, a dripping tap, the caterwauling or howling of a dog or a cat—whenever he heard a noise he ran to the piano, played what he had heard complete with all its overtones and returned contented to the game he was playing with Jacobi on the carpet. He was perforce enrolled in a music school, which he did not really mind, and Jacobi was often forced to play alone during the best hours of the afternoon beause of the music lessons. At his own instigation, therefore, he began to attend music classes himself. He proved a passable student, there was nothing wrong with his ear. But it soon became clear that Otto was a genius of the kind that is not born every hundred years.

But Jacobi found he was bored with the piano and switched over to the violin. The only problem with this was that he had to carry it home in a canvas case. When they were old enough to get to their music classes alone and were allowed to return the long way round, free to wander as they wished, the fragile instrument was always there, hanging from his neck. He still ventured up the hillside many times with Otto, violin and all, but it was a trifle in the way, it was a nuisance, that little violin.

Once it slipped out of his hands. They were climbing over a brick wall and he dropped the canvas case. Otto caught it, nothing much happened, the bridge had slipped out of place but the violin was not broken. Gosh, old boy! Darn it! They were really tickled pink, that time. His stomach ached, they had laughed so much that day, bent double, swinging their legs as they sat on the bench and later, running down the sloping walks, the steps at each bend in the hillside park.

He crossed over to Újvilág utca for a final time. On the crowded tram, watching the antics of a little boy, he had a brainwave. Jacobi was an inexperienced traveller on a tram, he lurched and staggered, allowing himself to be pushed here and there. Someone stood up, the little boy elbowed his way toward the seat by the window, tugging his mother behind him. "Let's sit down, mummy!" The young woman bent down and gently hushed the child. A fat woman sat down on the empty seat. The child continued to complain and when a new seat by the window was freed at the next stop his piping voice became louder. "Let's sit down, mummy!" His mother, embarrassed, attempted to restrain him. "Hush, sonny. There are others who are tired, older than you. Why, should you be the one to get a seat?" The child burst out bitterly: "I don't want always to stand between the bottoms!"

People began to laugh. Jacobi turned to glance at them. The young woman, her face crimson, hugged the little boy close to her, discomfited by the attention they were getting. It was true: whichever way he turned the little boy's face always came up against the posterior of one or other members of the milling, thronging crowd. Now he burrowed his face into his mother's lap and shook his face from side to side angrily, half crying. Jacobi squatted down among the bottoms for a moment and stroked his hair. He hunted in his pockets but all he came up with were some coins and a mute for his violin. The mute aroused the boy's interest but a whispered colloquy was necessary before he could be persuaded to accept it. "My name is Péter, what's yours?" Hepete, pepehe—even less could be made out from his answer for only the boy's soft lips had moved, and he had drawn a breath while saying something, full of awe, but Jacobi understood his question. "I am a violinist," he said very gently. The little boy, good-mannered, finally accepted the mute for a while they continued their journey at bottom-height.

That was a lucky day for Jacobi. He had at last seen a familiar object, the back of the neck of the old pianist. He had at last held completely rational conversation. ("If you're a violinist then I won't take your mute because you'll need it," the little boy had said. "Yes, but I've got a lot of them left." "How many?" "A lot. I don't even know how many myself." "Well, about how many then?" Jacobi paused—how many mutes did he have? "Three," he finally said, "or four." "That's not so many." "Not so very many, but see here, I can only put one on my violin at a time." This time the little boy paused to reflect. "That's true," he said convinced.)—Then he found Otto Grynaeus's house.

When he reached the dyer's shop window he squatted down as he had done on the tram. But it was useless; it did not lead him anywhere. Lamps made of copper, a samovar, a bunch, and who knows what else. This was not H. Millner and Sons, not even from a child's perspective. When up on the hillside in the park, he did not sit on the bench, but beside it in the grass. He examined the pebbles from close up. He slid closer to the grass. He looked for ants and beetles. He dug into the damp grass with his forefinger, then selected a pebble and slipped it into his pocket. Later, on his way back, as he walked along Újvilág utca once more, he tossed the pebble absent-mindedly from one hand into the other, then absent-mindedly threw it away. He bent low as he passed by several shop windows, as though he wanted to make out the price of an article, a sign. But he noticed that no one was paying any attention to what he was doing in the growing traffic so he squatted down once more in the doorways to reach bottom-height. And this was how he found the house where his friend had lived. He recognized a stone in the corner of an arched doorway.

5

The doorway was faced with large, symmetrical, roughly fashioned stone slabs. The pavement and carriage-way on the western side of the wide Újvilág utca was already in shadow, but here on the eastern side the façades of the houses were still bathed in the rays of the setting sun. There were places where the shadow had begun to creep up to the first storeys, but here, in the doorway of Otto's house, it just reached the foot of the wall. This twilight sunshine was clear but weak. It shone directly upon the doorway and as it brushed against the grain of the stone slabs—languidly, wearily—it seemed to blaze up from them, tracing long, black needles, finely drawn threads of shadow, patterns of unrivalled ferocity, making the stones sparkle and flash, bringing them to life as though it were illuminating the secret, tender, hitherto unknown but true spirit of roughness, of coarseness. Through the open doorway the setting sun cast an unfamiliar if temporary glow into the gloomy depths of the inner doorway. A brisk evening breeze darted down the street. Jacobi heard a lift door bang. The shape, the location of the staircase was familiar, but it was the stone that he had recognized. Not its grain, not its patterns of shadow, but its essence. Its content, its meaning, at all events its music. It was in C minor. "My God," Jacobi thought. He pressed his hands against his knees as he straightened up.

The rays of the sun became tinged with red. The noises of the street grew more distinct and scattered: a fourwheeler clattered by, clappetty-clap; the accompanying hum of the city had receded into the distance, beyond the Széna Market, across the river, echoing back from Easter Island. The Hebrides. From somewhere under the Southern Cross. "My God", Jacobi thought, "I have known this land."

He had stood in this doorway one evening in March. His family was busy with the preparations for a journey and he had suddenly been reminded of another evening in March a year before, coming back from the tennis-courts with Otto. Or perhaps it had not been a year before but earlier still. He was in his way home to supper. He had seen the city from a dwarf's perspective, from bottom-height. He too had sometimes felt overpowered, lost in the forest of humans on the tram, and on such occasions he too had been fretful and peevish with his mother. I want to be a war cripple, he had once said. Not because of the seat reserved for them. That strange deserted garden, the stone wall of which they had to climb, was an enormous, mysterious jungle, with dense, luxuriant shrubbery, vegetation run wild and now impenetrable. Within the walls they were always terrified. But they had to discover the mystery and in any case they liked to be afraid. It was while scaling that wall that Jacobi had once dropped his violin in its canvas case, from the top of the wall, as if from a parapet of a citadel, into Otto's hands. Gosh, old boy! Once they had left the church behind they burst out laughing. They laughed all the way down to Újvilág utca. They stopped in front of the shop-windows. Cigars, picture postcards. Artificial legs, prosthetic devices. The grocer's, the staircase, the nursery, and all from a dwarf's perspective, near to grass and carpet.

The odd-numbered side of the street belonged to them, all of it, the children who lived there, the shops, the side streets climbing up the hillside. The even-numbered side, the western half of the wide street, with other children, other shops and other side streets, was mysterious, almost alien to them. Unfamiliar doorways. A strange couple lived there somewhere, a couple who turned tables, conjured up spirits, or so Jacobi had heard. And a little girl, the green-grocer's daughter, who was said to be an exhibitionist; you only had to ask and she would lift up her skirts and show herself of her own accord. And a deaf-mute beggar, of whom at one time they were afraid.

But Jacobi had walked home to dinner on the odd-numbered side of Újvilág utca. He kicked at the snow covering the Széna Market. He stopped at all the floodlit Christmas displays. Cigars, picture postcards. Artificial legs. Cinema. Bolts of silk, great sale, that was boring. Buttons, hundreds of different buttons, they knew them all. A beggar in uniform, playing the harmonica. There were a lot of them. *H. Millner and Sons—Dyeing Cleaning with Guarantee.* A newspaper stand on the same corner. At one time Jacobi read everything he came across. Newspaper wrappers thumbtacked on the stand. Every letter written on the pillarbox. Then last of all there was the grocer's and he was home.

He skipped up the stair on one leg. When they were alone they often played at war cripples. They hobbled on crutches with an arm or a leg in a sling. Or they made their hands or heads tremble as though they were shellshocked. They did not do this in mockery, more out of jealousy. Jacobi had once said on the tram that he wanted to be a war cripple too.

Medals dangled from the shabby tunics. At one time a deaf-mute beggar used to sit at the end of Újvilág utca, on the even-numbered side, a beggar whom they discovered was a fraud. A dangerous crook, probably a spy. There was a sign hanging down his tunic, "totally incapacitated war casualty". He could only hoot at the passers-by; *oo-oo* or *hoo-hoo-eu*. When he was spoken to he shook his head: he could not hear what they said. His face was young, gentle; he wore spectacles. Jacobi took his courage in both hands and threw a coin into his lap. He was afraid that the man would boot his customary *oo-oo-oo* of thanks at him. But the deaf-mute soldier only nodded silently at the child; so from that day on Jacobi always carried a coin or two to give him in case he passed him by.

It was autumn, then winter, and still he sat in the snow. Spring came and the soldier was there every afternoon at the foot of the wall, sitting on his flat kit-box. But by then Jacobi and Otto had begun to spy on him. First of all, it was quite obvious that he was not a real beggar. You could tell from his face, hands, ears and neck. Secondly, he understood what was said to him. Therefore he was only pretending to be a deaf-mute. A young woman came to fetch him every evening. Who could he be, what was he, this soldier? A spy, a potentate? A pirate, a general? A marksman. They could tell from his stick. They followed him once or twice after dark. Where does he go, arm in arm with the girl? They'll turn in at the doorway of the necromancers. No, they've passed it by. Once Jacobi was really frightened. From afar he saw a policeman approach the soldier, ask him for his papers, begin to read. He's been nabbed. Run, man, he thought, terribly excited. Knock the policeman down and jump into that car tearing by. But no. The policeman returned the papers, saluted, and walked on. His papers are good, Jacobi thought. He's a big international spy.

Easter was approaching. There was school in the mornings, up in Háromforrás utca. Violin lessons in the afternoons. They were going on a visit with his mother, over on the other side across the bridge. He had a thousand other things to do; they could not spy all the time. Otto and he sent each other letters in code. Every Easter they went to visit his grandmother in the hills, to the town where he was born. But still, because they were little, close to grass and ground, it was easy to keep an innocent eye on the young soldier. One night—ten paces behind Otto, as though they did not know each other, his violin case tucked under his arm—Jacobi followed the couple, the deaf-mute soldier walking arm in arm with the slim young girl, on their long journey home. They crossed the Széna Market, turned the corner at the coffee-house and began to walk up a narrow little side street. Otto stayed behind to watch the stonemasons and carpenters working on the portal of the new Parrot night-club. Jacobi followed the soldier and the girl. He lost them in a side street that was even narrower and more dismal than the first. As he reached the corner, breathless, he saw them turn in at the entrance of one the three identical tenement houses.

Sleuthing was further hindered by the fact that they could not go out alone at night. Many times Jacobi's attention was distracted; other jobs of detecting had to be abandoned—they gave up the necromancers for good, the greengrocer's daughter proved a bitter disappointment; she blushed, slapped Jacobi's face and ran away when he tried to lift her skirt—he refused to think of it, let alone try again; it was an old sore that rankled even after forty years. One night on the dyer's corner of the street the headlines said: "Historical moments—negotiations have begun—tomorrow will decide the fate of the world." The newsvendor had gone home, the papers had been tacked up on his empty stand. So, Jacobi thought. It's to be tomorrow then. I must remember to look and see how it turns out. But the next day, perhaps because they came home the long way about, down the hillside, or perhaps because he had other things to attend to and did not have time to check the newsstand, or perhaps because he had completely forgotten the whole thing, he never got to know how the fate of the world had been decided. In any case it was quite possible that is was the week before's paper that he had seen.

They soon forgot about the deaf-mute soldier too. They set off for a final time one morning (they could not go at night) and found the house Jacobi had seen the couple entering. They climbed up to the top floor and took a walk around the gallery on to which the flats opened. Someone was chopping wood on the cobblestones of the courtyard. There was an enormous truck tyre propped against the wall. They could see into kitchens, into back-rooms. From one of them the tinkle of a piano could be heard. Someone was practising dance numbers which were in keeping neither with the house nor with the hour of day. *Yes, sir, that's my baby...* They listened for a while, then a woman appeared at the door of the washhouse so they went home, without being disappointed. It wasn't the right house after all, they thought.

After Easter, when Jacobi came back from his visit, they did not find their man in his accustomed place. He had disappeared for good. They gave up their sleuthing. Out of sight, out of mind; it had been the sight of the crippled young soldier sitting on the pavement with his head held in such a strange, beautiful way, deaf and mute, that had aroused their curiosity, that had drawn Jacobi like a magnet. And with his disappearance Jacobi's assignment was over. It was this that he had tried to spy out for the angels, or something like this: is there any person among men capable of holding his head up in such a dignified way? So motionless, so quiet. The rest was unimportant. Jacobi had noted the back of the young soldier's neck and his silence for his consigners, let them do with the information as they wished.

On one occasion, much later, he thought he recognized him somewhere. It was autumn, or perhaps the last spring he had spent in this city as a child. He was taken out for dinner to the big coffee-house in the Széna Market. He was bored with the protracted after-dinner conversation and wine-bibbing of the grown-ups, and went on a tour of the place on the pretext of looking for the toilets. He descended the wooden staircase leading down from the dining-room and found himself in the basement premises of the Parrot Club, which was part of the coffee-house. Here everything was still deserted. Photographs of semi-nude dancers hung on the panelling of the corridor-cum-lobby, dark because only a few of the lights had been switched on. Waiters and dance hostesses were coming in one by one, still in their street clothes; a cleaning woman was setting the tables in order. The empty ballroom gleamed dully with scarlet-velvety, expectant lights; at the far end a man with his back towards Jacobi was sitting at he piano. He was wearing tails and playing softly to himself. Jacobi stopped in the doorway to listen. He was waiting for the man to turn around.

There was something familiar about the back of his neck, and about one of the numbers he was playing. But the pianist did not turn round, though Jacobi lingered in the doorway for a long time; none of the arriving waiters or dance hostesses paid the slightest attention to him.

6

The Siboney? he wondered as he straightened up from crouching in the doorway. Oh, no the rumba was still to come. Like Estella, like the girl he had not married, like the deserted boulevard at dawn and the glass-domed lobby of the railway station. Those had all been in A major, this was in C minor. And even its tune was different, the tune he could not put a name to. Apple, window. He was going home to dinner. They had been on the tennis courts. The sound of a lift door banging, coming from afar. A mild evening breeze stirred. The rays of the setting sun burned red. All this was clear, spacious, acceptable.

My God, he thought, I have known this land. I have seen the twilight chafe a rough stone. You have shown me pebbles, grass, a child amongst the bottoms. And apples, and windows. But what was it that I recognized in this stone? I stood in this doorway, one day in March, we were about to set off on a journey, and it made me think of an earlier March; and I have now remembered that earlier recollection, or if not that recollection, then something else. A state, a quality that cannot be defined by human language. A feeling, a condition, a climate? A noun, an epithet, a verb, an adverb? The moment of creation perhaps, Jacobi thought, in the perfection, the simplicity of its namelessness. Something that precedes language, the sound of the violin, how can I then report it to angels? I must be satisfied with the tangible, minute particles of the moment, like what has this young crippled soldier to do with it all? However small the component, it is an elementary constituent of all that he recognized, and thus might prove important.

And in effect, though it was not the Siboney but the earlier hit beginning *Yes, sir, that's my baby* that had aided Jacobi in his immediate recognition of the back of the mute soldier's neck, in his stomach, his heart, his lungs, his cells he clearly felt, he sensed the truth. It was an attainable, a communicable particle of the elusive moment, this muteness of the young soldier, his motionless back of the neck. But with what kind of music should he express this silence? With what kind of dance this immobility? Who shall come to his aid, thought Péter Jacobi.

His dead friend came to his aid, and a story that was pure fiction. The first was the truth, the second a fairy-tale, a detective story. He did not go into the house. When he returned to the city for a short period at the age of nineteen, only Otto's aunt, the spinster sister of consul Grynaeus, and two of their old maids were still living in the flat. Otto was abroad somewhere, his parents were dead. Jacobi visited the old lady—she was a distant relation of theirs—Nanny and everything that remained in the flat, once or twice, but he did not learn much about Otto even from his Aunt Matilda. He never wrote letters to anyone. He had grown up into a strange boy. A few years after their separation Jacobi had met him one final time, but he did not like to recall that meeting. His friend had seemed awkward, stiff. Odd. There was no denying it—simply stupid. It was hard to conceive his manner, his behaviour in any other way. But one cannot easily conceive one's friend as a short-witted simpleton. And his face was still pleasant and winning. If Otto is stupid or subnormal, thought Jacobi, then so am I. I have not become a cleverer, more resourceful, brave or true Indian than I was when we were together. Otto's aunt gave him an address and he sent a letter and a card to his friend. Both went unanswered. Jacobi resigned himself to the fact that all ties between them were now severed. Later he heard that Ottó was dead. He also heard that consul Grynaeus had committed suicide after his wife's death, and that he had gone bankrupt during the slump. But if they had nothing left, what had Otto done for a living, how had the aunt, the nanny and the cook managed to make ends meet, how had they managed to keep up the flat which, if he remembered correctly, he had found unchanged thirty years ago? He did not go into the house.

A week later he went into the house after all. They had two days to go until the concert. The agent was in despair. "The concert hall will be quite deserted. Monstrous bad luck. No one goes to concerts on these occasions. Oh, that this had to happen now of all times!" "Why? What has happened?" "Events." "What events?" "Good Lord! Didn't the maestro read the papers?"

Jacobi, embarrassed, apologetically replied that he did not. He used to, earlier. But not regularly, even then. He had once read that the fate of the world would be decided on the morrow but had failed to inform himself of the sequel. "The President will be giving a talk on the radio on the evening of the concert," the agent said. "We must begin a little earlier so the people can get home in time to listen in."

The concert hall was not empty, but quite a number of the seats were left unoccupied. "There'll be many that'll sneak in towards the end, youngsters," said the old blind pianist. It was the first time Jacobi had seen him in tails and he simply could not take his eyes off him.

"I've found my friend," he said.

"Of course," the old man nodded.

"The day before yesterday, towards evening." The day before yesterday, towards evening, he had gone into the house. He had stopped in the doorway, then walked a couple of steps. He did not dare look around. "Looking for someone?" Jacobi knew he was behaving suspiciously. "No, no," he said. A woman came down the stairs and stopped beside the concierge. He should give some sort of explanation. "No," he said, "it's just that a friend of mine used to live here once." "Who?" "Never mind," said Jacobi, making a discouraged gesture. "What was his name? If he was a friend of yours you surely remember his name?" "Otto Grynaeus." The woman started off towards the doorway, disappointed. The concierge dispiritedly jerked his thumb towards the back stairs: "First floor to your left."

Retreat was no longer possible. There were three or four other families living in the flat. Unfamiliar names, cards stuck up one beneath the other. Someone led Jacobi into the old nursery, or rather opened the door a crack, pushed him in and shut the door on him from the outside. The man did nothing but point, trying to explain something to Jacobi in sign-language, since they could not have understood one another in any case because of the noise.

It was almost dark in the room but no one had switched on the lights. Pieces of furniture had been pushed up against the big folding doors on the left and the right. On the lefthand side was a reddish-brown mahogany wardrobe; pushed close to it stood consul Grynaeus's writing-table. On the other side of the wardrobe, wedged into the corner was a brass bed with the bedclothes turned down. There were three people sitting on the bed, hands folded in their laps. A man who looked rather like a tradesman, a frightened-looking older woman and a younger one whose age it would have been impossible to tell from her meek, uncomely face. They nodded to Jacobi and motioned him to sit. The armchair to which they pointed rocked under Jacobi's weight, made as if to collapse, then at a certain point settled. The piano took up a great deal of room and there sat Otto Grynaeus with his back to the window facing Jacobi. He was playing Chopin to his guests, stiffly, in a way that grated on one's ears. He did not look up as Jacobi entered the room.

Or if he had looked up his gaze soon fell blindly back to the keyboard. But he was not looking at the keys either. His shoulders jerked spasmodically; at times he raised his head and tossed it back. The window faced east overlooking the gardens. The man's high, domed forehead and long, jutting hawk nose stood out clearly against the bright square of light. As the sun sank slowly and the light faded in the room, the silhouette traced upon the bright pane, the angular profile of a balding old man became more and more distinct.

He played for a long, long time. With the buzzing inside his head and the loud noise outside it Jacobi could hardly believe that the whole thing was not a nightmare. At last, at long last all the guests stood up and politely backed out of the room. "Begging your pardon," they said, "the professor is so kind, you know, as to play for us sometimes."

"I play to them sometimes," Otto Grynaeus said. He shook his friend's hand, tittering, and winked at him, which was quite lost on Jacobi as the room was by then quite dark. Jacobi looked for the light-switch.

"Here, here, I'll do it," said the other. He squeezed his thin fingers behind the wardrobe and the lights went on. He wasn't so very old after all. And his smile was still warm and winning. "Wait a minute. I'll call Nanny. This is a surprise, my word!" He bustled off, cackling.

Left alone with the shabby old furniture packed so tightly together Jacobi found himself at a loss what to do. He knew every piece of funiture, every picture, every nicknack well. He did not want to look at them. He stared at the small glass cabinet then lost interest. He grew conscious of his aching head and realized it had been aching for some time. It had begun to ache when he had sat down in the lop-sided armchair. Or perhaps even earlier, when he had first heard the noise. I should squat down on the carpet, he thought, and look at the patterns from close up. But he had neither the strength nor the inclination to do it.

Otto Grynaeus came back crestfallen. Nanny had gone out. "Just imagine, old boy, good old Nanny! Over seventy, but she traipses around as fit as a fiddle, thank God!" He took out a bottle of liqueur, dusty little glasses. "There are only the two of us left now, Nanny and me. Old Vicky, the cook, imagine, has been gone these ten years. And good old Aunty Matilda's been gone even longer. But we've still got the flat. Though we've lived through hard times..." Jacobi wanted to light one of his own cigarettes but the other would not let him do it at any cost. "Wait, Péter, wait a minute." He began to rummage around in various drawers and cupboards. It took a long time.

"Oh, forget it, Otto. Come back and sit. I haven't much time."

"No, no. It's got to be here somewhere. Wait a bit."

He continued to talk as he searched. "It wasn't easy to keep the flat, old boy. You wouldn't know, of course, how could you know? Then I was ill one time. It frightened us a bit. That's when I persuaded Nanny. Because if I should die, well, what's to become of her? They'll put her out. No question about it. She hasn't got a pension or anything. Do you know what I did?" He found the little packet of cigarettes he had been looking for and triumphantly held it up for Jacobi to see.

"It was a present, you know. Foreign." He refilled the glasses with the sticky liqueur and they touched glasses. But he could not open the packet of cigarettes. He tugged and tore at the wrong end of the coloured paper with clumsy fingers. Jacobi wanted to take the packet from him but he pulled it away, would not hand it over. He continued the story. "D'you know what I did?" he tittered happily. "I married her. Good old Nanny, imagine. Now she's got her security. She'll have the flat and a pension. I teach music at the city school of professional training. In any case, we wouldn't have parted, would we?" He crinkled his eyes significantly at his friend. They had fooled the pension company, they had their security. Good for them.

Good for them. Though there was not much to the flat now, Jacobi thought, just the servant's room and this barricaded nursery. Perfect strangers appeared to be living in all the other rooms, even in the one which had been Aunty Matilda's. He began to fumble in his pocket for his cigarettes. But his friend had managed to tear open the packet at last and laid three or four mangled, half-crushed cigarettes in front of him. And he wanted to refill their glasses again.

"Have you hurt your hand, Otto?"

"No, of course not." He stared at Jacobi, suprised.

"Why?"

"It's just that—a fine job you made of these, old boy. Look."

In effect. He gave an enormous bellow of laughter. "Well I was never much of a smoker, you know." Then, who knows what made him think of it, he told Jacobi of how he had been unable to bear the strain of giving concerts. He had been a child still when the slump had hit them and his parents had died. He had had to give concerts abroad, in the country, in places that had gradually grown smaller, more out-of-the-way with every step. He had preferred to do anything rather than continue with it. He had even tuned pianos for a while—had done all sorts of things.

"But I couldn't stand giving concerts. Word of honour. You don't know, Péter, how could you know? Always the same thing, day in, day out, city to city... And I should have been studying still... Oh, you can't imagine how hard it was."

"*I* can't imagine...! I play the violin, you idiot!" cut in Jacobi angrily. "I'm a famous violinist, man!"

The words stuck in his friend's throat. He stared at Jacobi frowned. Then slowly, gradually, his face was wreathed in a happy, radiant smile. "The concert hall will be empty," flashed through Jacobi's mind. Who cares, he thought. But unfortunately he did care. He cared a lot. Success did not only mean money to him, did not only give him an artistic rank. It determined his intellectual, moral existence, his style and with these his spiritual bearing. In other words even his inner life. He had grown accustomed to the necessity of fame; when he was being photographed he automatically assumed a worldly yet wrapt expression. And this was in any case an especially important concert. Otto Grynaeus stood up and embraced him.

"Congratulations, Péter," he said enthusiastically, "so you're a famous artist! That's the ticket, old boy! Splendid!" He accompanied his words of approval with angular, clumsy gestures. It had taken him some time to understand the gist of what Jacobi had said, but when he did his joy was truly sincere. He refilled the liqueur glasses, we must drink to his, well I never, good old Péter! He tittered, shook his head as if in disbelief, winked at Jacobi.

His fervent joy had been so sincere that Jacobi, disarmed against his will, had begun to talk about a concert he had given the year before last. Then, in the middle of the sentence, he stopped. It was quite obvious that his friend was straining every nerve to pay attention to him. He had been sincerely happy to learn of his success but had immediately forgotten all about it. And he did not return to the subject. As if he did not even expect Jacobi to attach particular importance to his art.

All this was not only gauche, but embarrassing, even offensive. A bad dream, Jacobi thought. And yet, when he asked Grynaeus something, he was surprised to find that his voice bore no hint of resentment!

"Hey, Otto," he said. "Do you remember that deaf-mute beggar we used to sleuth?"

The other shook his head.

"One time we followed him to an ugly tenement house, behind the Széna Market."

His friend still shook his head. But as Jacobi continued to question him, outlining his whole theory, he listened with undivided attention, with effortless attention, even though he did not remember any of it at first. He could see that Jacobi was speaking in earnest.

In the end he forced his mangled cigarettes upon his friend. "Go to blazes," Jacobi said.

He thrust the cigarettes forcefully into the violinist's pocket, threw an arm across his shoulders and chuckled happily. He accompanied his guest to the door ceremoniously and lowered his voice in the entrance-hall.

"You were suprised, weren't you," he whispered, "to find me here in the flat? To find that nothing's lost, everything's the same, what?"

I really must decide, Jacobi thought, to give up smoking for good. He began to feel dizzy again.

And we've lived through hard times. You don't know how hard, Péter," Otto Grynaeus whispered. "But nothing's lost, everything's the same. You were suprised, what, old boy?"

"I was," Jacobi answered quietly. "Word of honour."

The pressure increased in his head. On the street he lost his balance for a moment, staggered. The next day he did not get up until late afternoon. He went for a walk, had some milk sent up to his room and lay down again. He woke up at dawn from a deep sleep. It was half past five. He was at pains to understand what had happened to him. He had been relieved of a great burden.

He did not feel anything. He had been tangibly stripped of all feeling of pressure, paralysis, bad emptiness. Inside he was cleanly, lightly, pleasantly empty, like the clean, light, unregistered dawn approaching at his window. The concert hall was rather empty. He did not think who cared this time. He knew very well that he did care. But he did not think it. "There'll be many that'll sneak in later, youngsters without tickets of course," said the old blind pianist. "I've found my friend," Jacobi replied.

The old man nodded, of course. He was in tails, and it sat on him so naturally that it seemed he had at last discarded all his disguises. Jacobi could not take his eyes off him. In the white collar his sinewy brown neck was infinitely tender, yet invulnerable, indestructible—the neck of a frail little boy and a terrible archangel.

"He's a good Indian. The kind that guarantees the safety of the world. He's my friend."

"Of course."

In the morning paper Jacobi had read, "Who will guarantee the safety of the world?" Even on the platform he looked at nothing but the nape of the old pianist's neck from behind his violin. The day before yesterday he had told Otto that he had recognized the old pianist, just as he had recognized the stone in the doorway. He had recognized the boyish nape of his neck, the way he held his head. Otto listened to him vigilantly; he listened to the whole of this story. He had listened when Jacobi told him he had become a world-famous violinist but it had cost him visible effort; he had been sincerely happy to hear it but when he was through had changed the subject immediately and did not return to it again. As if he thought it a matter of course that Jacobi would not attach particular importance to the whole thing. The violinist did not return to the subject either. He did not offer to get Otto tickets; he did not even mention that he would be giving a concert.

And yet he played well that evening. They clapped him long and loud as they always did. They had agreed beforehand to remain up on the platform until the last clap had died away so the blind man should not have to walk on and off. After concluding the C minor sonata the old man remained seated for a long time and, as at their first rehearsal, raised, then dropped his hands into his lap with a helpless sigh. The applause would not stop. At last Jacobi helped the old man to his feet. But the blind pianist, before turning to the audience, caressed the violinist's head with delicate, faltering hands. "Dear boy," he said. As if they were alone.

As if they were alone on a desert island.

The day before yesterday he had told Otto what he had discovered. The young spectacled soldier who used to sit on the pavement of Újvilág utca, in the afternoons at one time was not a deaf-mute. They had guessed correctly. He was a musician. He had lost the sight of both eyes in the war. His young wife came to fetch him every day. In the mornings he practised jazz numbers at home until he found employment at the night club. You could tell he was blind from the way he held his head. How long had he been the pianist of the Parrot Club? Who knows? Perhaps he had continued to practise in the mornings, not jazz. He may have become a first-rate pianist. And a professor of music in his old age. Who knows?

Otto nodded. It was true. He had good papers to show to the policeman. Totally incapacitated war casualty. Word of honour! But he was blind, not a deaf-mute. He begged incognito. He preferred not to speak.

The old pianist had not spoken much either until now. Jacobi had been praised many times in many ways: "You were astounding, Maestro. Heavenly, unsurpassable, I cannot find the words to describe..." No one had ever said 'Dear boy' to him before. They stood up on the platform, lonely, forlorn. A few people continued to clap, but from the doorways; the audience was flocking out. They did not demand an encore.

Jacobi suddenly turned toward his old compatriot.

"Do you remember this number, sir?" He began to play *Yes, sir, that's my baby,* energetically wielding his bow, on several strings. Yes! Sir! That's my Baby! The old man returned to the piano unhesitatingly and struck the first chords.

Those eight or ten young college boys and girls who still lingered in the deserted concert hall thought at first that the artist was just tuning his violin, but then had to accept, to their astounded consternation, that Péter Jacobi and the old, blind pianist had begun to play, in quick and dynamic time and with an almost severe unity of execution, an old foxtrot.

Translated by Eszter Molnár

AT THE MOVIES WITH FATHER
by IVÁN MÁNDY

He didn't turn toward him as they sat in seats eight and nine on the left. He simply observed the boy out of the corner of his eye in the drizzling incandescence. He touched his shoulder for an instant and asked, "Can you see all right, old fellow?"

KING KONG

"...and if you really must know, King Kong is still alive today, and he is constantly walking about, but only at night, and he is lifting roofs off and peering in everywhere because he won't rest until he finds the Blonde Wonder."

"Or Mrs. Rabnec."

"Mrs. Rabnec?"

"Mrs. Szecsey."

"Mrs. Szecsey?"

"Mrs. Tivadar Nagy."

"Mrs. Tivadar Nagy?"

"Mrs. Glemcsák."

"Mrs. Glemcsák?"

The usherette was lying in the cold, keen moonlight. She didn't know when she had woken up. She heard her husband's heavy breathing from far away, as if not from the same house.

Nothing was moving in the moonlight. Nothing was moving in the night.

Then in one swoop the roof of the house across the street was pushed aside and King Kong appeared. The gigantic apeman stood in front of the house like someone who has been searching for something for a long time and has finally found it.

"Oh!" said the usherette, and she sat up in bed.

King Kong was standing in front of her bed. He gave a shove to the room with every movement. The room billowed around her like an accordion.

The usherette was already lying in the palm of King Kong's hand. "But you are hunting for the Blonde Wonder!"

The apeman shifted her to his other palm.

The usherette trembled and closed her eyes. "You've got the wrong house. Everybody knows you have smashed several skyscrapers because you can't find the Blonde Wonder anywhere."

The apeman put her from one palm into the other palm.

"You've got the wrong house!"

The usherette fell speechless. King Kong strode over the window with her. Above the houses—out into the night.

CO-STARS

They were all there.

He was entering in his notebook every single one who at some time played opposite Greta Garbo. The name on one side, the film title on the other.

Lars Hansen *Flesh and the Devil*

Nils Asther *Wild Orchids*

There were quite a few of them. At times Greta Garbo seemed about to settle, on someone, but then a new name popped up again.

No, thought the boy, Greta Garbo, it seems, never finds the right man. Nils Asther played opposite her in two films, Gavin Gordon came next, then Conrad Nagel. Gavin Gordon played the part of a minister alongside her, Conrad Nagel that of a private tutor.

Notebook bound in blue paper, torn label, Károly Bonaja, arithmetic-geometry. The edge of the label curled-up. The boy licked it underneath, then tried smoothing it down. Meanwhile, he was thinking that Greta Garbo might take up with Nils Asther again.

"No," Nils Asther shook is head, "she'll never take up with me again. She can throw somebody aside in such a way... Ah, I don't even like to talk about it."

"She told me there is only one man in the world for her, and I was that man." The pale-blond Lars Hansen shrugged his shoulders. "After *Flesh and the Devil* she would have nothing to do with me. We were to appear in another picture together, but she threw herself on the floor and kicked up a storm."

"The divine Garbo!" nodded Gavin Gordon, who once played a minister opposite her.

"She wrings a man out and then throws him aside." Nils Asther was silent for a moment. "If I add that ever since I haven't been able to work with anybody else, that ever since there has been no other woman for me... well, you can just imagine!"

"It's the same with me," said Lars Hansen, "because one thing must be admitted: Garbo is a unique personality..."

"Yes, she is!" Nils Asther passed his hand over his face despondently. Names, names, one name after the other. The old partners vanished to yield their place to new ones.

"Keep them coming!" Nils Asther waved his hand. "None can do as well with her as I did in *Wild Orchids.*"

"Or I in *Flesh and the Devil.*"

But they were already through, finished. No new movie ever appeared again beside their names. Meanwhile, Lars Hansen spoke about Stiller, the director who discovered Garbo and brought her over to Hollywood from the North.

"Actually, they only invited Stiller, because at the time nobody had even heard of Garbo. Then there was no divine Garbo, just a big girl with bony hands and skinny legs who drove everybody to despair. At least film people." "Dear Stiller, I hope you don't really mean this." "But Stiller did mean it very much. He fought for Garbo until she got her first small role."

"She didn't create any particular sensation," Conrad Nagel interjected. "Besides, at the time everyone was eclipsed by Asta Nielsen."

"That's exactly why Stiller had to keep fighting for her. 'Maurice, I will never forget this,' Garbo said to him. But once she felt a bit more confident...!"

"Stiller might just as well have given himself up as lost."

"By then she was already picking and choosing her directors the same way she did her partners, and she preferred to work with anybody but Stiller."

"That's just like her." Nils Asther was plucking his mustache. "Really like her."

They fell silent. For a time, Garbo's old co-stars remained practically speechless. A new name had cropped up: John Gilbert.

The boy was barely able to write down all the movies next to John Gilbert's name. Apparently Garbo had found the right man at last.

"Haha!" Nils Asther broke into a laugh with scathing mockery.

Lars just smiled, but Gavin Gordon said: "My blessings on them."

The boy, perhaps in real tribute to John Gilbert, tore the blue cover off the notebook and rebound it. He put a new label on it. He licked and smoothed. Then he very carefully inscribed on it: Károly Bonaja, motion picture book.

He turned the pages back like someone suddenly remembering something.

Rhombus and rhomboid. There they were in back, slightly smeared, not completed. The boy merely looked at them. What's this? They really think I'm still bothering with them.

He erased the two geometric figures. Simply erased them. There's absolutely no place for them in the notebook. Especially now that the eternal partner has made his appearance.

"Haha!" Nils Asther laughed heartily. "The eternal partner."

Lars just smiled, but Gavin Gordon said: "My blessings on them."

"But he will be Garbo's destiny after all," said the boy.

"Her destiny!" Nils Asther laughed heartily. "Garbo has just one destiny, and that's Garbo herself."

He could say whatever he wished, but now only John Gilbert could be seen beside Garbo.

The boy simply couldn't understand the situation. "John Gilbert's mustache can't match Ronald Colman's!"

"Or mine either!" Nils Asther's voice was exasperated.

Mustaches around Garbo. John Gilbert's mustache quite close, Nils Asther's quite far away. Between them Lewis Stone's and Conrad Nagel's. Conrad Nagel's wasn't real, though. Just a one-role mustache. It really looked strange on that callow face.

Mustaches around Garbo. Then only John Gilbert remained.

Sometimes John appeared as a painter in a velvet jacket, sometimes as a slightly debauched young prince.

"A real Mickey Mouse!" Nils Asther nodded.

"No personality," said Lars Hansen. "And let's keep a sharp eye out because sooner or later he might even ruin Garbo."

He didn't ruin her.

Garbo's fixed, pained look drew away from John Gilbert's side.

"Incredible!" Gavin Gordon shook his head. "Everybody was saying they would marry." "Marriage!" John Gilbert's face darkened. "Garbo and marriage! Do you know what she said to me after all those?"

"After all those what?" asked Nils Asther rather sharply.

John didn't hear him. He just talked and talked and plucked his mustache. Just like Nils Asther earlier.

"She'd sooner enter a convent than... She just kept yelling convent."

"I can understand why," nodded Nils Asther.

"That's how she will wind up anyway," nodded Gavin Gordon.

John Gilbert was plucking his mustache, exactly like Nils Asther earlier. "Do you know who her co-star is? The newest one? A midget!"

"A midget?"

"What tales you tell!"

"We all know him. Ramon Novarro!"

For a moment startled silence. Then a voice: "No, that's ridiculous."

"Take my word for it. They are shooting *Mata Hari* together."

"But Ramon Novarro was Ben Hur," the boy said, "and when he licked Messala in the Roman chariot race..."

They all held their sides from guffawing. "He couldn't even peep out of the helmet."

The boy wanted to say something like nobody in the Roxy Theatre roared with laughter, they almost tore the place apart instead, and he even forgot about the candy he'd bought at the counter.

Gavin Gordon in a quiet, thoughtful voice: "What's wrong is not that he is so short but that he is such a lousy actor."

"Stiller would never have worked with him, he wouldn't have cast him even as a walk-on."

Gilbert: "That's exactly what Garbo wants, it seems. So she can shine all the more brightly."

Nils Asther very sarcastically: "Lately she has shined quite brightly enough."

John Gilbert didn't hear him. He was saying he made himself less than he was for Garbo. His talent, that is.

"Do you think that required much effort?"

This was Nils Asther again, naturally. Nils Asther, it appears, was determined to torment John Gilbert to death.

Gilbert's nose grew longer, just like a pencil sharpener, and kept repeating one name.

"Garbo... Garbo..."

The boy entered it in his notebook.

Ramon Novarro *Mata Hari*

A couple more film titles appeared alongside Ramon Novarro's name. But only a couple. Ramon disappeared through the trapdoor like the rest of them.

John Gilbert lived in the hope that maybe it would now be his turn.

"Garbo can truly shine only beside me."

"Because you're a backdrop!" nodded Nils Asther.

John allowed this to pass by his ear too. He waited, full of hope that perhaps... after all... Then something happened, something that... Garbo simply stated she wanted to play Anna Karenina again.

"But this time, it seems, you won't be her partner, dear Gilbert." Nils Asther stroked his mustache with short sly movements. "Some Frederic March. Yes, I remember now, Frederic March."

John was silent.

"Or rather, not just some Frederic March. The Man of the Century. That's what the newspapers are writing about him. Dear Gilbert, I don't remember, but did they say anything like this about you?"

And Frederic March, the Man of the Century, played that role with Garbo which John Gilbert formerly had.

Then the Man of the Century also vanished. New mustaches followed.

The boy entered every last one of them in the notebook. Name on one side, title on the other.

Then he no longer wrote anything. No name, no title.

"Embarrassing," said Nils Asther. "Garbo used up everybody."

They were silent, as if expecting something. Maybe for someone to crop up. Nobody did.

Suddenly the boy began drawing. A pair of glasses, enormous dark glasses.

"Yes, we know," nodded Lars Hansen. "Garbo put on dark glasses and withdrew. From everything, from everybody."

"Who can understand it?" asked Gavin Gordon. "When she had achieved everything... everything."

"The point is, it didn't mean anything to her." Lars paused for a bit, then blurted! "Stage fright."

"Stage fright? Surely you don't mean to say that..."

"She continually suffered from stage fright. Even success didn't help. Stiller had already said she'd have it as long as she lived."

"And now because of this?"

"This or something else."

They guessed, they kept trying to guess why Garbo withdrew behind dark glasses. Nils Asther also reported she was living in a place nobody could get to. Among cliffs, in some kind of bay. Occasionally an old girlfriend can visit her. On one condition: she can't talk about movies.

John Gilbert, who, it was thought, would become the right man, the eternal partner, suddenly exclaimed, "If only I could perform with her just once more! As a supporting actor... even as an extra."

Then he fell silent because the boy erased him.

The boy also erased Nils Asther, Lars Hansen, and the others.

Nothing remained, just the dark glasses.

THE DEATH OF ZORO

Two jolly fellows in the movie foyer. Zoro and Huru, the two staunch companions who never so much as take a single step without each other.

The boy stopped in front of them. He put his hand out as if he wanted to pat the cardboard cutout Zoro and the cardboard cutout Huru.

It was morning. He was alone in the foyer. Around him on the walls were photographs of film actors and actresses and scenes from next week's attractions. But all these vanished beside the life-sized Zoro and Huru. They were standing at the cashier's window. Somewhat offended at being left all by themselves in the dim foyer.

Perhaps the others are sitting in the darkened theatre this forenoon. Rudolph Valentino, Vilma Bánky, Barbara La Marre, Richard Dix... They are sitting there in front of the curtain drawn over the screen, staring straight ahead silently. No noise of any kind reaches them, only the beating of a carpet from a distant courtyard. They are sitting there in the long rows of seats. Rudolph Valentino, Vilma Bánky, Barbara La Marre, Richard Dix...

Zoro and Huru in the foyer. The gangling, mustached Zoro and the merry, chubby Huru. The buttons were torn off their coats long ago, and were held together by some sort of string. Little satchels in their hands. What can possibly be in those satchels?

The wall is covered with pictures from their film.

"Beach Photographers."

The two noble companions are in striped swimsuits in one picture. Zoro's head is stuck under the camera's black cloth, while Huru poses women from the beach for a shot.

"I bet," the boy thought, "Zoro and Huru are playing tricks on the beach. Maybe Zoro won't even take his head out of the camera, and Huru is only interested in the girls. He positions the arm of one, the chin of another, meanwhile promising to marry them. It's quite possible Huru is proposing to more than one girl. It's quite possible he will bamboozle the whole beach."

"Beach Photographers."

Photos from the film, captions next to the photos.

Zoro and Huru, who had already tried their hand at so many different things, decided to sally forth as photographers. They packed up their nonexistent belongings and set off alongside the Northern Express.

Zoro and Huru were trotting between empty tracks. Huru was

looking ahead confidently, Zoro with a vague distress in his eyes. His long mustache hung down droopily.

Zoro and Huru, the two inseparable friends, arrived a couple of days later than the Northern Express at the bathing resort, where as beach photographers they again underwent ever funnier situations.

Ever funnier situations...

Huru's face so plump, Zoro's stiff as if benumbed with cold.

"It all started with his eyes," spoke up someone behind the boy.

The boy didn't turn around. He knew it was the old projectionist. He had left the projection booth and climbed down. Once in a while he would climb into the booth early in the morning and inspect the projector and reels. Or he would start showing the film, just to himself.

Now he was standing in front of Zoro in his loose-fitting coveralls and round cap.

"One thing's sure, he'd stood before the klieg lights for many more years than the other, this chubby one. He was already a famous actor when this other one..."

"Didn't they begin as a team? Zoro and Huru?"

"How could they have!" The projectionist looked at Zoro as if wanting to ask his forgiveness. "Oh, we still remember very well when pudgy here dropped in on Zoro to ask for some kind of work. Maybe not even in pictures, just so he has something. Meanwhile he told heart-breaking stories about his dear mother who is ill and must be provided for. Everybody knew, that's exactly what Zoro was a pushover for."

"You mean, somebody just starts in on his mother and Zoro...?"

"The thing is, Zoro lost his own mother very early. His house is full of his mother's portraits and statues."

Then the old projectionist said that Huru got hold of this tip. He got hold of it and faked everything. It came out much later that Huru never gave so much as a penny to his mother. Not even when he was a world-famous movie star.

They were standing next to the cashier's window. Zoro who lost his mother very early and Huru who never gave so much as a penny to his mother.

"The old lady died in a poorhouse. Neighbours took up a collection to pay for her funeral. I don't have to tell you you would've looked in vain for Huru at the funeral."

At first, Huru got just bit parts beside Zoro, and nobody had confidence in him. But it is also true that Huru worked the public hard.

Huru visited schools and joked with the children. He sat at a desk (in his sailor suit, of course) and acted awfully nervous about being called on to answer questions. And he was called on (prearranged, of course), and he hemmed and hawed at the blackboard so much they made him stand in the corner.

Somehow Huru forgot to take Zoro along on these excursions. True, Zoro wouldn't have gone with him. Zoro told him off. He said he also liked children but didn't care at all about playing the fool. Huru just grinned and fell silent. Then newspapers began publishing reports that Zoro had contempt for his audience, especially children. And between the lines, yes, between the lines, was slipped the hint that Zoro was jealous of Huru's ever-growing popularity. A that point, Zoro stuck the item under Huru's nose. "What is this?" Huru protested he didn't know anything about it.

The boy leaned on the railing at the cashier's booth. The window closed. A sign above it: balcony, stalls, easychair...

"There's no doubt Huru mounted a real campaign against Zoro... on the sly, naturally. By then he had frequently been warned to be on guard, but he still didn't want to believe the vague rumors. It never occured to him how strange it was that after several film previews school children marched ahead of Huru carrying their little pennons. Ahead of Huru! Not Zoro and Huru together! Not even what the children were shouting roused his suspicions: 'Don't be afraid, Huru! We are with you!'"

"Huru swore he knew nothing about it, and that was enough for Zoro."

The boy swung himself over the railing.

"In the meantime, Huru invaded Zoro's married life." The projectionist whipped his hat off and dug his fingers into his hair. "This is what nobody can figure out to this very day. Zoro married a Danish actress of astonishing beauty, Dalma Dagmarson. Their marriage was unclouded until... Yes, even now Zoro didn't want to believe the whispers. He threw the unsigned letters away."

Zoro was pacing in his room, wearing a lounging robe that reached his ankles. He held an unsigned letter in his hand. Occasionally he would glance into it: "...your wife and your partner are seen together very frequently these days. I must note that lately they don't even care about keeping up appearances." Zoro took a step toward his wife's room, but then he tore up the letter.

He didn't want to believe the gossip, the slander, the whispers. He didn't want to believe his wife when one day she walked up to him.

Dalma stood squarely in front of Zoro and looked into his eyes. "We can't live together any longer."

She also told him the why of it, namely the who of it.

Zoro grasped the edge of the table, his head slumped forward.

The ravishing Dalma and Huru! How in the world was he able to sweep her off her feet?

The boy whirled around on the railing at the cashier's window. Huru above him. "By hook or by crook I swept the ravishing Dalma off her feet."

"Zoro didn't stand in the way of the lovers. He let his wife go. He continued to make movies with Huru. It's true, he hardly spoke to him outside the studio. At this time he was being racked by terrible headaches. Headaches and insomnia. When he wasn't working, he lay behind closed shutters with a cold pack on his forehead. Or he walked. He walked from one room to another with long, drawn-out strides. But his eyes grew weaker and weaker, he saw with increasing difficulty. At his friend's advice he turned to a doctor."

Examination followed upon examination. They had him read letters from a chart, they stuck different kinds of lenses before his eyes. "Is this better? Can you see more clearly now?" They took him into a dark room where he had to lie for a long time. Robed figures moved around him. For an instant his wife seemed to stand beside him. Huru's round face seemed to pop into view. A lamp's small sphere in the dark came closer and closer, like a klieg light. At the end of the examination, they announced: "Surgery is unavoidable."

The projectionist walked back to the double-door where the public is admitted. He opened it for an instant. The long passageway with its columns ad buffet counter could be seen.

"They threw Zoro on the operating table."

The projectionist said this.

The boy slipped off the railing. He didn't get up right away, he stayed on the tile floor for a while.

"A famous professor of ophthalmology operated on Zoro. Not quite free of charge. He touched him for a tidy little sum. I must add that by this time Zoro wasn't in exactly the best situation. You can bet his wife didn't leave him in just the clothes on her back. The operation... ah yes. As they say, it was successful. Only, Zoro couldn't see any better."

"Did they operate on both his eyes?" The boy had hoisted himself back on the railing again.

The old projectionist disappeared behind the double-door. When he returned, he was striking an empty pipe against his palm.

"They kept Zoro in the hospital for a long time after the operation. Did he have any visitors? Of course he did. But he was waiting for only a certain somebody."

Zoro lay with bandaged eyes in the darkened room. He waited for a particular voice, for someone to touch the covers and sit down beside his bed. He waited in vain. Not once did Dalma Dagmarson, who had left him for Huru, open the door and enter.

Huru, he was something else.

Huru really turned the hospital upside down. He came at the head of a merry company. In the corridor he pinched nurses, passed out autographs, opened bottles of champagne. It was only natural that he was accompanied by a pack of reporters, it was only natural that the newsreel was also with him. The Eye of the World.

As he entered Zoro's room, he stopped in the doorway. For a moment he just stood there motionless. Then he spread his arms out wide and threw himself on Zoro's bed. "How awful to meet under such circumstances!"

The newsreel camera whirred, and during the following week, everybody could see there was no more faithful friend than Huru.

The Eye of the World also showed Huru weeping. "I won't leave until I can take Zoro with me."

The Eye of the World didn't show Huru slipping out of the hospital that very same day.

Zoro stayed there.

The operation was successful, though. But the doctor decided to try his hand at a new surgery. They took a crack at it. They experimented with at least three different operations.

The projectionist was now poking his pipe with a little piece of wire. Then he struck it against his palm again. He looked up at the boy, the pipe remaining in his hand.

"The result was that he left the hospital with a glass eye."

Dark glasses, scarf, topcoat, small bag. Zoro stood like that in the hospital entrance. The Eye of the World wasn't on him. No reporters paid any attention to him when the nurse took him by the arm and led him out of the hospital grounds. For some reason, even his friends, those few who still remained from the old days, forgot to come.

Leaves circled listlessly on the hospital grounds. He stopped and reached for a leaf hesitantly. He would have liked to linger in the yard for a bit; perhaps he would even have sat under a tree. But the nurse led him on.

A small stubby-nosed taxi waited at the entrance. The hospital had hailed it. They still did that for him.

The nurse straightened his scarf, gave the driver his address, and then squeezed him into the back seat of the taxi.

His housekeeper shrieked. She clapped her hands together when she saw her master with his little bag from the window. She rushed out to the gate.

"Dear sir! Oh, my dear, dear sir!"

Zoro allowed her to lead him in, he allowed her to set him down for some tea with her. He asked her to open the mail and read aloud the letters that had arrived during his absence.

She couldn't open any, none had come. Not from the studio or anywhere else either. Later she finally brought forth a letter. Zoro's bank wrote that they regret to inform him of the unwelcome news that his shares had fallen, not just fallen but crashed, and that the funds on deposit, which had already greatly declined...

He waved his hand to say it's enough, she should stop. He wanted to be left alone. All he wanted to do was curl up in the corner of the sofa.

He could curl up there all he wanted to.

If he had few visitors in the hospital, now he had...

The boy was perched on the railing.

The projectionist was standing in front of him, seeming to want to leap instantly on the railing too. But he merely shrugged his shoulders as he said:

"The day came when Zoro went to the studio. Don't think they sent a car for him. He had to tap his way to the studio, he who was one of its founding members. The porter greeted him but didn't come out of his booth, he seemed to retreat even more into the corner. It was the same with the others he encountered in the courtyard or the corridors. They muttered confusedly and then stepped aside. He even came across some who wanted to stop him: 'Stop! We're shooting!' But he continued on anyway among the cameramen, makeup people, and extras."

Sad was Zoro's passage through the cameramen, makeup people, and extras. Suddenly he did come upon someone, and then he really had to stop.

A long-legged fellow with a mustache hanging down the sides of his mouth and a sour countenance. A sailor's cap on his head unlike any in the world, with a long ribbon hanging down.

They stood in the corridor, Zoro and the one with the sour countenance.

Suddenly shouting was heard.

"We're starting to shoot! Shooting!" They didn't stir for a while. Then suddenly Huru appeared. He also had a sailor's cap on.

"Don't you hear we are shooting?"

With that he pushed Sourface onto the set.

Zoro drew into the collar of his topcoat and didn't say a word.

Huru caught his breath and straightened his sailor's cap.

"The boy is working out splendidly and the public is already used to him."

"Used to him," nodded Zoro.

"Putting it more correctly, they didn't even notice that I had started a new Zoro on his way, that I had launched a new Zoro."

"Launched?"

Huru spread his arms out. "Old chap, we couldn't wait for you. The public—this thousand-headed Caesar—is impatient. You know that as well as I do. You know what the audience is like. In short, you still need time to pull yourself together."

"I must pull myself together..."

"Besides," Huru bent closer to him, "that glass eye... The public notices such things. You know how it is. But come now, take a look at the new Zoro!"

"I am Zoro!"

Huru grinned and nodded. "You are... you are!"—he seemed to sing it, "You are... or somebody else is!"

Huru vanished. Zoro remained alone in the corridor.

"I am Zoro!"

Suddenly he collapsed. A pain stabbed him in the head so hard he fell against the wall. Someone took hold of him, led him into the courtyard, and sat him down in a chair.

He sat on a little chair in the courtyard. He pulled his shoulders up and spread his hands out. He could still hear the hubbub on the set, the horn, as the clapboard slapped. Then he got up and left. But he didn't go home. He went to the Film Cemetery.

The boy slid off the railing next to the cashier's window. He is now going to hear something the old man has never related to anyone else. Something he will pass on to Gyuri Streig and the others in the evening on the square or in front of the street door.

"Lots of people think the Film Cemetery is in California, somewhere in Film City. Well, that's a big mistake! The Film Cemetery is up North, in Zoro's native land. From all parts of the world travel to this place those stars who can't keep up anywhere but still don't want to wind up in an old people's home. In greatest secrecy they travel to this place, in greatest secrecy they make their way across the suburb toward the Grove. The first stop is a shabby little movie theatre. No picture is ever shown in it. Its walls are covered with old posters. Every movie star finds the one bearing his name in the biggest letters. He rolls his poster up and takes it with him."

Don't think you will find crosses and gravestones in this cemetery. Broken klieg lights, twisted cables, rusted derricks mark the route. Caved-in studios with discarded props.

A room with crumbled walls, with split-legged tables and broken chairs from a baron's house. Rows of burned-out suburban streets, collapsed floors, abandoned arbours and promenades where nobody ever walks. Only an actor or actress grown too old. He walks the length of a promenade. He is in the studio again. He walks and walks until he reaches a room. On the wall are photos of his greatest roles. The room itself is the set of his most successful film. By then he has nothing more to do than sit down in an old easy chair. To look at the pictures on the wall, to gaze into the air. Meanwhile, he can even light up a cigar or a cigarette and also find some beverage in one of the corners. There still remains a bottle left behind from takes of *Hussars in Ingolstadt.*

Hither came Pearl White, the most elfish gamin, when they froze her out of the silver screen. Theda Bara, the true vamp, and Milton Sills, the pirates' captain, the old sea wolf. Pearl White found her old ball and jumping rope, Theda Bara her feather headdress and the divan on which she could stretch out full length, and Milton Sills the shipwreck with its tattered pirate flag.

Hither came Zoro. He crossed the suburb, the Grove. To the movie theatre, the theatre where he chose his poster. The one in which he is fighting the windmills with lance in hand. The poster of *Don Quixote.*

Zoro rolled it up and took it with him.

He carried the poster with him among shattered klieg lights, corroded cables, blinded lamps, burned-out searchlights. Torn ribbons of zigzagging streets, collapsed stairs of caved-in houses marked his route. Shattered statues, headless statues, armless statues, crushed heads, split foreheads. A hollow-ringing rail area with a broken glass roof, an unstocked department store, crumbling columns and balustrades.

The Cemetery for Sets was left behind.

He arrived at a barren, empty field. A kind of whinnying sounded. The outlines of a horse appeared, the outlines of a yellowish, impossibly scraggy horse. His bones running into one another at the slightest movement. Next to it on the ground were a lance and shield.

Zoro knelt down and bowed his head on his palm. He remained like that for a time. He slowly straightened up. And then he was soon sitting on the horse with his lance and shield.

Windmills off in the distance.

Zoro's scarf became untied, the tails of his topcoat fluttered as the horse started out with him.

The windmills were turning. They were waiting to fly him into the air to pass him on from one to the other, from one to the other.

The wind blew, Zoro's topcoat fluttered as he headed for the windmills with his lance held high.

The shadow of a horse, the shadow of a horseman on the broad, empty field as he rides toward the slowly receding windmills.

There was silence. One couldn't tell when the projectionist had fallen silent, but now silence reigned in the foyer at morning-time. Pictures of actors and actresses on the walls, pictures of the movies appearing the following week. Zoro and Huru beside the cashier's window. The two staunch companions who never so much as take a single step anywhere without each other.

It was silent in the theatre at morning-time. Then the projectionist spoke.

"It seized him while he was shaving. Yes, they found him like that, with his throat cut." He took hold of Zoro's shoulder. "They had been watching him for some time, he had already aroused suspicion at the studio, and then while shaving... They say he couldn't forget that day when the old Zoro, the real Zoro, stood in front of him in the studio corridor. From that time on, they say, he practically begged for them to give him something else, even if it is a worthless bit part. He would rather be an extra, just so he won't be Zoro! As for the one who came after him, something happened to him too..."

The projectionist's hand slipped off Zoro's shoulder.

The boy hoisted himself onto the railing at the cashier's window.

"What's wrong with all the Zoros, that they always...? Please tell me what's the matter with the Zoros. Please tell me!"

No reply came.

He flopped down from the railing. He looked up once more at the figure with the blank look and the long moustache; then the theatre door slammed shut behind him.

Translated by Albert Tezla

REQUIEM

by FERENC KARINTHY

The chief physician hadn't planned to attend. He was home for a short two days, a brief respite between a convention in Copenhagen and a ski trip to the mountains. That was when he received the invitation to attend the requiem service in the Coronation Church in memory of Albert Gyulafy, who had passed away in Montevideo on January the 7th. Nothing more, just Albert Gyulafy. No address, no rank, not even a "Mr'. He promptly forgot it, checked in at the hospital to take care of a few pressing matters, but was immediately syphoned off to a consultation, then signed his name to a batch of papers and letters, at least forty in all. He finished at two-thirty, rushed over to the ministry, had some cold chicken in the buffet, then drove home for a short nap before his two private patients were due that evening. But he had barely closed his eyes on the couch when an old memory unexpectedly emerged from the primeval waters: ruddy-cheeked Uncle Berci, dressed in the special Magyar gala suit, sword at his side, at Ubul Brenner's wedding, as he gave him a reassuring little nod, his way of letting him know that his scholarship to Switzerland was okay. In those turbulent war days that took quite some doing, even for a minister. Actually, he had escaped the siege of Budapest and the battlefield due to this support in the upper echelons, and it was the two years spent abroad that had started him on his career. In fact, he had those same two years to thank for poor Helga, that sad, now irrevocably clouded period of sunshine in his life. He brought her back with him from Switzerland, and it wasn't until later that he realized his wife couldn't acclimatize, she was a flower that couldn't be replanted, her frail physique wasting away in this hot soil... And suddenly, a bittersweet nostalgia, a feeling of gratitude surged up in him, and perhaps curiosity as well. What would it be like? Who would attend? A challenge, a time of reckoning. How much had survived of his youth? The telephone lay nearby. Soon he had called off one appointment, postponed the other, and was driving up to the Castle.

It was cold, crisp winter weather. Dusk fell early. Uncle Berci was his uncle twice removed, his mother's cousin, and so, a Gyulafy by birth. He had been the pride and joy of the combined Brenner, Gyulafy, and Korbuly-Mersich clans, a minister of many years' standing. In private, he was an entertaining gentleman with a Bohemian temperament, an acknowledged hunter and womaniser, a fin-de-siècle anachronism. At least, that was what he'd heard; he rarely saw Uncle Berci in the flesh. As a politician he was a liberal, a sly fox, the silent representative of a British orientated policy in the government, and the hated target of the Hungarian fascists. At the time of the occupation, in '44, he was deported by the Germans, that was how he ended up in South America. He was never declared a war criminal at home. Still, it wasn't politic to pride oneself on being his relative.

Several people had already gathered at the side entrance of the Coronation Church. He was flabbergasted when he recognized an obese, porky man as Aladár Zetelaki of Zetelak, or Zaladár Etelaki of Etelak, as everyone called him, wearing a closely-cut coat with frogging, and his wife, Zamália Etelaki of Etelak, in a worn seal coat. Though he hadn't given the old man much thought since God knows when, he could have sworn that the former chief school inspector, the apostle of the "Magyar Goods in Magyar Homes" movement and editor of the Zetelak Young People's Almanac (the Etelak Young People's Zalmanac) was no longer among the living. He must have had a hormone imbalance or something. Bursting at the seams he was, his pudgy, flabby cheeks, small toothbrush moustache, sickly-thick stump of a neck, tiny puffed-up eyes, idiotic, vacuous stare as he blinked in return to his greeting (obviously not realizing who he was), made the chief physician think the man is a porker ripe for the knife, an open sesame of bacon and lard... And good Lord, Loránd Korbuly-Mersich, the "butcher"! Uncle Lóri had been deputy police commissioner of Budapest, though in private he was a gentle and softspoken man and an avid collector of insects. Then, in '51, the *Szabad Nép* came out with an article in favour of relocation and published a list of some of the sworn enemies of the state who had already been sent out of the captial to live in the countryside. The list included Korbuly-Mersich, the "butcher" commissioner (or so he had been inadvertently promoted). The family had called this white-bearded, lean old man living on raw food and herbs and fifteen-mile constitutionals by this epithet ever since.

"Egon, dear! So you've come!"

Dear, sweet Babuka. Dear little Baba Kézdy, the orphaned, penniless, old maid baroness who had been like a nurse to him after his mother's death. They kissed. Poor Babu hadn't got any younger either; she was even more diminutive in black, and completely grey. Even her old-fashioned hat couldn't hide that. But it was nice cuddling up to her, and there was the same natural sense of belonging... She had sent the invitation herself, she said, and the chief physician decided he'd stay by her side, hold on to her, and not let go of her reassuring presence.

A ghost came over to him, or rather glided, floated over, an incorporeal other-worldly shade. And, extending his cold spirit hand, he mumbled something about his wife's cure and couldn't you, old boy, see about a bed in a good sanatorium... He'd never have guessed who the man was, were it not for Babuka whispering: it's Guszti, Guszti Huszár, sub-prefect Dr. Chevalier Ágoston Ladányi-Huszár. Could this man with both feet in the grave be the former Tartar khan of the raven-black eyes and moustache and prominent forehead? The one whose retort to a discussion on the Gulf Stream—"It's nonsense! The brainchild of Jewish scribblers! It's all I can do to believe in America!"—became part of family lore?

Babu quickly supplied the essentials. Guszti is down and out, an incurable alcoholic, and so is his wife. They frequent taverns and bars, drink with bums and do the most distressing things. Last year Guszti fell down the stairs of a pub in a drunken stupor, broke his hip, wore a cast and was dependent on crutches for six months, but made his daily pilgrimage to the pub just the same. He's always the first in and the last out. As for Mrs. Huszár, née Lula Korbuly-Mersich, a once-celebrated beauty, the star of the society pages, she takes up with all sorts of filthy, drunken carters and others of their kind, even now, at seventy, wherever she can, in a ditch, on the road, last autumn she fell asleep in the park and

almost froze to death at night, that's what's caused her rheuma...
Babu pointed her out in the distance: a shaky, skeletal figure, and
even by artificial light you could see the heavy coat of makeup and
the ghastly frozen smile on her larva face. The chief physician remembered what they used to say back then, that alongside many
of her other scandalous affairs, the captivating Lula had also
found time to be Uncle Berci's lover.

They walked into the church. The mass was being celebrated
up front, at the main altar illuminated by candles. The partici-
pants sat facing each other on the benches, on two sides of the
apse, fenced off by a small balustrade. He was surprised by their
numbers, a hundred and fifty or two hundred at least. He moved
as far to the rear as he could with Babuka, as he had always done.
Mrs. Huszár, on the other hand, sat down dramatically in the first
row. And on her right, now, who was the woman so elegant even
in mourning, veiled, with flowing ribbons? Could it be Minci Jacobi? Correction. Countess Vayk, after her fourth husband. Yes,
indeed, the two Jacobi girls, Trudi and Minci. Had eight husbands
between them. Trudi was living in Canada now. She had married
the owner of a chocolate factory and supplied her younger sister
with clothes, among other things, though Minci would look swell
dressed in a sack. To this day, whatever she might have on, her in-
nate elegance was a natural, organic part of her being. What lovely,
enchanting women they were! They must have had a secret way
with men. Minci, in fact, was still going strong; the tall, thin, quiet
Oliver Vayk, also in attendance, was a good fifteen years her junior...
The chief physician liked her, he found her bizarre humour entertaining, like the time he had met Minci in town. She was going about
some business, carrying a tiny bag in her hand, and in aswer to the
standard "How are you?" she began to talk in full earnest:

"Just think, Egon dear, the minute I woke up this morning,
I found myself all square and covered with polka-dots!"

However, she'd been covering up more of herself lately, that
was how she selected her clothes, shawls and hats. The veil must
have come in handy; now, too, she was virtually hiding behind it,
only a strand of her blonde hair visible, and the flash of her impish
eyes. She, too, had been a great friend of Uncle Berci's and Trudi
as well, or so gossip said, both at the same time.

And there was the third widow, Mrs. Linger. Her husband, the famous industrialist millionaire, was carried off in the first confused days after the siege of Budapest and was never heard from again. Gizike had been mourning him close on thirty years now. She spent half her time in church. The other half she used to spend writing to Uncle Berci in Uruguay. She'd been desperately in love with him ever since her teens. Their correspondence became especially lively after Ma Orsi, the old man's wife, died. In a sudden onrush of sentiment, Uncle Berci invited Gizike, and even somehow managed to scrape her air fare together. Mrs. Linger took leave of all her friends, including her spiritual advisers and father confessors, and was accompanied by at least thirty old women to the airport of Ferihegy. But she was back in four weeks. It wasn't hard to guess what had happened in far-off Montevideo; all you had to do was take a good look at this long-necked, hopelessly silly, proud, busybody mother goose stewing in her own fanaticism. They say she had refused to sleep with Uncle Berci even before, she being of the opinion that such things must wait till after the wedding ceremony, and even then should be attempted only with the express purpose of begetting an heir. Otherwise it was lechery... Nevertheless she now laid claim to the title of widow number one. She had already broken into such profuse sighs during the Oratory, mumbled her prayers so loud and wiped her eyes with her black-bordered handkerchief with such emphasis, that anyone could see—she had suffered the greatest loss of anyone here; she was the real widow, the other two mere undeserving self-appointees, unauthorized trespassers.

Behind the three mourning women sat the loose-limbed Vayk brothers, Oliver, Minci Jacobi's engineer husband, and his older brother Jenő, a corporation lawyer. And wedged in between the two counts, the latter's wife, whose various metamorphoses had been followed with great excitement by the family for years. No point in denying it, her dad's name was Sámuel Freund. Following in the footsteps of his ancestors, who were in the leather trade, he also dealt in leather goods and was later founding partner in the Sámuel Freund and Co. leather firm. This was later shortened to Sam Freund and Co., and when her father struck it rich with his war contracts he converted to Catholicism and bought himself into the nobility. On his visiting card, under the five-pointed crown, appeared the name, Soma Freund of Barát. His daughter, elaborating on this, assumed the name of Éva Baráti-Freund, and later under the People's Democracy, when such things were no longer taken so seriously, she became Éva Krisztina Baráthy-Freund, and finally, since her lucky marriage, Baroness Krisztina Vayk Baráthy... There was a story about them that their maid said to a visitor who came to call on them:

"The doctor and the comrade engineer are out, but milady the baroness will see you."

There was nothing distinctive about her. She was rather chubby, but still a relatively well-preserved, energetic woman wearing a short sporty fur coat, cropped hair, and a large gold ring with a coat of arms on her hand folded in prayer. Her twin brother, Chevalier Ferdinánd Baráthy, the respected dog breeder and recurrent sailing champion, cut a more distinguished figure with his crisp moustache and the discrete Maltese Cross in his buttonhole. Ever since Nándi could remember, his main aspiration in life had been to be admitted into the Knights of Malta. But despite all his efforts and connections in high places, in the old world his ambition had remained unrealized. However, he never gave up this aim, not even under the building of the socialist way of life, and persevered until he obtained a visitor's passport to America where, with the help and recommendation of the still-active Hungarian branch of the Order—some ancient gentlemen sans wealth but with impressive-sounding names—for a modest contribution, something like a hundred dollars, he was inducted and initiated into magisterial knighthood. Having thus attained the chief ambition of his life, he returned to his beloved retrievers and hounds as a descendant of Raymund de Puy, the crusader, of Villiers de l'Isle, the hero who defended Rhodes against the Turk, and La Valette, the liberator of Malta.

During the Gospel the chief physician stood up along with the others, but did not cross himself. He caught someone whispering:

"That's Boriska Gyulafy's son. He's a communist."

He glanced that way. Some dark-eyed old women were whispering in each other's ears. He couldn't place them, though. And then, further off, at the other end of his bench, yes, it struck him like lightning, his knees began to tremble, as years ago. Perhaps they even gave way.

Kati Kerecsényi.

How did she get here? He thought she was living in the country, in Kiskunfélegyháza or Kiskunhalas; ever since the relocations, she was a teacher or something down there. Had she come up just for the mass? Of course. She was another of Uncle Berci's protégées, the apple of his eye, in fact, and possibly even his god-daughter. Carefully, inconspicuously, he studied her profile for signs of aging. But despite his scrutiny, he could discover nothing substantial. He found her almost as beautiful and exciting now, the mother of three grown children. Or was it just a reflection of the old glory? Still the clear, well-defined contours of her face, which emphasized the noble curve of the neck, her skin tight and smooth, her blonde hair barely a shade darker, though greying, only her unbelievable, unearthly thinness had filled out ever so slightly... Yet how this woman had fought for years on end, alone, with her children, just to survive. A year after he left for Switzerland she married Pubi Lippai Kreiss, a fatuous and lazy lounge-lizard and sports dude. He got her with three children, then, after everything was nationalized and his money was gone, he ran off with a waitress. Later, he died in a car crash in New Zealand or New Guinea. Kati stayed. She refused to become a burden on anyone with her three children. She accepted her fate and first worked in a nursery, then, through superhuman effort, finished the academy and became a teacher, and today she was a school principal, or so they said. And she did it all alone, in the provinces, away from her relatives. The chief physician hadn't seen her in over twenty years, and only knew about her through hearsay.

Babuka was quietly explaining who was who, but he wasn't paying much attention. There were four or five former generals and colonels present, most of them night watchmen and overseers now. And Dénes Antal, a chaplain general. He had held out the longest. He wasn't forced to retire until 1950. He had been appointed prison chaplain in '45 and spent the night before their execution with the war criminals including an army commander sentenced to death at a spectacular trial, to whom—having been absent when they handed out brains—Uncle Dini said the following by way of parting as they left death row at dawn: "My most sincere apologies, Your Excellency!"

A good-looking man of gigantic build in an elegant winter coat lined with fur: Tamás Teleki. The son of Kálmán Teleki, once the owner of a huge estate, member of the Upper House and chamberlain, he was now—Babuka was rapidly giving him the lowdown—a furniture mover; a plain haulier, but with a difference. He had organized a special team with a few friends, all gentlemen like himself. Their specialty was that they never used coarse or unseemly language. Regardless of what they might have to lift or carry, they did so efficiently and with the utmost ceremony, to the great astonishment of their customers: "Go on, dear fellow, a little higher, if you don't mind... many thanks, dear colleague... the back of the chest, if you will..." and so on. Their reputation spread quickly in this rather menial profession, and besides, they were quick and worked with clockwork precision, on the basis of scientific principles. They had more customers than they knew what to do with, and needless to say, they made as much money as they wanted. They all had cars, their own apartments and summer places.

There was an old clipping from "Theatre News" among the chief physician's photographs, a picture taken on the beach of Földvár. Some young men making a pyramid in the Balaton, he at the bottom, the two Telekis, Tamás and Tibor, standing on his shoulders, both lanky, sunburnt adolescents. Tibor making a funny face. A few years later he was shot down as an air force pilot... Kati was also vacationing there that summer; he was introduced to her only in passing, which gave him the right at most to greet her along the promenade or the pier, and she nodded back condescendingly. He adored her from a distance. How could he hope to approach the beautiful, spoiled, very popular, tennischampion, queen-of-the-ball daughter of a fabulously rich champagne manufacturer and stable owner, he, the poor, just tolerated cousin from the periphery of the big family, the medical student son of Dr. Brenner? He thought up all sorts of adventurous ways of meeting her. For example, they get into the same compartment, and the train stops in a tunnel, or Kati sneaks down to the shore at night because she's fed up with the company, and he accidentally comes by, or the girl's horse bolts during the morning's ride, and he appears among the poplars and rescues her, and so on.

Then it all happened quite differently and much later, just before he left, on that two-day boating excursion on the Danube. He was so nervous just before departure, he almost called it off, but he had promised, and they were so insistent, and the early September was so brilliant, he didn't have the heart. They had decided to go island-hopping. About fifteen of them gathered at the Római beach, and his heart fluttered to see Kati Kerecsényi among them. But rowing up the Szentendre branch, he hardly saw her. There were three girls sitting in a keel, and he was alone in the kayak. They spent the night at the Huszár's villa at Visegrád. Nothing happened, though; Kati didn't even notice him during the hayride. The next day they discovered that the keel was damaged and out of commission, and the girls had to split up. He managed to get Kati into his boat. In fact, through various tricks and machinations, he fell behind the others right at the start, and though they had agreed to row down the main branch of the Danube and the others made their way towards it, he turned to the right at the tip of the island, back to the Szentendre branch. By the time Kati realized what had happened and he had made his excuses, it was too late—too tiring and long a way to row back and catch up. So they had a full day and thirty kilometres ahead, just the two of them.

They drifted downstream slowly, the weather was heavenly, the early autumn mist hovered above the tiny ripples of the almost perfectly still water... Gossamers, gleams of sunlight, seductive peace and tranquillity. The fact that he was going to leave in a few days, which he had already told the girl, turned to his advantage; it added a special aura to their words and dissolved Kati's tension. Kisoroszi, Bogdány. The shallow river wound its way among sandbanks and shoals. The dry, white ridges of the riverbed, not visible at other times, and in the distance, the soft outlines of the tree-studded Pilis mountains. At Goat Island, the Danube spread out into a lake, its mirror shining bright in the noonday sun and dotted by thousands upon thousands of wild ducks. As they drifted quietly towards them the ducks took off, clacking, quacking and gabbling in unison. They anchored on an abandoned stretch of grassy beach across from Leányfalu.

How they got to that point is now lost to memory. Kati broke out unexpectedly in her bitterness. She wasn't satisfied with her life, she was fed up with the role her situation and family forced on her, and what they expected of her. She was sick and tired of meaninglessly drifting from one ball to the next, from one cocktail party to another; she'd had it with the petty intrigues, the gossip, the light, superficial flirtations, the same conversations time and again, the incessant pursuit of pleasure, the late night parties. And she envied his work, his career, the fact that he had an aim in life and even a scholarship. She wore a two-piece orange bathing suit. With her tiny waist, very long arms and legs, she represented the ideal woman of the century. On her tanned skin he could spot some scattered, sun-bleached hairs. She lay relaxed in the grass by his side, her eyes closed. All he had to do was reach out. But he didn't even kiss her. He merely squeezed her hand once, and Kati squeezed his in return.

For a couple of days after this, he seriously considered calling off his trip. Once he even called the girl. Had she been at home then, perhaps everything would have turned out differently. As it was, though, he got caught up in a whirl of last-minute errands, visas, offices, school, applications. He was living in a rarefied atmosphere. The decision would have had too many consequences. In the end, he didn't even say goodbye.

He discovered many more new faces in the dimly-lit church. Ubul Brenner, sweet, wise Ubul, once the manager of a great estate and lord of half county, today a translator of scientific literature, in five languages, both ways. Miska Gyulafy, stepbrother to the deceased, the "crazy Gyulafy" to the other's "clever Gyulafy", who wanted to prove that the Magyars had originated in Australia, and who danced the Lambeth walk with so much energy. That was the dance in which you had to stop from time to time and jerk your thumb behind your head. Kocsárd Barcza, the "Red count", who divided his two-thousand-acre estate in Szabolcs County among his reluctant peasants in the autumn of '44, months before the land reform came into effect. But he landed in jail anyway. And Baron Gorlitz Pasha in a loden coat, Tyrolese hat in hand. Christ, is he still among the living? He must be past ninety-five! His wife, the notorious Baroness Goritz, ran an illegal gambling club and house of ill repute. She had paid everyone off, the city council, the police, even the electric company, so that they wouldn't remove the old-fashioned, flickering gaslamps from that part of Bajza Street, to guarantee the visitors some measure of anonymity. And Uncle Iván, unable to get a divorce, became a Mohammedan so he could marry his masseuse... And many, many others, acquaintances whose identity was now lost to him, and total strangers as well. Who were they, and where had they come from?

When the bell tolled during Transubstantiation, the entire row knelt down, except the physician and Kati Kerecsényi at the far end of the bench. Had she seen him? Did she remember him and that outing of thirty years ago? In some way he now felt it important, symbolic, that only they were standing, in this, too, differentiated from the others. A hot surge of emotion gripped him, and he fell in love with her all over again. He had left Kati, or at any rate let her go. They had exchanged a few letters, some rather explicit, but later, in more chaotic times, even this became impossible. And then he found Helga in Switzerland, and Kati met Pubi, that toothpaste-ad windbag. The war handed them a one-way ticket.

Maybe he should have stayed after all? Was that it?... The wounding question, like a dagger pointing at his heart, flashed like a threat through his mind. Although the three years with Helga were unforgettable, could they have been merely a sidetracking, a step in the wrong direction? The dear, frail creature who grew up in rarer air had perished here, in this dense atmosphere; the cause of her illness was never satisfactorily diagnosed. Could that have killed her? But then he was to blame, too, perhaps that was why he lacked sufficient strength to keep her? And Kati... Was this what she deserved? Should he have burst into her life? Rescued her from idleness, grabbed her hand when he had the chance, instead of driving her into the arms of that clown? It was his fault, too, he alone had been in a position to lift her out of her rut.

But maybe he himself was loser number one. He felt a wild bitterness, a choking pain with no relief in sight. Was that the original sin, the fact he left, and did not share the common fate? It was undoubtedly an advantage at the time when the war swept over Hungary; in those two years lightning would have struck around him too, and who was to guarantee that one flash would not have struck him? He sat in Zurich in comfort and security, and it was an advantage in a narrower, professional sense as well, from the point of view of his career as a doctor. But from a wider perspective, if you consider life as a whole, it was a horrible disadvantage, an irrevocable error. That was why he could not really understand things here, why he had always been a stranger, an outsider. He had never gone through the rite of passage! Can a person escape, desert the ones he loves in the time of danger, then dance back in after the storm?

But these *ancien-régime* waxworks, *ci-devant* remnants, archaeological finds and antediluvian fossils, these other-worldly spirit-bodies, he might laugh at them, but they had stayed at home then, and had never left. They all had a chance to slip out, sooner or later, to some country where they could have turned their past and rank to advantage, or where at least these things would not have been a liability to them. Yet they accepted being slighted, persecuted, humiliated, stripped of their wealth, even imprisoned in internment camps and gaol. They accepted everything with true *noblesse oblige* and dignity. They handed over their entailed estates with less reluctance than a fishwife her stand at the market. And though no one bothered them any more, history had broken them in body and spirit, time had laid waste these genuflecting wrecks who would never again straighten themselves, and who probably knew very well that they could expect no recompense... And even if it was fruitless, senseless and of little significance, he too must accept them, yes, fallen as they were, these absolute losers, since he had basked once, however slightly, in the light of their brilliance. After all, their former greatness still discovered itself from time to time in their erect posture and soft voices, in the way they carried their heads, in their handshakes, their glances—a last ray of light from the Eden of their youth.

The tolling and chiming and clinking of bells. Flaming candles cast fantastic shadows on the Gothic arches and pillars. The lamps were transformed into colourful Chinese lanterns, the mournful organ music became a waltz, the hard stone slabs of the flooring melted into parquetry. Servants came and went with soft drinks and champagne on trays, dancing couples floated out of the Béla Chapel. Everyone was bright, young, beautiful, wearing gorgeous clothes, the ladies and gentlemen both bejewelled. Dressed in a flaming red jacket lined with ermine, tight-fitting light blue trousers and soft leather boots and looking just like the time he was photographed on the balcony of the Alexander Palace with the other ministers whenever a new cabinet was formed, Uncle Berci was watching the crowd with pleasure and an amused smile. Ma Orsi stood beside him in seagreen velvet from cap to toe, with a train and diamond diadem. Ubul Brenner in tails came up the aisle with his snow-white bride, under the drawn swords of his fencing comrades. He wore a tuxedo and a white carnation in his lapel. Guszti Huszár of Ladány's long, pointed moustache and Tartar eyes shone black: in a decolletée turquoise ball gown, Lula floated past flirtatiously on the arms of deputy police commissioner Korbuly-Mersich, dressed in a black Magyar jacket. The music turned into a din. With arms outstretched, Trudi Jacobi was doing the Charleston for her own entertainment, Minci with her blonde hair gently pressed against her partner as they danced the tango. In his ceremonial national jacket, Zaladár Etelaki was doing a fast Csárdás, which he accompained with frequent yodelling. Miska Gyulafy danced the Lambeth walk and jerked his thumb behind his ears. Tibor Teleki was doing the foxtrot in his air force lieutenant's uniform, while Pubi Lippai Kreiss, in a dinner jacket, was gliding through the English waltz with Kati Kerecsényi... He came up to them, bowed and asked Kati to dance. The girl nodded, freed herself from her beau's arms and turned to him. They began slowly, feeling each other's rhythm and tempo. Kati wore a strapless orange tulle gown, her long hair flowing free, her arms and shoulders bare. She was light as air: he could barely feel her weight beneath his palm, only the warmth of her skin. Without words they danced past the others, towards the stained-glass window; there, he squeezed Kati's hand, she smiled at him, squeezed his hand in turn, they swam through the glass and out over the Fisherman's Bastion standing silent in the crossfire of spotlights, over the dark, icy Danube, past the Parliament, towards the throbbing city sprawled out below in the cold glitter of the night.

Translated by Judith Sollosy

LAMENT FOR A MOTHER
by MIKLÓS MÉSZÖLY

It was sixty-four years since the fox died—*So clammy was that evening, moist and red...*—the young wife, the belle of the county, was twenty years old, and during her first pregnancy they would steal along the bed of the Séd brook to the doctor, because there was no telling whether the Reds might shoot at them for breaking the curfew or a lurking White might fire out of hysteria when he heard the crackling of their footsteps. Later, forty years afterwards, the rococo-framed painting hung heavily on the salt-petre-encrusted wall of the back kitchen she had been allotted in a half-derelict peasant cottage. In the picture she has been married for ten years, a light silk scarf hangs from the soft, bare shoulder, and the fingers of the two hands resting in her lap, with hesitant artistry, just manage to avoid an electrical discharge: they are not clasped, even the tips of the fingers do not touch each other, but they are just polarized sensuously for a never-ending moment. One little finger is twisted in an unnatural but gentle sprain—as the queens of the air descend into the sawdust and for a breathtaking, motionless instant undertake the impossible: with stiff grace they express their thanks for the ovation by not bowing, though they do nevertheless bow, magically bringing to earth the weightless acrobatics of flight and dreams. The lack of dimensions. The superfluity of dimensions. Even during those years the young wife was unhappy, and nothing came of flight and dreams; the inscrutable, silent man who radiated a desperate predestination towered beside her, a sure support, like the Calvinism of defenceless concealment. A parable of foam and iceberg. The memorable film-shot of these years recalls that noonday parade one summer Sunday when her two boys in sailor-suits raced with each other to climb the iron electricity pylon and she—with a blue-spotted sunshade in her hand—pleads with them in vain to come down and they take not the slightest notice; they never miss an opportunity of putting danger to the test. They cling obstinately to the cross-struts a couple of centimetres below the high-tension cables. The sun shines murderously, as in a wrecked paradise. A cross-fire of smiles, a crowd gathering, general encouragement, voluptuous malice, a degree of erotic humour. The young wife grows prettier each minute from fear and pride. The carriage from the office happens to pass that way just then, with the measuring-rods poking out behind the sprung seat like a bunch of sausages. The old driver recognizes the lesson to be learnt from the situation, swings close to the pavement and holds out the long-handled whip—"Just catch their bottoms with that, madam!" A confused feudal consternation mingles with the laughter, and that seals the fate of the advice proffered from below, as is true of this kind of prescribed feudalism. The driver continues on his way in dull perplexity, the face of the young woman goes sallow and blood-red. They cannot deny that only they live in isolation. The other, long-distant scene is the marshy area between Ózsák and Borjád-puszta, full of centuries-old black poplars. There was news of a three-year-old stray dog-fox that had settled in a deserted earth; it had more or less finished working at the entrance, but had not touched the inside, the burrows and the depression that served as living-quarters. It was in the February mating-season that they had heard it barking, then the flood-plain seemed to have swallowed it up. Only at the end of summer did there come a new and confidential report that it was prowling around "with a mincing gait", and when it was in good spirits it even barked, when it suspected that something was wrong it whimpered. But nobody had seen it slipping into its earth, so there could be no question of listening for it, digging a shaft to its lair and disposing of it with a blow to its muzzle: the only compensation was this expertise with which they prepared for its fate. At the end of August it spent more time than usual lying around outside its earth, not suspicious of anything in particular, but just enjoying memories predestined to the darkness of instinct. It seemed to be facing up to its future without wanting to. It was still young, but it had gained a fair amount of experience and knew what raids, hunts, being outlawed and the lot of a scapegoat were all about; it had learnt the basic elements of being a culprit, and knew that the world is hardly capable of showing mere curiosity and respecting what is different. That was enough for its mind to be occupied with thoughts other than those of a professional hound. The furrier and the tanner—the latter still used old-fashioned vegetable materials and proudly proclaimed on his signboard that he was a furrier—suggested a time which happened to coincide with the first ball to celebrate peace, in February. Just such a February in which the fox last panted after the vixen on heat, pounding the powdery snow high into the air and whirling around with her like a glowing reel. So the choice fell on 8 September, so that the boa might be ready in time. Of course, there was no guarantee that they would succeed in killing it in the first drive, but all the company were good shots and the foxhound Rolf knew exactly what he had to do. They took the young wife with them as well, though she was reluctant to go. She longed for the boa, but even more for a bloodless miracle. Towards seven in the evening Rolf caught the scent. The rifles were set up with mathematical precision and there was no gap in the line of fire. Here too expertise was evident in every movement, yet it was not the fox, but the young wife, who was the centre of attraction. She stood slightly to one side, yet on the rock of Gibraltar of the scene of action, from which everything could be followed. She was wearing high-heeled laced shoes, a long beige skirt and a simple hunting-green jacket. Her multicoloured straw hat melted with deceptive mimicry into the background; she might even have been an exceptional landmark as she stood apart, awed and immobile, at the barbarously simple, straightforward place of execution. It would be a romantic idea that it was she whom the fox noticed first when Rolf, after a nerve-tingling scamper, finally found the invisible direct line which is straighter than a stretched rope and not merely leads, but in a vulgar way gallops, to the target. Yet this might approach what the young wife thought she saw: that their glances met. Not for long, but just long enough for her to feel a pang in the pit of her stomach; as she would feel later in the great hall of the county hall, when she had to start the first waltz—or when the fur kept appearing and disappearing like a bullfinch-ornament in the throng round the buffet, as if it were a fragile guiding principle. The fox realized immediately that it was surrounded and did not think it necessary to rush more than twenty or thirty metres; it suddenly slid to its belly and pressed itself hard to the ground, waving its tail wildly for a moment or two, then giving that up too. *In acrid smoke resounds / The shot; the meadow sways before his eyes, / As from the bush with rushing, mighty wind / And thunder far and wide the grapeshot flies*—just as the ball too went on its prescribed way with such a sense of unreality. The organizers still recalled, like a kind of historical inheritance, how to turn a mirrored room into something crazy, how to transform the staircase leading to the gallery into a magical, fern-decked tunnel of love; they remembered the disciplined orgies of the great Redoute and souvenir balls. The girls and women, who scarcely two years before had been knitting gloves and pullovers for the front-line troops, supported their powdered breasts and made them resplendent with tight "trimmed brassières", and from the darker valley between them there arose the concentrated perfume of chafing curves lower down. These competing scents flashed in the air like so many visionary morsels of forgotten nudity. And in the large room it was indeed possible to feel that it was May, though the night was sparkling white, and between Ózsák and Borjád knife-blade cracks criss-crossed the ice covering the uncultivated meadows. Perhaps it was at this very ball that it first occurred to the young woman that winter lies in wait behind every season, and it was winter even on that eighth day of September. *With a thin tracery of blood that face / Emerged primeval, wild, upon the snow*—or, to be absolutely businesslike, it was as if at that ball she had once again rendered an account for her fur.

After that the boa lay in a cupboard for years.

Years passed. She had no daughter (though the child she miscarried might have been a girl), so there were no more balls in her life; so too the only time she went abroad was when she was able to join a party of underfed wartime schoolchildren on a summer holiday in Fiume. That was so distant that its recollection returned even when she was in hospital for the very last time—the jetty, the man in the linen shirt who presented her with a giant seashell to take home the sound of the sea. And a white rock on which only black birds landed. These petrified birds were capable of flying away after every wave; they could never really be washed white, they were snow-white and blackish-grey like the cigarette-smoke that enforces the frame of mind on evenings when guests are expected, curling above the festive dining-table; it billowed out with ever new promises of hope and seemed to belong to that false peace that did not last ever for twenty years, to that consolidated eve of tragedy, like the emblem of exorcism—"Nothing's the matter, you see. *The little lark in the field cried her eyes out, both of them...*"; meanwhile they might have been young, not on occasion, but once and for all, since their turn had come to play the repertory of Youth, pushing aside the favourite Chopin and Mozart scores and obediently running their fingers over the yellowed keys of the red and black Bösendorfer so that the lurking silence should not be heard and the man's self-torturing toasts should not sit heavily on the damask tablecloth which had been ironed stiff with such care. Later this is how she remembered things in that back kitchen transformed into a warm nook, which the rats gallantly respected (since she did not use poison, but inventively stuffed the holes full of broken glass), and into which, at the cost of a little rough sawing, she had somehow been able to squeeze the piano. But she sank with Atlantis that summer afternoon when she tried voluntarily to cross the Threshold—she was scarcely thirty years old. In the yard of the two-storey block of flats her younger son had just finished his great work: he had filled five beerbottles with water and, having straightened the caps with tweezers, had forced them on the bottles again with mechanical precision. Today it is difficult to reconstruct what might have been the deeper reason for this careful deceit. Most probably it was an artful demonstration of the fact of mystery, of unanswerability. From the upstairs corridor she watched the secret operation for some minutes, and only rapped on the railing with her wedding ring when the boy had covered the bottles with his shirt, awaiting a suitable moment to smuggle them into the ice-chest. She waved farewell with a blue muslin scarf; she was incapable of doing anything more, then she hurried back into the flat. The boy felt he had been spied on, and that he too had been initiated into a secret event. Annoyance and fear made him almost unable to move and he dashed up the stairs only when they were trying to force the door of the bedroom with an axe. The sickly-sweet smell of medicine was seeping through the cracks. They gave in to his plea that he should climb across the air-shaft on a plank let into the lavatory window opposite, to approach the bedroom from that direction—an adult would not have been able to get through the narrow hole. The only way he could jump down from the high little window was by clinging to the chain as he jumped. The water, like an ominous Niagara in a distant country, suddenly assailed his ears. Before he opened the door into the living-room, he stole a momentary glance at the sight that was for him alone: the beautiful body radiated a nightmarish whiteness as it lay on the rumpled bed dominating the darkened room, as if it were on a bier in a fairytale wood. Only when the door was opened did the saliva dribbling from the corner of her mouth gleam like a snail's track on cooling gravel. He had grown up so much at this that the adults who rushed in could only stand around him as if he were a sturdy dwarf. It took hours for them to bring her back to life and all of them felt that this day would remain a special date, even if it were not recorded. They propped up the new wife with pillows, gently merciless; they were conscientious and attentive, and somehow everything became more blatantly muted, more decidedly ceremonial. And as time passed the world too appeared to begin to assimilate to the pitiless end-game. Frankness turned into frank self-decep-tion. She had to tremble at the war, she had to trust in the future; her sons were called up. Her husband, at the peak of his pro-fessional career, must have felt with grim satisfaction that he had completed what could be done before his time was up. If the world still wanted an operation, that might also be a celebration of the verdict; as the trial approaches there is always some twisted sense of relief. But there was never any further mention of that unrecorded summer afternoon—when they were to face it without wishing to. Nor was there of the fur; except that each year the mothballs were changed in the paper bag. Then one night the entrance was smashed to allow lorries to stand in the yard, the lamp-standards were rewired and the smell in the streets changed. Another morning she caught sight of a huge pool of oil from the upstairs window; it was only a couple of metres away from the statue of St. Sebastian in the market-place. It was as if some monster had bled to death on the cobbles, only a couple of metres away from her bed, her dresser, her sewing-basket too; certainly they had dragged away the corpse, but they had forgotten to sprinkle sand on the place. Her terror increased when she also discovered traces in the garden beside the petunia-beds and the same smell belched up out of the kitchen sink. The next thing was that not a single postcard arrived from the front for a whole eight months. And there followed a hard winter. In this war it was not customary for women to knit "heart-warmers", and that was not longer their name anyway. But the cold promised to last and made no distinction between the front and the folk at home.

So it was that the fur was brought out of its mothballs. The old furrier had died by now, but his son had taken over his shop, and he cut it carefully in two—*Convulsively he raised his head on high, / His tongue grew stiff upon his open wound*—to make a really heart-warming, sleeveless jacket out of it.

The war ended as usual, with contradictory hopes. And law and order were able to perform their eternal role: while embodying new justice in the law, they did not forget those injustices which, it is customary to believe, protect the new justice. They soon discovered that the husband, with criminal intent, had allowed water to inundate the fertile plain around the town at the time of the spring floods. The court, however hard it tried, could not make anything out of the show-trial, but it served its end anyway. The sluice was his life-work; they charged him with operating it with ill-intent; in vain was he cleared of the charge, he never recovered from it. He brushed any defence aside, but left doors and windows open for death. It took five years for the guest to arrive. His agony lasted for several days, during which the woman became dazed. And like her son on that day long past she became almost incapable of movement, she gazed *fixedly* at what was happening and suddenly lost all her previous competence. A single fly circled over the sick-bed; it did not settle, but waited like a disabled, hysterical vulture. When death ensued, the woman tore her clothes and had a fit of tears and laughter; she kept insisting wildly that only Borját and Ózsák-puszta had not been flooded. It was then that she moved from the official flat into the back-kitchen she had been allotted. All the same, the trial had far-reaching effects, and she was unable to find work for a long time. There followed a period when women left in widowhood betray with enigmatic calm that they know immeasurably more than men, and not only about the cradle; when with incredible tenacity they manage to tack together a silhouette out of death, a silhouette which is "unharmed by snow and ice" and has much more to do with the minutely-detailed organization of endurance than with happiness. She had received a balanced inheritance from her ancestors: she was able to combine growing vegetables (and sending the surplus to market) with continuing her music (even taking on a few pupils). It was an event when she succeeded in finding a job washing up in the canteen of a local factory. She calculated that if she became disabled the two pensions would allow her to put aside money for the funeral. Some time later it occurred to someone that they could use her expertise at the piano in celebrations at the factory, and her knowledge of drawing in the crèche. She seemed to take on new life with the extra work, for which she was given no remission of duties or lighter work; on the other hand she could be more certain that she would not be given notice. The children doted on her, trotting after her with linked hands in a long line; if she crossed the yard of the crèche with the food-trolley, they helped her, back and front, to pull it along. She felt she had never risen to such heights. It was now that she really received compensation for being denied the sacraments because of her agreement that the children should be brought up in another faith; and only now was she able to forgive herself for having lived in adultery. Her new situation gave her more warmth than the fur jacket, which in the meantime had become quite shabby, a witness to the passing of time—*His tail fell like red ashes to the snow*—but stubbornly kept going and lost its hairs only gradually. Then with the approach of the end of her last year of employment and her pension, she wanted to celebrate her retirement. She borrowed the neighbour's living-room (the best room in the derelict peasant cottage) for the afternoon of the second day of Christmas, to entertain the crèche children in two parties. She prepared for this in secret and only told the children at the last moment that there was going to be a surprise at her home. For an hour and a half she sat around beside the flower-decked table, but nobody came. The cream went thick, the cocoa grew cold and the currants fell clumsily out of the slices of cake. Somewhere high up in the factory her unusual idea was regarded as sensitive, and still because of that old trial. "A place of work is different; there one can keep an eye on everything, you must understand that." In the end she upset her stomach with the cream, and so hardly noticed that she was crying and kept repeating parts of Beethoven's D minor sonata until well into the night, particularly the final Andante moderato. It was then that she suddenly realized that her hands and fingers were almost completely ruined with lifting saucepans, and would hardly be fit for her to play in front of a pupil. And her fingers had become sensitive to the slightest hint of cold. Then she decided to sacrifice the fur jacket. This last operation, however, she did not entrust to a furrier, but did it herself.

So the remains of the boa became a muff, which she carried night and day hung round her neck, and kept warming her hands in it.

She lived for eighty-five years. Like a full glass, she had no desires or complaints. In her last years she put it this way: "My solitude is endless; I have to delve everything up from myself." She regarded it as a piece of good fortune that from the end of the garden—where the brim-full earth-closet with its piercing stench was not emptied by the authorities because the house was in any case due to be demolished—she could look out over the Ózsák floodplain. Somehow her memories always started out from there. When the day came—*Congealing blood boomed hazily above him*—most probably she felt the same as the fox: *The taste of rotting carrots in his mouth...* Even without the rococo frame the picture is a strong one; both of them are resting in the tussocky meadow before continuing their way—*clammy is that evening, and red*—not too near, yet not too distant from each other.

Translated by George F. Cushing

OLD PEOPLE
by ÁRPÁD GÖNCZ

"This doctor," she said half aloud as she was smoothing the cream onto her hand, "is a genuine God-send! What's it called?" She lifted the jar and drew it closer to her eyes. "Ne-o-gra-nor-mon," she deciphered. And then to herself, shaking her head: "It is a genuine miracle that Bernát has no reaction to it, that it doesn't constantly give him a rash there." She nodded her head. "There." She spoke emphatically as if someone were attempting to deny her assertion. "And it is good for the hands too. My hands aren't chapped any longer since I started using it." Raising her hands to her eyes, she turned them palm outward. Then she started to rise and with narrowed eyes gazed at the clock. It took a while before she became aware the clock had run down. "When I no longer can climb up there and wind it up..." she said, and interjected, as if defending herself against some unspoken accusation, "I'm not going to climb up there just for that. What if I fall? What would happen to you then? Who is going to take...?" Her eyes roved about and sought the alarm clock. Quarter past nine. "They wrote they would be here by ten. Fortunately, I checked the mail..."

She folded her hands in her lap and patiently sat still. Her facial muscles eased. The room was quiet. One could hear just the sibilant rasping breathing from next-door. And only a fly buzzed, stumbling unhurriedly to and fro.

"I don't know," she said, "I really don't know..." She straightened herself up, and her face tightened. She glanced furtively at the alarm clock with a hunted, suspicious look. "Good Lord..." Suddenly she rose. She removed her nut-brown, heavy robe and stepped in front of the large wall mirror. Now, dressed only in her slip, she appeared positively gaunt: her every bone stuck out, her clavicle was exposed, her shoulder blades sharp as knives. Her legs were skinny and had varicose veins.

"One turns ugly in one's old age." She spoke half aloud, in her accustomed manner. There was no bitterness in the observation. Not in this one.

She opened the top drawer of the chest, removed a silver-handled comb, and untied her sparse, carelessly made-up hair that was neither grey nor black. "People turn grey slowly in my family," she observed with a determined nod. "Daddy and Mommie as well!" She repeatedly combed through her hair and arranged it to disguise the bare spots on her rosy scalp. Then she fastened the knot. Turning her head from side to side with self-assured, well-practiced movements, she placed the finishing touches on her hairdo. Then, walking over to the three-doored wardrobe, a little bowed down, a little insecure, and noticing that the key was missing, she returned her attentions to the chest, opened the top drawer, stopped, pondered, pushed the drawer back, opened the second drawer, fumbling about, searching with progressive nervousness. "Where did I put it, where on earth did I put it?" she mumbled, still standing in her slip. "Yesterday, when I..." She removed a leather purse, opened it, closed it again, removed a tin box and dumped out a dozen or so keys. "This is it, this is going to be it..." she said as she turned toward the wardrobe with the key, fitted it into the keyhole with great difficulty, opened the door and lifted a black and white silk dress off the hanger. Then she stood in front of the mirror and raised her arms. Then her face froze in agony, but overcoming the pain, she slipped into the silk dress. "There! And Anette wanted me to buy that silver dress. But of course this was much nicer... And cheaper." she added, as if to defend herself before an unseen audience. "But then she did have to concede that this one was much nicer, didn't she?" She glanced at the mirror, but she only saw Anette, Dödi's granddaughter who last summer came to visit with that Spaniard, her husband. Anette had taken her to the summer sales, and with the self-assurance that only the young and the rich have, she had cut through the Hungarian–German–Slavic language barrier, and the barrier of perspiration and, without as much as a moment's deliberation, she had selected a grey dress from the rack and later, when she recognized that the old lady didn't like it, she had pulled off this one. Anette had laughed, thrown back her long, blonde hair and had the salesgirl wrap the dress before she had an opportunity to inform them that she didn't need any dresses, that she was perfectly... that those few old rags she had were perfectly... you see... perfectly... "This is the first time I'm wearing it." She nodded to herself in the mirror and then reaching back and amidst sighs she buttoned her dress at the neck. Then she dropped her arms. "At least she didn't buy it for nought," she said. She wished to leave but couldn't tear herself away from the mirror and turning left and right, she smiled imperceptibly. "Ah well," she said, with a wave of her hand, and returning to the chest, she stopped and pondered, "What was it?... Oh, yes."

She retraced her steps, stopped at the wardrobe, hung up the empty hanger, pushed the door to, removed the key, stepped over to the chest, opened both the top drawer and then the second. She reached into the leather purse and opened it. "No, not here." She closed the purse and replaced it. Then she lifted out a tin box and placed the key amongst the others. Then after abruptly closing the drawer she just as abruptly opened it again. She fumbled about in it nervously. "Where did I put it? Where on earth did I put it..." she mumbled. "If I didn't put it here ... if... if it got stolen..." She finally found what she sought under the leather purse; it had slipped there: a small golden chain with an amethyst set in gold. She reminisced, while she held the chain in her hand: "Dödi... this is what Dödi... from the front before he got wounded." She was startled and glanced around with a bad conscience. She placed the chain around her neck, stopped in front of the mirror, peered at herself, turned from left to right, adjusting her hair all the while. "Dödi," she said, talking to herself and smiling faintly. "Mommie." Then nervously she said: "They are going to be here in a minute and I..." She walked away, wringing her hands, then sitting down helplessly, said, "Yes, well, it's good that already at six... otherwise it'd not..." She placed her hand on her forehead, then drew it across her eyes as if to wipe away the sense of being hunted. Resentfully she sighed, "I have been up since six in the morning... and all night I didn't sleep a wink..." Then she continued half aloud and as if in a chant: "I went to the market, bought some of the chicken legs for Bernát, bought coffee, changed Bernát's bed, gave him breakfast... I'm glad I baked the cake yesterday and that I bought the wine... What would these people say if... Good Lord, did I grind it?..." She jumped up nervously. "I don't know..." She hurried as well as she could into the kitchen with wooden, somewhat insecure movements, stepped into the pantry, and opened the coffee bag's yellow cover. "Yes, I did. Good, then... then—yes, the coffee pot..." She removed the pot and muttered: "This is the best coffee, even if it is the cheapest. Even then, in spite of that, it is the best. And when I buy it at the market... fresh... it is always..." Abruptly she put down the coffee pot. "What now? Ah, yes, I'll have to make the coffee now, so that I won't have to when... and I'll have to set the table before they come... so that I'll not have to when..." She pulled the tray from under the sink and placed it on the table. "My, I completely..." She went over to the sink, then came back, unscrewed the coffee pot, filled it up with water, put it on the countertop, walked over to the cabinet, removed a coffee spoon, returned to the table, put it down, returned to the cabinet, lifted the coffee, brought it to the table, then searched for the pot, "Where did I... Where on earth did I..." She kept repeating herself, but then she recalled, shuffled over to the sink, then to the cabinet, looking for the coffee pot.

"Well, of course... on the table..." she said, then returned and put coffee in the pot, screwed it back together, lit the gas, and put on the pot, then she lifted the tray and went into the room. "Where did I?..." she said, knitting her brows. She looked for the key in the chest, opened the three-doored wardrobe, and took out a tablecloth. "Mommie..." she said to herself. "This too is from her... part of my trousseau..." She reached up and took down the Turkish brass smoking set from the little smoking table. "This is what Bernát... still in Istanbul when..." she said and placed the richly embroidered tablecloth, yellowed at the folds and crumbling in spots, on the table. Then stopping in front of it, she dropped her hands, nodded, and said: "Last year, when Anette and that Spaniard, her husband... he must be a fine man... that poor Dödi..." Then she shuddered, took out four napkins and placed them neatly, with calm self-assurance, on the table; then she lifted the tray and tiptoed into the room from where the breathing came. She opened the carved cabinet's door; when it creaked, she reproached it: "Psst! Bernát is still..." She put four china coffee cups, four saucers, and four small silver coffee spoons on the tray, then removed the sugar bowl and the silver sugar tongs that had aged to a dark blue color. "They take sugar-lumps nowadays... that's the fashion... I brought home some so that..." She pondered for a while, then removed four cut glass goblets and retrieved the bottle of Riesling she had bought the day before, placed a corkscrew next to it, carried everything into the other room, and arranged them all neatly on the small table.

"Good heavens, the coffee!" She slapped her hands in fright. Her face, again, showed that hunted look, and she hurried as well as she might into the kitchen with insecure steps. The coffee pot was boiling wildly; every second a wild coffee-geyser burst forth from under the darkened plastic cover. She viewed it in despair and was about to reach for it.

"The cake knife!" She suddenly remembered and turned to rush to the other room. But her movements froze, she whirled around, turned off the gas from under the coffee pot, then hurried back into the room, leaving the door wide open. Then she removed the cake knife. At this point the cake knife inevitably reminded her of the four dessert plates; the four dessert plates, alas, also reminded her of the four dessert forks. She crossed over to the other room, lifted the tray, returned to the cabinet, placed everything on the tray, then carried the tray in and arranged all the goodies on the table. "Good Lord, the coffee..." she suddenly remembered. She retraced her steps, returned to the kitchen but forgetfully left the tray behind. Here she ruterned for it, lifted it and carrying it into the kitchen, placed the coffee onto it. Then one more trip was devoted to the pantry where she took a long cake tray upon which was placed a butter-cream cake and carried it into the room. She placed this latest addition in the middle of the table; then she successfully took from the drawer the cigarettes that she had bought the day before. "Something Porti... the tobacconist said that's what gentle-folk smoke nowadays..." Gently she put the cigarettes into the cigarette box and placed the matches nearby.

Tired, she sat down and stroked her forehead. "What else... what else... Good Lord!" Jumping up, she tiptoed into the other room, opened the blinds and dragged the portable toilet sitting next to the old man's bed into the bathroom. "There is no need for them to see this..." she mumbled. Then she stopped beside the chair and wavered: "Eh..." Then she grabbed the cross sheets from the easy chair and carried them into the bathroom. With all this finished, when she was on her way back, she cast a long glance at the old man turned towards the wall and breathing quietly. "Bernát..." she said quietly, "... Bernát... They'll be here in a second... They've come to see you... don't you understand?" The old man's eyes fluttered but he remained asleep. She didn't have the heart to startle him out of his sleep. She sighed and her hand shook; then she stroked her forehead, went into the other room, and mutely sank down into the armchair next to the smoking table.

"Good heavens," she said, "...the flowers... And I bought them today, at the market... from the country woman..." Restlessly she scuttled into the kitchen and said, "They are going to be here in a second..." The vase being already at hand, she filled it with water, opened the bouquet, and arranged the flowers. "Peasant flowers..." She made a slight grimace. "Common peasant flowers... but these are the ones Mommie loved too. And in Szogi, peasants had them in front of every house... marigolds, that's what they called them... there must be another name... but I only know them by this... And she let me have it for one-and-a-half forints..." she added defensively. She took the bouquet and placed it on the center of the table. Slowly she lowered herself into the chair, all exhausted, and wiped her forehead. She sighed. Quite abruptly she glanced up at the grandfather clock, squinting to see better... she could read it, written in carved gothic letters above the Roman VI: Ferenc Niewelt, master clock maker, Sopron... or was it that she knew the words by heart?... It took her awhile to comprehend that the clock had stopped. "I am not going to climb up there to wind it. I am not going to fall just for that. Sure, then who would..." she remarked, annoyed and defensive. Her eyes sought the alarm clock. Ten to ten. "They'll be here in ten minutes."

She placed her hands in her lap. Her gaze wandered and settled on the marigolds. It seemed as if the yellow flowers had soaked up the sunshine of thousands of years. They glowed orange-yellow in the black vase on the perfectly starched but yellowed embroidered tablecloth breaking at the folds. Around the flowers everything seemed to take on new colour: the red-brown of the book-case, the Biedermeier wardrobe, the pot-bellied inlaid secretary, the four armchairs with their now greasy, faded covers, the ornate daybed, the darkened family pictures, Grandpa in white uniform and Grandma in lilac headdress and, under her feet, even the worn Persian carpet with holes in some places. And it was as if the light came not from without but from within, as if it were the street that received its light through the smoke-covered, un-washed window of the room.

"Mommie," she mouthed slowly, half-aloud. "These were Mommie's favourites too... the peasants in Szogi... they had them in front of every house..." Tired, she closed her eyes. "I haven't stopped since six in the morning. I've been on my feet..." She was complaining to Mommie. She opened her eyes. "All this," she said, "all this is from Szogi... the secretary... the daybed... the car-pet... the wardrobe... the silver... and also the tablecloth and lin-ens... all of my trousseau. It's a wonder that it is still in such good condition since it lay exposed for so long. The clock... while it was working, even struck at a quarter to the hour. But now that it doesn't, so be it..." she mumbled perturbed. "I'm sure... then who is going to care for... that too... the Schiller bound in gold..."

Somehow her thoughts had emptied themselves. With closed eyes she rested, her hands resting in her lap. "Daddy..." she said quietly to herself without opening her eyes. "I got it from Daddy in Szogi. He'll live by his brains like his father, the notary. She'll be the wife of a professor... there hasn't been a woman married to a scholar in the family... not a single one... but for her he'll do anything. Only the Eördögh family looked down their noses... they wanted me to marry Dödi... poor Dödi... but no, Daddy was never stuck-up..."

The de luxe edition of Schiller glittered behind the marigolds. "... In front of the house, all in a pile... all of it... the whole library in flames... a big fire fed with the books..." she mumbled. "That they were soldiers? That it was all the same?... That... after having in-spired the soul, it was time for them to warm the soup... and after all, they were hungry... and cold... if they weren't cold, they wouldn't have made a fire... and since they didn't find anything else... naturally they took the books!..."

But Bernát was no soldier. "No... But this Schiller belonged to Daddy... He hadn't been to Szogi since that... Last year when Anette, Dödi's granddaughter, came home from Argentina with that man driving the car... they asked me to accompany them. Why should I? The boxwood trees are uprooted anyway... and the chapel... you know... the chapel there in the midst of the yew trees, it was blown up at the front. They placed guns behind Granddaddy's and Grandma's gravestones... that, too, was Bernát... that it was 'reasonable'... it's better for the stone to be blown to pieces than for a man... it would be more of a pity if people... Dödi wouldn't have placed machine guns there... he wouldn't have even though he *was* a soldier. An officer. A gentleman."

Her hands touched the amethyst. "Before he was wounded... Then he returned to Monte Grappa. His servant said, in 1919, that his body was never... The child, Dödi's and Mária's child, was very small then. And Anette... Anette is very beautiful... she could have been my granddaughter, not Mária's... if Daddy hadn't... then. The trees, the gravestones, the chapel... the house is now some type of office for the cooperative... as if Bernát had planned it... something about historic justice: repaying debts. But why does history demand justice for Grandpa and Grandma? Why? What did they owe history?"

The bell rang for the third time. "Good Lord, it might be them." She jumped up and, becoming slightly dizzy from the sudden movement, she pressed her hand to her heart and then started for the door a little insecurely, a little wobbly.

*

She sat with her hands resting in her lap, her head tilted to the side. The lines of her face relaxed; the wrinkles around her mouth deepened. She heard the car door slam downstairs, the motor start; then that, too, faded and in its stead deathly silence settled in. Only the old man in the other room wheezed and a fly buzzed nervously about the cake plate.

In front of her on the little table stood the four uncleaned coffee cups, the four plates and forks covered by remnants of the cake, the open bottle of Riesling, barely sampled—only two inches were missing—and the four wine glasses with a little yellow fluid at their bottoms.

"... My dear colleague... my dear uncle Bernát... on this very special day, your ninetieth birthday, as well as the sixtieth anniversary of your appointment to the university, the Hungarian Academy of Sciences wishes to pay its respects... to you, who as a guiding light... the cultural inheritance of our spiritual ancestors... for the epoch and its social customs... Ady, Bódog Somló and Oszkár Jászi... always ready to sacrifice... always among the first to resist the expansionist policies of fascist barbarism... as a modest token of our love and respect, of our heartfelt gratitude, to commemorate your unforgettable achievements..."

"But then, of course, when they determined the amount of his pension, then they forgot," she mumbled, annoyed and half aloud.

She stood up, straightened her dress and went into the other room; she returned with the tray and started clearing the table: plates, forks, coffee cups, sugar bowl, wine glasses. Then she sighed and again sat down. "Lady," he had said, "Dear lady?" Exhaustion, like a gray boulder, obstructed the flow of her thoughts. "Why did he say that? What was his aim? What did he want of me?"

Her thoughts again halted. "It's easier to remember than to think."

"That other man, the one from the ministry... he was not..." she mumbled. "And that little blond man... what did he say he was? President? President of the Bernát Kostyál society? That man, he's not... He was so very common... He kept looking... kept looking... at the books. Why was he interested in our pension? In what we get?"

She straightened herself in her seat and blushed a little. Her head trembled more violently now. "They can't take *that* away... Bernát worked his heart out for them..." Then she almost shouted: "I told him, I told this young man that we are no book peddlers. Bernát Kostyál bought and received books as gifts; he gave some away but we never... never books... not even when... until then... What business is it of this comrade when I... he can't be wishing that I... Did I have any direct descendants... And what about any personal correspondence... those are Bernát Kostyál's letters... I won't have anyone else read them, not even fine gentlemen. They are his... Bernát Kostyál is not a memory... when he becomes a memory... then... then they won't even have to... and it's not that much longer... that they are establishing a Bernát Kostyál memorial library... What will they think up next?"

Her head shook uncontrollably. She remembered those awful two hours when they were sitting on their packed-up suitcases waiting in the stripped flat for the pickup truck. She remembered their friends scurrying about, carrying off a good part of the library to save it—just in case—and then they received that phone call, heard the fateful decision that they didn't have to... that they would be permitted to remain in the city... that the minister, personally... and there wouldn't be a pickup truck, no policemen..."

She rose, lifted the tray, carried it to the other room, opened the door to the china cabinet. "... No... not here..." she mumbled, "...where was I going... oh yes, I wanted to take it into the kitchen..." she turned around and started for the kitchen but got waylaid in the room; she laid the tray down and started carrying off the dirty china, the four plates, the forks, the coffee cups, the sugar bowl, the glasses; she moved with self-assured security, beautifully. "Good Lord... I am... I am completely..." she mumbled, and fell into the armchair. She wrung her hands in despair.

"No matter that that man looked at it like that... and even the professor... saying that eventually, at some other time... But then the minister intervened, he didn't allow it... I shall explain to him if he visits again... I shall, that the minister is not going... yes, Sir, he did intervene and that is how the library was saved and the correspondence also... and the minister is going to... again... if he wants to know, I'm going to explain to him that's how the library survived... and I'm going to explain to him just that... he can't force me... and he can't touch Bernát's pension either..."

She froze; all the blood drained from her cheeks. "And what if they can? What if they take it?... the library, the pension, everything?... Then who is going to care for him?..." Terror focused her every thought. "Everything!" she mumbled, "Everything... the books... the pension... the *flat!*" she exclaimed quietly "... the flat!" And she burst into tears.

"He said... he said... that it is a national treasure," she cried. "The books... the correspondence... and that it must not be allowed to... they are all conniving... and then, who is going to care for..."

Somehow, the alarm clock entered her field of vision. "Good Lord!... I'll still have to wash the dishes. And before that... Bernát's lunch... I bought him ..." she said half-aloud. But she didn't rise, she didn't have the energy; she didn't collect the dishes. She wiped her brow and dropped her hands into her lap again. "I have been on my feet since daybreak... since six... I haven't had a moment's rest... I am no longer... not any more... and I can no longer carry things as before... I haven't slept a wink the whole night..."

"Whoo-ee?" clashed the old man's voice from the other room. Startled, she jumped up, then becoming a little dizzy from the sudden move, reached for her forehead. Dizzy, she lurched for the other room.

"Who were these people? Who?... They came from the Academy, Bernát. To see you. To congratulate you on your birthday." She spoke slowly, deliberately, shouting the words so that the old man would understand them. "And look, look here what they brought for you. Do you see it?" She showed it to him, held it up for his view. On the plaque a naked young man glittered, bearing a torch held high. "Are you pleased? Are you pleased with it? You see, they love you."

Through his cataracts, the old man smiled beatifically, staring blindly. He extended his hands and, shaking uncontrollably, reached, groping for the plaque. When his hands touched it, he grabbed it like it was booty. "Shiii!" he shouted.

"Good Lord." Her hands flew to her face and she stroked her forehead. "Now? You are already in it? You couldn't have controlled yourself a little longer? At least until they left?... Let me see..." She lifted the cover and the stench overwhelmed her senses. She dropped her hands and stood there. "I, too, am only human, you know; I, too, am over eighty. You should think of me too. What's going to happen to you if I ... if I can't endure it any longer? If I... Why couldn't you have controlled yourself a little longer? At least until they left. And at the very least you could have said something."

"Shiii," the old man shouted impatiently, and his taloned hands, grabbing the plaque, beat impotently, angrily, at the cover.

"Ca-ca, all the time... just a minute... wait a minute," she said and she started moving toward the bathroom, still a little dizzy. She returned with the portable toilet, raised the cover, and put a new rubber cover upon it. She carried a pail of water into the room and tied an apron in front of her new black and white silk dress. Then she removed his cover. "Put down that whatever-you-want-to-call-it," she told him, but the old talons stubbornly clung to the plaque. "Put it down. I can't lift you like this!"

"Myy!" the old man shouted.

"Of course, of course it is yours. No one wants to deprive you of it." And she clutched the plaque and began to wrest it away from the old man.

"Myy!" The old man shouted desperately, but he lacked the strength to resist.

She deposited the plaque on the nightstand, inhaled deeply, reached behind the old man and, slowly, with her face crimson from the effort, first lifted him slightly then rolled the helpless body over onto the toilet seat.

The old man sighed, his tremendously large head sunk into his bony shoulders. His face turned purple from the straining; he rocked his upper body, and the stool creaked under him.

"Be careful, or you're going to fall off. I can't lift you back up into the bed..." She burst into tears. "Couldn't you have waited until they left? Now I'll have to wash everything all over again. Do you think I still have someone to do the wash? How would I pay her? From what? From your pension? And what's going to happen if ... if they take that away too? And if I no longer can care for you? What's going to happen to you? Who is going to care for you? Because, of course, you didn't want any children. Always only your work... your scientific work... only your great scientific work... and humanity..." She cried now without restraint; her tears dropping on her new black and white silk dress. "Because children... there are none... and now... who's there... who's going to... if... Good Lord... Mommie, Dödi... I ... dear Mommie!" She exclaimed in pain.

"Out!"

"All right, all right, well done, I'll put you back in bed." And she looked at him with her little grey eyes, bleary from crying and almost entirely buried in her wet, teary face. She quickly removed the soiled cross sheets, replaced them with clean ones; with quick, efficient movements she straightened them out and reached under the old man's armpits and pulled him up. "Hold your legs in place," she ordered him and turned him over. Together with him she almost fell on the bed. "Turn over." The old man stretched himself. "Myy!" he shouted.

"It's yours, of course it's yours. I'll give it to you, here," and she put the plaque in his hands.

With practised, almost desperately exact movements, she turned, washed, creamed, and powdered the helpless, wrinkled-up old body, and then pulled up the covers over him again and stood at the end of the bed. She dropped her hands, the tears flowing.

"Dödi... Mommie," she mumbled very quietly.

The old man didn't hear her.

His head rested on the pillow motionlessly; his eyes stared into nothingness, his taloned fingers jealously encircling the plaque. "Myy ... myy," he kept repeating, smiling beatifically.

Translated by Katharina M. Wilson and Christopher C. Wilson

BLUE-WHITE LOVE

by ENDRE FEJES

The tiles burned the palm of his hand as he crept across the rooftop. The girls threw pieces of soap at him, called him a bum, and worse, from behind the shower room window where they stood laughing. It was summertime, the end of the dayshift. They liked the boy. He was handsome, a dreamer with a gentle look in his eyes.

In the yard Kendur, the guy with bowlegs, slapped him savagely across the face and walked away. Not many of them saw it. Only a few men, a girl in a spotless white blouse, and the bookkeeper, Pál Schnirer, who commented loudly, "I've had enough of these tasteless jokes."

The boy smiled wanly and tried to say something silly which would make the other laugh. But nobody paid any attention, so he stopped. Listlessly, with uneven strides, he walked over to the Hump where his buddies were playing pool. He drank a glass of cold beer—Pali Vitok's treat, for the rooftop joke. Gróf, the old redhead, was of the opinion that wars were always caused by women. He cited examples from history. Little Rotyi spoke up too: "Why does he have to spy on other people," he said. Hábetler spat on the floor. "Someone ought to puncture Kendur's lung," he said. Little Rotyi hunched up his shoulders: "Hábetler, you have yellow eyes. Nobody likes you." He bent over the billiard cloth, his neck quivering. The others laughed. Little did they know that in his dreams Hábetler habitually beat up Little Rotyi.

They knocked around the ivories all afternoon. At stake was a pitcherful of beer. They quarrelled endlessly. Right before sundown young Feri Preisz left the game. "Well?" Hábetler asked sarcastically. For a few moments Preisz stared at the oil-stained floor, his head bowed low. He caressed Hábetler with his dark eyes. "I cannot hate people," he said softly. "Nor do I want to." Smiling apologetically, he stepped out on the street. He was known as an honest man. Words formed beautifully on his lips. He stumbled on a charmed path.

One early autumn evening, after seeing a play, they sat down for a glass of wine. Hábetler was still grieving Romeo and Juliet's death. Sullenly, he asked for another bottle. Lajos Stanec griped about his gout, the fall weather, the early morning fog. "Every day a ray of sunshine passes over my machine," mused Feri Preisz. "At two in the afternoon it says good-bye and climbs up the wall. Now I'll have to do without it till spring." The women looked at him and the girls too sought him out with their eyes.

Later, on their way home, in an underpass, Hábetler told them to shut up; he had a dirty joke for them. They laughed because he also made silly faces. Kendur was the only one who didn't join in. The bowlegged one rarely laughed. In front of the red-brick hospital building a fat girl put her arm around Preisz. "You with the gypsy eyes, how about a little sweet talk?" "I can't," he said. "Only if I love the person." "Come on, you love everyone," the girl said and laughed. "A hypocrite is what you are, a... a pharisee."

The girls got all excited; they shook their fists and rattled their silver bracelets. With a laugh that was furious, chromatic, they cried into the silent night, "Pharisee! Pharisee!"

He looked them over with his dark eyes. They quieted down. "It's no use", he said brusquely. "I am never getting married. If I say I'll die in the summer, when the stars are beautiful, you start blubbering and abuse me for not being the marrying sort." Having said this, he took off. They watched him run in the light fog, his gait ever so supple. Only the woman shouted after him, "You'll get married all right, you pharisee; there's a church waiting for you down the street." With her laughter still ringing, she took Kendur's hand. The wind grew cool. Kendur turned up her collar and quietly said goodbye to the others. They began walking home on poorly-lit, dreary Szabolcs utca.

The New Year's Eve ball was again a success. After midnight the marble-paneled hall was filled with laughter. The Kucuk brothers danced the night away. Whenever one of them fell down, he shouted, "Constantinople." Their ancestor was a Turkish pasha in Eger. They commuted to work from an outlying district. At every soccer game they got into a fist fight.

At the raffle Preisz won a bottle of champagne. He put it on the Kucuk brother's table. "You are a decent fellow," Lajos Kucuk said. "Still, Kendur hit you. Are you scared of that bow-legged bastard?" At the next table Kendur raised his head. He gave Preisz a menacing look but didn't say a word. Preisz raised his glass in slow motion. "I've been slapped quite a few times," he said gently. "I am not trying to brag, but when I start paying back, all hell will break loose."

A little later Pál Schnirer turned on him. The previous morning Preisz built a snowman in Schnirer's office, and this, naturally, caused a sensation. The cleaning women refused to shovel snow out of a second-floor office. They said Schnirer should turn off the radiator in the room and then he'll be all right until the spring. Schnirer, white with rage, yelled at him, "You climbed up on the roof, too, just to spy on the women."

Preisz waved his hand in annoyance. "Yes. And next time I'll take you up with me." He sat down at the tables, which were pushed together by now, and listened to Little Rotyi give him a piece of his mind. Sándor Ruzsó, the party secretary, also told him what he thought of the snowman affair. He didn't answer him either. Squinting his eyes, he watched the dancers on the floor. Then he drank a glass of wine and fell asleep, nestling his head with its frizzly mop on his two arms.

The woman woke him up. Few people were left in the hall. The redheaded Gróf was wondering about the weight of one's soul. "Let's say a man who weighs 130 pounds dies. What would a highly sensitive scale show?" "You have your lung and your stomach," Hábetler said. "Plus other stuff. There ain't no soul."

He got another bottle of wine and sat down again next to Ancsura. Kendur got involved explaining to Little Rotyi all about the theoretical aspects of driving a car. "Do *you* believe your soul can be weighed?" the woman said, laughing. Preisz looked at his watch. It was a quarter past one. "I am tired," he said. "I probably have a slight fever... I was never sick in my life."

Stanec felt Preisz's pulse and decided it was normal. Then he wanted to sing, but the others wouldn't let him. "We lugged four sackfuls of snow on our back," he said in his raspy voice muffled by a cleft palate, "because Preisz wanted to teach Schnirer a lesson in humanity." On this long, crazy night they still liked the boy; they had fun with him. Gróf, the old redhead, explained to him patiently, as to a child, that a common cold was not an illness. Hábetler blew into a noisemaker and laughed coarsely.

"You with the gypsy eyes, don't you worry," cried Ancsura. "You *will* die in the summer, when the stars are the brightest." Everyone laughed, even those sitting at tables farther away. The woman leaned back as she laughed. He looked at each of them, one by one; his eyes settled on the woman's flushed face. A shy little smile appeared in the corner of his mouth; then he got up and left the room.

The woman caught up with him in the checkroom. He looked handsome, pale, like a rebel. They moved behind one of the marble columns. The music from the ballroom could be heard through the wide double doors. The band was playing its theme song, the final number. The woman in the coatroom sleepily adjusted her wire-rimmed glasses.

A mean frost settled over the city. The moon didn't want to move, it shivered on top of a smokestack, somewhere over Újpest. On the street the woman pressed close to Kendur. Her eyes flared with menacing blues; she wanted to see her child. Kendur embraced her and felt her trembling. He, too, was cold, and he said fretfully, "Such a waste of time, these parties." They walked home without saying another word to each other.

Just where the Number 14 streetcar turns with tiny shrieks toward Angyalföld, in a quiet café, the two of them hid every day for months, terrified, ashamed, intoxicated. Preisz loved the woman, loved her with the grateful, happy love of a lonely man. She got less talkative, lost weight. This wondrous, blazing love of his troubled her deeply.

In August they stopped seeing each other. They could no longer take the pain, the hopeless, daydreaming, the forbidden, snatched moments. She cried; her eyes got all red and puffy. It was a hot afternoon; she wondered aimlessly on the soft asphalt, then went up to her sister's place and told her everything. It was quite late by the time she arrived home.

She kissed her husband, as she had every night for six years, but for the first time she felt a need to account for the time she'd spent away from the house. So she said she had been shopping for bed linen downtown, and looked for an apron for their girl a little bit farther on Bajcsy-Zsilinszky utca, and even looked in on her sister.

Kendur was in bed already, watching her undress. She stopped talking, lowered her head resigned, and turned off the light.

For two days they avoided each other. On the morning of the third day, an unshaven, tormented Preisz walked into the press machine shop and turned off her pounding machine. "We'll go away, Mária," he said.

She smiled; tears welled in her eyes. She got up from her little stool, and with a lovely, touching motion swept the metal shaving off her apron. The girls watched in silent dismay through the many-paned window as the two of them, clinging fast to each other, walked away calmly, disappearing behind the severe iron posts of the pipe storage room.

That evening she gave back her wedding band to Kendur who said only, "I knew it that night. And I haven't raised my head since. Stay with me. I love you." With her hands trembling, she got her little girl dressed, picked her up and fled. She moved back to her parents' house.

The next morning everyone knew it. They talked about it on the streetcar. In the dressing room all was very quiet. Preisz laced his shoes anxiously, defiantly. He went over to his machine where a fistful of sunshine was waiting for him. He gave it a yank and the machine was spinning.

At ten o'clock Kendur came over to him. The sunlight showed the time of the day; it had already moved quite a ways from the armature. Preisz let go of the switch. He didn't step back but kept his eyes on Kendur. "Have you met her parents?" "I haven't; not yet." Kendur gulped down mouthfuls of milk from his bottle and wiped his mouth with his oil-stained hand. "Don't say anything bad... to my daughter." He left, playfully knocking the milk bottle against the machines. The workers listened to the panting motors. It was a scorcher of a day, they were all sweating.

In the dressing room the redheaded Gróf asked in a loud voice, "How's your daughter?" "Fine," Pali Vitok said. "Does she look like you?" continued Gróf. "You think I stole her?" Vitok countered. They were both bachelors.

Preisz didn't say a word. He opened his locker and began dressing. In the yard he received a wedding present: Stanec spat on him. Outside, past the factory gate, amid the hubbub of the departing crowd, Pál Schnirer told him with embarrassment: "Wipe your face, will you?" Preisz nodded his head, bemused, and took out his handkerchief.

Many of them demanded, loudly, adamantly, that Preisz be drummed out of their circle. A few days later, towards the end of the workday, the party secretary asked to see him. Preisz told him how they had both gone through hell and tried to break off. "For three days I saw her everywhere," he said, "on the wall, on my machine, on my pillow." "What about Kendur? Don't you ever think of him?" "Not any more. I don't care." "And the child?" "He can see her: twice a week if he likes." Preisz stepped up to the window. In the yard a truck was backing up: men stripped to the waist carried on noisily. The sun had gone down, the motionless air was waiting for night to arrive. He said, "You guys spit in my face because I can't live a lie. But I am not afraid of you. You can't do anything to me."

He left. They stopped hiding: after work they waited for each other and took walks in the city, dazed by their love. On the last day of August, emerging from behind a telephone booth, Kendur appeared suddenly before them. He got thin, his eyes grew large in their sockets. With an embarrassed smile, and in his meek, beggar voice he asked for his daughter. "My mother could pick her up Saturday..."

She fixed her gaze on him and spoke softly, with emotion "You can take her, Jóska, any time you want to. But please send her back Sunday morning; we are seeing a puppet show." He said good-bye shyly, politely. He didn't hold out his hand, though; he just walked away.

Kendur didn't send back the child. Hours passed; the more concerned they got the less they talked. They avoided each other's eyes; sobs choked in her throat. Before ten o'clock she ran home one more time, and when she came back to the café she brought her sister along. Preisz introduced himself, then said angrily, "He wants to lure her home, back to the apartment." The sister was quiet and kept looking at her thumb that had been mangled by a hatcher. "He is crazy about Mária," she said finally.

Preisz went for the girl himself. It was a muggy night. High in the sky heavy rain clouds rushed from every direction, gathering over the city. He rode a streetcar as far as the Jewish Hospital and from there walked briskly down Szabolcs Street. To the caretaker who blinked his eyes suspiciously he handed four forints and said he was looking for Kendur and would be down in a few minutes.

He never forgot that meeting. The front door was open. Passing through the narrow hallways he opened a door painted brown and stopped. He was greeted by a mass of roses; heavy-scented flowers lay on the tables, the chairs, they were all over the floor too. Kendur, sitting in an armchair, tried to smile, but what he produced was no smile. They kept looking at each other in complete silence for as long as it takes to count up to ten. Then Kendur stood up, smoothed down his Sunday suit, turned his back to Preisz, and walked over to the window. He listened to the wind acting up again outside. Preisz, in the meantime, took a building block out of Katinka's hand, picked her up, and with his head hung low sneaked out of the apartment.

It was pouring outside. Every minute almost, the departing summer tossed down a thunderbolt. Preisz was off and running, and though soon out of breath, he didn't care, and raced through the puddles under the yellow glow of the dancing streetlamps. After a few hundred yards he stopped under an archway and put down the child. "It's all right," he said softly, "we'll be home soon." Katinka gave him a questioning look, a raindrop quivering on her long lash. "Home?" They waited for a streetcar.

The first week of September Mária said to Preisz: "Mother wants to see you." Sunday afternoon he bought ten carnations from the corner flower-seller. In a cobblestone street in the ninth district he found the ancient, noisy tenement: he walked up the filthy stairs. Mária opened the door. In a dark corner a rawboned though barely gray old woman coughed asthmatically. Preisz kissed her veiny hand. The old woman looked at him; her gaze, though lusterless, was sharp and penetrating. "Give our guest some wine," she said. Mária turned pale. "Mother, he's not a guest." The old woman didn't answer, just reached for the jug of wine standing by the cupboard, put it on the table, and filled three glasses to the brim. Her hand trembled and her face also revealed excitement. "Not long ago," she began, "on Jóska's birthday, we turned on the radio and he danced with my daughter. You are the second groom here... I don't know about such things. I've lived with my husband for forty-two years, and I never looked for another man."

He was shocked, and his thoughts scattered. He looked for them on the embroidered sampler hung on the wall, on the scrubbed kitchen floor, on Mária's white face. He fixed his gaze on her prying eyes and said in a hollow voice, "I didn't mean to hurt anyone."

They kept looking at each other with a hard, expectant look. The old woman reached for her glass, then broke down and cried. He said good-bye quietly and waited for Mária in the dark stairway. They stood under the lamp, in the dim light, like two outcasts. "There are only the three of us now," he said softly, "Katinka, you and I." The woman nodded silently.

December rolled around. In the quiet café warmed by an old tile stove, Katinka asked for a baby carriage, a sleeping doll and a handbag. "We'll see," Preisz said. He kissed her sweet-smelling little head, ordered a portion of chestnut puree for her, and told her about a fairyland where a very stern-looking bird in a silver coat sits at the gate and withholds the lunch subsidy from anyone who is late. Katinka laughed. "Daddy is never late. He shaves early in the morning." Mária patted her on the head. "Eat, darling," she said. They talked about the divorce proceeding.

The weather turned bitter. There was still no news from Kendur; he didn't send for the child. Mária had bad dreams. Preisz saw how scared she was. A few days before the holidays he poured himself a glass of beer, drank it, and looked at her. "I'll try to find him tomorrow," he told her. Mária smiled at him gratefully, held out her hand, but the anxiety didn't lift from her face.

The next day Kendur called her on the telephone; he asked to see her one more time, privately. His voice was calm, almost apathetic. She was overcome with fear. She put down the receiver and just stood there, anxious as ever.

Her eyes were red from crying when Preisz met her in the café. He turned pale with anger "What does he want then? Haunt me for the rest of my life? He's not a cripple, he's not deformed, why does he play the martyr?"

Mária answered quietly, "He didn't get over it yet; it still hurts." He lit a cigarette and eyed her suspiciously from across the table. "Do you love him?" he suddenly asked. She looked into his eyes and grew pensive. "In a way I always thought of him as a son," she said. "I even told him at times that I had two children." With a far-away look in her eyes, she began to smile, and tidied a few strands of hair around her temples. "See, I am turning gray," she said, laughing quietly. "The bride is turning gray." He just stared at her fragile, girlish figure. "I can't live without you: not for a single minute." And he kissed her hand.

They went to the meeting together. Kendur sat in a corner. He had a new suit on. He helped Mária with her coat, shook hands with Preisz, and ordered three brandies. He told them he was a busdriver now on an intercity line and was rarely home. He made as much as 2,800 a month.

The waiter brought them their drinks, they clinked glasses. Preisz's hands were shaking; he looked around, embarrassed, but no one noticed. Kendur emptied his glass at once, took a sip of seltzer water, and for a few minutes drummed the table absently with his ring finger. "I'll be working Christmas Eve," he said, just to say something. "Why did you want to see me?" she asked. He thought about the answer, stole a glance at Preisz, and almost imperceptibly shrugged his shoulder. "Don't know myself. It's hard to believe that my child will be raised without me." "She won't be raised without you," Mária said. "You can have her any time you wish, we settled this already." "I thought it's worth discussing a little more," he countered, "being that she is our child."

This time she answered somewhat impatiently, "Katinka loves you. And she'll go on loving you, we'll make sure of that." Preisz hurriedly asked for three more brandies. Mária didn't want him to, but Kendur agreed with Preisz that it couldn't hurt. "Your mother all right?" she asked Kendur. After seeing her husband nod, she continued: "I always liked her, you know; I never hurt her feelings. Please ask her not to spread filth about me. She went to the factory and called me all sorts of names."

Kendur didn't know about this and was clearly annoyed. "That's dumb," he said. "I'll have a talk with her." "Dumb and unnecessary," Preisz offered. Kendur took another drink, put down his glass and moved it away. "You mustn't be angry," he said with gentle irony. "Try to be more understanding. My mother is old, you have to consider her point of view." He looked at his wife, with an ugly smile this time. "Her only son was kicked in the rear, her grandchild taken away... She prays at night, and asks God for cruel retribution." He called over the waiter and paid for the drinks.

A biting wind blew on Mester utca. They shivered as they looked at the shine on each other's face. Preisz glanced up at the green neon letters. "It makes you look pale," he said quietly. Kendur bowed and walked away in silence.

The morning before Christmas it began to snow and didn't stop until noon the following day. Preisz bought himself a new shirt, went to the barber, and got his dark suit out of hock. He made sure he was all set for Christmas Eve. And although Mária promised that the family would be more than happy to see him, he stopped in at a pub and downed two shots of cherry brandy. He got there early: the family was still sitting in the kitchen. The old woman had an awful cough and was groping for her medicine in the kitchen scale's dish. Everyone knew, including her, that one bad night she was going to choke to death, but she wasn't afraid of that. She kept her intelligent eyes on her grandchildren.

A four-year-old boy stood on tiptoes by the door, his little legs shaking. Katinka, in a flutter herself, pulled him away from the keyhole. "Did you see Little Jesus?" she asked. "I did." "How did he look?" The little boy thought hard about this, knitting his brows in concentration. "He's black," he said. "Black?" Katinka opened her eyes wide. She looked at her mother, but she was busy pouring drinks into skinny little glasses. She touched Preisz's glass with hers, they both laughed and kissed. At this moment he caught the old woman's glance. He wanted to say something, lest the others think he was afraid of that placid pair of eyes, but he just shrugged his shoulder. Though annoyed, he couldn't wipe the awkward smile off his face. The old woman kept staring at him; wrinkles fluttered around her mouth. "In our house, you are at home, son," she said.

They drank. The old woman put down her glass, and with sudden anger shook her bony fist, banged on the table, and in a belligerent voice, almost without melody, she began, "On the blessed birth of our Lord Jesus..." It was addressed to the sinners, her husband in particular, who one spring evening sneaked drunken into Jolánka's house. On the second day of Easter the woman next door blabbed out their shameful secret, and now, twenty years later, there still lurked in the voice of the old carpenter's helper the eternal guilt for what he had done. He cried out, excited, alarmed: "Just a minute! Just a minute! Somebody poured water on the sparklers."

Preisz's eyes were hazy from all the liquor. He talked about his enemies, maintaining indignantly that you can't live in a lie. He was arguing with himself, loudly, ramblingly. "I have a right to be happy. They can spit on me, tell me anything they like, but I am not giving her up; while I am still alive, I tell you, I am not giving her up." His face turned a sickly green, his hair hung down over his forehead. A frightened Katinka watched him from a dark corner near the cupboard. Preisz's devotion to the family was best understood by the old woman, for she, too, had grown up without a family.

Every second Saturday Kendur sent her widowed mother to pick up Katinka, and Sunday before dark she brought her back. While there, she would chatter away, show off her fur-lined boots, complain about her kidneys. Only the look in her eye told a different story—lurking in those sleepy eyes was helpless rage, and hate.

Preisz negotiated lawyers. One of them asked for 3,000 forints, another wanted 3,500. They expected it to be a difficult case. The old woman was furious, called the lawyers crooks and highwaymen, and said she would not allow good money to be thrown away. The old carpenter's helper had a different view on the matter. He felt Jóska didn't want a divorce and would insist on keeping Katinka. There was sure to be a hassle over child support and various other complications, for which they would definitely need a lawyer. Preisz agreed with him, while Mária sided with her mother. They argued for a long time. Katinka got sleepy, began to cry, and told Preisz to go home already. He kissed her and returned to his rented room.

The new television set caused quite a surprise. On March 17, the old woman's birthday, at eight o'clock in the evening, delivery men arrived with the set. Preisz signed the receipt, gave the men a twenty-forint tip, made room for the walnut-coloured box, pulled out the indoor aerial, and winked mischievously at Mária—their little plot had worked. He turned off the light. They heard the strains of waltz, ice dancers glid across the screen, and the two old-timers, holding hands, watched. A bluish light fell on their startled faces.

It was a lovely evening. Later, in his solitude, when he had trouble falling asleep, Preisz picked it out of all his memories and contemplated his once happy self.

At the end of March, they worked feverishly for hours on end composing their arguments, building up their case. Afterwards they would just sit around in the kitchen. Preisz would talk, Mária would listen and giggle softly. Every now and then they would kiss, their eyes aglow with restlessness, like those of patients getting ready for an operation.

They asked Kendur for a meeting. They waited for him at the City Gate café. He showed up in his busdriver uniform and didn't even look at the handwritten sheet of paper presented to him. He said they could say anything they liked about him, he'd accept it unread. He and Mária had lived together for six years, after all—he had no desire to play dirty now. All he was asking for was that after the divorce went through they burn all those papers, so that Katinka wouldn't read untrue things about her father. Mária understood. They were quiet for a while; Preisz lit a cigarette. "Naturally, I will take care of all the expenses," he said. He picked up the check too. A few stars began to twinkle over Calvin Square by the time they were ready to say good-bye. Mária wanted to say one more thing to him, but her bow-legged husband disappeared in the crowd.

The warmer days were followed by warmer nights. Katinka now played with the front door open. Sometimes she would bashfully ask Preisz to go out in the hall, and then she'd ask for the chamberpot. But she didn't make anything, just gabbed with her mother. Actually, she did this quite often. The old woman was of the opinion that it wouldn't hurt to give the sensitive young lady a good spanking, and as a matter of fact it wouldn't hurt Kendur either, because obviously he was egging her on. "Jóska is no heel," Mária said. "When we'll be together, living under the same roof, she'll be all right." She put Katinka to bed and snuggled up to her for a little while herself. Then she came back to the kitchen and opened a bottle of cherry brandy. They planned the wedding for August. Mária thought they might go to Hajdúszoboszló afterwards. All she wanted was some peace and quiet.

During the first hearing the judge decided to question Kendur's younger brother and the widow Mrs. Antal Kendur. He also asked the woman seeking the divorce to name her witnesses. After a few moments of anxious reflection, she named her sister and Ferenc Preisz.

In the shop rumour had it that they broke off. It wasn't true, they loved each other. The city became their home: during their long walks fresh dreams were born. And after midnight, when the streetlights dimmed, the glimmering pearls seemed to nod at them; the first ray of dawn also welcomed them. And when it did, they kissed.

Who knows how a rumour gets started? But it does, and goes round and round. It swells and becomes colourful, like a soap bubble. Grown-ups like to spread them—it's their game. Little Rotyi was firmly convinced, and tried to prove to everyone, that the bow-legged Kendur was waiting for her unhappy blonde wife to come back. Lajos Stanec laughed off this absurd contention. The red-haired Gróf felt, on the other hand, that it didn't pay to guess what was going to happen—with lovers anything was possible, even death. Hábetler felt sorry for the kid. The girls at work cursed the pharisee, that scoundrel, and secretly tried to catch his glance as he stood by his radiant machine. They felt that the piercing May sunlight made him look older. Katinka's growing hostility was also a warning signal. Preisz felt he was in Kendur's hand, and he knew that that hand, if bent on getting even, would be clenched into a tight fist.

A few days before the second hearing he went to see Sándor

Ruzsó. What he had to say was brief: he wanted a flat of his own. He sat down in an armchair and lit a cigarette. His words filled the room with restlessness and fear. He couldn't account for his fit of candour. Maybe it was the quiet in the room that brought it out, or the unusual sparkle of the pretty crystal vase on the table. Or the barely moving pair of eyes that was now fixed on him. He talked about things that were likely to happen, though he didn't stress any one scenario, indicating thereby that he wasn't really troubled by guilt. He trod on a well-worn path: what he said was said many times before him by others. Take yesterday, for instance. Katinka unexpectedly announced that her mother's name was Mrs. József Kendur, and that's what it would always be. The old woman kept cursing and said they should hire a lawyer at once. He himself sized up the situation more objectively—the prospects were not rosy. With Ruzsó now he sometimes got confused and repeated himself. Thoughts flashed in his mind, and swirled and collided and merged. They grew large like rain clouds. Ruzsó listened with growing sympathy. With his talk of TV sets and children's toys, the exhausted, grimly determined young man tried to prove to himself, to all the world, that he did indeed have a right to some happiness. He had been living in his dreams, and his torments barely left a mark on his soul, which, come to think of it, may not even be that unusual. But now that suffering became more real, threatening him with renewed force, he felt the gravity of the struggle.

He didn't use big words; he prepared for the coming battle with the unyielding obstinacy of a Jesuit. He said he would give up his right to ask for child support. For Kendur this would mean a saving of four hundred forints a month for ten years. He hoped Kendur would get the message and leave them alone. In his heart of hearts he believed that they could avoid an unnecessary, and probably bloody scuffle this way. Responding to Ruzsó's comment, he admitted that coming to blows would solve nothing. But the truth was that his patience was wearing thin. The rumours floating about didn't really concern him. He knew that his housing request would not be signed by the shop steward or by the local party secretary; it would not be supported by the department of social services either. Yet he talked about his future home with the calm self-confidence of an accomplished lathe operator. He wanted modern-looking steel-tube furniture for his new flat and a healthy corn plant to go under the window. He pondered his chances at the trial. He didn't feel much pity for Kendur. When love is gone, he said, both parties are to blame.

They talked for a long time. When they said good-bye, they both thought that their talk would make a difference in the way their lives, the lives of all four of them, were going to turn out. Well, it didn't make much difference. Ruzsó did actually get Preisz his flat, though not without a hard fight. When the factory bulletin listed Preisz's name among the happy new apartment owners, the people in the cutting shop said it was an outrage. Pál Schnirer, however, disagreed. In fact he went as far as stopping Ruzsó and telling him that Preisz did not commit a transgression; their love stood every test, he said, and to support it was the decent thing to do. With that he shook Ruzsó's hand, and with an embarrassed, forced laugh disappeared in the bend of the narrow corridor outside the office.

Before the first snowfall of the year, Sándor Ruzsó confronted Schnirer, and sarcastically, bitterly demanded an explanation for that absurd statement of his. And then, Pál Schnirer, this sternly religious man, this active churchgoer, took full responsibility for what he had said, and surprisingly enough, despite the Bible and all, proved the validity of his position with frighteningly rational arguments.

They got through with Kendur fairly quickly, in less than a half hour in fact. Preisz presented his proposal in a cautious and pretty clumsy manner, so Mária quickly took over from him. Somewhat snappishly, she declared that no power on earth could separate them now. And if the law decided against them, they were just going to live together. Kendur was a little taken aback, and in a sincere voice though with a tiny smile he tried to impress it on them that he had no intention of throwing obstacles in the way of their happiness. He didn't mention Preisz's proposition, and again asked them for just one thing: not to talk about him in front of the child. The last time he saw her, he told them, she cried and said, "You are all alone because you don't love Mommy any more." After a brief silence Mária answered him quietly, "We never talk about you." Kendur acknowledged this with a nod, put out his cigarette, shook hands with them, and left. The two of them stayed a while longer in the beer garden.

This meeting took place in the middle of June, the day before the second hearing. Kendur kept his promise. On the tenth of September, at two p.m., the court dissolved the marriage. The two of them descended the stairs in solemn silence, and even in the streetcar spoke little. On Haller Square, they sat down on a bench. The sun still showed its strength: the tarboard top of the vendors' stalls glistened. The rings creaked on a nearby swing set. Mária didn't take her eyes off her man. "I am a single girl again," she said. "If you abandon me now, my chances of getting married are ruined." They both laughed at this.

Thirty days later the court's decision became final. Preisz took out loans. They bought bedding and steel-tube furniture, and they told Katinka that pretty soon mommy will have a new name. She didn't ask any questions. She got a slide projector and film strips from her father, and these kept her busy. But when Preisz left the house, and mother and daughter slipped under the covers, Katinka very quietly told her mother the big secret: It was Aunt Erzsike who bought her the films. Aunt Erzsike taught small children, she went swimming with Daddy, and she had long brown hair. But she quickly added, "You are much prettier, Mommy." Mária smiled and caressed her face in the dark. She felt it was wet. She rocked her to sleep with soothing words, and she too fell asleep, holding the child in her arm.

Preisz found himself in a tight spot. The family, but mainly the old woman, turned on him; they wanted to know why he was willing to sign away the money that was Katinka's due. He answered angrily: He didn't feel like taking Kendur for a ride. If two people couldn't support a child, he said, they might as well hang themselves. This time not even Mária took his side, but very persuasively defended the child's interest, arguing that he didn't have the right to deprive Katinka—they could have put those monthly payments in the bank. Besides, the fact that the divorce proceedings went off without a hitch had nothing to do with Kendur. They had the long-haired Erzsike to thank for that.

The wedding took place on the fifteenth of October, but their vacation started the day before. That morning Mária stood by the tub and washed till noon. The old woman bought four chickens for the big day. Tied to a short piece of string, they toddled about in the kitchen. Katinka pestered them with a pencil. She was bored. In the afternoon Preisz arrived. In a playful mood, he kissed the little girl's hand, called Mária Mrs. Preisz, wrung out the clothes, and together they hung them on the clothes line. Then the three of them went out for a walk. They never once talked about this walk afterwards.

An uninvited guest—silence—moved into the bright new flat with them. The cold weather had already banished the fleshy corn plant from their window when Preisz realized that he would not be able to get rid of this silent tenant. He sat in an easy chair with his legs crossed, motionless, and kept rolling in his mind the memory of that autumn afternoon. He was struck by a silly, absurd notion: maybe it was all a dream.

The day was lovely, memorably so. It was on the leaf-strewn Mester utca that Preisz came face to face with hate. He didn't even defend himself, no angry words left his lips, he acted as his tired soul bade him. Now his imagination rang with every word uttered that afternoon. He saw Katinka's pitiful face, every twitch on that face, even the slightest. He saw her drawing away from them, leaning against the wall in front of the barber shop and looking at them in a way that made Mária break into quiet, queer-sounding sobs. They returned home timidly, in silence, avoiding each other's eyes in the fading sunlight. In the stairway scribbled all over with chalk Katinka again begged them to let her go back to her father. With her new patent leather shoes she began kicking the railing, threatening to tell everything and never coming back. Mária kept pulling her, dragging her by force, her chest heaved, her face broke out in a sweat by the time they reached the third floor.

She hit the girl with the flat of her hand. The sound of every slap could be heard out in the kitchen. "What's that you will tell?" she demanded. "Everything I know... everything." "What, what will you tell?" They were screaming in a high-pitched, reedy voice. The others closed the kitchen door; the plain cotton curtain let in little light, but they didn't turn on the electrity. The old woman put some still-warm cookies on the table, and they ate them carefully, over an earthenware dish. Then she curled up again in her nook by the cupboard, coughed a little, and said to Preisz, "When you pick up the television, be sure to take a taxi." Later, the hysterical screaming abated, the smacks stopped resounding. Katinka now sobbed with heart-rending anguish. Then she too quieted down. At this point the others walked into the room. Mária sat on the sofa, deathly pale, her lips quivering, repeating the same question in a whisper. "What's that you will tell?" Katinka just stood there, staring at her stiffly. There was no longer hatred in her eyes, or reproach, only emptiness.

They were married at city hall. A few weeks later, without Mária knowing about it, Preisz returned the child support money to Kendur. They met in a tavern. Kendur ordered a spritzer; he was sleepy, his eyes bloodshot. He cursed the weather, the slick roads. Then fell silent. They sat facing each other. Later, Preisz looked up, as though about to say something. Perhaps he only wanted to catch the other's glance; he couldn't open his mouth, so he just looked away, dispirited. They drank their wine and slowly headed for the door.

It was a cold, sightless night. In front of the tavern a single, fixed beam of light cut through the dense winter fog.

Translated by Ivan Sanders

GOD IN THE WAGON

by FERENC SÁNTA

When the peasant had almost reached the top of the hill, he looked back and saw an old man in his wagon. The peasant was heading home alone and hadn't picked up anyone along the way. And yet, there sat the old man, his back draped against the side of the wagon, his legs stretched out, a bag in his lap.

"Well now!" the peasant said. Leaning on the seat with his hand, he turned around. "How did you get into my wagon?"

The old man—shapeless heavy shoes on his feet, a billed cap on his head like the kind worn mostly by workers, a white villager's shirt with two buttons at the neck, a gray, shabby coat thrown over his shoulders—raised his eyes, calmly looked him over from head to foot, and then turned away without a word and gazed listlessly at the bushes running along the side of the road and at the green cornfield behind them.

The peasant raised his voice. "I'm talking to you, grandpa!"

At this moment the horses crossed over the top of the hill, and reaching the decline, they broke into a run. The peasant grabbed for the reins, pulled them into his stomach with both hands, and then bending sideways—and meanwhile calming the horses—he tightened the brake on the wheel. The horses slowed down, and the wagon followed them, creaking and groaning. The peasant turned around—the wagon was empty, the old man had disappeared just as if he had never been there.

"What the...!" The peasant looked around. Silence was everywhere, birds flitted about in the sky, butterflies fluttered above the bushes, the whole area was at peace, and there wasn't a trace of the old man as far as the eye could see. The peasant peered at the empty wagon, arched his eyebrows, then spat on the road and turned to his horses again.

"Come on. Easy now."

The horses descended the hill, cantered on the level road, and then ambled. The peasant heard a little thud and then the wagon side creaking. He turned around: there was the old man with his bag in his lap, stretching his arms high and yawning mightily with his eyes closed. "Hey!" he shouted at the old man.

He grabbed for his whip, took the reins in his other hand, leaned on the seat again with his hand, and turned all the way around.

"Why are you playing jokes on me!"

At that moment—exactly as before—the horses, crossing over a hill, broke into a run. The wagon rattled and jolted downhill. The peasant hardly had time to turn around and grab the reins and tighten the brake.

"Whoa! Whoa!"

By the time he turned to the back of the wagon the old man had disappeared again. Not a soul was near, not a rustle in the bushes, not a crackle in the corn. The old man was gone just as if he had never been there.

"I'll be damned!" The peasant looked around. He blinked his eyes rapidly, pushed his hat back on his head with his finger, and rising from the seat and leaning on both his hands, he glanced around the area.

"I must be losing my mind," he said, looking at the empty wagon.

When the wagon had crossed the flat land and reached another hill, the peasant jumped off, hung the reins on his arm, took the whip into his hand, and pulled his hat down over his forehead. He trod alongside the wagon and didn't look back, but his eyes darted around the area and he held the whip firmly.

The horses began climbing the hill. They had barely started up the hillside when from the back of the wagon came the sounds of stirring and a weak, weary sigh like that made by someone settling down in a comfortable place.

The peasant's eyes opened wide, then he shut them.

"I'm crazy, I'm sure I must be crazy," he said, and stopped. The reins jerked on his arms, the horses took a couple more steps, then stopped. The wagon rolled on a little, the harness tightening on the horses.

"I must be crazy," the peasant repeated. He turned around very slowly, and when he came face to face with the wagon, he cautiously opened his eyes.

The old man was sitting in the same place; the bag in his lap, some bread atop it, and a small piece in his hand. He was having a little snack and gazing at the peasant very placidly. His feet peeped out of the wagon, and the stripes of his white foot-cloth could be seen above his shoes and above them his gray, frayed trousers.

"Damn it!" said the peasant in a dry, choked voice.

"Be careful now!" said the old man. He broke off another piece of bread and put it into his mouth. He blinked at the peasant, then turned away, and calmly gazed ahead with the tranquil mien of old men. His face was full and fine but brown like that of a man who walks in the sun. The bones were strong and hard, and stretched his skin smooth, and the corners of his eyes were embellished with delicate wrinkles. His mouth was as gentle as a child's, but its corners were marked by two very deep, strong lines as if someone had engraved them there. His forehead was high and furrowed, his hands were large and corded with veins like a peasant's.

He looked up. "May we go on?"

The peasant hung the reins on their hook.

"I asked you to tell me who you are!"

The old man sighed and put the left-over bread into his bag.

"No, you didn't."

"Then I ask you now. Who are you?"

The old man tied up his bag and set it carefully on the plank beside him. Then he looked at the peasant and said:

"I am God."

He rested his eyes on the peasant for a little while, then turned his face toward the sun and closed his eyes.

"Let's go on."

The peasant's mouth hung open. He stared at the old man. Then he pushed his hat back on his head, wiped his moustache, and gripping his whip, stepped to the side of the wagon. He leaned against it. He closed one eye and said quietly, "I don't mean to hurt your feelings, but would you mind repeating that?"

He dangled the whip inside the wagon, alongside the old man.

"I would be glad to," said the old man, continuing to hold his face to the sun. "I am God."

"I see!" said the peasant.

"That's the way it is," the old man said.

"Really? ...God?"

"Yes."

"The Lord God?"

"I am called that too," the old man replied.

The peasant rested his chin on his arm—his arm was resting on the side of the wagon—and his eyes flashed. His face flushed with amusement, and he said quietly, emphasizing each word, "Well now, that's something! But...if you are God, then who do you think I am?"

The old man opened his eyes. He turned sideways slightly, and glanced at the peasant, then turned back and closed his eyes again.

"You are... Ferenc Sánta."

"Well!" The peasant stuck his chin out.

"Aren't you?"

The peasant turned pale.

"How did you know?"

"I told you. I am God."

"God?"

"God."

The peasant bent over the side of the wagon, pushed his face all the way into the old man's, then pulled it back and stared intently at him.

"You aren't from around here," he said, looking at him with ever-widening eyes.

"Can't we go on?" asked the old man.

The peasant stepped back, closed his eyes for a moment, then looked at the old man.

"Well, as I'm concerned..."

He shrugged, and looking doubtfully over his shoulders at the old man, took the reins in his hand and still glancing back, got into the wagon. He whipped the horses. The wagon lurched onward.

"One of us is lying," he thought, "either he or I; one of us has gone crazy today. How did he know my name if I never saw him before? I am positive I never saw him. He's not from around here as sure as I am sitting here in this wagon!"

"Wouldn't you like to sit up front?" He turned around. "You know, when the wagon starts downhill, it shakes very hard, and I don't think that will do you any good."

The old man didn't look up. "You are right. But I'd rather go to the bottom of the hill and wait for you to come down."

"That's the way he disappeared before," thought the peasant, "and if I let him go ahead, I'll never know what kind of fellow he is because he might not come back."

"Please come and sit up here. I'll hold the horses back and we'll go down so smoothly, you'll think you are traveling on water. Come on, please."

The peasant stood up and began arranging the blanket, leaving most of it for the old man.

"Come, please!"

The old man got up, panting softly. He took the bag into his hand, climbed over the seat, and settled down beside the peasant.

"I like spring very much," the old man said.

"Yes," answered the peasant, stealing a look at him, "it is really beautiful. If only we had such weather all the time!"

"That can't be," the old man said.

"No?"

"No."

The peasant thought, "He speaks as if it were really up to him whether it can or not. Yet he is so dignified! I have never seen anyone so dignified. He talks so earnestly, and his voice is like a big bell, it fills a man. Maybe he really is God!"

He whipped the horses.

"Are you telling me the truth?"

"What do you mean?"

"You know, about being God."

The old man looked at him. His eyes were clear and very sad. "I am."

Then he looked away past the horses, and stared straight ahead as if he were alone; with no peasant, no wagon, no world around him.

"He is very sad," thought the peasant. "His eyes were so very sad when he looked into mine that deceit just doesn't go with it. But I'm smart enough to know I'm not crazy, so he must be lying!"

He took out his tin case and rolled a cigarette for himself. He lit it and blew out the first puff. Meanwhile he stole glances at the old man. Then he hung the reins on the wheel-fork, flung his leg on the seat, and faced him. "Listen to me!" he said.

"Yes."

"Do you see the road there ahead of us?"

"I do."

"Well, if you do, then listen closely to what I am saying. Make a big hole there for me, there on the road, and then make it level again so we can go ahead on it. Do you understand me?"

The old man lifted his head higher.

"A big hole?"

"Yes."

"Do you really want me to?"

"I do, what do you say?"

The old man turned his eyes to the peasant. They were brown, deep like the woods. He gazed into the peasant's eyes calmly, wearily.

"Suit yourself!"

Raising his eyes above the horses, he cast his look at the road. "Is this what you had in mind?"

Twenty or twenty-five meters ahead of the horses the ground tore open with a horrendous crack. The banks receded, the road-side trees and bushes vanished one by one into the yawning pit. A tall oak leaned on its side for an instant, and then, with crackling branches, quivering top, and roots rising high, it toppled over. Up ahead the hillside whined and groaned, shattered, then disappeared in a single massive landslide, leaving only a void.

"Is this what you had in mind?" the old man asked again.

"Close it up quick!" shouted the peasant. He was hanging on to the side of the wagon with both hands, his ears were filled with the endless, vast thundering and rumbling of the soil and the air. "Quick! Close it up quick!"

"Is this what you had in mind?"

"Yes, but hurry, close it up!"

"So be it," the old man said, and by the time the peasant got the frightened horses under control, everything was growing again in its place, the sun was sprinkling its brilliance on the white road, and farther on, the hill grew tranquilly verdant.

"Can we get going now?" asked the old man.

The peasant jumped off the wagon and ran to the horses, shushed and patted them. Meanwhile he gazed at the old man. He wiped his brow with his arm, adjusted the harness, and finally returned to the wagon. A slight, flickering smile appeared on his lips and slowly spread to his whole face as he took off his hat. He smoothed his hair down with his palm and said, "Don't be angry. I didn't mean to offend you."

"That's all right," the old man said. "Sit down and let's get going."

The peasant put his hat back on, and as he picked up the reins, he said, "I didn't think you looked like this. You are just like the old people around here. You look just like them!"

"Let's go," the old man said.

The peasant climbed into the wagon, sat down a bit farther to the side of the seat, and called out to the horses, "Giddyup! Giddyup!" He looked at the old man, sitting there beside him, his head sagging, his eyes closed. His coat—an old, tattered thing—hung loose on his shoulders, the bag was in his lap, and his large brown, veined hands were resting on it.

"Do you know my grandfather?"

"What?"

"I asked if you know my grandfather. He died a long time ago, when I was a boy."

"Yes, I know him. I like him very much."

"You do? Well, we didn't notice that very much."

"It doesn't matter."

"What doesn't matter?"

"Nothing. Nothing matters!"

"You think so?"

"Yes!"

Leaning his elbows on his knees—his chin on his palms—the old man stared ahead at the ground running under the wagon. The pressure of his hands wrinkled his face, his eyes were contracted by the crowding skin. His shoulders were tilted high and forward, his brown neck was also deeply engraved by furrows, his gray hair was tousled on his coat collar.

"He is very sad," thought the peasant, "but he is not as old as one might think. With this kind of build our old people still hoe the fields, and most of them still work with the scythe."

The old man was looking straight ahead with half-lowered eyes, above the horses' heads. He had taken his hands from his face, and his chin was resting on his chest. His hands were folded on the bag. His back bent forward, and his whole frame had shrunk in size. The peasant whipped the horses to a canter and just took in the surroundings bathed in sunlight. A small breeze was stirring, swallows were flitting about, a sparrow took flight from the dusty road, and silence reigned everywhere.

"Ferenc!" The sound seemed to come from his side.

"Right here!"

The old man didn't move his head, he continued to stare straight ahead with bent, sagging face.

"Ferenc!"

"Yes!"

"You have two rooms, don't you."

"I do."

"I should like to sleep in one of them tonight. In the morning I'll move on."

The old man glanced at the peasant. His eyes flickered. First he looked into the peasant's eyes, then at his face, and next at his gray shirt. He reached up and buttoned the two collar buttons of his white shirt. Then he slowly turned back, raised his hand and looked into his palm the way mostly old peasants have the habit of doing.

"Just until morning. Then I'll move on. Just for tonight."

The peasant pulled back on the reins until the horses were moving very slowly. Then he hung the reins up, took out his tin case, opened it, got a cigarette paper, and sprinkled some tobacco on it. He snapped the lid of the tin box shut and straightened himself up and put it back into his pocket. Then he said, "You...you can stay with me as long as you like." He took out a match, lit up, and throwing the match away, he shouted at the horses, "Get going!"

The wagon began to rattle, and thin, small clouds of dust fluttered high in its track. He asked the old man calmly, "Have you been gone a long time?"

"No, not very."

"You see, I hadn't noticed you'd left."

"It doesn't matter. You weren't the only one... No one else noticed either."

"That's the way it is."

The old man waved him away gently and closed his eyes. He bent his head to one side, almost to his shoulder. He held the bag firmly, gripping it with his fingers. The peasant glanced at him, moved closer to him, and supported the old man's shoulder, so to say.

"Listen, from now on we go straight home, and the wagon won't be jolting. I'll spread the blanket in back, and you can nap on it peacefully."

"Do you think so?"

"Just do as I say. You will think you are riding in a coach."

The old man stood up, pressing the bag into his lap. The peasant brought the horses to a halt, got into the back of the wagon, and arranged the blanket.

"Just lie down now."

He jumped out of the wagon and fixed the blanket through the slats. The old man stepped over the seat, and taking hold, went to the end of the wagon and slowly stretched out on the blanket. The peasant placed the bag under his head.

"Just a minute," he said. He took his coat off, and folding it, put it on the bag. "There! Now you'll really be comfortable."

He adjusted the coat carefully under the old man's head. Then he stood without saying anything on the road beside the wagon and watched him fall asleep. The sun touched the brown, furrowed face. The two furrows cast deep shadows around his mouth. Where the hard bones stretched the skin tight the sunlight shone with a tender, soft radiance. His eyelashes—under very tightly drawn eyebrows—threw soft shadows on his face.

"Rest peacefully," the peasant said, and gently, carefully, he covered the old man's chest with the lap of the coat, which had slipped off him. "We will fix you such a bed, a nest couldn't be better."

He got into the wagon. Holding the reins tight, he started the horses up as slowly as possible. He restrained them standing up, and sat down only when he saw they were ambling easily.

When they arrived at his place and pulled up in the courtyard, he jumped off the wagon. His wife was standing in the doorway. She came into the yard.

"Fix supper and prepare a bed in the room."

She stood looking at the old man in the wagon.

"And who is this?" she asked.

The peasant looked at his wife, then at the wagon. He shifted from foot to foot, hesitating. Then, pushing his hat forward, he took it off, to give him time to look here and there for a while. At last he said, "This... He is the Lord God Himself!"

His wife let out a loud laugh.

"Oh, you silly thing, you!" And because the old man had stood up in the wagon and was preparing to get down into the dusty yard, she turned to him and said, "Please come right in."

Translated by Albert Tezla

MOTHER IS DRESSING
by ERZSÉBET GALGÓCZI

The metallic clatter of the mail train, the cooing of the turtle doves in front of the window, the swaying street lights on the wall, joy cosing like blood in the head, under the ribs, around the belly—the old woman awoke to find herself still alive. Twice already had she been brought back to life by the doctor's injections in bright daylight: clean night shirt, identity card, soap, cutlery, glasses, ambulance, hospital—o, my God, never again! On leaving hospital she had been told to move about a great deal, even if she had to force herself, because resting in bed is death itself for someone of seventy-seven if she spends more time in it than on her feet.

She had been lying on the bed since seven the night before —and not the other way round—yet it was she who was crumpled, and not the bed. Her hands felt like sticks, the vertebrae were rusty at her waist and the blood faltered along the channels of her varicose veins. The bed was pulling her back, it would have had her float there till the end of time. It was as if she were dragging a full sack of wheat, this half turn towards the reading lamp. By the light of the opalescent bulb the corner of the room came to life: a tiled stove, a wardrobe half covering a door leading to the adjoining room, a scarlet rug by the bed with a footstool and shoes on it. On the bedside table under the small circle of light a book with glasses in it and next to it a lyre-shaped mahogany pendulum clock that had to be wound every eight days, without its glass; it did not matter where the hands pointed, for her it was good enough to set it by the mail train which passed at three every morning. Her engineer daughter had bought it for their golden wedding—it was the clock that reminded her of her husband every morning. She was no longer irritated as she was while he was alive, nor missed, as she did for one or two years after his death, the snoring, coughing, hurrumphing and catarrhal throat clearing from the other bed, to be followed immediately by the scraping of the match being struck and the stench of his first cigar. Her husband had been older by seven years. She did not want to count the years, but her grandchild, born on the very day of his death, skipping about from morning till night, was a constant reminder: she had so far outlived the deceased by six.

She balanced herself with her hands into a sitting position, dragged out her swollen feet from under the eiderdown, let them dangle and tried to draw the footstool nearer, but only her big toe could reach it. She raked her false teeth from under the pillow, removed the circular comb from her sparse knot and smoothed the scanty, knotted strands of hair. (After her second stroke she had called to her daughter-in-law: "My teeth...? The children...? My money...?") She had had a bath the evening before and in the clean night shirt and with her skin refreshed she felt almost well now, if only she were not so heavy, like so much mud.

She was the youngest of three hundred pilgrims when she went on a pilgrimage to Maria Zell at the age of seventeen. They marched barefoot under the gold-embroidered, deep fringed, shining banners and the crucifix; hymns welled up all along the long procession, undulating over the June meadows; the chant snaked to a different rhythm from that directed by the choirmaster, even the words were changed; it was neither the text nor the tune that evoked devotion, but the joy of forgetting oneself, singing as part of the multitude of people. On the carts which brought up the rear there were bundles containing provisions as well as the crippled, the epileptic, the aged and the footsore. She could still see the seven-spooled well; they camped there one afternoon, drank its water and washed their feet. When the gaping villagers only spoke German it was clear that they had left Hungary behind—Hungary still belonged to the Monarchy at the time. An Austrian innkeeper and his plump, sad-eyed wife wanted to adopt the late-August-born girl, this chit of a young thing, a barefoot little cricket, whom they had only seen for an evening. They were charmed by her nimbleness as she came and went, taking dinner to the weary-footed elderly. She often wondered, when she was burdened with cares, and one worry would bark awake seven others at night, what her life would have been like had she stayed with the innkeeper's family. The Mother of God embracing her Child in the church which rose on the summit of the awe-whispering mountain, the knee-bending gratitude, wonder, high clergy robed in rustling splendour, the dazzling vision of the church interior floating in incense and hallelujahs, like an enormous Christmas tree covered with a million candles warmed the memory and turned into an irrepressible wish to reach the true source, Jerusalem. The Holy Land!

She inched her way out of bed, leaned her palms against the tile stove, and shuddered with joy: it was warm. Her joints crackled like a cogwheel clogged with sand. The neatly folded clean clothes filled the shelves of the linen closet. She looked for underwear to go with her just-washed nightgown.

The old woman lived in one room and a kitchen, the rest of the house being occupied by her son and his family. It had been built with three rooms in the thirties—the largest in the street—her daughter-in-law, however, finding it small and impractically divided, had changed it beyond recognition as soon as she had felt sufficiently at home; had the old man come back to life he would not have been able to find his way home from the cemetery. For her a bathroom was also necessary and a pump costing twenty-five thousand forints because the village had no drainage. Now her daughter-in-law had taps in the kitchen, by the well and in the former stable, where the coal and oil were stored and the ducks fattened—only her own kitchen had no tap. "You can get your water from me, Mother," her daughter-in-law had said; after all, both kitchens opened on to the same veranda. But what for? The tap in the yard or in winter the one in the stable was good enough for her. In any case she was alone all day and even though her daughter-in-law had pointed out many times where she kept the keys she would never be able to bring herself to open a locked door. Why was the tap left out of her kitchen only? Of course, as soon as she dies they will be able to add this minute space to their room. She complained about this only to her eldest daughter who came to see her every week, laden with a sack packed with wine, pastry, smoked sausages and coconut chocolate. In one way or another her daughter-in-law had got wind of this, but was quite brazenly lying to her face. "But Mother, it was you who would not let us install the tap there. You were afraid you'd have to pitch in two thousand."

She sank down on the footstool and with a lengthy effort managed to pull up the chosen fleecy lined knickers she favoured over her varicose-swollen feet and well-fed hips which had preserved their man-teasing curve. Warming her back against the tiles she could forget herself on the footstool; it was only after her husband's death that she had had the courage to speak aloud of the dream that she had nursed for fifty-three years, since Maria Zell: the Holy Land! Since they had joined the co-operative and her dominion had shrunk to the flower garden in front of the window, she had taken up reading; her daughter-in-law, knowing of her longing for the world of the ancient Jews and early Christians, supplied her with the Bible, the *Jewish War, Ben Hur, Quo Vadis? Joseph and His Brethren, La Gerusalemme liberata,* half a dozen lives of Jesus by different authors, the *Catacombs of Rome*—so many emotional attack brought to the surface an obsession which had turned into a goal.

And what happened? Her daughters, sons-in-law, sons, grown-up grandchildren and daughters-in-law betrayed no shock, they neither rebuked her, nor waved deprecatingly: Israel? It was practically on the doorstep, and the travel agency would take care of everything. Mrs. Garam went by herself to Japan last year to see her son; she flew via Moscow and Vladivostok, and for a change decided to come back by a route she had not travelled yet, namely India and Turkey; although she only spoke Hungarian and that with a pronounced Tósziget-Csilizköz accent, nothing had happened to her, except when she lost her way in Budapest trying to get from Ferihegy Airport to the Eastern Railway Station. Her engineer daughter would have gone with her, the twenty thousand forints in her mother's savings account would have covered the expenses. Yet she had hesitated: her husband needed a tombstone. A new cemetery had been opened recently and although the first row had not yet been completed in the direction where the wood lies, her eldest daughter and son, as heirs to the family prestige, succeeded in having a second started for their father's. Her husband now lay at the head of the second row, directly in front of the mortuary, almost in a place of honour, where not just any monument would do. This was what she wanted to devote her twenty thousand to. And yet there they were, just an arm's length away, the Mount of Olives, the Sea of Galilee, the Temple in Jerusalem where the twelve-year-old child had spoken to the scribes, the tomb of the Virgin Mary... After many months' hesitation she still could not make up her mind until history did it for her: the Arab-Israeli war broke out.

Her son had vacuumed the rugs the day before, so the old woman shuffled to the window in her bare feet and looked into the November dawn. She was curious about the weather, about how many underpants, bodices, slips, skirts, vests, pullovers, coats and overcoats should swathe her sensitive body, but also noticed the plaintive cooing of the wild doves. It was she who told her grandchildren that the wild doves were mourning Christ—the poor man was killed, killed. The sound was coming from the top of the fine, tall pinetree standing in front of the window; she twisted her neck in vain, the street lamp revealed neither the nest not its inhabitants. What could they be wanting? Not food; just like with her hens, she took care of that with the maize.

She slipped down on the foot-stool, pulled on her black stockings and her fur-lined lace-up shoes. Her grandchildren never got tired of lacing and unlacing these big shoes. They pushed and shoved each other in their excitement, and got the laces so tangled up, it was more work untangling them than if they had not touched them in the first place. Her schoelaces seemed longer than a sleepless night. From time to time she went faint and pressed her back against the tiles.

The reading lamp lit up more of the room—had the darkness outside softened? Above the beds were two Munkácsy reproductions: *Christ before Pilate* and *Christ on the Mount of Olives*. She had bought them during the war for half a pig from a refugee lady from Transylvania; the lady's son, a major, had been drowned in the industrial canal the very next day. Before moving in, her daughter-in-law had had the two empty rooms whitewashed, without a frieze, so that she could decorate them with her own things. She put back those two works of art on the snow-white wall as a wedding present—after all she herself had received from her mother-in-law a Virgin Mary, and a Head of

Christ as well (the sunlight was eating away their colours in the loft). But, before the new bride had even changed her dress or the lorry finished unloading, she had taken down those pictures and brought them into her room. "Don't be offended, Mother, but I would go mad if my child had to stare from his cot at a man being whipped and crucified. He'll have enough time for suffering, for other people's too when he grows up."

And so she had hung the walls with fancy homespun, rugs, glazed plates, church etchings, gay calendars and Egyptian queens dangling on chains. She placed brick-red statuettes among the books. The shelves, laden with pots of cacti and vases, might crash down on the children's heads at any time. The old woman had thought that her daughter-in-law would forbid her to make the children kiss the blue-mantled Virgin Mary statue, or to tell them the story of Holy Christmas. But that did not come to pass. The children's capacity for stories was like the appetite of the man in the folk tale who could consume one hundred and twenty plum dumplings at a single sitting. The young woman complemented the tales their father remembered from his childhood with adaptations she found in books of collections from Hungary, Transylvania, Moldavia, the Bánát, Baranya and the Csallóköz, while their grandmother was free to recite the life, death and resurrection of Christ. "Go ahead, Mother," her daughter-in-law had said encouragingly. "I shan't be the one to deprive my children of the timeless values of culture. When magnificent creations such as Bach's *Passions,* Dante's *Commedia,* Leonardo's *Last Supper,* the churches of Lőcse and Bártfa or the *Confession of Saint Augustine* call out to them, I don't want them to stare back blankly, but to become their echoes, and meditate on them." They banished the Munkácsys. They never went to church. Who could understand these young people?

Groaning, the old woman struggled from the footstool and again rummaged in the wardrobe. She put on two warm petticoats and a shaggy white waistcoat over the yellow flannel night dress. She tied the strings of the petticoats tightly round her waist. Then she tottered to the window. The window of the house opposite was lit up, so it was already past four o'clock; Miska Süveges always left by the five o'clock train for the wagon factory.

Her gaze strayed to the ground. From the spring to the early frost she had been digging, setting out, hoeing, weeding and watering; and since they did not keep animals any longer, when the herd passed by and no one was looking she had often sneaked into the road to scoop up the cow dung and throw it over the fence to pamper her little garden with stolen manure. She had planted the pine fifteen years ago; there were evergreens for the edges and each season was hailed by a different kind of flower, from the March violet to the chrysanthemum. No garden in the whole village was richer, except Bözsi Sós's plantation of roses, carnations and gladioli, but those went by the bundle to the market on the back seat of the Skoda.

Several coffins were removed from the old to the new cemetery together with their tombstones, but none could be better than that of her husband, red marble, the finest work of the Pilis stonemason, a cross resting on a squat foundation stone. On the smooth plate, under her husband's name, was engraved, *"and his wife Gizella Ráckevi 1895–".*

There had been a singing in her ears for ten years, a kind of buzzing. Sometimes she could not even make out what people were shouting directly at her. All Saints' Day while she was arranging the wreaths on the grave, her engineer daughter had whispered to the elder one, "What a barbaric custom. She's fit, has never been ill, knows influenza only from hearsay, and yet has her name with her date of birth engraved on her tombstone as if only the final figures were needed to seal her fate." "What do you mean, barbaric?" exclaimed her fifty-year-old daughter, herself a grandmother. "You and I and she will die, as surely as the sun sets. Look round. Old women prepare for death just as they did for childbirth in their youth. Have you ever seen a young expectant mother who was not getting ready with swaddling clothes, nappies, little dresses and bonnets? Look around this graveyard. If the wife dies first, the husband's name is never carved on the cross. Only old women are pregnant with death, men never."

She squatted down once more on the footstool. The warm voice of a man filtered through the door which was hidden by the wardrobe. Although the words were not intelligible she knew that is was five o'clock, her son was up and had switched on the radio.

She hurried to extract her green and brown check flannel dress from the pile on the sofa; by the time the ringing tread of studded boot heels reached her door and the sharp raps reached her ears, she was already smoothing the stiff, thick material around her waist.

"Good morning, mother dear," and even the air resounded. "There was a frost last night."

At one time she also used to wake up the family with a weather report: "Every two froze into one during the night."

In his right hand a small bottle holding about a third of a pint, in the other a glass hardly bigger than a thimble; he poured it full spirits and offered it to his mother.

"Good morning," returned the old woman. She did not reach for the glass but arranged the dress over her hips and thighs. Her son placed the bottle on the carpet and squatted at her feet, one of his hands pulling down the hitched-up skirt at the back. "It's November. Why shouldn't the nights be frosty?"

She wetted her lips with the spirits and handed it back immediately. "Thank you." In hospital they had also ordered: no wine, no spirits.

Her son searched her face. No, it did not seem to be ready for the grave yet.

He drank up what his mother left.

"Mother dear, would you feed my ducks? They have not digested their last feed yet." His voice was like a flute.

How did her son know? He had not even had time to step out the house. Shining boots, grey breeches, light poloneck sweater, that was not how one dressed if one intended to go near ducks splashing about in the dirty stable.

"Of course I'll feed them." Her face was serious and serene. And immediately she began to look for her shawl. Her son turned lightly, "Goodbye, mother dear!" and she was pleased to have work to do. Her daughter-in-law also let her get on with jobs that demanded no hurry, but required skill and a great deal of trouble and could be done sitting down. She cracked the nuts for strudel, spent a week stoning the sour cherries for preserves, stirred the sugar and raspberries for two hours, plucked the slaughtered ducks, put blue patches on the knees of children's red

track suits and red ones on the blue, boned the chops with match-
less skill, sorted the potatoes for sowing, husked the maize for the
squawking mob of chickens, threw the wormy plums and
overripe apricots into the starting tub, picked peas for soup, banished mud from ten pairs of shoes; sometimes did things on her
own with exasperating, disastrous results. Her daughter-in-law
had scattered grass seed over the yard; to her it appeared to have
become overgrown with weeds, and remembering the Hungarian
curse: may God give you a weedy yard and a bad neighbour—she
got a hoe and flung herself into the work. Her daughter-in-law
recoiled at the sight: her crippled mother-in-law sweating
profusely added nothing to her good humour. "But Mother, grass
is no longer a sign of poverty." The old woman thought it over,
went out to buy seed and after the first shower sowed it surrepti-
tiously. The others thought the grass, which had been imperfectly
hoed out, had simply recovered by itself.

With an apron over her warm clothes and thick scarf on her
head, she went again to the window. She opened it to see if she
would need any more clothing for feeding the ducks. The turtle
dove was cooing on top the pine while its mate paced and
searched among the dying flowers. "You little fool! You don't
think there are still worms there? The earth is frozen now." The
bird listened attentively to his mighty patroness, who to him was
as much part of the yard as the well was. The patroness also knew
that they were unmistakably hers, no matter how many other
birds raided the yard. Just as she could pick out her own broom,
preserving pan, clothesline, basket or flower pot from among a
hundred others: she was in touch with all organic and inorganic
beings and things in the house, drawers, barn, yard, and in the
small and large garden. Her daughter-in-law had once even
remarked, "Mother can tell her own rainwater from others."

One Sunday, as she was sitting here on the footstool, lacking
courage to switch on the light so early, she heard her engineer
daughter's faltering voice from behind the halfhidden door: "I've
been home for a week now and see that mother takes three whole
hours to get dressed every morning. I wonder if there has ever
been a time in my life, whether at seventeen, thirty or forty, when
I would have put up with this three-hour torture every day, this

self-resurrection each morning, merely for the sake of keeping alive. Never! We are nothing but shoddy copies of Mother. She is the original."

"Life is never *merely,*" the old woman muttered; she put on her greasy but back-and-waist-protecting fur-lined jacket, went out, looked about her on the stairs and became at one with herself again. The great acacia tree, higher than the draw-well, the chimney or the television aerial, had been the reference point of her dominion, defining the space. Its vast crown gave ample shade to the yard, which was the size of a football pitch. For fifty-eight years she had been able to forecast the weather from the trembling of its branches. The shock reverberated through her like a siren: the great acacia was gone! Even fifty-eight years ago when she herself had come to live here, with her mother-in-law, it had been the great acacia and not just any tree in the backyard. Now it came back to her: her son felled the half-dead tree last Sunday; then the electric saw cut it up for two whole days, and its logs took up half the barn. In three of its hollows they found birds' eggs, desiccated nuts, a small pair of rusty scissors, a copper curtain ring, and in the fork of the thigh-thick branches over the barn, there was a pigeon's nest as big as a plate.

See, the homeless pair of birds now live there, and one can see they would spend the winter in the pine in the small garden, but what would they make their nest of? Since the threshing of the corn had been done by combines the birds had not been able to find a single intact blade straw either on the threshing floor or the road or even among the sweepings in the ditch. That was why they complained all the time. It looked, though, as if there were a few scraps of straw under the disused, decaying cart that even the co-operative had no use for in one corner of the barn. Her son did not overlook any rubbish, but luckily the handle of the broom did not reach there. Wearily she got down on her knees, groveled under the cart, pressed in further and further, and with her fingers raked together a handful of long, shiny, crisp straw. She slipped out into the flower garden, placed the straw carefully under the whispering pine, moved back and lingered until one of the birds swooped down to pick up a straw.

Translated by Peter Szente

THE GREAT ADVENTURE
by ISTVÁN GÁLL

Two men lean close in the underground passage and whisper.

"Password?"

"The Great Adventure."

"Time?"

"This afternoon."

"Place?"

"Lujza Blaha, bottom-view."

The chubbier one with the beard can't keep a straight face. He guffaws good-humouredly.

"Oh, you donkey!"

"Oh, you ass!" responds his friend with relief. "You haven't changed. As far as your gray matter's concerned, I mean. And what now, Fer..."

"Shhh! No names!"

"Why? What's wrong with it? Is it Hungarianized?"

"This is a secret operation," the fat one warns him severely. "Didn't I tell you? Double oh-oh."

"Yess, siree, Chief!"

"You see, Beanstalk, you're not a bad conspirator after all, though you're in your infancy still. You haven't stopped growing, I see."

"Neither have you, Chief Widthwise. And that beard! Looks like a flea market reject."

"It's the Hungarian blade."

"The air's running short down here in the underpass. It's afternoon high-hubbub time again."

"Let's surface."

The two men join the stream of people.

"Fire away! What are your plans? Curiosity killed the cat," says the tall, lanky one.

"Wait and see. Trust the Big A."

"You're as mysterious as a lead article in the Sunday papers."

"You think I asked you along on a wild goose chase? I never congregate if I can help it. You know our national history."

They roll along the Boulevard with the crowd in the direction of the Western Railroad Station. Two men in springtime, for it is spring now; moreover, they have not yet reached the summer of discontent of their lives. They are confident that on this afternoon, on which they have managed to find time to be together at long last, something will surely happen to them.

"I haven't seen you in a year and a half, Chief, if my memory cells serve me right."

"It's been over two. When the peach trees were in bloom," the man with the beard corrects him.

"How time doth fly! Like camel shit in the desert."

"If Alexander Graham hadn't invented the telephone, you'd still be sitting on your ass. I had a hell of a time getting you to come."

"The rat race, Chief. And the family. I think twice even before I breathe."

"And in the meantime, you've grown worn as a doormat."

"And you've got basting thread in your beard. Why don't you tear it out in the morning?"

"I do... You know, Beanstalk, sooner or later it's going to be Closing Time for us, too."

"Eh, you'll love it in your urn. You can stretch your ashes."

"Still, we're closer to thirty than to our Christmas bonuses."

"Thirty? That's positively antique! We'll turn into our ancestors. Think it can happen to us too, Chief?"

"Sure thing. Life is like a drawbridge. Up one moment, down the next."

"Life is also like the common cold. You can't get round it."

"Yes, siree, ladies and gentlemen! That's what I call Truth. But no sentiment, Beanstalk, no panic. The afternoon is ours."

"We'll fool around like we used to. Like in the Ice Age."

"The Great Adventure awaits us!"

"Funny you should mention it, it was just fermenting on the tip of my tongue. What have you cooked up?"

"I didn't want to say over the phone," whispers the rotund one with the beard mysteriously, "it might be bugged."

"You needn't spell it out. I'm prepared for anything! My trigger's cocked!"

"You won't need your trigger at the bank. We'll be using gas and dynamite. You didn't leave any telltale signs, I hope. Sure Interpol isn't on to you?"

"Definitely not! Not Interpol. My cleaning lady, perhaps. I owe her money."

Nonplussed, the one with the beard loses his train of thought as he glances anxiously up at his friend.

"What makes you say that? Don't you want me to ask you for a loan?"

"I didn't know you had intended to," answers Beanstalk, playing the innocent.

"What makes you think I had? You the National Savings Bank or something?"

"Chief, I honestly don't know who I am any more. Haven't known for some time. But I can assure you I am definitely not the Savings Bank."

After a long pause, Beanstalk sighs.

"The assumption has nevertheless hurt me to the quick."

"Chief...!"

"I just wanted to see an old pal. Have a chat. Bosom to bosom, soul to soul. To discuss the various ways of saving the world. And clean out the World Bank. Free the Zulu tribes. And then..."

"Oh, Chief...!"

"And then, my pal presses his purse to his heart's core because he thinks I want to ask for money! In other words, we spend a month planning, telephonig, synchronizing watches, listening to mutual reproaches about how we never meet any more, reminding each other of the sacred oath we took in the Sweatshop that our beloved teachers should live as long as we stay friends, we went through all this so now I should come and ask for money?"

"Stop playing on my emotions, Tiny Tim, or I'll cry... All right, so you didn't want to talk about money."

Tiny Tim snaps back at him.

"Aha! So *you* did? A friendly little handout, eh? And you

passed on the right so you'd come out ahead? Now was that a nice thing for a Comecon member to do?"

"Forget the mercantile trash, Chief. We went to the same sweatshop, resisted our teachers' efforts like true heroes, and though Time's winged chariot's hurrying near, friendship stands eternal! Let us take a solemn oath on it."

"A peck on the right cheek, a peck on the left," says the fat one mechanically.

"And arm in arm, let us face the Great Adventure!"

"Full speed in reverse!"

"But where?"

"We're together aren't we? United we stand. With a whole afternoon at our disposal... Life is like an unopened telegram. Full of mysterious promises."

"Bologne! Life is like the cleaners. You take them a new shirt and get back a pair of torn trousers. But let's have a stroll anyway, Chief. You're bound to let me in on your plans sooner or later."

They walk along leisurely, like loose-limbed marionettes ignorant of who or what moves them, or why. With the wild self-confidence of youth they know only one thing—that chance will surely throw something their way.

"It's hot," pants the heavy one with the beard. "Like an oven."

"And in your case," jests his friend, "the sun's got more to shine on."

"We could've gone out for a swim, like we used to."

"Great! Let's go."

"You ever go swimming these days?"

"Regularly. I even went the summer before last."

"I should've known. A busy father uses water only for brushing his teeth."

"So now you know why I want to have some fun today. How about that swim?"

"It's too late."

"It wasn't my idea."

"I didn't say we should go. I said we could have."

"Provided?"

"Provided we had agreed beforehand and brought our swimming trunks."

"We can rent them."

"I refuse to wear somebody else's."

"At one time, you went girl hunting in my nylon shirt, Chief."

"Think you still know how to swim, Beanstalk?"

"Better than you, at any rate. You swim only with the tide, don't you, Chief?"

"You don't trust me, Jack the Bean. I told you, the Great Adventure is just around the corner."

They come up to a crowd of people.

"Look! The old movie theatre. It's still here?"

"The Rat Hole. We spent a lot of time in there."

A boy sidles up to them.

"I got just two tickets left," he rattles. "My girl couldn't make it, you can have them for what it says. The box office is sold out. What about it, boys?"

"We'll think it over, son. Take out your barnacles, Bean, and spell out for your old man what's on the menu."

" 'Stress.' Shall we go inside, Dad?"

"What on earth for?" asks the fat one with mock consternation.

"Because it's there."

"Like Everest, I suppose."

"They say it's dynamite. We've got to trust public opinion, you know," argues Beanstalk naively.

"We're not that old yet," counters Tiny Tim.

"You want these or not?" the stranger asks impatiently.

"Business must be slow today, sonny boy."

"Buy my tickets first, pauper," says the ticker tout as he backs away, "we'll issue a joint communiqué later."

Beanstalk pretends disappointment.

"I thought you wanted to go to the movies, Dad."

"Not now. I'm hankering for a greater adventure."

They saunter along the noisy crowded street.

"Swimming's out, the movies ditto... What else did we do in the good old days?" wonders Beanstalk. "I got it! The games. We used to go to the games."

"The games? What games?"

"Soccer games."

"Soccer? What on earth is soccer?"

Beanstalk catches on.

"It's rather hard to explain. They used to play it with the feet."

"I see. Like the organ. It must've been some kind of religious spiel."

"Something like that. It was the Hungarian national religion. Had millions of followers."

"If it's gone, why discuss it?"

"Have you a better idea?"

"A tiger hunt. Sleighing on the ice. Parachuting. Flying Dutchman."

Beanstalk interrupts him with a shout.

"Dancing! Dancing! It just dawned on me. Dad, we used to go dancing! Rock'n roll an' do da twist, and other such imperialist opiates."

"Today, there's just disco," shrugs Tiny Tim. "Pressing out cabbage leaves as you stomp your feet in place. Behinds clashing in the night. That's no dancing, that's dodge'em! Besides if I start throwing my weight around, they'll have to renovate the premises."

"You know, we're as dull as a running debate in the Sunday papers. Perhaps you will be good enough to reveal what your plans are, Chief. Come on, give! What about the Great Adventure?"

"Don't get ants in your pants, Comrades! Everything is progressing according to plan, Comrades. The Great Adventure? You'll get it, Comrades. Right away. Actually, it's happening bit by bit, Comrades. Permanently! We denounce pseudo-adventures, Comrades!"

"You mean you just wanted us to knock around?"

"Considering the difficulty we had agreeing on a time, that's no mean achievement. And once we're *tête à tête,* I figured something's bound to come up. And it will. Just wait and see, it will."

"I had great expectations...Tickets to the flicks. You with a new wife... Or inheriting half a million, and needing someone to help you carry the gold bullion home from the pawnshop."

"Money. You're talking money again."

"I'd gladly talk all day for a mere hundred. Not that I'd mind a hundred-thousand."

"Sorry to disappoint you, Beanstalk, I just wanted to be with you and gab, like in times of yore. That's all. We'll just have to be satisfied with that. We've grown richer by one more experience, and that's like money in the bank. Let's walk along like wise old gents and be grateful we've got the sun in the morning and the moon at night. Such is life."

"No. Life is like chewing gum. It's so utterly boring, you never get tired of it... Okay, let's walk and enjoy the quartz substitute. I dig the sun."

But they are not enjoying the sun now as they squint and blink and wrinkle their brows and turn their heads to avoid the glare. After months of overcast skies, the city is suddenly as suffused with light as a stove with embers, and it takes time to adjust to spring too.

They stop under the cool awning of a furniture store. Behind the plate glass several armchairs flaunt themselves in poses as vacuous as two politicians debating before the cameras.

"Take a seat. These have been waiting especially for us," says the fat one with false nonchalance. "Won't you be seated?"

"Only after you, Chief," answers the lanky one as he pushes his friend closer to the shop window.

"Take that tall chair so you can let those long legs dangle."

"And I suggest you take that armchair over there. It's ample enough for your behind."

"Did I ever tell you, you'd have to gain weight just so I could call you a skeleton?"

"I could scrape some of the blubber off you. That way, we'd both come out ahead."

The short one, who looks fat because for the past fifteen years—ever since he got tired of growing—all the extra weight has settled around his hips, is looking hard at something further inside the store.

"See that set? It's forty-eight thou. A sofa, two armchairs, an ottoman and coffee table. Five pieces in all. What has that set got to offer for forty-eight thou?" He raises his voice. "Can it come running when you whistle? Can it conduct a conversation? It's so priggish, you'd have to send a letter of apology before you could touch it!"

"It's pure leather. It takes nerve to sit cheek to cheek with pure leather." Balancing on his long legs, Beanstalk squints down at his friend treacherously, like a room painter from the top of his ladder. "You got exhibitionist excrescences like these in your office, Chief?"

"My office is a pigeonhole. A glass pigeonhole. It's so tiny, I have to step out the door every time I pull open a drawer. It was meant to be a telephone booth, but it turned out too small. Even the ringing won't fit inside. The moment I hear it, I grab the receiver, it makes such a racket."

They continue walking. The tall one murmurs pensively.

"Still, you're the only one from the bunch with his own pigeonhole, telephone and key. You're as high up, Chief, as a sputnik! Reaching for the stars, eh?"

The short, fat one with the beard (with time, the too objective teasing of the aesthenic type always gets under the skin of the endomorphic type) stops dead in the middle of the pavement.

"You're nuts, Beanstalk, an ass and everything!" He flails an arm up in the air, where his friend presides. "For your information, I'm fed up with this shit! You called me Chief on the phone too. Some funny joke! Can't you force something else out of your grey matter? ...And don't interrupt! It's my turn. Tell me what's bugging you. Why're you needling me? You must think I'm off my rocker. We studied technology together, the whole bunch of us. But for the rest of you chaps, work stinks, that's the point. So get off my back with the you've-got-your-own-cubby-hole number. If you'd condescend to visit me in the shop, you'd hear how those machines clank and pound, and then maybe you'd get it through that pea-size brain of yours why I need that glass cubicle. Otherwise I couldn't hear what anybody said whether I was on the phone, or facing him, mug to mug, if you know what I mean. Besides, there's such a draught in the shop, if they open the door at both ends, all the diagrams and requisitions, all that goddam paperwork goes flying off my desk all over the place." His summary is bitter now. 'You're acting superior because I stayed with production, I stuck it out in the plant. 'Your own office,' and 'Chief' ...Very amusing, ha-ha-ha."

Beanstalk bends down to him, sympathy gleaming in his eye.

"But aren't you chief of the Fart Distillery division?"

"No!" The fat one realizes his answer was too abrupt, and blushes behind his beard. So he repeats himself, just for spite. "No. What do you think of that?"

"Sorry, Tiny Tim, I must've been misinformed." Beanstalk apologizes with relish, it's his ballgame now. "You know, I reckoned you had become alienated from the Masses. Your own office. Armchairs with built-in ass-warmers. Oriental rugs. A bar. A redhead secretary who comes equipped with the Pill and everything else needed for the earnest retardation of progress. But if things stand as you have outlined above, respect goes right out the window as far as I'm concerned, anyhow. I won't call you Chief any more if you're still the same old Tiny Tim, the fattest fatso in the class, and if you're just stagnating, like the national income."

The fat one's eyes flash up at his friend.

"Stop beating about the bush. You sound convincing, I admit, but it's just the dregs, no meat. Since I threw a nice juicy problem your way, why don't you deal with that? Work stinks for you guys, is that it?"

Beanstalk flaps his two thin arms as if he meant to fly away.

"Active rest, that's what you said over the phone, and that something's bound to come up once we're together again. That's what I'm programmed for. There was no previous mention of a political screening."

"The Champ works at a gas station, right?" asks Tiny Tim abruptly. "And Phil?"

"Married a share in a chow house."

"And Patchouli?"

"Drives a cab," admits Beanstalk.

"And you're a supplier at a producers' co-op. None of you sweat under the arms from a little hard labour."

"Punch and Judy fought for a pie, Punch gave Judy a bash in the eye." The skinny man drops his weasel head. "I've got to make ends meet, Chief, I picked up a loan at the bank against a promise of three kids. We had one when we got the flat, and pulled off the second soon after. Erika's on maternity leave with him. And this year she'll have to litter the third. It's breeding time again."

"Are you bragging or complaining?"

"Take it as you will. But there's five of us, and that's a fact. Four club members, and the fifth in reserve in mummy's tummy. A mortgage on the flat, and the furniture bought on the never-never. My in-laws took out a loan for us, and we'll have to pay them back, too. We spend the first of the month filling out money orders and lugging the dough to the P.O. in numbered bags. Every moment of my day, including the time I spend fooling around with you, is being financed by the National Savings Bank. Continue your questions, and I'll just pop down for another loan so I can answer them. Go right ahead, ruin me. Friendship comes first!"

Tiny Tim stops and scratches his beard thoughtfully.

"You wouldn't happen to have a picture of the kids on you?"

Eagerly, his friend reaches for the inside pocket of his coat. His hand freezes in midair. "Shithead," he murmurs, and retrieves his empty hand with a begrudging smile. He's been trapped in his father role.

"I was just wondering whether the kids look like you or the National Savings Bank," grins Tiny Tim.

"Well, they don't look anything like you, thank the Lord! They happen to look intelligent."

"Good boy. Bravo! But for the sake of the record, let it be noted that Erika was some dish, it couldn't have been much of a sacrifice killing two birds with one stone."

"Why're you using the past tense?"

"Are you trying to tell me that girl-hunting is out?" asked his friend like the devil's advocate. "Where does that leave the Great Adventure? I was hoping we'd pick up some chicks."

"Well, count me out! I haven't got a vacancy!"

"We wouldn't have any place to take the little charmers anyhow. My landlady sits at home all day, dusting her picture frames. I bet she spends the nights, too, up on the wall, sliding around, inspecting them."

Beanstalk sees his advantage, and his spirits soar.

"I hope you haven't turned into a saint! Anything, even marriage is better than that."

"That's what Mari says." Tiny Tim slows his pace. "And she says I should go back and start all over again. But I won't want to play hanky-panky with her family any more. The warmest greeting I ever got in that house was from their refrigerator. Maybe if we had our own apartment... I could be one of the bank's customers now, like you."

"With a picture of the kids in your pocket."

"With a picture of the kids in my pocket," the fat one says with resignation.

"Okay, we're quits," sighs Beanstalk. "Ooooh, you donkey!"

"Ooooh, you ass!" Then the fat one stops and expands his chest like a cock in the ring. "No! We will not surrender, Bean. Let us shake off our shackle of slack! All is not lost! Our troops may be beaten, our planes blown to smithereens before takeoff, our tanks shot to pieces by our own men in the fog, but our fighting spirit stands firm. We'll throw in our reserves!"

"Reserves? What reserves?"

"Search your noodle, man! I'm thinking of spiritual reserves." He continues with eloquence.

"Are we forced to the negotiating table? So be it. We'll have a business lunch! Today, there are no final defeats, no lost causes. At the negotiating table, everyone can force through a nice little dietetic compromise." He looks at his partner soberly. "We'll have lunch. A gigantic lunch. I wouldn't call that a Great Adventure, but it's something."

"But I... She's expecting me, Erika has cooked lunch, and..."

"It was my idea, you're my guest, I'll foot the bill."

"That's not what I meant."

"Yes, it is. It's written all over you."

"Well, if you insist. I can't resist brute force."

"Besides, I've got to talk to you," confides Tiny Tim with embarrassment. "That's why I called you. There's something I want to talk to you about."

"That makes two of us." Beanstalk is uneasy too. "Actually, that's why I called *you*. It's urgent... You see, there's this chance of making some money..."

"Hold your horses! Let's attend to spiritual matters first! It's late afternoon, and my spirituals are famished. Let's grab some lunch." And he goes through the menu, practically drooling at the mouth. "Chicken soup with quail's egg, bird's nest, shark fin, followed by steak à Chateaubriand with Cumberland sauce and goulash à la puszta, then trout with sponge cake and whipped cream, stuffed Csárdás with strawberry frappé, vintage wines with champagne, cognac and a double portion of bicarbonate of soda."

"I've graduated to Di-Gel ages ago!"

The spring sunshine seems too expansive for the narrow streets; it has hardly enough room even on the wide boulevard. A yellow tram glides ecstatically along its shiny rails, springing off the ground now and then as if in pursuit of the sky. But the two men don't care, they pass through the reluctant door of a restaurant.

"Not a soul."

"So much the better. Maybe we'll get treated like a capital investment." Tiny Tim sticks to his high spirits as he looks around. "Just look at that waitress, Beanstalk," he whispers with satisfaction. "All breast and thigh, and no unnecessary garnish. My mouth begins to water. Something tells me she's going to be our Great Adventure."

"What'll it be?"

Fixing his glare on the tightly-wrapped hips of the waitress, Tiny Tim goes into action.

"We wish to have some lunch, miss," he cooes ingratiatingly. "And don't bother your pretty head about the spoon. I'll eat my soup with a fork."

"Excuse me, sir?" The waitress's eyes, indifferent until that moment, open wide. "Why a fork"?

"So the soup'll last till closing time. I don't assume you can get off before then."

The waitress gives Tiny Tim the kind of look she usually reserves for a stained tablecloth in bad need of prompt removal.

"The boss takes me home in his sports car. If you happen to be a long-distance runner, sir, you might try following." She turns away from them. "I'll call the wine steward."

"Hey! Hold your horses!" Tiny Tim shouts after her. "We drive around ourselves in a car at night. You can have your pick of brand names."

Beanstalk stretches his long legs under the table.

"You've fallen on your ass, like the rain in Spain."

"I had no intention of catching her, I just threw her a line."

"Sure. Because you didn't know she was the big man's broad. What did you want to talk to me about?"

"Let's concentrate on lunch first. Besides, the girl's probably bluffing."

A bald waiter shuffles over. He is as red in the face as a turkey. The girl must have passed the word.

Something's gone wrong. Several waiters appear in the empty restaurant, along the back wall.

They move around ominously, rearranging chairs and keeping an eye on the two men.

"Cocktails? Beer?" the waiter asks.

"The menu! I've already told your colleague. Couldn't you send her back?"

"The kitchen's closing soon. Beer?"

"Fine. And bring the menu with you. Me and that waitress were just coming to an understanding."

The waiter stands staring into space.

"You'd better make up your mind. The boss, you see... Not that I care. Ask for something ready made. Like two consommés, two porkchops with vegetables." He grinds this out and leaves the table, shouting to someone in the back. "Two beers coming up!"

Beanstalk looks around with apprehension.

"There's a lot of movement back there. The waiters had a good look at us."

"The guy in mourning must be the boss." Tiny Tim grins. "What does he need all that breast and thigh for?"

"Even the washroom attendant's staring. Shouldn't we make a quick exit?"

"Ugh, she's already hooked, the little darling, just keeping it a secret," says Tiny Tim, leaning back in his chair. "Sooner or later her little hams will quiver like aspic, the heart-stew in her bosom will go pit-a-pat, and she'll throw herself at me. Just wait and see."

Beanstalk grins meaningfully.

"This girl reminds me of Mari. You know, your ex."

"Now that you mention it..." Tiny Tim is playing with the fringe of the tablecloth. "I guess this type must be coded in my genes."

They spoon their soups dejectedly.

"This reminds me of the school cafeteria. There's something in this soup, all right, but it ain't meat!"

"Very thin stuff... And how much longer, I wonder? When will we get something more substantial?"

"The finish line! Pick up your speed, Tiny, here comes the meat!"

"How long does it take for rat poison to be absorbed? D'you think the boss could have... If you know what I mean."

But the waiter just smiles. When he speaks, his voice is ingratiating.

"Two prime porkchops. Dessert-coffee-two-more-beers?"

"Two more beers."

Beanstalk glances at his retreating back.

"He's so obliging all of a sudden."

"He'd gladly cook... He'd gladly serve up the boss's pussycat himself," murmurs Tiny Tim as he chews and swallows. "Money speaks. A tip ennobles and depraves... You pour!"

Now that their stomachs are full, they feel relaxed once more. They gulp down their ice-cold Kinizsis and stare with glassy eyes as the foam slides down the insides of their mugs.

"What did you want to talk to me about?"

Tiny Tim is busy with his digestion.

"I just wanted to gab, that's all. It's the gab that counts, not the what... We've lost touch. I don't see any of the boys any more. At one time we had nothing to discuss, but we were together all the time, and talked until we went dry in the mouth. But now..."

"Things were different when we attended the Sweatshop. If we wanted to hear anything worth hearing, we had to do the talking ourselves."

"Remember Outer?"

"Outer the model teacher? How could I forget!" answers Beanstalk in a throaty gurgle. "*Out,* boys! Parades are *out!* Rioting is *out,* get my drift?"

"But on March 15th, we marched anyway."

"And the cops gave us a run for it, even though the shindig was organized by the Young Communists' League. But Outer's paternal heart could feel the imminent danger, bless his soul."

"Ugh, he couldn't know the cops would be all over us. Of course, shouting *Che Lives* wasn't part of the programme. The shopowners quaked and quivered for a full hour."

"And their shopwindows went slam-bang!"

"And they salvaged their display shoes and junky knits..."

"We created a stir, and then, nothing..."

"Don't say that," snaps Tiny Tim. "Those were the days, my friend. In Paris, the students occupied an entire arrondissement. In West Germany the city guerillas kept the population popping. In the U.S. of A., there was shooting on the campuses. And in South America, the Tupamaros thinned out the ranks of the police. That was something! The world was afraid of the young. And we in the Inner City, in beautiful downtown Budapest, were in sync with those out in the big wide world. Don't you see? That was our past, and it was something, after all! But Europe is silent, silent again, her revolutions gone, as the poet said. And behold, next came the Seventies, then the Eighties, all stuffy silence, not a spark of revolutionary fire."

"Not so loud. The Mortician's men are listening in over there."

"They can shove it... Yes, old boy, we were witnesses to great times. The kids today don't even know that we fought for their long hair."

"And for the hitchhikers, so they wouldn't be picked up by the police."

"The beat concerts at the Metro Club, remember?"

"And the old Illés Band. Their song that went, *It hurts, hurts, huuuuurts!*"

"Don't even mention it, or I'll start weeping through the ears."

"To make a long story short, things were different in our day, old friend."

"For us, who were there at the Don, during apple blossom time."

"And at Doberdo, in a shower of arrows."

"At Világos, in the dead of night..."

"And with Attila the Hun on the first IBUSZ trip to the West..."

"Oooooh, you donkey!"

"Ooooh, you ass!"

"Comrade in arms, how about another round? Waiter, two more beers," shouts Tiny Tim. "It wouldn't do, him eavesdropping for nothing."

Beanstalk heaves a melancholy sigh.

"Life is like ulcers. It never passes without a trace."

"Life is like the elevator at home. Neither up nor down. We push the buttons in place."

The headwaiter brings their beers.

"We're changing shifts, gentlemen," he says, slapping his leather billfold open in his palm. He is as fat and stout as an advertising pillar, and blocks the restaurant from their field of vision. Neither of the two men would be enough to fill a cavity in one of his teeth.

Tiny Tim makes a gesture of annoyance, but Beanstalk prepares his long legs under the table for a speedy departure.

"Six beers. Isn't that right, gentlemen? I hope you don't mind, gentlemen, but we're changing shifts." The headwaiter's manner is obsequious, yet threatening. "We're closing, but you just go right ahead, finish your beers. Take your time."

"Don't blunt your pencil," says Tiny Tim as he flings some bills on the table. "And keep the change."

Although they are by themselves again, Beanstalk shifts his weight restlessly.

"Well, what is it? Come on, out with it, I've got something on my mind too, you know."

But Tiny Tim is in a state of beer euphoria, and responds with an unhurried, philosophical belch.

"What was it, what was it...Let's see now...I've said it, Bean. Neither up, nor down. We're punching the buttons in place. I'm not kidding, Bean, I'm on the level. I've been worrying myself a lot lately, asking myself, what else is there? Is there anything else? I sit in my pigeonhole from morning till night while outside the rest of the guys work the conveyor belts. In the afternoon I vegetate in my room, while next door my landlady slides up and down the wall among her paintings. At night I stare at the boob tube, and then, off to sleep. And the following day, the same merry-go-round goes round and round again. Sometimes I feel like asking somebody: isn't there a terrible waste here? Because if someone

were to tell me to whitewash the sky, polish the sun, sieve through
the sand of the Sahara, sprinkle the North Pole with salt, I
wouldn't ask why, I'd ask, will tomorrow do? Instead... Put the
kids' pictures on the table, Bean. Right here, in front of me. Show
me some hope for the future. If Mari and I could have another go
at home-making, maybe I could talk her into delivering triplets,
and we wouldn't have to fall behind..."

"So that's what's bugging you. Mari! And you need somebody
to encourage you. Tiny, go back to her! Please, I beg you! I'll go
down on my knees if I have to."

"Hold your horses! It's not as simple as that. I won't go to live
with them again. Dadsy-mumsy are detrimental to my health. Believe me. I know."

"But any other solution would mean money."

"Ay, there's the rub," recites Tiny Tim, leaning his bulk over
the table. "I know of a flat. The owner's going abroad for two
years. I'd have to pay one year down. But where should I get the
dough? Ask mumsy-dadsy for a handout so I can abduct their
little darling? And the car needs repairs. It'll be six years old this
fall, and the testing takes money, as you know... I didn't want to
ask you, though, that's not why I called."

Beanstalk sees his chance, and takes it on the run.

"You couldn't have called at a better time! I need money, too,
to pay off my debts... Look. I have a business proposition. That's
what I wanted to talk to you about. You drive a sedan, don't you?"

"A Moskwich sedan. But it's old."

"All it's got to do is roll. Listen! I know a greengrocer who
needs some shipping done. And that means good money."

Tiny Tim shivers.

"You want me to fill Ivan Ivanovich with lettuce leaves?"

"Lettuce is big business. And fruit. At dawn, we'll go out to
Bosnyák Square and load up."

"What do you mean by dawn?"

"Two o'clock. Maybe three. We'll take the stuff into the store,
unload, and go to work. The widow will pay through the nose. Saturday and Sunday we'll go down to the countryside. From the
farmer to the store, that's double pay! The widow needs us bad,
she kicked out her previous shipper. She'll dish out anything we

ask. Might even give us an advance. Ten a head. Probably even more. We'll be millionaires by autumn... Well, what do you say? We could start tomorrow. Let's go to the widow right now and strike a deal."

Tiny Tim shakes his head morosely.

"I need my beauty sleep."

"So you'll hit the sack early, and watch less TV."

"No. Beside, there's such a thing as self-respect in this world."

"But you can't turn it into capital."

"And pride! Remember Outer lecturing us on pride?"

"Yes. In his threadbare pants."

"And how about socialist mentality? Would you have me sweat for a capitalist?"

"The public interest demands that the stores be well stocked."

"For all I know, this thing could even be against the law."

"Think of your triplets. How will you support them?"

Tiny Tim continues to resist, but with less conviction.

"I just can't see myself huddled inside a car stuffed with wilting cabbage."

"Then try seeing yourself inside a brand new car, you fat, indolent swine!" snaps Beanstalk. "If you continue this shilly-shallying, someone'll snatch the business away right in front of our noses. I told the widow we'd go see her today. If you're pig-headed, she'll find somebody else. It's a goldmine for anyone with a car."

"Before we were just talking about lettuce and cabbage, now it's gold."

"Listen. The widow promised ten grand a head in advance. But we could get thirty. And you can have it all. We could settle our accounts later. You'll rent the flat and move in with Mari. And from then on, when you go home, Mari will be waiting with dinner. You'll stuff those calories down and hit the sack. You'll work on the triplets, then sleep. At dawn's early light, you'll leave for Bosnyák Square fresh as a daisy. And by six, you'll be at the factory. Well, what do you say?"

"When do I breathe?"

"I'll tell Mari," says Beanstalk with a sinking heart, "that you refuse to make sacrifices for her sake."

"Don't bother. She knows. Ever since I stepped out of the family frigidaire."

"In that case, do it for my sake. Do it for an old pal," pleads Beanstalk. "I need that money... Do you know how healthy it is to rise early? And how gorgeous a sunrise is? Dawn in purple mantle clad?... Come to your senses. Let's go to the widow, all right?"

"It's too late," says Tiny Tim, leaning over the table meaningfully. *"Don't move! We've got the house surrounded!* I should've settled for your lettuce instead of the boss's moll."

Beanstalk looks up questioningly.

"A cop at the door?... What's going on?"

"The Mortician locked us in and called the fuzz."

Meanwhile, the boss is eagerly explaining the situation to the policemen.

"They're sitting right over there, Comrade Sergeant. They acted and talked pretty suspiciously. Said that they go around with a car by night, that's what they said, word for word, Comrade Sergeant... And since you mentioned how there's this gang of car thieves in the neighbourhood... Well, we believe in vigilance, Comrade Sergeant!"

The waitress, too, puts in her shrill two-cents' worth.

"Yes, they told me, too. They said we have a car too, at night... Or go after cars at night... They're the ones, all right!"

Tiny Tim nods with satisfaction.

"You were right, Bean. She looks a lot like Mari. And you want me to sit in a carful of wilting lettuce for this? Ooooh, you donkey!"

"Oooooh, you ass," whispers Beanstalk nervously. "If I act quickly, we can still make it to the widow."

Saluting stiffly, the policemen towers over them.

"Good afternoon. Your papers, please."

Tiny Tim winks at Beanstalk.

"It's gonna take time, that's the problem. We might as well make a clean breast of it, they'll write that to our credit in court, and we won't get the Chair." He turns to the policeman. "Comrade Sergeant, life is like every big adventure. All our dreams end at the police station... We give up. What do you want to know? We're international drug smugglers, and white slavers, not to mention wanted terrorists. And patricides! But we never deliver lettuce and cabbage, we'd never stoop that low. That's extenuating circumstance, I hope!"

The policeman ignores him as he leafs through the two IDs, subjecting them to a thorough scrutiny. Then he takes a good look at the two suspects. After a long pause, he gives back their IDs and turns away from their table.

Tiny Tim and Beanstalk are barely out of their chairs before the disappointed headwaiter bulldozes them towards the door.

Outside, the afternoon crowd sweeps the two men along. Out on the street, they are just like all the others to whom, just like to them, nothing extraordinary happened that day, except that the spring sun shone on them perhaps more brightly than usual.

Translated by Judith Sollosy

KERBSIDE

by ISTVÁN CSURKA

Something told her to glance towards the door of the pub. She hardly ever did this if she could help it, because when she was sweeping the section of street in front of the pub and her eye travelled there, she found herself going in after it, and that regularly led to trouble: she would lose something, fail to do her daily stint till evening so that the inspector would scold her, and every other sort of inconvenience and bother that can plague a poor lonely old woman overfond of cheap brandy and other tipple besides. This time, however, something different happened: through the door came one of her mates—old what's-his-name—who had been sweeping up along the 8th district side of the street right opposite her beat for quite a number of years. Though not exactly drunk, he staggered on emerging into the open air and daylight; then, catching sight of the old woman in her orange-and-white striped warning cape, he went straight up to her. She got in first with a question.

"How many did you have?"

"What?"

"Glasses."

"Three."

He dropped his chin with a crescent-shaped sweep just for emphasis.

"So what?"

Without replying the man just stood there in front of her. The old woman straightened and propped her broom against the cross-bar above the handle of her litter-pan.

"Found anything?"

"Yes."

"What?"

"A lighter."

"Of all the...! You're damn lucky, aren't you?"

She flung him a look full of hatred.

"No chance of me damn well striking it lucky like that."

The man stepped down off the kerb. He felt uneasy on the pavement. Vehicles hurtled past on the busy road, the drivers taking notice of them and respecting their rights of the road; but the pair paid no attention to the traffic's various roarings.

"Where?" she pressed him further.

"Here in front of No. 18, in the dustbin."

"A good lighter in a dustbin?"

"Not a bad one. It was filled just yesterday."

The old woman gave the old man a look. Something was puzzling her, but she could not say what. She was thinking, searching the man's somewhat sad stubbly face, crazed and vinegary, his eyes, as he stood there, sunk deep in the groove of a thought. 'How could it be done?' was his thought. How could he wheedle at least two forints off her? He had two more in small change. 'A small glass.' That was the visual part of his thought. He could see the very glass on the tin bar-counter, saw the slender form of the little brandy-glass, its silvery glint, the delicate fluting around the base of the diminutive glass, felt the strength gathering in his hand with which to raise the small cylinder clean off the wet surface, and, of course, felt on his tongue the fruity taste, the aroma, and kick of blended brandy.

The woman was unable to find her way through the whys and wherefores of incomprehension leading to her puzzlement, while the man deemed the moment inopportune for the two forints. So they just went on standing there by the kerb, facing each other yet very far away too, amid the exhaust and din of the traffic, lost within themselves and sunk into nothingness. Perhaps the only thing they shared in those minutes flying by in senseless silence was the longing for a drink. The man wanted to go on drinking, the woman to begin.

Whole minutes went by. Cars, lorries, buses, Volkswagens, Trabants, Skodas, Volgas, Warszawas, Opels and Ford Taunuses kept roaring, rattling, gliding past them in an endless stream like the years.

"How many did you sell it for?" the old woman came to at last.

"A couple."

"You were taken."

The slightest twinge of pleasure, of a warm feeling around her heart now. She said it again.

"You were taken. Five brandies plus two beers would've been fair. Or perhaps one brandy a day for a week."

"Maybe."

Almost cheerfully now:

"What about the third?"

"That came out of my own pocket."

A sudden itching fit came over the old man, and he scratched his backside energetically all over in a way he didn't try to conceal.

"Got the crabs again?"

"Maybe."

"Why don't you have a wash? I've got a bathroom in my place, you know."

"Must be quite something. How many bathrooms you got?"

"What do you mean 'how many?'"

"How many? Tell me. How many bathrooms you got in your place?"

The old woman put on a stern face. The man dropped the idea of the two forints for the time being.

"Cut it out, will you?" she flared up. "What are you hinting at? Nobody never got the crabs from me! I'm a clean one who washes herself regular. Anyone can come and see me for himself. My man didn't leave me 'cause I didn't wash, it wasn't that at all."

"I never said it was."

They looked at each other. Somehow or other that was enough now to make it up between them. The man began quickly.

"Lend me four forints till the first."

He asked for four to get two. But he drew a blank.

"I won't."

"You've got it but you won't?"

"I have, but I won't.

"Why not?"

"You never give back."

"How much do I owe you? Up to today?"

"Do you think I keep account? Either I give if I have a mind to and take the loss, or I don't. You never once came over and said, here, this is what I owe. Never. You're forever asking."

"Just last week I stood you a brandy."

"That's true. All right, 'cause you'd won on the races. 'Cause you're the one who has the luck. You find a lighter, you win at twenty-five to one on a three-forint ticket on a long shot. Go back to work and see if you can't find something else."

"I'm sure I can't."

"Nothing's sure but dying."

"Still. Whichever way you look at it. It's not sure I found the lighter."

She threw him another of her most piercing looks, because she sensed that the conversation was once more taking an unpredictable turn. The man on the other hand was filled anew with hope, perhaps by this very look, that he was going to get the two forints after all, or possibly even four, because he would appear as a hero in a minute and make the old woman grin, and when she did that his cause was as good as won, because then she'd act nice and charitable and generous. However, first he'd like to light a cigarette. His rummaging in his pockets was a mere formality, a hint; he knew well enough that he hadn't so much as a dog-end in them and hardly any tobacco dust either. The old woman let him search thoroughly; she produced her packet only when the lean old man who looked older than his age finally gave up. There were five cigarettes inside. She pulled out one with great deliberation and passed it over. Then one for herself. The man at once found matches and offered her a light. Both or them puffed away vigorously, and as the nicotine's daze quickly spread within them, their gaze rose from the ground in front of them, travelling up to the windows, the eaves and finally to the sky, as they yielded and threw themselves open to joy and drugged delight.

"Did you steal it?" the old woman had meantime found the solution which came as a surprise to her too.

"Yes," the man agreed automatically, because he was still thinking of the half box of matches he'd given a light from a moment before, and which be had just slipped back into his pocket. Then the woman's expression suddenly turning sour made him realize that they were talking at cross-purposes, and that her thoughts were still on the lighter.

"Not the lighter; I didn't steal that," he said without any sign of emotion of being offended. This made it even more of a puzzle for the woman. The man thought it better to make a clean breast of it at once with a proudly heroic confession. As cockily as he could, he looked the woman in the eyes, head thrown back.

"I chucked it in the dustbin last night."

"What?"

"The lighter."

She could only shake her head slowly to and fro in disbelief.

"It was mine."

"First you lose it, then you find it," she said, not as a question but as a statement of fact. "Damn me if that's not lucky, too. If I lose a thing, I never find it."

"No," he said with a show of even more majestic pride. "I chucked it on purpose so I could find it this morning."Cause I never sell nothing that's not mine in the pub, only what I find. That's a rule with me. I promised my late first wife, back in 'thirty."

Standing in front of the woman, sombre, erect, a little moved by his own so well-regulated habits, he waited tensely for the effect. It did not fail to come, though it fell far short of his expectations. The woman did not grin at all, on the contrary, with sadness in her eyes, head shaking in wondering amazement, withdrawing as it were behind some falling curtain she reached slowly, very slowly, into the breast-pocket of her uniform, and from a thick wad of papers, letters, lottery tickets torn and crumpled but nonetheless greatly prized, she produced a ten-forint note.

"It has to be changed," she said. He did not reach out for it yet, and he did not ask how much, whether two or four forints, he was to get after it was changed. For a second he looked through the gaps in the stream of vehicles towards the other side of the road where he had left his broom and litter-pan instinctively, evidently because his going back into the pub had become a not too distant possibility, and on such occasions he always made it a point to inspect his equipment.

"Couldn't we make a go of it, together?" the woman popped the question right at that moment. The man started. He hadn't expected it. Only the week before, he could recall clearly, he had rejected her latest self-recommendation, which she'd made goodness knows how many times before; on that occasion the refusal was made more roughly and rudely than usual—and now again?

Steeling himself, he stepped back onto the pavement, higher up, aloof. If you stood those few inches higher, he thought, it was like you were not standing there at all. You were in a world apart.

"You don't like my cooking, do you?"

He did not reply.

"There's room for two in my place. Two wages is two wages. You wouldn't mind if I kept you clean, would you?"

From the man still no response. The old woman held out the ten-forint note in front of her lap, as tenderly as if it were a flower.

"I hate it to seem I'm trying to hook you with the things I've got, but think it over again. What's going to become of you? You'll go to the dogs, you'll get lousy. You're a nice decent man really. It's just that you're such a thriftless sort. You're too happy-go-lucky."

"That's me," he said with conviction, hoarsely. "That's what I am. My sort doesn't make a good husband. You'd have a bad time of it if we got married."

"Don't be hasty, just think it over again."

She held out the ten-forint note.

"How much for me?"

"All of it."

The old man flinched.

"I'll give it back on the first," the same concealing hoarseness in his voice. Seeing he was ready to leave her, the woman quickly added:

"Winter'll soon be here. I'll have fuel. I can make the room as warm as I like. All our clammy old soggy things'll dry in front of the stove during the night. I have no worries during winter."

"Nor have I. I was in charge of fifty to sixty snow-shovellers last year." He repeated for emphasis. "Fifty to sixty men."

"You could keep the extras. We'd only put the two wages together. For rent, board, fuel, light. We could even buy clothes, underwear too."

He did not want to offend her. He stooped down with one foot onto the road again.

"Aren't you coming?" he said with as much warmth as he could manage.

"Are you asking?"

"I'm asking."

She hurriedly swept up into the litter-pan what was left of the street garbage as far as the grating over the drain, then having arranged her things together and bracing herself with her hands on her knees, she stepped up onto the pavement.

They started together towards the door of the pub, seeming to swim or float along. They uttered no word, though they had plenty to speak about. The man had already decided during the few steps that this time he would repay all ten forints on the first, and that he would not deduct anything for what he was going to spend on her. The woman for her part was happy and hopeful, on account of what she could not quite find words to express. She was thinking that she was only sixty-three and the man just turned fifty-eight, but that the difference didn't mean anything.

Then, as they were approaching the door, having turned their backs on the road which was their life, there grew in them an overpowering excitement far beyond any anticipation, hope or imagining about alcohol diffusing warmth through their bodies, but from the simple fact that they were about to, were able to, enter the world, the society of people, from their outside place on the road's margin, from their world of stampeding traffic, garbage and pot-holes.

With melancholy lazily huge flapping wings, like two colourfully striped crows of fantasy, they sailed on towards the door of the pub, then inside, the larger giving way before the smaller one already slightly withered.

Translated by László T. András

THE OUTPOST
by ÁDÁM BODOR

The day she sets out, everyone has a word of praise for Gizella Weisz. Even the great Comrade Onaga gives her a meaningful look.

"Now that's something," he says appreciatively. "Your ideas are excellent, your plans first-rate. You're a born leader." He curls his wormy lips, smiles sourly, and lifts his champagne glass. "And now, hurry. It's time. And good luck."

It is getting dark. Gizella Weisz is driven home in the company jeep. As soon as she disappears through the gate and up the stairs, the driver backs into the thin shade of a leafless acacia and kills the engine.

Gizella Weisz doesn't bother to take off her gray loden coat as she walks around the apartment, looking through open closets and pulled out drawers, picking out clothing and underwear. She puts a few pieces on top of the commode near the phone. Soon, she picks up the receiver and waits for the dial tone, then puts it down again.

She packs away a change of underwear, socks, sneakers, a few books, some yellow apples and her handbag with all its contents inside a faded brown travelling bag. She straightens up and looks at her watch. She steps out of her shoes, walks to the hall in her stockings, pulls on her gray waterproof Halina boots and ties a white kerchief round her head. Before she pulls the curtains to, she looks outside. The pavement is damp under the street light, the net of barren twigs casts a shadow on the canvas of the jeep.

Gizella Weisz studies herself in the mirror, runs a hand over her cheeks, looks into her own eyes, and picks up the phone. She waits, presses down the fork repeatedly, dials at random, then with a frown, puts down the phone. She pulls the plug of her night lamp out of the wall socket, turns off the light in the living room and the hall. She steps through the door and locks it.

Out on the upstairs gallery she raps on a window. The mist from the kitchen sits condensed on the pane; here and there, it runs down in tiny rivulets. On the inside, a palm wipes some of the steam away. Gizella Weisz leans closer and shouts.

"I'll be gone for a couple of days. My sheets are up in the attic. I'll bring them down later."

The woman knocks back from inside.

"You'll do what later?"

Gizella Weisz waves an arm. "Nothing. I'm just off for a few days."

"I figured I'd wait," says the driver at the gate. He opens the front door of the jeep, takes Gizella Weisz's brown bag and dumps it on the seat. Then he opens the back door.

"Oh," says Gizella Weisz, "who's that?"

"Just me," says a man in a hat. "Hello."

Gizella Weisz bends down and glances under it. "Oh," she says. "Where are you going?"

"I'm going with you," answers the man in the hat, "we'll be travelling together."

Gizella Weisz sits down next to him in the back. "Good."

The driver starts the jeep, makes a turn, and takes the road leading to the railroad station.

At the station the driver, carrying Gizella Weisz's bag, leads the way.

"No bags?" asks Gizella Weisz of the man in the hat.

"No. Nothing. I'll buy whatever I need there."

As they walk, Gizella Weisz studies the man in the hat, both hands sunk in the pockets of his overcoat.

"So you're coming without your things."

"Yes. Just like this."

Out by the tracks, the driver hands Gizella Weisz's bag to the man in the hat, but follows them along the cars and down a corridor until they find an empty compartment. He waits on the platform until the train pulls out.

"Where would you like to sit?" asks the man in the hat.

"Makes no difference," says Gizella Weisz, "I want to sleep."

"I prefer to sit facing forward."

Gizella Weisz unties the kerchief under her chin and leans her head against a corner of her seat.

"Let's turn off the light," she says.

"No," says the man in the hat, "let's not."

Gizella Weisz turns up the collar of her coat and takes another quick look at the man.

"What about your hat?"

The man in the hat shakes his head.

"No. I have a fungus. The doctor said to leave it on."

During the night, the train stops at a junction. Soldiers stand in the steam shooting out from under the train, other soldiers check the wheels.

"Are you sleeping, Comrade Weisz?" asks the man in the hat.

"No," answers Gizella Weisz, wide awake.

"I've been watching you" continues the man in the hat, "sitting there, as if you were sleeping. And I'm a little envious."

Gizella Weisz opens her eyes and looks under the brim of the man's hat, but can't see his face. The pale light of the compartment falls only on the tip of his gray nose.

"Of me? What on earth for?"

The man in the hat coughs.

"You studied at the Lomonosov in Moscow. And in no time, got everything you wanted."

"Yes," nods Gizella Weisz. "That's true. They spent a lot of money on me."

The man in the hat nods. "And you're full of ideas. The boss likes you."

Gizella Weisz stands up and digs into her bag. "Yes," she says. "I like my work. How about an apple?"

The man in the hat shakes his head. "No. No thanks. Sets my teeth on edge."

"I like them even frostbitten," says Gizella Weisz and bites into her apple, "core and all. But not the seeds."

"Must come from a good family," says the man in the hat.

Gizella Weisz chews the apple until only the core is left in her hand. She flicks the seeds into the litter box.

"Well," she says, "actually, I never knew my parents."

At dawn, the man in the hat shakes Gizella Weisz awake. In the dim light of daybreak, the rush of the water beyond the railway bed is barely visible. Water oozes out of one of the compartments, too. The man in the hat steps outside, looks at the puddle on the floor, stamps his foot in it repeatedly, opens the door a crack and looks inside. Gizella Weisz is right behind him. Inside, a couple sit drenched to the skin, shivering in a terrified embrace. Water drips from their clothing and hair.

The tracks soon leave the riverbank and are enveloped by soft, thick, furry fog. Along the ditch, the remaining snow is buried under brown leaves and fallen crow feathers.

"The water must still be cold," says Gizella Weisz.

The man in the hat stares morosely out the window.

"We'll be getting off soon."

"Somebody threw them in," says Gizella Weisz, "they wouldn't be this wet otherwise."

The man in the hat is already standing at the door. The train heads over the points towards the station.

"You were dreaming, Comrade Weisz."

At the junction, in the heavy fog, the early morning light is barely visible. Yellow mist rises from the halo of the station lamps. Gizella Weisz walks alongside the rails in her loden coat, white kerchief and gray waterproof Halinas. The man in the hat walks by her side, carrying her bag.

In the waiting room Gizella Weisz buys a newspaper with a message from Malenkov and Bulganin on the front page. She asks for her bag and stuffs the newspaper inside.

A lonely bus is waiting in the hazy dimness outside. Its ignition is on, its headlights quiver on the bumper.

"This is the one," says the driver as they approach. "There's nothing else leaving here at this ungodly hour."

"Well, so long," says the man in the hat.

"Oh," says Gizella Weisz, "you're not coming along."

"No. I'm going someplace else."

"And here I thought..."

"No. This is where I stop."

"Well, so long then."

It is noon when the bus finally emerges from the fog and reaches the mountain pass along a drying road. The water boils in the radiator. Carrying a bucket, the driver plods along to a small snow-covered mound, brings melted water from under it and pours it into the radiator. On the other side of the road, in a ruined chapel, sheep bleat. Dogs walk lazily from the shelter of the wall and in a fanlike formation approach the bus. The driver chases them off with stones.

From here, a black road shiny from pits and puddles leads to solitary, haystack-shaped, partly-extracted mountain peaks. On top of some of these maimed summits, crests rise to the sky—pieces of long forgotten forests. Under them smokes the settlement, Borgova, Borgova Two, B Two for short.

"This is it, you can get off now," says the driver just before he comes to a stop near the small road to the settlement.

Along the access road, over the sea of splashing mud, the unsteady network of decaying plank, tar paper and crumbling cardboard, tramples Gizella Weisz. At times, when she slips, like a bird she flaps her arms. The abruptly melting snow has transformed the road into a sheet of slippery mud. This one, too, which leads among steaming slag heaps to booming machine shops and muddy storerooms.

"Yes, this is it," says a man upstairs at the head office to Gizella Weisz. "This is settlement B Two."

Legs extended, the supervisor sits behind a yellow-stained, empty desk. His brows have just a few hairs, his face is yellow and translucent, like parchment. His wrinkles are black from coal-dust and oil.

"I'd like to wash my boots off," says Gizella Weisz in the doorway. Thick mud covers the gray Halina cloth of her boots. Pieces of dry mud lie on the floor, and spilled slag in front of the iron stove. Rubber boots, tied in pairs, sit on a bunk.

"The outpost you're going to run," explains the supervisor, "isn't here, actually."

Meanwhile, he gazes out the window. Puffs of smoke from a train whistle swim lazily across the yard. The sun penetrates right through them.

"Actually, it's further out," says the supervisor. Then he glances at Gizella Weisz's boots. "But tell me, what's with your boots?"

They're a little heavy," says Gizella Weisz. Meanwhile, she notices the thick black crust on the supervisor's boots and on his pants, too, drying in flakes up to the thighs. And she adds, "but once they're dry, they'll be lighter."

"Sure," says the supervisor.

Somewhere outside a window shatters with a sharp crack. The hum of the compressors escalates. Startled birds take off from the rooftops and fly across the yard. The supervisor stands and looks out the window.

"There'll be a rail car out the work site in the morning," he says. "It's taking rubber boots. It'll take you too."

And with that, he hurries out of the office.

Gizella Weisz tries to catch a glimpse of him through the window, but hears only the squelching of his boots under the eaves. Small steam engines move there and back between the machine shops, up to the axle in mud. The mud eddies in their wake, too. The tracks must be submerged under the mud. The horses' legs, too, are sunk in the mud knee deep; from a distance they look as if they were walking on very short legs. They're hauling an empty tin wagon along the high pile of coal, on whose northern side the early morning dew sits grayly.

Gizella Weisz takes a handkerchief from her handbag, goes down the corridor and opens the washroom door. The basin is dusty, and covered with a filthy crust; the faucets blurb dryly; in place of the mirror, just at shoulder's height, a coal-dusted finger has drawn a skull. Under it, with coal-dusted fingers, stand the words: *I'm still beautiful.*

The supervisor plunges into Gizella Weisz's open bag. He crumbles a panty between his fingers, raises it to his eyes, and studies the small tag.

"What the hell is this?" he asks when he sees Gizella Weisz in the door. "The letters are so tiny, I can't make them out."

"Oh," says Gizella Weisz, "just some names." And she spells it: "Dior, Paris. That's what it says."

The supervisor purses his lips as if he wanted to touch the lined part of the panty which hides Gizella Weisz's most intimate secrets. He purses his lips and says, "In that case, we'll rip it out. So."

And taking the tag between two fingers, he rips it out of the material with a flick of the wrist, like a tooth or a nail. He even smiles a little.

"I forgot to take them out," says Gizella Weisz. "I could've cut them out at home, but I forgot."

"Well, now you don't have to any more," nods the supervisor. He pushes the stuff to one end of the desk and digs into Gizella Weisz's things once again.

"And you think," he says, "you'll have time to read?" He hems and haws as he studies the books in his hand. "Besides, what's the use? You know enough already, from what they tell me. I got what you need in my drawer. *The Problems of Leninism.* Put that under your pillow. The rest will stay here."

"I don't mind," says Gizella Weisz. "I'm only here for a short time anyway."

"Time's always short," says the supervisor. "Under all circumstances."

The supervisor looks inside the stove, sees that it is cold and empty, shrugs and leaves the office. Gizella Weisz watches till late afternoon for his figure to appear among the engines moving in the mud, discharging their veils of steam.

"Come," says the supervisor, "I'll show you the canteen."

The supervisor goes up front, Gizella Weisz follows. They go down to the yard, pass under the eaves, supporting themselves against the wall with one hand, and go around the building.

Behind an open door, above a table dull with filth, hangs a barren bulb, shedding its light behind the counter, the canteen attendant wearing regulation clothes, and the shelves.

"Give me a rum," says the supervisor, "and an orange liqueur for the young lady."

He takes the two tumblers and stops with his back to the counter.

"Did you hear? I said young lady. But I even know your husband's name. Anyway, is the orange all right, or would you have preferred the fennel?"

"I really don't know," says Gizella Weisz, "I don't like either."

"Well, you'd better make up your mind quick. And buy a bottle or two," says the supervisor. "And buy yourself a stick of that salami. Two pounds of cheese, some zwieback, marmalade, if you like it, and crackers."

"And who is going to eat it?"

Gizella Weisz inspects the shelf behind the counter, the muddy bottles with their torn labels, the moldy, herniated salamis, the crumbling crackers in the barren wooden boxes.

"You'll be hungry," says the supervisor. "You'll want to eat everything you see here now. A whole basketful of everything. Of course, you won't fit on the rail car with baskets. As I said, it's taking boots out to the work site."

The supervisor takes Gizella Weisz back to the office. He locks the desk drawer and pockets the key. Then he looks out the window. The sky is green in the twilight, the base of the lilac slag heaps is black.

"You'd better catch some sleep. Want me to throw these boots off of here? Or can you sleep on top?"

"On top? Maybe. I'll try."

In the early morning a rail car stands in front of the office; it seems that there must be rails everywhere under the mud. It's a kind of handworked rail car with forked drives, two seats, a small loading stage, just enough for fifty pairs of waterproof boots and Gizella Weisz astride them. Two helmeted trainmen push the car over the mud-covered points out to the open tracks and jump up behind the drive shaft.

The car climbs slowly on the narrow-gauge tracks. Before long, they pass the haystack-shaped, capped mountains and roll squeaking past sleepy mountainsides. Among budding wood laurels and pale bushes, licked down by the melting snow, the grass crouches under its shiny membrane. As soon as they reach the forest whose resin-smell hit them several bends back in the road, they stop the rail car.

"Now we'll change," says one of the helmeted trainmen.

He jumps off the seat and climbs on top of the boots. Gizella Weisz takes off her loden coat, sits behind the drive-shaft, and covers her legs. She rows in her sweater. Soon the sweat appears on the fleecy wool over her shoulder blades and freezes in translucent, milky drops. Above them, icicles hang from the pine branches; a white crust covers the tiny gradients and coves of the rivulets they pass. Once, when the subdued trickle of one of these rivulets falls out of hearing distance, the tracks under the rail car begin to screech.

"Watch out!" shouts the trainman from atop the rubber boots.

They pull back the driveshaft, secure it with a hook, and pull in the brakes so they won't slide back down the slope. The screeching of the brakes gets shriller as another rail car appears up ahead, winding its way among the pines. Two men are sitting on the other car, both pulling on the brakes, but easing up now and then.

When the two rail cars stop, their buffers almost collide.

One of the men is wearing a helmet, the other is travelling bareheaded. His long, dirty, graying hair falls to his shoulders, his faded reddish beard reaches to his swollen belly. On two sides short braided pigtails stick out from under it. He is wearing a wadded coat tied round his waist with a piece of rope.

"Hi there, Bucko," shouts the trainman to him, the one riding on top of the rubber boots. "Where to?"

The fleecy bearded man studies them suspiciously through narrowed eyes before he answers in a thin, coughy voice: "Home."

He yawns. You can see right down his throat. There's not a tooth left in his mouth.

"You never can tell," says the man sitting next to Gizella Weisz.

The other rail car is carrying timber. It is laden with gray, snow-covered, rough boughs. The whole looks like a shipment of frozen elephant tusks. The rubber boots have to be flung down by the railway bed and the rail car moved off the tracks, so the other car can pass with its big load.

After they reload, the two trainmen change places. The one who was riding on top of the boots now sits next to Gizella Weisz. He pokes her in the ribs.

"You didn't greet our colleague," he scolds.

"I don't know him," says Gizella Weisz.

The man shakes his head and laughs.

"But you do know Doctor Potra," he adds after the car is in motion again.

"Of course I know him," says Gizella Weisz.

"See? I told you you know him."

"He doesn't look anything like this."

"Well now he does."

They reach the settlement in the afternoon. One of the rails passes through a tunnel or some sort of drift, the other makes a detour to a barracks-like stone building with a shingled roof. The two rail car men haul the rubber boots into the office and drop them on an empty bunk bed. Meanwhile, Gizella Weisz pulls on a pair of sneakers and washes off her Halinas with water dripping from a trough near the building, rubbing out the mud with sand. She hangs them up inside, on a hook.

When the man who heads the office enters, first he glances at the drying Halinas, then the fifty pairs of rubber boots lying on the bunk bed.

"You can't go any further today," he says to Gizella Weisz. "You'll sleep here. In the morning Jani Kuptor, the charcoal burner, will pick you up in his cart and take you out to your squad."

"Fine. Tomorrow, then," says Gizella Weisz.

"What's the size?" asks the supervisor, pointing to the boots drying on the hook. "Because should they be size thirty-six, and they look like it, I'd like to buy them for my wife. Not for money, of course, but for a pair of good rubber boots. I wouldn't want you to go barefoot."

"Fine," says Gizella Weisz. "When they're dry, take them off the hook."

"Thank you very much," says the supervisor. "If you get a hole in the rubber boots, you get them replaced free of charge. So you got yourself a good deal. And now, come with me. I'll show you the canteen."

A candle is burning on the plank counter. Its light flickers on the lowered lids of the canteen attendant.

"A rum," says the supervisor, and wakes him. "And an orange liqueur for the young lady."

They stand with their backs to the counter and the candle light, their two tumblers sitting on the windowsill. They gaze outside, into the frozen dimness of the valley.

"I said young lady," whispers the supervisor, "but of course I know how things really stand. This way, at least, you won't want to write anybody. By the way, is the orange all right, or would you have preferred the fennel? Tell me if you like fennel better."

"I really don't know," says Gizella Weisz. "The truth is, I don't like either. And that makes me hesitate."

"I suggest," whispers the supervisor and looks around the canteen, "that you buy yourself a bottle or two of both, regardless. And buy at least ten cans of sardines, with tomatoes and also with onions. Ten or twenty of each. And buy yourself at least thirty packs of cigarettes."

"I don't smoke," says Gizella Weisz.

"You will," says the supervisor.

He lightly touches her elbow and guides her out of the canteen.

"I think I'll have a look in your bag," says the supervisor back at the office. With his right hand he plunges into Gizella Weisz's belongings, lifting out the pieces one by one. Then he replaces them neatly, all except for two articles.

"Just a change of underwear," says Gizella Weisz.

"I see," says the supervisor, and takes one of the articles from the desk, the bath soap wrapped in cellophane, and smells it.

"This won't lather in our water," he says. "Besides, once it's gone, what will you do? Right? I'll give you a good three pounds of scrubbing soap instead. And the same goes for this bra, it's called a bra, isn't it? I'll give you a pair of fur-lined mittens in exchange. You'll get everything in the canteen tomorrow. Everything will be on the counter in a small hemp sack. Don't forget, the charcoal burner will pick you up in his cart tomorrow morning. He'll take you almost to your squad, where they'll be waiting for you."

"Fine. Tomorrow, then," says Gizella Weisz. "But tell me how many men are waiting out there?"

The supervisor looks at Gizella Weisz and raises a finger.

"One."

In the morning, Jani Kuptor, the charcoal burner, is waiting in front of the canteen in his cart. The small hemp sack lies on the counter, with a three-pound cake of scrubbing soap and a pair of fur-lined mittens inside. Gizella Weisz buys two bottles of orange liqueur, two bottles of fennel, forty cans of sardines, twenty with tomatoes and twenty with the onion, thirty packs of cigarettes and ten boxes of matches. When she climbs up on the dickey, the charcoal burner wraps a blanket around her booted feet. But she kicks off the blanket and runs back to the canteen. She raises a hand to her forehead, as if trying to hide her eyes.

"I'm a bit confused," she says. "I didn't pay for it. I don't have money."

The canteen attendant picks up the sack and hands it back to her.

"You don't have to. Here, we just deduct."

Gizella Weisz climbs up on the dickey. The charcoal burner wraps her legs in a blanket. The ride on the car begins uphill, and the road soon narrows into a gully. Stones, branches and pieces of ice brought here by the snow crack under the wheels. The horse stumbles as it drags the cart uphill, from time to time it lifts its tail, and with a long hiss or a mournful drone, lets out some wind.

"The horse is the cleanest animal there is," says the charcoal burner when this happens.

Around noon, they stop in front of a gray wall of hard-packed snow. It must've come from somewhere up high, from red-rimmed ledges, because it is full of stones with red veins, crushed clumps of grass, broken pieces of ash trees and pepper-grass.

The charcoal burner unharnesses his horse, and with Gizella Weisz's bag in one hand and the small hemp sack over his shoulder, starts out on foot, kicking steps with his boots into the frozen snow as he climbs. At the top of the wall of snow, he waits for Gizella Weisz.

"Don't be surprised if you find something in your bag you didn't put there," he says.

"Okay, I won't," says Gizella Weisz. "Thank you for telling me."

"It's just four onions," says the charcoal burner. "Don't think of anything bad."

"Thank you," says Gizella Weisz.

They climb over a gradually rising, snowy, rocky precipice, with Gizella Weisz in the charcoal burner's wake. At first they sink knee deep in snow, then only to the calf, and at last, near the wind-swept ridge, only to the ankle. They stop when they can climb no further. The charcoal burner throws the sport bag and the hemp sack down at his feet.

"You see where you have to go, don't you?"

"I think so," says Gizella Weisz.

From the green-frozen lake, stakes driven into the ground spiral to the edge of the crater, from the edge of the crater, stakes placed at regular intervals spiral down to the lake, like the curves of a whirlpool. Above the lake, in the perpetual calm of the deep, sits the mist in motionless layers.

"I will come for you some day," says the charcoal burner. "And then you can go home. It was I took Mr. Bucko down the other day. So we'll be seeing each other again."

The door of the stone house is unbolted; Gizella Weisz knocks on the rough board in vain, nobody answers. She stops in front of a makeshift table. A light-gray animal is perched on top, looking straight at her. A weasel.

The weasel doesn't know Gizella Weisz, yet it does not move, even its shiny button eyes do not shift. Only its fur changes colour in the light breeze stirred up by her arrival.

There are two bunk beds in the house; one is strewn with small, black, cylindrical droppings, chewed shavings from the bed boards and bits of fluffy blanket. This is the weasel's bed.

Gizella Weisz puts her brown bag and the small hemp sack on the weasel's bed and pulls the door shut. The gloom is stuck inside, the tiny windows barely give light through the blueish-cream grime of the panes. A torn paper bag rustles on one of the paneless windows.

Through the blueish grime of the windows, the clouds passing above the round crest seem brown. The snow falls from them in dove-gray flakes.

"Where are you?" asks Gizella Weisz of the weasel, because the table is empty, and there's nothing left of the weasel but a few new droppings, shiny as tar, and the sound of scurrying feet. Gizella Weisz bends down, feels the dark underside of the bunks, but sees nothing, feels nothing, not even the weasel. But she finds a black wash basin full of litter, dried-out flies and bugs.

When she glances out the bluish windows, Gizella Weisz notices that the stones outside have turned gray in the snowfall. Over them, the tracks of a ribbed rubber boot lead to the door. Gizella Weisz opens the door right in front of the nose of a sallow-skinned man with a thinning beard.

He stands on the threshold, a heavy tool box on his shoulder, sniffing a little like an animal.

"I knew," he says, "that somebody was coming today. But I didn't know it was a woman."

He leaves the door open; the melting snow swirls in tiny whirl-pools above the threshold where he stood.

"Well, it is, as far as that goes," says Gizella Weisz.

The man hangs his toolbox on a hook. From the corner of his eye, he glances at Gizella Weisz. Gizella Weisz closes the door.

"I need some hot water," she says.

"Hot what?"

"Hot water."

The man with the thinning beard shakes his head.

"We can't make a fire in here."

He sits on the edge of his bunk bed, staring obstinately into space.

"You closed the door," he says, "so the water could warm up."

"I haven't got any water."

Gizella Weisz touches the rim of the black washbasin with her foot.

"It's outside," says the man. "Where it belongs."

"It needs warming up."

The man with the thinning beard shakes his head.

"We can't make a fire in here," he says. "The heat drives the weasels off. The house is theirs."

"Just as warm as my skin," says Gizella Weisz.

"Okay. But no warmer," acquiesces the man with a frown. "Okay. I'll start a fire, but just this once. Just so you'll see the harm it does. Just this once, I'll start a fire."

He jumps up from his bunk bed with a soft, animal movement, opens the door and leaves it open. Up by the edge of the crater, in the distant stray sunlight, yellow streamers of snow swirl in the wind. Above the green lake, the purple sheet of fog is velvety and quiescent.

Gizella Weisz takes the newspaper she had bought at the junction from her brown bag, crumbles it up and stuffs it inside the stove. The man brings snowy juniper roots and frozen kindling, throws them on top of the paper, and lights a match. But before the flame touches the paper, he throws the match away, grabs the newspaper from under the kindling, and smooths it out on his knee.

"Who's this Malenkov? Who's Bulganin? What does this mean?"

"Take a guess."

"So he's dead," sighs the man with the thinning beard. He crumbles up the newspaper, stuffs it under the kindling, and lights it.

"Heat's no good," he explains softly. "Heat is the most terrible thing there is. If it's warm inside, it's cold outside. And that mustn't happen. You'll see tomorrow, when we work the stakes."

"I haven't decided yet what we'll do tomorrow," answers Gizella Weisz. "I'll let you know in the morning."

"We're going to put up more stakes," says the man with the thinning beard. "There's nothing else to do here. And in the shade, I hope. It must be April now."

"It'll be April in a few days," says Gizella Weisz.

"I thought so. In that case, for a few weeks we'll stay in the shade, even in a southern exposure. All the way on top, though, the sun is pretty strong. But never down here, don't worry."

"You know that better than me. You must be down here for a long time."

"This is the middle of the world, Gizella Weisz."

"You know my name?"

"You could guess mine too. After a while, I'm sure you will."

"So we know each other."

Gizella Weisz pulls the chewed blanket off the weasel's bed and shakes it out outside of the door. She unpacks her bag and the hemp sack and puts the sardines, the cigarettes and the four bottles out on the table.

"How about a bite?"

"I already ate today," says the man with the thinning beard. "But since there's a fire, I might cook up some corn grits. And spill it out in front of the door. You'll see, it'll be all gone by the morning. Not even a tiny yellow speck will remain."

Gizella Weisz goes outside with the empty basin, leaving the door open. She brings it back filled with snow and puts it on top of the stove.

"If you have a piece of string, you could help me," she says, and puts the three-pound bar of scrubbing soap on the table. "It's got to be sawed up. I'll give you half."

"What for?"

As the top of the iron stove heats up, the water drops begin to pop under the basin. Gizella Weisz sits on the weasel's bed, the man with the thinning beard sits on his. They pull the two ends of the string and the shavings fall in their lap.

"Isn't it cockeyed?"

"It's cockeyed."

"Because I never saw cockeyed soap yet."

"Okay. Let's start from scratch."

"Where's the water closet?" asks Gizella Weisz when they finish sawing the three-pound soap into twenty-four equal pieces.

The man points out the bluish windows.

"That's all the water closet. The whole thing. But you'd better stick to one spot. That way if you notice some muck, you know there's been a stranger up these parts."

Gizella Weisz takes the basin off the stove and puts it down on the floor.

"Turn away now," she says.

"I'll close my eyes," growls the man from the shadow of his bunk bed.

Gizella Weisz opens the buttons round her waist, pulls off her clothes, flicks the water with her fingers and sits inside. Under the water, she runs a hand over her body and looks at the man with his lowered lids, and shudders. The water ripples around her.

"You can look if you want to," she says. "I don't mind. You can open your eyes."

The man opens his eyes. First he tries to catch Gizella Weisz's eyes, then looks at her bare, taut knees and the water rippling around her waist. He looks as if he were looking at a weasel.

"It's getting dark," says Gizella Weisz. "What do you use for light around here?"

"Nothing."

"I'm sorry. That was a stupid question."

"There's no need for light here."

Gizella Weisz sits on the weasel's bunk, shivering silently. "Excuse me. Let me ask you another thing. Have you got a can opener?"

"I have a couple of sharp knives," answers the man with the thinning beard.

Gizella Weisz rummages among the cans, picks one at random, and holds it to the light of the fire.

"Sardines in tomato sauce. Like them? Open it please. And I have orange liqueur, and fennel, which one would you like? Open one."

"Oh, no," says the man, "I won't abuse my constitution with that stuff."

He cuts around the top of the can with a knife and puts it on the table. He takes one of the bottles and pushes the cork in with a finger.

"Here."

"So start eating," says Gizella Weisz. "Eat while the fire gives us some light."

"I told you, I already ate today. But if you don't like it, leave me the liquid. I need the salt."

Unsettled by the contact with the light and warmth, the man huddles in a corner of his bunk bed. For a long while, Gizella Weisz doesn't see anything of him, except his thinning beard and dark eyes as he lights a match, and then the tiny flares as he pulls on his pipe.

"Here's the liquid."

Gizella Weisz hands him the almost empty can. She waits until he slurps it up. "I like the smell of what you're smoking. Stuff some for me. I'd like to try it."

"I bet you would," says he man. "Leaves swept up by the wind. Gathered them myself. When the weather permits, the leaves sometimes swirl all around up high, in the sunset. At times like that I know they're mine. They'll float down here soon, and I can pick them up."

"I'd like to try it," says Gizella Weisz.

"Take a puff, if you're such a pipe smoker. It's the only pipe I got, so have a drag at this."

Gizella Weisz takes the pipe, moves the mouthpiece around between her teeth and takes a drag. "Oh my god," she says, "where can I spit?"

"Anywhere. On the floor." The man leans forward on his bed. "You're laughing?"

"Oh, God," says Gizella Weisz, "I think I am. All right, come and have a drop, Ocsi, or Petya. You're either Ocsi something, or Petya something. I almost remember now who you are."

"I see you recognize me," says the man with the thinning beard. "I'm one of the two. But I won't drink. I won't abuse my constitution. I want to outlive those who sent me here. But that's enough. Let's not talk any more."

Gizella Weisz takes a good swing at the bottle before she speaks again.

"Doctor Potra, or Bucko, as they called him around here... How much time did he spend here?"

"Be quiet," whispers the man irritably. "You were sent here so you'd think about why you were sent here yourself. And don't put any more wood on the fire. The weasels will run off, and I'll be left all alone."

Gizella Weisz lowers her arm to the paling circle of light by the fire and looks at her watch. She unstraps it, winds it up, and puts it on the table. "It's almost seven," she says. "It's evening. I'll come over in a minute, and sit next to you. And we'll chat. No one's going to hear us."

"Don't bother winding your watch," says the man hoarsely. "Put the damn thing somewhere so I won't hear it. Take it away from here. Bury it."

"I'll hide it later," says Gizella Weisz. "I'll hide it under the green ice outside, so it won't tick any more. We'll discuss that too in a minute. You said you'd make some grits and throw it in front of the door to show me that it'd all be gone by the morning, every speck of it."

"I don't remember. I said no such thing. I never wanted to cook anything."

The ambers moulder away; they barely glow any more under the gray, trembling ashes. In the silence and diminishing heat, the paper bag rustles repeatedly in the window; the cooling stove cracks and pops. The buttons on Gizella Weisz's waist pop, too, as she unbuttons her dress.

"You're getting undressed," whispers the man. "You don't have to get undressed here for the night."

"Well, I am," whispers Gizella Weisz. "I'll be coming over soon."

"Don't." The man turns to the wall. "Don't you dare!"

"I will. I'll come over for a spell. Tonight."

"Stay where you are. Stay in your bed. Wait till I want you."

"You'll want me once I'm there." Gizella Weisz stands somewhere in front of the bunk bed of the man called Ocsi or Petya. "Where are you? I can't see you. I can't see a thing. But I'll find you."

"Don't touch me."

"You've got to be here somewhere. Right nearby."

"Don't touch my skin. I don't want you to."

"Let's just try it," whispers Gizella Weisz. "Tonight. Because tomorrow is tomorrow. Just give me your hand, and I'll warm it up somewhere."

"Be quiet," whines the man wetly into his palm. "You should be ashamed of yourself. Don't touch me, or I'll scream."

"I said, don't!" growls the man called Ocsi or Petya. "Wait till I forget Bucko."

Gizella Weisz's hand is in mid-air. Slowly, it drops. She touches her own knee. She leans against it, and pushes herself back, towards the weasel's bed. She feels around for her clothes, pulls them on silently, lies down, squirms around in the litter, and covers herself with her blanket.

"Will it take long?"

"Long? Who's to say what's long?"

"But you're bound to forget him sooner or later."

"Maybe. In a couple of years. Maybe."

Gizella Weisz buries her fist between her thighs and lies, huddled in the litter, floating off to sleep. Sometime during the night, she hears subdued whimpering, quiet, plaintive whining, the soft approach of feet. She feels a light touch on her shoulder and abruptly sits up.

But the man called Ocsi or Petya is asleep on his bed, breathing regularly; he is not crying, he is not whimpering, he is not whining. He is not groping his way to her, he is not approaching. Male and female weasels are playing catch on her legs, waist, and under the torn blanket, squealing as they pursue their love-play.

Gizella Weisz's fist is between her thighs. From time to time, she feels soft stray fur. Sometimes she shudders in silence. At last, she calms down. Things are going to be like this for some time to come.

Translated by Judith Sollosy

FAMILY PORTRAIT AGAINST A PURPLE SUNSET

by PÉTER NÁDAS

When I get off the bus, I must take a good look around. The even numbered side of the street seems to face the mirror of the odd numbered side. In the narrow street, the houses all look alike. I do not know the house number, but I think I can safely rely on my instincts, be they ever so muddled. I can start. I can look up and find the third-storey window. The two facing windows, for only in this way can I decide. But I must always cross to the other side of the street—it seems to alter sides in the meantime, always it seems to confuse me on purpose, prompting me to lose confidence in my own senses—I must cross to the other side where they keep potted plants in the third-storey window.

On the staircase two elderly men are carrying a sofa, their faces are red, and they are holding their breath. They are accompanied by a young girl. I must press myself into a corner to make room for them. I can feel the smell of the two men, the girl has no odour. Then I push the bell.

My maternal aunt, at the time of my visit, is just seventy, and, as if she weren't a real aunt at all, she sits in a huge armchair uphol-stered in claret velvet right in front of the window, with her back to it. The armchair has stood there for a very long time—at least, ever since I can remember. And everything is in its exact appointed place. Like all her visitors, my aunt sits me in the uncomfortable, backed chair. Her crutches are leaning against the piano, and should either she or her courteous visitor, attentive to her slightest stirring, reach out an arm, the crutches are within easy reach. I have never seen my aunt stand up.

The door is opened by Adél, the little woman from next door—she too is some sort of relative—and as we pass down the long, dark hall, we could agree on a lot of things without exchanging a single word.

In the soft velvet of the claret armchair, right under my aunt's hand—her fingers just have to worm their way under the fold of the armrest—is a button. A kind of alarm bell. It serves several purposes. It alarms the caretaker downstairs. But when my aunt is not alone, then, for the sake of greater security, Adél sits with her by the stove, crocheting. She stiffens the little lace baskets with sugar water and stuffs them with lace flowers and lace birds. These are made for sale, but two especially nice samples are displayed in the room, one in the *vitrine,* the other on the piano—a testimonial to my aunt's brilliant girlhood, like the mummy of a basket of flowers received at an important concert. Adél sits on a stool, and though she keeps to herself, her eyes narrowed, hiding her sharp glances behind wrinkles, she smiles determinedly, and when my aunt nods, she begins to speak rapidly, jumbling her words. But in the same way, with a nod, she can be made to stop. And when she is not allowed to speak, her presence is not disturbing; she leans against the stove, hunched; her smiling glances can make contact only with the back of the visitor sitting across from my aunt. Or meet my aunt's own eyes.

On overcast days, the back lighting illuminates my aunt's heavy wreath of whitish-grey hair only dimly, on brighter days, more pronounced, but the face always remains in shadow. My aunt lives off her past. She is not only the recipient of a high decoration—the result of the same merits that caused her lameness—but she has also received a pension much higher than the average, and thanks to her impeccable upbringing, can even teach Latin, Greek and German, and therefore—since the family fortune too is in her hands—she could easily be considered a woman of means. Halfway between the stove and the claret armchair, the pupil or visitor sitting in the highbacked chair is scrutinized by two pairs of invisible eyes. But if the attention of the pupil or the visitor is steadfast enough to withstand the glare of the backlight, if it searches for the eyes in the shadow of the face, it will see, in the course of its scrutiny, a bony, almost manly face in strength, and thin, colourless lips—as if ceaselessly, these lips had to hold back some renewed pain yearning to be expressed in words—above the lips a rather pronounced little moustache—the old-age growth of that light feathery formation which can be so titillating above the lips of a young woman—a hawk-nose with a pronounced curve, and finally, reaching the goal of the scrutiny, the veiled, colourless iris as yellow as the whites of the eyes, which lends the seemingly aggressive face the pleasant uncertainty of the dullness of old age. My aunt is as motionless as if her whole body were paralyzed. But her glance is impalpable not only because of the half light. It does not flash but moves slowly, avoiding living things and sharp objects. It feels best in midair.

On the third floor of the house opposite, a lace curtain is pulled aside behind the window, but for a long time, nothing happens. I watch my aunt's hand on the claret velvet of the armchair and gauge distances.

Then unexpectedly a man in his undershirt opens the window—from the windowsill and the blackened stucco figures of the façade the pigeons stir and lazily take to the street—the man leans out, looks around, spits, then quickly closes the window.

Not a sound to be heard. There is silence in the room as well, for nobody speaks while I'm silent. The crutches just an arm's length away, leaning against the piano. My aunt can't even be short-sighted, and she never complains of illness. The door is at some distance. "Well, I'm glad you're here!" she says with satisfaction, like someone anxiously waiting, and lo and behold!, I nevertheless appear before The Presence in the best of health. If I were to grab the crutches now and hit her over the head... I look at my aunt's hands. One single movement wouldn't do; grabbing the crutches, I'd need another movement to direct it at the head, only thus could I level the blow. In the undiscernible pause between the movements—and this rhythm cannot be erased with any legerdemain!—not only would Adél scream—though I could just as well count on her becoming a silent party to the crime—my aunt's finger would find the push button, unless of course fear should paralyze them. I stir my tea.

"But if it's not the money, then what?" I ask.

The snow descends in big, fluttering flakes.

At my aunt's I'm served not just good tea—they serve candied fruit, sour cherries and peaches even in summer—they also know how to set a table. However, I get no answer to my question. On the little table which moves on coasters—which the pupils pull up, too—on a golden yellow silk table cloth is bone china, a crystal bowl, a dessert fork with which to spear the fruit glassy with sugar, and silverware.

"Some toast and butter?" my aunt asks, and she seems to nod.

"It would be so easy that way!" Adél says. "Oh, yes, so easy! I don't think I've even told Henriette, it's so terrible, so humiliating, hearing such things, and some things one prefers to bury for ever, or at least, one hopes it can be done, isn't that so, Henriette?"

She falls silent, and my aunt makes no response.

"I can't, no, I can't keep it to myself any longer, I'm sorry, Henriette, I'm going to tell you. When he said that now, though his defence attorney would surely talk him out of it, but if it could be done, if it could help in any way, after all, both the prosecution and the defence have reached an impasse, he would like to talk about his emotional life, and the reason I didn't talk about it till now is that I'm afraid once I tell it I'd falsify his thoughts, or his feelings, and thus, by shaping the facts after my own image, I'd become involved myself, I preferred to just think about it quietly, no, I did not forget, on the contrary, I tried to make it more vivid and lasting, but it's so shameful that in him, as he said, in his emotional life, tenderness and death, cruelty and life are related like when an angel and a devil are forced to have intercourse all the time, and he felt something like this for the first time, he doesn't want to mention other, earlier such memories which nevertheless are relevant here, when they were washing his mother, he's never seen anything more maddening, ever, the wet washcloth left drops of water in the folds of the body, the hair became dewy, and never did the living and the lifeless show up their differences as sharply as then, for the material of the body overcomplicates itself in such a mysterious way all in vain, when water is eternal, and here he should make a detour and talk about the relationship of the simple and the complex, but as his last wish, he's going to ask anyway that in the condemned cell he should get the chance to write down his latest thoughts, the most abstract ones, but now he's going to stay on the level of sensual perception, of memory, because when he realized that the body could no longer absorb these drops, the pores have closed off the flesh once and for all and will never again press out any drops, as if death had oiled the body over, then, yes, it was then he felt it for the first time, though he was till a child, or perhaps because he was a child, though naturally, he did not comprehend his feelings, a live body should be laid out like that! or if he were laid out like that, naked! dipping the knife into him, or if they would dip the knife into him! like salami, in slices! to feel one's superiority over the transitional process that changes the living into the dead and the dead into the living, for this superiority can be apprehended only in the guise of a transition and if he wished to spice his message with a touch of the spiritual, he'd think it possible that yes, turning into God, and that's why the autopsy room left him cold, but that's why he was more attracted by experiments, vivisection, the oligochaetons worms, for instance, this seemingly insignificant type of animal, the simple earthworm, for instance, which can be sliced up and it's not murder but the multiplication of life, in short, the divine providence ruling over its existence can be freely studied, though, since we're here, it's murder, like the others, from a moral point of view, after all, the earthworm is a creature of god or nature only in its original, we might say, evolutionary length! thus, if we cut it into pieces and in this way multiply its life, we're up against an excitingly paradox form of murder after all, for the criterion of morality can never be either the goal or the result, morality cannot be revolutionary, it must keep the singular, the individual within view, and honour everything living in an ascetic manner, but of course nobody can answer the question: must all organic formations be regarded as individuals? before he had mentioned the earthworm there was silence, but then people exploded with rage, they stamped their feet, and the judge too felt that this confession was so delicate and so devoid of a message, that he had the court emptied, though apparently that's when he revealed that he, contrary to the story that his lawyer was kind enough to make up, not only did not hate his victim, but if by love we mean a fatal, an all-encompassing passion for any class or rank of living being that cuts across all intellectual barriers, then, from that point, he was in love a little, and he asks that they should not look for deep psychological connections, because though the resemblance to his mother may have played a role, but he was much more excited by the problem of the power over life, the transition and its gradations, and if they should hang him now, all that would happen to him is what every lover fervently thirsts for, but in his fear, since after all, what he wants could only be realized with their mutual deaths, he'd contaminate his love with life, making it equally unseemly, but he doesn't want that, for him fear is just something mercifully thrown into the bargain, a lust which enlightens the psychology of transition, a pleasure that cannot even be approximated by the rubbing of the genitals."

As if I were touching their bodies, my laughter is met by a strange silence. Adél lets the thread wind sleepily off her finger and fall into her lap; she pulls her dark brown flannel dressing gown tighter around the neck. She presses herself against the stove; the stool squeaks unpleasantly on the edge of the tiles. My aunt is motionless, though she has raised her head slightly, nevertheless. And even the way I imagine their lives, based on the gleanings of their insignificant communications seems untrue; the pre-noon potterings about, till lunch, the arrival of the pupils, the coffee with brioche after dusk sets in, turning down the bed, Adél's leaving, the snap of the safety locks, coming in from the hall, mixed with the sweep of the car lights from the street across the ceiling, the piano sprawling lazily in the dark, and the night.

"Why are you laughing?" my aunt asks, her voice hoarse.

"Was I? No! Maybe because it surprised me, and it doesn't seem to be true, though it appears very amusing and rounded and maybe you know why, but I bet Adél made it up."

"Adél!" shouts my aunt.

Adél does not answer, but my aunt is not daunted, we must listen to her wheezing reprimands.

"Look here!" she says, perhaps a shade louder than she had meant, but stops short, her body helplessly shuddering on the dark velvet of the armchair, then changes her mind again, turns her head unexpectedly to me, but I can no longer see anything of her face, only her hair glows. "As a rule, you plan your visits to last an hour and a half, and if my calculations are correct, we've still got approximately ten minutes. Please give me these ten minutes. I won't go over time. It would be a great treat, because I have no right to speak. That's why I keep silent. I just live. I want nothing more, nor less. I eat just enough to ensure this condition. And I see nothing extraordinary in my situation, everyone's in the same shoes, they just haven't made the necessary deductions. They haven't come to the point where they regret even what they must shit out, because that too just goes to waste, it's material, and so my aim is to reduce its quantity. And anybody who, as young as you are, will not heed the sensible caution that we might call practical material management, that is, life maintenance, and who doesn't just stuff himself inordinately, I see how you gulp down a whole bowl of candied fruit which I have served only because I know my manners, but even tickles his senses to nausea, and more's the pity, there are always adventurous souls to lend a hand in this! hetairas! he, yes, he will croak like a dog! Quickly, without a trace. Which, in itself, is not regrettable. And consequently, I have nothing to say, really. I can't even waste these ten minutes on you. Go on, stuff yourself! You forgot a cherry!"

I can feel Adél stand up behind me.

"Someone should really kill you, Henriette!"

Moaning plaintively, yet with pleasure, my aunt leans against the back of the armchair. For a long time, nobody speaks.

"You gave yourself away at last, Adél!" my aunt says later. "I won't ring, since I know everyone's sharing in your plan. Strike me. But the crutches aren't hard enough. The axe is there, by the stove. You lied, you said you'd protect me with it, but I knew better. I knew why you wanted it. Why don't you move, my dear beloved nephew? Didn't you hear the story? Though I might as well admit it, for years I really believed that Adél was telling the truth, because one night I woke to a terrible struggle, but she made it up for you! and in the morning I asked Adél, and that's when she made it up, that there's a young man living above us, 'the same age, Henriette, as your nephew,' he's an orphan, too, and stood in the reputation of a serious young man till then, he always greeted me in the corridor, had a bright scientific future ahead of him, so young, and a doctor of biological sciences, 'and if now we were to tell your nephew this, Henriette, we'd frighten him away, he'd get lost at last, he'd think we suspected him of murderous intentions,' because it's no use, it seems, emphasizing to young gentlemen like him that we haven't got a damned penny under the pillow and it's just a waste of time, it's no use wasting money on those ingratiating carnations, at this time of the winter, they're at least twelve forints a piece, when he sees the silver we use on the table because we know our manners, it's all right, Adél, and my emotions towards Adél rise, and it just might work, after all, she knows me, I thought she knew the torment I feel seeing how you gulp down my candied fruit to no purpose, and drink the English tea by the potful, and you still haven't learned German properly, though you know very well how important it is to me. I consider it *de rigueur.* But nobody learns it properly here. They just stutter and stammer because they're lazy and obtuse. Where was I? Adél! I wanted to say something, but not this! Don't you know what I meant to say?"

The street lamps aren't lit yet, it is dark in the room, but the crutches do not dissolve into shadows, by all odds, the snow will surely last. And I can soon stand up.

"Can I pour? It must still be warm."

"Yes. Please. Go ahead and pour, Adél, I'll have another cupful."

"Yes! Now I know what it was," says my aunt, and in Adél's hand the spout of the tea pot knocks against the rim of the cup. "I still have a few minutes, don't I, Adél? When I give a lesson, I make sure not to waste any time. Every moment must be filled with words. But now I'm speaking only because in the lewdness of your laughter I can feel the power that will make you perish before your time. You must use time wisely. I'm no longer worried about Adél, she'll manage somehow if I keep a close watch and don't give her wishes free reign, but she'll die soon anyway. I'm going to outlive her because I'm more cautious. I don't tickle myself. I can press this button any time, and I don't think you could have won the caretaker over to your side, he wanted to be my lover, you see, but I wouldn't give in even then, because I knew that if his passion survives, I could take advantage of it. You, on the other hand, belong to the dumbest kind of the living. You're even dumber than Adél. You're afraid of fear, that's why you luxuriate in the candied fruit, that's why you laugh so greedily, that's why you drink the last drop of tea. You mistake every one of your fantasies for thought, and would like to act upon all your fantasies, to prevent them condensing into thought. That's why you haven't got a single thought in your head. Nor that it bothers you. Your whole life is illusory light, smell, sound. Yet there is a perfect thought in which every detail, interconnection, and the whole itself is to be found."

My aunt falls silent because I spear the last piece of cherry on my dessert fork, lift the crystal bowl out of the silver basket, and reach it out towards her. I lean forward, lifting it up high, up close, so she'll notice. She smiles sadly, the line of her lips swells with the smile, and with palms pressed against the velvet of the arm-rest, she too navigates in my direction. We see each other; in the purple reflection of the snow, everything appears sharper.

"It's not that piece of cherry I begrudge you, you fool. Go on, eat it, gobble it up! I like watching people eat. It's just that I'm afraid. Like that, down the hatch! The bell, too, that's why it's here. Of you, too. And Adél, too. Of everything and everybody. All the time. Because nobody knows bounds, and I don't know what happens, what more can happen to me. And I hate every-body. That's why I'm so glad that I could finish with Adél too, at last. And if I were to ask you, after all, I've never asked you anything till now, besides, we're passed discovery, to be good to me, would you do what I ask?"

She must shift the weight of her body in order to stroke my face with her ringed palm.

"You know, you don't want to kill, just play! Has it ever occured to you? Answer me this, just this!"

"Don't torture yourself," I whisper.

Yet my breath brushes her face, and her lips part, as before a kiss, but she can't lean towards me for such a long time, and falls back into the shadow. From there, she laughs.

There's a long wait.

When the lamps are lit on the street and their blueish glow fills up the space between the furniture, I stand. My aunt seems to be napping. A shame. I wanted to take a look at the picture. The pic-ture is in the casket, the casket on the middle shelf of the linen closet, under the sheets. My aunt keeps the keys of the linen closet and the casket in an old silk-embroidered velvet pouch in the other room, under the divan.

When they open the casket so I can see the picture—on the pic-ture I seem to see myself, my face earnest, though I'm not wearing my own clothes, it looks like a mascarade! and the lady sitting in an armchair in front of me, holding the pouch in which they're safekeeping the key to them in her lap, resembles my mother, and my aunt too, yet is too much of a stranger to be mine, or too familiar; one hand sunk informally in a pocket, the other resting on the back of the armchair, and I need only reach out my ring finger to touch my lady's neck—if, in short, the casket is opened, I can steal a glimpse of my grandmother's jewelry as well. I have a handsome, thick, dark moustache on the picture—emphasizing the earnestness of my lips—but my eyes are gentle. I more or less look the way I am. And in a couple of months the same age as my grandfather was then, for the picture couldn't have been taken much earlier.

I support my palm right next to hers on the plush of the armchair, lean over, and kiss my aunt's forehead. Adél too rises from the stool. As if this door would never have to be opened again.

"When you come again in the spring, I can continue. But bring potted hyacinth instead, or sweet violets. Something that'll last," whispers Adél in the hall before I kiss her, too, on the forehead.

Translated by Judith Sollosy

WITH MY FATHER AT THE GAME
by GYÖRGY SPIRÓ

June 13th, 1973

Today is the last time I am going to see a game with my father.

We are on Dózsa György út, with me driving and glancing sideways at times. He looks weary, there's no colour in his face. The jacket of his grey suit is on the back seat. A handkerchief hangs in the pocket of his short-sleeved shirt, over his heart. It makes me edgy that he keeps it there. From time to time he wipes his forehead.

"What's on today?" I ask.

"I had a radiation session."

"And?"

"I am going for the last time tomorrow. The doctor said it's getting better."

We are close to the Szabolcs utca hospital now, that's where he is going to die, it's all fixed.

"I brought the set," I tell him, "Szepesi will do the commentary."

I'm hot, and the bunch of keys in my pocket presses against my thigh. The keys to the upper and lower lock, that of the lift, the front door, and the mailbox. The ignition key dangles right in front of me, with the car-door keys and that of the safety lock.

We pass through the demonstration square, there are the stands. The pedestal is empty. This is where the Stalin statue used to stand. My grandmother, who committed suicide, got a piece of the earlobe in '56. I looked after it for a while, then it got lost somewhere.

A bunch of cops at the end of Dózsa György út. They are diverting us to Ajtósi Dürer sor.

Népstadion út is also sealed off. We have to go to Hungária körút. Traffic has slowed down to walking space. All three lanes are crowded, in front of us a bus is edging by, filled with fans with boards, behind us lorries, and cars on both sides.

"We should not have come this way," father says.

"Makes no difference," I answer, "cars must be diverted in other streets as well."

I light up. The air is awfully sultry. He never drank, or smoked. He kept fit. If there's justice, he should have got cancer of the throat in the Csepel air, spending twenty-five years in the smoke and soot there.

We are still stuck. He keeps wiping his forehead. I gaze in each direction but his, and yet I watch him all the time. I want to note his features. He is practically grey but at least he hasn't grown bald. His face is so familiar. I know every little wrinkle on it. Yet nights I wake up to realize that I have forgotten him. There is a tiny swelling on the left side of his nose, a reminder of childhood chicken-pox that he scratched. His ears stand apart. I wonder if his ears will also turn thinner.

His fingers are thick and pudgy, and I know they feel warm. These days their mere touch makes my flesh creep. In the morning when I do touch them, I wash it off, and shudder thinking that the touch is contagious. I feel that worms of cancer are swarming all over my body which, I feel it logical, can do more harm in hot water. I also abhor father's blue shirt, which could be full of cancer spores. Mother is not likely to throw out his socks and handkerchiefs, I shall have to use them, and fear possible infection for many years. Someone we know died fifteen years ago, and I inherited some of his socks. I wear those most often just to prove to myself I am not scared.

His watch will come down to me.

It makes me shudder. I shall throw away the band, it has touched father's skin. Of his clothes I shall get his fine suede jacket, he never wears it, he takes too much care of it. Since I know it's going to be mine, I wear mine more often, I used to try and save it. I must admit: it gives me a good feeling to know I will own new objects. I inherited an old, worthless Sanyo set from my grandmother, his mother. I knew it years before that I would inherit it, and though I owned transistors, two of them, I was still glad of it.

The line of cars starts to move, we roll about five metres, then stop again. The two outside lanes are moving, but we are still stuck in a bottle-neck.

"We'll miss the prelim," I say.

It's like in a coffin. He is sweating, and he keeps wiping his face. That handkerchief will also be mine. I need some consolation. How good he won't have to die old and helpless, no longer himself, bedridden for years, blind, paralyzed, after a stroke, senile, etc.

We start to move, and get to Thököly út, where the lights are against us. The air is sooty, the decaying tenements are shabby. The sky is grey even when the sun is shining like now, the cars around us look miserable, with the indifference of middle age showing on those driving them. Father had to live his life in such surroundings. A shocking revelation. I look back on my father's age in astonishment.

I can fully inhale my next cigarette. The lights turn green, and we cross Thököly út. Hungária körút narrows and I just manage to get ahead of the bus and return to the line. In front of us a string of unending red brakelights. We're in second, but have to change back to first. I slip the clutch, it won't do any good to the car, but father is not paying any attention, he is just sitting in a completely resigned way. The heat has been eating at us for forty-five minutes now. Walking, we would have got there long ago.

We have to stop again. Not a word. I have no idea what's going on in his mind. I should question him closely on what is keeping him busy these days. Everything is important. Yet I cannot question him, that would be too obvious. I don't even remember when we last had a good talk. Now it is too late to make up for what we missed.

Sleepiness gets the better of me, and night images overwhelm me. I dreamt that he had shrunk. My mother and I visited him in a strange polygonal ward. There must have been at least twenty there, and father was walking with a stick and lying with a stick—why precisely a stick? And he was getting smaller all the time. My mother pretended she did not notice father was as small as a garden gnome. Father was grinning, then vanished, only the stick survived. Why the stick? He never used a stick. I cannot recall his roommates, but vaguely remember that they were observing with interest how a man vanished into nothing.

"Let's get going," he says.

I come to with a start, and we're off.

I make an effort to relive my Sunday happiness.

I always used to wake up hearing him clear his throat, sharpening his razor blades, in the bathroom. I felt an unexpected joy and decided to remember him that way, scratching around—that's what my mother called it—on Sundays in the bathroom. Come what may I will remember him as a lively man, who could make the time to scratch around. Three days ago, that's all.

At last we can turn right. The side-street is dug up, with pipes ready to be laid.

"Move a bit forward," he says, "a truck might hit us, there's so little room."

He lumbered out. I passed him his jacket, it could turn cooler in the evening. What would happen anyway if he caught cold? He slams the door shut, and I lock the handle. Below the left backseat I switch on the electronic anti-theft device and lock the doors. He tries the lot to make sure. He checks if I stopped close enough to the kerb, but not too close, that's no good for the tyres. He doesn't say a thing.

Half past five. A large crowd in Népstadion út. People are waving the national tricolour, but green-white Ferencváros colours as well. He walks more slowly than usual. I notice now, he is wearing those rotten yellow perforated shoes. They're at least eight years old. The colour always gets my goat, but I can't talk him out of wearing them.

I stop and jot down József Lengyel in a notebook that I always carry. I have looked over our bookshelves time and again but I thought the short stories in *Forfeited Obligation* are the only ones I want him to read. The rest is literary. I don't really know if it makes sense for him to enrich his mind. That adventure story set in Hungary by Jules Verne occurred to me. In 1956 in Saint Roch's Hospital a boy with an abdominal wound asked mother, who went in to see father to get the book for him. I owned it, my mother took it in. I was afraid it might get lost; the boy read it; liked it, and died. We're inside the fence, groups of people clatter by, and we draw aside.

I thought again that I'd buy a black T-shirt, a black watch-strap and black jeans. If white were the colour of mourning as in ancient times, I'd be longing for white jeans. I will have to hide the black things for a while yet. But I want to mourn in advance. Maybe to get it over with as soon as possible. Or maybe because it's exciting. I should like to know how I will look in black. And I want to mourn just like other people. The way it's done. Feeling I was one of them might give me strength. Perhaps I just want them to know.

We are behind the players' entrance, right next to the stadium. On the training pitch some of the players are kicking a ball about, cerise guernseys, white shorts, green stockings, and white numbers on their backs. A young player is looking around lost, with a ball in front of him. He looks like a cub.

"That's András Tóth," I say, "I wonder how he'll perform."

He looks at him absent-mindedly, and steps across a stone.

Father, pale, stepped across the line four years ago, just four years ago, when we buried his mother. A line was drawn on the ground right in front of him, and he had to step across it ceremoniously for some reason. That was the only terrible moment during the whole funeral, the rest was plain boring. Perhaps it started that moment.

We are going up to the level of the elevated passage, he's a bit short of breath, but I see, he takes no notice.

"Maybe I can play a little tennis in the autumn all the same," he says. "Before that," I say, then start to laugh. "You're a real boy. You're upset just because you can't play for a few weeks. You are spoilt because you have never been ill. And you are a little impatient, don't you think?"

He seems to cheer up.

"Does it show?" he asks.

"Why do you think your blood pressure goes up?"

"Don't tell your mother, but the registrar took it and said 250 and not 220."

"Why do you upset yourself? The wonder is you never had any trouble so far."

"None now either. My weight is right too, I am not as overweight."

He is losing weight. Funny, but I had not noticed it.

His photo should be taken now when he still looks like himself. But taking photos can also be suspicious. This morning I looked at a picture-postcard of Elizabeth Bridge at a tobacconist's and I kept looking for our car among the others, and for him among the pedestrians, could be he was there when the picture was taken.

We are under the stands already, you could cut the crowd with a knife, a lot of filth, rushing hordes, lots of drunks. I keep turning my head, I'd like to guess from the fleeting faces if their fathers are still alive. Whoever told me that story? There were two octogenarians, and they were writing their wills. They were twins, and when the notary public asked them if they had any relatives, they had a good cry and said, we are orphans.

I wonder why he steps on the scales? I secretly glance at him.

For a few seconds my gaze followed him until he disappeared at the turning of the steps. More than a month ago he put on his black gaberdine and black beret, he carried an overnight bag. He went for an in-patient check-up and I saw him to the door. He was walking heavily and unsure of himself, and I felt in my insides that he knew. I looked at his beret, it will come down to me, and I shall wear it at the funeral. Since then a few weeks have passed, and as I see it, he knows less and less. Yes, he has become senile, I calm myself, he has demobilized those brain cells that apperceive death. I look sideways again, but I can't penetrate his mind. What could be going on in his head? Who knows, perhaps a man becomes more clever before death, and finds out the essantial things.

"My mouth is dry," he says, "I want to drink something." He has a good-looking mouth. In the terminal ward his mother's mouth stuck to her dentures, and it was so dry that she lacked the strength to move it. Will his lips shrink to his teeth as well? Perhaps, about to die, he will be like his mother, and lack the strength to talk, or even to lie down. Even lying down was an effort for my grandmother.

There are long queues at the bar, a lot of jostling and shoving.

"Half an hour at least," I say.

"I'll have some kind of juice all the same. Give me one of the tickets, I'll follow you."

I shouldn't leave him on his own, what will happen if he faints in this crowd? He looks pale, and breathes heavily. Still, I fumble in my pocket and produce one of the tickets. I want to run away from him, even now.

"We'll meet up top," I say.

I start up the stairs to sector 25.

I'd love to change places with him. I'd try what it's like inside when you're dying. A change of roles would not even be too great a sacrifice on my part. I want to escape from the natural mourning that lies ahead of me. Let him do the mourning. People are shoving me. The whole thing is a fraud. By wishing to be in his shoes, I can only imagine his death and not mine. I'd die in his place, then get back inside my own skin, enriched by the experience.

At the turn I go into the gents, half a centimetre of liquid on the paved floor. I stand on my toes waiting my turn. This gents is a historic place, I say to myself, my father's son is pissing in it. When I first went to the stadium, I also went to the gents. My father took me, those were still the Golden Boys, we beat the Rumanians 5 to 3. Time and again Puskás stopped with the ball, body swerved to the left, then to the right, and the Rumanians rushed around, not knowing which way to go. That was at least eighteen years ago. What would my father have said then if somebody had told him he still had eighteen years to go? Would he have settled for that much?

No ticket collectors at the central grandstand entrance. Two policemen prop up the wall. A crowd, jostling, and I pop up at the top of the sector, it is full, people are standing and sitting on the stairs, and the pitch is empty. Some in front of me are trying to move down, and I bore into the crowd with them. People are uselessly waving their tickets right around me. A new lot gets in above me, pushing us downwards, a lot near me lose their balance. I turn back and see the policemen loafing around. Young louts are screaming and waving flags. Father cannot come here. We not only cannot reach our seats, but won't have a place to stand. I turn back, the pressure is great from the top, the young louts twin up in packs, and the loners packed tight dare not kick back. Head down, like a battering ram, I fight my way back to the policemen who cheerfully prop up the wall.

"Where are the ticket collectors?" I ask.

"Gone."

"Why don't you watch it on the box?" the fatter of them suggests.

There are still some empty seats in the upper grandstand. Perhaps I can manage two. I rush up, no ticket collectors there either. Then I hurry back to the rails to see if father has got there. The two policemen are standing around below me, another lot arrive, screaming rhythmically. I am waiting for father to appear in the grinder, keeping an eye on the empty seats.

The two line-ups are beginning to appear on the scoreboards. Another seven minutes before kick-off. At last I see father, who starts to fight his way downward among the people crowding the stairs. I jump on the rails, shout, but he does not hear. I don't even know how to call him, I wouldn't like to deliver up his name to the crowd. I whistle the family signal, but I cannot even hear myself.

The crowd closes around him, I only see the crown of his head, it is as easy to break as an egg. He does not look up. He'll never see me. He thinks I have got down to my seat. I am breathing fast as if I had run a lot. Finally he turns back, and struggles backward. I have taken away days from his life. It takes one or two minutes before he reaches the policemen, I whistle to him, and try to touch his head with my feet, but no go. He is about two metres from me. He says something to the policemen, who only shrug their shoulders. I have nothing to throw at him. Funny, I can see him move. He turns back and looks downward. I lay my hopes in mere chance, people are shouting at me to sit down, but the pitch is still empty, there is a slight movement in the players' entrance.

At last he looks up. I beckon to him to come up. He beckons back that he understands and disappears.

Sighing with relief, I run upwards. In the middle of the sector I find one and half seats at the end of a row, I sprawl on them to stop someone sitting down next to me. In front of me a group of ten or twelve people take their places, unfolding their flags, blocking the view to the pitch. I am really sorry I talked him into the game. I had hoped he would enjoy himself.

Finally he reaches me, he is gasping for air, his shirt is wet through and his face is grey. He could die. We squeeze against each other. I lean back on my right elbow to stop him being kicked that much from the top.

"This is a scandal," he says. "It's this you should write about in the paper."

"What did you have?"

"Raspberry syrup. It tasted bad."

Perhaps there's a bad taste in his stomach.

People in front stand waving their flags, turning their rattles, and hoot away on an old car-horn. "We won't see much," he says.

Six o'clock. The line-ups are still there on the scoreboards. The sun shines on the Népstadion út board, so it is hard to recognize the names.

Bicskei—Török, Kovács, Vidáts, Szűcs—Juhász, Bálint—Kozma, Bene, Tóth, Zámbó.

Larsson—Olsson I, Olsson II, Nordquist, Grip—Grahn, Tapper—Magnusson, Kindwall, Edström, Sandberg.

They are jumping about in front of us again, which suggests the teams have come out. We are sitting somewhat more comfortably, then we, too, stand up. Busying people in the middle of the pitch. The two teams stand next to each other. I say a prayer for victory, maybe father will like it.

The Swedish anthem. We stand. *Huj-huj-hajrá!* The Hungarian anthem. Singing on the other side, slow and drawn out, our side joins in. I am gaping, in case anyone objects. The Hungarian anthem falls apart, as if the stadium were singing a canon. It ends in bits, undisciplined. Screams, rattles, bells, pipes. Petards go off, and a line of smoke. They are tossing up at the centre. From the back: sit down, sit down.

I switch on the radio, Szepesi's away telling his story, but the noise drowns his voice. I switch it off. I'll turn it on when they score. I feel a pressure in my throat like years ago when, though I mocked at myself, I still rooted for the national eleven. Then the pressure eased. At the Munich Olympics when the Arab—Jewish—German bloodbath was on, I nodded with approval, at last it was clear the Olympics was all lies as well. Yet I sit here with my fists clamped tight and look steady at the players to inspire them to victory. This is father's last game.

The Swedes' goal is closer to us, we see it diagonally from the back. I glance sideways at him. He seems less grey, his face shows he's interested. If I could only tie down his attention for ninety minutes, it would be worth the trouble. If I could get him to the car quickly after the game.

The storm of sound barely outlasts the ball being passed a couple of times, then it stops. Dull midfield play.

"The Ajax–Juventus game was better," people behind us say.

I watched it with him on the box, and he enjoyed it. Five minutes have passed. It turns out that Bene, No. 9, is out on the right-wing, and Kozma, No. 7, is the centre-forward. That's a smart move. We easily lose the ball, and so do the Swedes. In attack we are slow and clumsy. Only the extra-tall Edström is in the Hungarian half, with Kovács treading on his shadow.

"Maybe we'll see some action now," my father is confident. Our first sound attack: Juhász nods the ball to Bene, who's off and centres. Vidáts moves in, draws the whole defence, and Kozma, left unmarked, scores. Goal!

We jump up too, and scream as well. We are ahead, already after just eight minutes of play.

Father smiles, then grimaces.

"It's now we'll stop playing," he says.

It is obvious this is happening after the game is restarted. We are attacking in a manner, but without punch.

"Pretend football," he says.

Perhaps we'll manage to hang on to the lead, I think anxiously. Half an hour has already gone. Not a real chance in front of goal. Next to us Szepesi says his stuff in a large portable, as if something were happening.

"We'll get a hiding," they say behind us.

Slow push-ball, with the ball out in touch more often than not. Tóth has a few good moves, but it's eff you Jack as far as the others are concerned.

Ten minutes left of the first half. The ball is kicked forward by the Swedes, Edström heads it down, there is a great mix-up near the edge of the box, we can't really see, it's so far. It seems Bicskei got a hand to the ball and one of the Swedes, with all the time in the world, puts it in the net.

Silence. Kindwall's name appears on the scoreboard. A draw is good enough for the Swedes, we have to win.

We manage to keep going to half time without another goal. We stand up, moving restlessly.

"This lad, Tóth, distributes the ball cleverly," he says, "he could be educated to become a second Bozsik. He can see on the pitch and knows how to take a kick."

"They'll manage to destroy him."

"They will, all right. Kozma is pretty good. Too bad he doesn't use his head."

We sit down again. Half time is not over yet. There is a faint murmur all around the stadium. I glance at him, he is turning his head without suspecting a thing. All of a sudden I almost cry out. I want to tell him straight: you've got cancer, and you are going to die. I bite my lips, and my hands squeeze my jaw and cheekbone, just to keep silent. Three words mockingly and with sadistic relish would put an end to the whole comedy. I jump up. He stays in his seat. I grate my teeth. I want to cause him pain. What does it matter? He'll die anyway. Why have I been lying to him for weeks now? He is lying too. Let him do the asking, if he cares.

Let it all be finished, I can't stand at his side, I ought to run away before I do something mad. What would happen if I just grinned in his face? Why can't he die of a heart attack?

Breathing deeply, I sit down and take out that morning's Party paper. Chess. Even geniuses can be beaten. Spassky said that about his chances playing Fischer. I open my mouth, and move it a little. I almost got lockjaw.

Sports briefs. Washington. Avery Brundage, the former president of the International Olympic Committee, has announced he will soon marry. The 85-year-old ex-president has chosen for his bride the 37-year-old Princess Marianne de Reuss whom he met during the Olympic Games in Munich. After the wedding Brundage will move to West Germany.

I'd like to tell father, go and get married fast, take a 17-year-old tight bike before you kick the bucket. He should be grateful for that advice. In America they tell you are going to die. This is just a European imbecility.

Rudolf Illovszky, the Team Manager has taken a bold decision... Basing oneself on past performance changes had to be made in the Hungarian Eleven. Should these new faces fail to win, nobody can blame Illovszky. He did everything he could...

The players have not come out yet.

How would he take it? Would his face fall apart? Would he suffer a heart attack?

I turn the pages, it helps me pass the time, then I slowly fold the paper. Death notices. I look at the names. I feel only a moderate elation, on better days more people peg out before father. How much does such an ad cost? I shall have to draft one. I don't want a funeral in winter, the snow is too white then.

A murmur, they've appeared. People in front sit down. The ball is placed at the centre.

I put down the paper. I won't tell him now. I feel a shudder. As long as it doesn't get me again.

I am watching the world. Tóth and Kozma have not come out, and yet they were the best. Szőke and Kocsis are the substitutes.

The storm of voices soon subsided. Nothing much happens out there. Szőke takes a free kick, the crowd holds its breath, the ball rubs the crossbar. The Swedes attack, just below me, one of them passes the ball, another puts it into goal, neither is interfered with. Our defence is nowhere. Silence. Sandberg's name goes up.

"Bunglers," father says, "the Swedes are no good either, they could have been beaten."

Now we are starting to play. The idea could have occurred to us sooner. We put the pressure on, the Swedes defend. Suddenly the whole stadium explodes in a shout. Have we equalized? It seems we have. The other goal is a long way off. Vidáts. A tempest of shouting.

"Now we'll have to keep up the pressure," he says, "we can win by goals."

The Swedes cross the half-way line. The fools. Too many free kicks. Some say Lo Bello is whistling the game apart. Fifteen minutes to go. We ought to leave now before the crowd. Bene passes the ball to Zámbó, who puts a boot in, a shout of joy: it beat the Swedish goalie. We are leading. We've only got fifteen minutes to play out.

Father is warming up.

"We've got to go on attacking," he says, "we mustn't fall back into defence."

We defend.

Grahn lobs the ball. Right in the middle of the penalty area Edström rises to head, lots of ours around him stand and watch. The ball leaving from the tall Swede's head takes its time towards the near post. Bicskei stands rooted to the ground and watches. As if we were watching it all in slow motion. When the ball reaches the goal-line, Bicskei dives but how slowly.

"It is all over," father says.

The public are silent, no whistling. Father looks around in a bad mood. Szepesi moans.

That's it.

We didn't make it to the World Cup finals. Not once beaten but we didn't win even once either.

The public scatters without demonstrating. We move three or four steps a minute towards the exit. The flagwaving mob continues to scream and ring bells, it's all the same to them. A few working men look grim as they leave.

It was eight by the time we reach the bottom of the stadium. Half of the crowd hurries toward Verseny utca, the other half toward Népstadion út, and we find ourselves in a crossfire position. We are edging our way around black government limousines which were allowed to enter the stadium area. The crowd presses us against the line of policemen. Outside the line there are mounted police, steelhelmeted riot police in a truck some yards away. A few ambulances. We are pushing our way out among the survivors.

On Népstadion út groups of drunks are bawling. Some of the mounted policemen head their horses for the crowd. Cars are moving more slowly than people, hooting as they go. Dust everywhere. No relief to the sultriness, yet it is getting dark. The lights in the stadium are still on. Father is moving along next to me weary and dejected. He won't be able to see the World Cup on television. We should have won all the same. Funny, how a draw can make you feel empty.

We cannot turn into Kerepesi út, the police edge us off. We reach the underpass on Hungária körút where we come to a halt once again. It takes fifteen minutes before we can turn right into Kőbányai út. My left foot is numb from working the clutch so much. It is turning dark fast, I switch on the lights, put my foot on the accelerator, over eighty, but he doesn't notice. I desperately hold the steering wheel to have time to hit a bus or lorry head on. Let us die together. Father does not sense the danger. I have no right, I keep telling myself, and pray lest I swing the wheel left.

We get home by half past eight. We get out. I look back on the red Skoda, S 100, licence number IG 20–27, I don't know why, but it is important now. It's parked in front of the house. That's what tells me father is alive. It will be a strange feeling not to see it there one day. That must have been a more human age when a man left a horse behind. I can well imagine: a horse would mourn his master, perhaps die. I look down from the third-floor passage and stand against the wall. My father messes with the key, his neck looks thin to me. I don't bite it.

The heat settled in the room and yet the window is wide open. I start to count my sins. I feel remorse because of the draw. That's all I could give him. Maybe he will die because I wished him to be dead as an adolescent, just to mourn him properly. That is what I am doing right now. Speaking nonsense, I search the faces of my friends to watch them change when I let them know after father's death in a few modest, simple words what I have gone through. Then they will love me and respect me for my human nobility, because I concealed my sorrow so beautifully. I will be a hero. A month ago I almost told the lot to a tart in the Olympia bar. I just wanted to boast, I kept provoking her to ask me why I was looking so low. That evening I wasn't really upset, quite the contrary.

It was a rotten day. Still it would be fine to start it again. His life would last that much longer. We would not go to the game, we'd play chess. Perhaps.

The stick he left behind appears. Dreams attract one another. There is a damp mattress in a dark room, on which he was dying, with a bloated face, I remember, but it is gone. People say I killed him with a poisoned pin, I shall have to go after him. I go out into the street, I stand on the Danube embankment by Parliament, but this is not the real Budapest, only a counterfeit. It has been set up in America, and I was asked as an expert to check if everything was in the right place. I laugh at them, I see Elizabeth Bridge in the place of the old Kossuth Bridge, they are incompetent. I took a tram No. 2 toward Váci utca, that is where I have to meet him, I will find the damp mattress there, but I know he will wear a suit. I am looking for him. They pretend not to understand. They have conspired against me, he is no longer alive, but they act as if he had never lived. I am running among colourful shop windows, the cobblestones are of marble, and my steps have a glassy sound.

I stand paralyzed: I hear steps. The kitchen door opens, father is pottering about. I must go out to him. I must not hide. I have to go out.

He is in pyjamas, his hair is dishevelled, his face wrinkled, he blinks into the light.

"What's up," I say jovially, "can't you sleep?"

"Not really."

He sits down on the kitchen stool, leaning against the tiles, crossing his legs with the right on top. His hands are folded. I drink some water.

"It is still sultry in here," I say.

"My blood pressure is playing up."

His face displays a strange, bewildered look. He pulls up his eyebrows a little.

"We didn't have a good game," he says, "we could have won."

He smiles funnily, awkwardly, sadly. His neck is wrinkled. His ears too will get thinner for sure.

"We did not get into the finals," he says.

He stands up, nods to me, half-smiling, then turns away, slowly shuffling out of the kitchen, closing the door behind him.

Translated by László Jakabfy

THE TURNED-UP COLLAR

by GÉZA BEREMÉNYI

It was glorious weather—the October sun shone with a brilliance that brought the summer to mind. And Magda Szukics was not allowed to go to school. Shutters closed against the heat, she had spent the summer vacation in bed with a persistent myocarditis. She had hoped to get well before the autumn term began. Her parents had enrolled her in a model secondary school and had urged her to put up a better show in the future. But her illness prevented her from attending the opening ceremony, and schoolday after schoolday passed until her unknown schoolmates had got so far ahead of her in the curriculum that by October it looked as though she would have to repeat the year. She found the continual, compulsory state of repose difficult to endure. Books covered her blanket; she would begin to read one only to discard it in order to start another somewhere in the middle. At the time she had fallen ill she had had a dream that continued from one night to the next, but later the dream became jumbled as well. She had no visitors; the fresh linen on her bed every week was the only change in her life. She got well suddenly, when everyone thought she had fallen behind for good.

Still she went bravely to school. Into her bag, following the timetable set for the day, she placed exercise-books with blank pages, textbooks that had never been opened, and a ruler for the new, unfamiliar subject, technical drawing, the last two classes on that Monday morning, given by a teacher she imagined would be strict, Dezső Villányi by name. The sun was shining brightly on the other side of the door. Magda Szukics was happy to walk the few steps to the tram stop, happy to be wearing sandals and nothing but her panties under her blue school smock. On the crowded tram only the noisy groups of blue-smocked and capped pupils could catch and hold her attention. She tried to guess which of them would be her future classmates.

Pintér recollected seeing Magda Szukics in the classroom for the first time, but his memory was playing him false. Though it hadn't been more than a glance that had passed between them, their first meeting had taken place on the staircase of the school at the time the first bell had sounded. Pintér was talking to a fourth-form senior and had his back to the new girl who was just arriving. The sunshine, the jostling crowd of pupils at the school entrance and the unexpected semi-darkness that had met her as she went in, a gloom that only cleared on the mezzanine, where the dazzling light streaming in from the large windows transformed the shuffling pupils into mirage-like apparitions, had made her dizzy, so she stopped on the first landing, flattening herself against the wall to let the jostling, rowdy crowd pass.

When she looked up she saw a tall, good-looking boy, elbows resting on the banisters, who stood among milling blue shoulders and uniform caps. Many girls would have found him handsome; Magda Szukics did not. But it was good just to watch him standing there, halfway up the staircase, facing her and looking upwards. He was speaking to someone—nodding his head at another boy who stood couple of steps further down on the stairs. The handsome one was so engrossed in the conversation that he would not have noticed the new girl for anything on earth—not even if she had begun to walk up the stairs and pushed him as she passed. Magda Szukics was curious to see the other boy—what could he have in him to fascinate such a good-looker to the extent that he doesn't even notice a girl nearby? Then suddenly the crowd was gone, a few latecomers ran up, taking two stairs at a time, and with them the clamour receded into the distance. Only the new girl remained on the landing, and the two talking by the banister.

The other boy stood with his back to Magda Szukics, speaking to his handsome friend with his chin raised. His shiny brown trouser-legs stirred restlessly. The collar of his short blue smock was turned up. What a stuck-up thing to do! Can't he think of something better? The two boys laughed, the handsome one facing her doubled up for a minute, the other threw his head back. The first bell went. Its last echoes had died away but still Magda Szukics did nor stir. The two boys stayed. The one with his back to her had a schoolbag under his arm. A long ruler stuck up out of it, pointing straight at Magda Szukics. The new girl made to move. Just then the one with the turned-up collar changed position and the ruler continued to point at her. And she had a ruler too. A shorter one, one that fitted easily into her bag. And according to her timetable her class would have two hours of technical drawing last thing that day.

At last Magda Szukics started up the stairs, she passed slowly by the still-laughing Pintér with the turned-up collar, who did not see the new girl look at his face. Just glance at it for a minute. Then hurry on up the stairs, her bag pressed tightly to her breast, scuttle along the corridor to find shelter in the new classroom.

Pintér continued his conversation with Pierre, the tall fourth-former, until the second bell went. He knew that Miss Lovas, who took the first class that morning, was always a few minutes late. He and Pierre had a last laugh together, took leave of each other as the last bell went. By the time he reached the classroom Magda Szukics had already asked someone which seat was vacant in the girls' row, had sat down and introduced herself to her neighbour. When Pintér with his turned-up collar burst into the classroom the new girl took another good look at him and thought that she couldn't really like him as much as she thought she did. She only wanted to see his eyes and to know when he would notice and look back?

Miss Lovas came into the classroom, the monitor brought the class to attention, the pupils stood up from their desks. The white-smocked, spectacled schoolmistress glanced around the room as she listened to the monitor's report. Her experienced eyes rested for a moment on the new girl, then passed on quickly so that no one should notice her thinking. Oh dear, oh dear, she's not going to be easy, that one. Wonder where they found her?

The homework that had been set for the day was a poem by Petőfi.

Everywhere in the school monitors were making their reports. Whistles shrilled in the gymn, balls thundered across the floor. The fourth-form corridor prefects were the only ones allowed to remain outside their classrooms. They bawled at the late juniors scurrying along the corridors, checked the toilets to make sure they were all empty, the stamp of their running feet resounded down the echoing corridors; one of them gave a last loud whoop and at last they too disappeared. The corridor-prefects wore blue armbands with a big P embroidered on them in red wool by the female members of the parent–teacher association.

Pintér's school was silent. Until the next break. The old building was founded upon tradition, but ist weatherbeaten walls had consented to admit the achievements of many new eras. It housed a primary and a secondary school, a consequence of its ample size being that inexperienced children of primary-school age would lose their way from time to time in the labyrinths of its corridors. Which was why the prefects always had a last check after the third and final bell had gone.

At the end of the day the school would release its pupils. In the afternoons there was extra physical education for those who wanted it in the basement gym; study circles were held in the laboratories. The feeble glow of lightbulbs in the corridors would mean parent–staff meetings were taking place in some of the classrooms. Every now and then a dancing class or class party would break the sound of silence with the faraway tinkle of a piano or the loud blare of a tape-recorder. But finally all would be silent and dark in the building once more.

So its days passed.

When morning broke the sunlight would form pools upon the green oil paint of the walls and benches and would settle on the pictures nailed to the walls. Their mute, infinite ranks covered every possible inch of surface. Pictures, each in its uniform brown frame made of plain laths, each under its sheet of glass, all the result of decades of afternoons spent in the woodwork circle. The roving eye would light upon them everywhere in the building. Over the years they had completely inundated the school, becoming so congested in places that the frames almost touched, forming a jumbled tableau; then thinning out again the line would continue, slowing down unexpectedly only when some larger, broader specimen broke the uninterrupted flow that continued around the corners, into niches and hollows, into the darkest nooks; its labyrinthine course mapped out the whole school from the coal-cellar door to the attic. There they hung, as if conscious of the inconsistency, the disregard of chronology and values which had determined their position in the procession-pictures of great moments in Hungarian history, portraits of prominent figures who had distinguished themselves during those moments, portraits of the great examples, cheek by jowl with characteristic paintings from each of the representatives of Hungarian and foreign schools of painting. In a plain brown frame hung Ladislas the Fourth of Hungary on horseback, tending his hand to Rudolph from the House of Habsburg, to whose aid he had gone, celebrating the victory of Marsch Plain; a couple of turns of the corridor and there were the Hungarians again, but the revolting Kuruts armies this time, cutting down Habsburg soldiers in their three-cornered hats, harrying the army that had become strong enough over the centuries to attack those who had once come to its rescue; all this taking place soon after the battles along the frontiers with the Turks, which were represented, in addition to a few paintings in oil depicting the courageous defenders of fortresses in action, by the portrait of the great poet, Bálint Balassi, carrying within himself the contradictions of his age mirrored in his work, to be found somewhere on the second floor, next door to pictures of international revolutionaries. Soviet soldiers waving their weapons in greeting from their tanks, and the crowd greeting them hats off and kerchiefs in the air, which hung facing the photograph of the marble bust of the enlightened philosopher, Voltaire, renowned for his vitriolic pen, followed by a reproduction of the Impressionist masterpiece entitled 'Picnic in May' and a drawing of Attila József, poet of the proletariat, in ink. But in the company of those who sought and found the way out, of those who sang in praise, those who followed and those who were steadfast, a place was found for those who made vain attempts to remain uncommitted and sought refuge in the ivory tower of *l'art pour l'art;* a place was found for the vanguard, for those forced to recognize the contraindications of ages long become a lesson for today, for those who pointed them out, at them and beyond them, for those who, all in all, in spite of their class limitations, had been progressive in their fashion, who had passed beyond the boundaries of their class prejudices, who had portrayed the complexity of the long-forgotten conditions and tragic problems of their age, problems only resolved by the present—a place was found for the geniuses who, with lasting validity, because with visionary force; the ages which had carried the germs of, the prophets who had interpreted it in their way, and the revolutionaries who had recognized it and created it in spite of transitional regression—a place was found for all of them. Some of the pictures depicted typical scenes from critical moments of history, periods when the course of development was only recognizable with great effort, when ideals were glowing embers under smothering ashes, glowing only in the best minds of the people. The geniuses represented on the walls desired the collaboration of the progressive forces, the standard-bearers reached their hands toward the oppressed, and were replaced by others when they preferred death to compromise. The pupils of the school often referred to these paragons when questioned, but seemed to forget them at break, when they would repeat one name, and one name only: Pierre, Pierre.

"Have you seen Pierre?" Pintér heard the arm-banded corridor-prefects shout to each other above the racket produced by the juniors as they ran by them.

"Do you really think Pierre's all there, do you?"

"Do you know what Pierre's gone and done again?"

"Is Pierre going out with Kati or has he still got that platinum blond bird of his?"

Pintér heard the name repeatedly from the fourth-formers at breaktime. Their classrooms were on the top floor; it was from there that the loud-voiced big boys came down when the bell went for break, to watch over the juniors. They walked in pairs, talking to each other with voices raised against the uproar. When they lost patience they rolled up their soft-bound textbooks and hit the nearest boisterous youngster within striking distance on the head. "Steady on, kid!" Then they continued to stroll down the corridor, because they thought it more important to discuss Pierre's latest doings. From the snatches of conversation overheard by accident Pintér spun an elaborate web of fancy around the figure of Pierre.

The first-formers discussed him too during breaks in the toilets where they retreated to smoke. Most often it was little Körmendi who began; he liked to draw, and made no secret of it, boasted of it even, and so had been christened Cocky. Cocky Körmendi thought Pierre was like the hero of a penny dreadful; he said Pierre had once bent a coin in two with his thumb and forefinger under the nose of a grey, defeated teacher nicknamed Ficere and had promised to do the same thing to him if he dared plough him at the end of the year. The old, grey-haired teacher has been trembling with fear ever since, as anyone could see for himself—you'd only got to watch him walk down the corridor in his brown smock, starring straight in front of him, his head trembling like a leaf. According to Cocky, Pierre planned to join the Foreign Legion; he spent half the night running in the park so as to be in form for marching in the desert. He played in a band, his father was in prison and his mother was persecuted because of her origins, they had their ancestral estates taken away from them. Cocky Körmendi would take Pintér to visit them one of these days, but first he had to ask Pierre because he was a bit suspicious of strangers. He'd got his reasons for it though. He'd had some trouble with the cops. "Hey Pintér, you really don't know which is Pierre? He just went by. Weird you didn't see him, he even said hello to me. Didn't you notice? If I don't feel like coming to school he always gets me a medical certificate. He's got this doctor girl-friend. She's great!"

Pintér stared at all the prefects during breaks. Perhaps that one in glasses was Pierre. He'd got a deep voice and he was really strong. But he wore glasses. That one there was too fat, he was disgusting. He picked one of them out at long last, a blond one that the girls in his class, by a quick vote, had found the most attractive. Pintér, after he had named him Pierre to himself, followed him everywhere at break. He eavesdropped on his conversations, meditating over the way his companions treated him. But he soon lost interest. Finally he watched his candidate greet Rajnák, the deputy head, and heard Rajnák's reply. After that he wasn't surprised when he saw another fourth-former give his chosen one a friendly thump on the back and say cheerfully, "Don't piss in your pants, man, Pierre's not mad at you. He was just having a bit of fun, you know how he is when the mood takes him."

Pintér took extra gym with Cocky Körmendi. One day they arranged to meet on November 7th Square. Dusk had settled in early that day, the streetlamps were lit and it was raining, not heavily, but in a steady, disagreeable drizzle. Pintér waited for Cocky at the top of the steps leading to the underground station. He wore a leather coat that was much too big for him, and his uniform cap. For a while he banged his gym bag against some railings which sent up clouds of steam into the cold, heavy air. It was the rush-hour, and it seemed as though the traffic jam on the square could not get any worse; as though all the cars in Budapest had converged here on the gleaming wet asphalt to obey the signals flashed at them by the traffic lights. Herds of cars zoomed thundering at the first blink of green, impatiently sounding their horns, spattering the brightly lit trams with mud as they overtook them. Because of the weather Pintér wasn't in the mood to cavort about in the gym, but for some reason the gym teacher was not overfond of him and his good will, said Pintér's mother, must at all costs be won, through paying the fees for the extra gym course and through showing a lot of enthusiasm for the subject.

Cocky Körmendi was late and Pintér, bored stiff, began to examine the photographs displayed in the photographer's window beside him. The simpering children and the smiling women, dominated even here by the stern, manly faces of fathers and fiancés' sporting moustaches and clenching pipes, failed to hold his attention for long. He turned instead toward the crowd waiting to cross the street in order to appraise those coming towards him, one by one. The biggest crowd of people the day had seen so far surged across the street in the rain; there was nothing in their faces or their clothes to catch the eye. The crowd flowed around Pintér, brushed by him or jostled against him and he stood in the midst of them, their words an incoherent babble in his ears. By the time the traffic lights had turned yellow they were all on the pavement. On the gleaming, empty asphalt only the cars waited, legitimately impatient, headlights flaring, ready to spring.

And this was the moment that a solitary, perturbing figure chose to cross the street. As he stepped off the kerb the lights turned red for him and justly green for the cars, but that did not bother him at all. He walked sedately, at a leisurely pace, oblivious of the shouting around him; even stopped in the middle of the road, in the glare of headlights, turned to face one of the files of cars and spread his arms wide, stopping them all. "The public is warned," he shouted, but the rest of his words were lost in the din of cars whipping past him. And he punished them for ignoring him, bringing his palms down on their tops with a bang; afraid of a collision, they could take no revenge, and sped on, seething. The other files of cars could not move for the figure with the outstretched arms; people jumped out of the first car, tugged at the jaywalker, almost pushed him under the cars passing on the other side of the square.

We know now that this was Pintér's first meeting with Preston. He could not take his eyes off him; he was drawn to the edge of the kerb, gym bag swinging from his hand, to watch him being dragged off the asphalt. And as one is wont quite arbitrarily to fix a name to a character in one's dreams, regardless of whether the apparition bears any resemblance to the bearer of that name in real life or not, so Pintér was certain that the conspicuous figure in the square could only be Pierre. We know that the delusion lasted a few days only, but it was a characteristic mistake, as characteristic as Preston's behaviour.

After having forced a file of cars to wait for the next green light, and after the rest of the cars had moved on, Preston shook himself free of his pursuers and walked straight towards Pintér. From behind and beside Pintér pedestrians moved forward because the lights had changed again. Preston knew his way around; he too recognized his man in the crowd. He took one look at the boy in the school cap and stopped in front of him. He was tall and dripping wet, only his usual dark blue jacket covered his bare chest. Pintér would have been shaking with cold in his place. They did not say a word to each other. Preston performed one of his characteristic gestures, one with which we were all familiar: he extended his arms and placed the edges of his palms together, which meant "give", or, rather, "give if you want", staring all the while with the unblinking eyes of a priest celebrating mass into the eyes of the honoured chosen one—honoured since he did not ask just anybody, and always in a good cause. A lot of our money wandered into his pockets this way.

Pintér thrust his hands into his pockets. He had four forints put by to go to the movies. He took out the two coins, discoloured with age, and placed them into Preston's extended palm. Then, suddenly remembering, he silently lifted a forefinger for Preston to be patient. He had a silver five-forint piece in the pocket of his trousers, a rare treasure at the time. He held it up, then dropped it on top of the others.

Preston recognized the distinction between the two gifts. He slipped the two-forint pieces into the pocket of his jacket, then took the silver coin and placed it slowly, ceremoniously into his breast pocket, smoothing the material covering the coin twice to emphasize that it would there be held in esteem. It was a practical trifle—or a solemn promise, hand to breast. Pintér could decide as he wished. With a nod of the head Pintér agreed to join the disciples. In answer Preston performed the rites of initiation before moving on. He really knew how to go about it. As they stood in the square, soaked through, he took hold of the boy's collar and in the tumult that surrounded them gave a shake to the jacket, as if adjusting it. Then he turned up the collar and walked away. A thousand duties awaited him.

Pintér watched him walk away and believed he had met Pierre. He made a note of the light duck trousers and the blue Czechoslovak tennis shoes. At the time Preston did not care for ties and winkle-picker shoes. For practical reasons, perhaps? The main thing was that his clothing should be original. We couldn't say a word, he'd invented himself.

For years afterwards Pintér always wore his collar turned up. His teachers often warned him that he would have to leave the class if he persisted in wearing his collar pointed toward the sky; after all, it rarely rains in classrooms. Pintér always took heed of the warning but as soon as the bell went for break, up went his collar again. He wore his coats the same way.

"If that was Pierre you saw then I'm Pierre too. It couldn't have been Pierre on November 7th Square because Pierre was at the seniors' parti, OK? He couldn't be anywhere else, there was a bird he's after, at the party. You really don't know where it's at, do you?" Cocky Körmendi underwent an extraordinary transformation every time he spoke of Pierre. As soon as he had uttered the name his whole body began to shake, he humped up his shoulders, his head turned this way and that, and his voice became throaty, guttural, as if he were singing a pop song with a maddening rhythm.

He wanted to express a singular feeling, enchantment, enthusiasm, an idealised passion that must be devoutly protected from the whole world. While he was speaking the conductor asked to see his ticket, and Cocky Körmendi, because he was speaking about Pierre, thrust it at him with a recklessly insolent gesture, although he was normally a bashful boy. He even began an impudent dispute with the conductor. "Who asked you, anyway?" just to be true to his chosen ideal. Pierre gave him courage and strength. Occasionally, he delivered Cocky from the glazed look, he acquired during class, rid him of his odd grimaces and changing moods, gave him a secret language, a pledged, private code; incited him to make provocative, witty rejoinders. With Pierre's help the fat, bespectacled Cocky Körmendi was able to ignore the gibes and sneers of his classmates, the lectures of his parents; was brave enough to face any conductor on any tram. And this help he tried to requit by measuring up to those exalted feelings which he could express when dreaming of Pierre. His body shook and his voice became throaty even when he was muttering to himself—and not only in front of the mirror. He used the role bestowed upon him with growing confidence, as if within himself; woke with it more and more often in the morning, began to consider it his own, his true self, made it his only pride and joy. He was faithful and unexpectedly conscientious. Pintér jealously watched him tackling the bad-tempered conductor, unperturbed by the interjections of the rest of the passengers, calling him a hysterical, wretched old fool, and knocking his hand away so adroitly that he even escaped a slap on the face. He grudged Cocky Körmendi his Pierre.

The rain did not seem to want to stop. It was still pouring heavily when they came out after gym. Pintér turned up the collar of his leather jacket and mumbled something about a girl he was to meet, in order to get rid of Cocky. He walked a couple of steps in the opposite direction and when Cocky had disappeared around the corner ventured back into the darkened building.

In the school only the landing lights had been switched on, illuminating the first few pictures of the endless procession aligning the walls; the battle-scenes that had made history, the geniuses and other illustrious figures of the curriculum were lost in shadow. Pintér took the stairs one by one, sliding his hand along the banisters as he walked. From around the region of the first floor he heard music and the growing sound of voices singing, the sharp notes of a guitar and somebody screeching. The darkness deepened as he neared the source of the sound. He swung his gym bag in rhythm to the music. The seniors' party was on the third floor, where the lights had been switched off even on the landing and the sound of singing became dangerously loud. An only-just male voice was belting out a song in English in an incoherent falsetto with delightful shamelessness, as though he were crying and did not deem it necessary to control himself, as though, lost to the world, he were celebrating his sorrow, demanding, in an exorbitant desire for immediate satisfaction, more and more from the feeling of anguish, because it was his and his only, because it was a pleasure to lose himself in it, a true experience, an adventure, an adventure that raises one above duty and obligation and achievement and constraint and inexorability and goals and aims to be transfigured, realized, to bloom henceforth only for oneself; to disintegrate and let one's desires wash over one, to celebrate that one is liberated from a law and order and their standards, to experience with one's body that one is at last left alone with one's sensual needs. Pintér proceeded into the cavernous depths of the top floor corridor, and when he could no longer see a foot ahead and felt he could not stand the smallest increase in the volume of sound he stopped and leaned against the wall. He stayed there for an incalculable length of time.

The first thing he could distinguish was a green eye. The only source of light was the tiny lamp of the tape-recorder, shining, as it turned out, from within a classroom which had the double door wide open. The desks had been carried out and in their places the white shirts of the final year boys swirled, closely embracing the blouses of the girls who had been invited. The song ended, the bright pieces of clothing stopped and waited for the next song to begin. Then from very near Pintér heard a girl's voice whisper "Pierre!". The voice came from a window recess close by and was at once full of fear, curiosity, reserve and admiration. Pierre must have done something which she was not expecting but would now have to accept reverently. Then she began to pant, and moan a little, softly, but loud enough to be heard above the new English number blared out by the tape-recorder. You could clearly hear her whisper, breathless, full of wonder, "Pierre!" The third time she cried the name out loud. But Pintér strained his ears in vain for the slightest sound that would attest to Pierre's presence; he did not betray himself with a single word. Whatever he was doing he did silently and mercilessly. He was playing with her as one played on an instrument; he wanted to coax his name out of her, and that was all.

Pintér drew one of his three cigarettes out of his pocket and lit it. He felt capable of everything. He thought the gesture with which he had struck the match and flicked it away into the darkness had been grand. In a flash, like the sudden flare of the match, it came to him that soon, any moment now he too could arouse the admiration of someone; he too would hold a girl close, feel her body and make his own felt, would find someone to his taste at last, one of those from in there. Soon, any moment now. He was sure, there on the dark corridor, leaning back against the wall again after his last puff while a singer inside, much taken with himself, sung in English, that faceless somebodies had already formed a line, were preparing themselves for an unparalleled, un-precedented meeting with him, and the discoveries soon to be made awakened a feeling of superiority in him. He felt strong and was excited. How will it happen to him? He did not try to guess be-cause it was the uncertainty, the feeling of risk that gave the most pleasure. That they would present themselves incalculably at last, through a superb freak of fortune, and the choice will not be made for him. Not even by him. He will simply be set free.

"I'll be off soon," thought Pintér after the last puff before he threw the butt into the darkness. Then he pushed himself away from the wall, and strolled slowly to the end of the corridor, away from the blare of the tape-recorder and the girl who was still re-peating that name.

Translated by Eszter Molnár

THE WHIMSIES OF ONIRISM
by LAJOS GRENDEL

To the memory of René Magritte

In a certain sense I am but a reflection of the man who allowed himself to be lured into a small basement gallery in the city centre to see the elderly onirist artist's exhibition. I was stopping over in Budapest on my way to see relatives in Miskolc in the north and was to have taken a train in the afternoon. I was sucked into the tumultuous morning bustle of the city as into a vortex, and had walked past the Basilica when I stumbled into an old Budapest friend of mine, Zoltán Markó, who abducted me to reminisce over faded memories of our old days in a coffee bar. We had not seen each other for all of three years. Enough time had barely gone by for us to warm to the theme when he started to press me to come and see the master's exhibition, his first show in thirty years, which was a bare five minutes' walk from there. By then I ought to have been dashing off to catch the Miskolc express. My indecision was compounded by having only a very vague notion of what onirism was about, and the elderly artist's name meant no more to me than most commonplace names to be found in the diary features of the dailies. That was the first time I became convinced that I could only be a reflection of the man whom my friend Zoli Markó pushed and bundled down the steps to the basement, and that the slave is relieved of any responsibility by his dependency.

"Well, what do you say to that?" he shouted full of enthusiasm immediately indicating by a majestic sweep of the hand what he expected me to say.

I simply nodded, for although the paintings in the manner of Magritte were to my liking, I didn't fancy them as much as my friend did, who was given to picking quarrels and once wine had gone to his head, would brook no contradiction. I allowed him to put his arm through mine and lead me on; stopping at each of the canvases I had a word of appreciation and even flipped through the catalogue. The majority of the paintings exhibited were from the late 40s, the rest came in from the 60s and the more recent past. The style of the later works scarcely differed from the early ones, the master merely rang the changes on his well-tried ideas and manners. It chagrined me greatly to see that neither the passage of time nor changes in styles and fashions had left any trace on his work. It wasn't so much this bizarre quality of theirs, however, as their timelessness, their atemporality, that put me off. Each picture was different in its own way, yet each appeared to copy the one before it. This dispiriting and wearisome monotony made me restless. I could not help thinking that man was doomed to live his entire life enclosed in the same body, exposed to his own flesh and skin; and that wasn't a comforting thought at all. In order to overcome these gloomy sentiments of mine I was moved to say something nevertheless.

"René Magritte is one of my favourite painters."

While I said this I was poring over one of the paintings. In the middle of the picture there was to be seen a double-hinged gate opened wide with a naked woman, her face utterly dead, stepping out into a wooded landscape ablaze with vernal colours. Behind the gate the sky was ink-blue with the shining sickle of a new moon atop an obelisk.

"Congratulations," I heard somebody behind me say in a hoarse voice and felt the palm of a hand descend on my shoulder.

The master was standing behind me.

"Nobody who likes Magritte can be a bad man," he jested and winked.

I bowed and said my name, which the maestro repeated twice, rolling the "r" in it.

"You like her?" he then asked shooting a glance at the naked woman and without waiting for an answer said, "You can make Bella's acquaintance tomorrow. Come and see me at four in the afternoon."

In my short existence, which can be extinguished at any moment without the world batting an eyelid and without the girls' hearts missing a beat, I have often been faced with a choice that afterwards proved to be decisive. In my younger days I enjoyed assaying my freedom and despised those fussy fault-finders who considered me irresponsible for it. I explained to the overcautious that freedom was something you must meet half-way if and when time and will were ripe to confront destiny. So I did not spend much time thinking over the master's offer: I stayed on for another day in Budapest. I felt no more at ease in Budapest than anywhere else, though not any worse either. And even if it was nice to hear everybody around me speak my mother tongue, I had long since given up the solemn illusion which in my eyes used to transform even a bandit should he happen to speak Hungarian. I thought it natural that I was, am, and can never be anything else but Hungarian. I had got used to being a transit traveller everywhere and never felt, beyond nostalgia for long outgrown intimacy, greater emotion in my native town than on any of the open balconies running in tiers round the walls above the courtyard in some old, rundown tenement houses in Budapest slums. I knew my Miskolc relatives less well than Zoli Markó or others unrelated to me by blood, therefore I liked my kinsfolk out of a sense of duty and propriety only. I had resigned myself to being lonely even among the members of my family and even to my wife and children being different from me, much though we could read each other's thoughts. I had acquiesced in the idea of mundane life not having begun with me and also in having to die one day. So I could well be governed by whims and be unpredictable, and got to meet freedom half-way without taking much risk.

The next day I waited for the master at the appointed place and time, outside the Astoria Hotel. He did not arrive but instead of him there came a young man who introduced himself with, "I'm the master's secretary, please come with me."

We took the Metro to the Buda side, where we got on to a tram in Moszkva tér. The master lived in a detached house in fashionable Pasarét; the garden around the villa was running to seed. The secretary led me up a few steps to a verandah, then as soon as he'd done so he disappeared and before long the master emerged in his place robed in a purple patterned cotton tunic distending on his protruding belly. Not only was his hair and beard tinted but he used lipstick as well, like many of the officers in the former royal Rumanian army. If I hadn't known him to be a painter, might have mistaken him for an oriental magician or a nasty confidence trickster. He complained of a backache and shoved two cushions behind his back at the wall and settled reclining onto a divan groaning loudly.

"I'm all in ruins," he began amiably, and enumerated all his twelve different ailments. "The body refuses to obey any more, not even in bed," he complained. "The body is ready to shuffle off this mortal coil."

Conversation could hardly have begun with less ease. Where did I go to, I asked the man I am the reflection of, I the slave, the incorrigible rationalist. The master noticed my confusion and tactfully changed tone.

"So you came here from Pozsony?"

"Yes," I said.

"And are there any Hungarians still living in Pozsony?"

"There are some," I said gruffly. "Me, for instance."

"Strange," the master mused. "I was in Pozsony once."

"A long time ago?" I queried.

"A very long time ago. In a dream."

"And in reality?"

"Dream is reality," the master asserted. "Why, you've seen my work, have you? Dreams are the truer reality, more authentic... I've been to many places in my time. Chicago, Hong Kong, Papua New Guinea. Without a passport," he said and laughed. "Dreams are in here, and whatever's inside no one can deprive us of. Dreams are the revenge we take for our ill-favoured history. Don't you agree?"

An icy silence descended between us. I was reassured by the observation that the windows of the verandah were being occasionally rattled not by some dark and ungovernable power but by the rush-hour traffic in the streets; that the tram as well as the green of the trees in the garden had real life colours, the green not some imperfect copy of the piercing greens, expressing and evoking anxiety, that glared from the master's canvases.

Outside it was afternoon, the slightly muggy heat of summer failing to bring on a thunderstorm by the evening and merely making the scent of the linden trees heavier and more pervasive in the air. I thought of my wife and children at home, then of my relatives in Miskolc waiting in vain for me for supper yesterday as well as today.

"What did you come here for?" the master asked me, unexpectedly, though not rudely.

Since he received no answer, he went on asking more questions.

"Why do you usually travel?" And,

"What is life?" Then, "What do our words death, love, Hungarian mean?"

Since he still received no answers to any of his questions, he supplied them for me.

"Well, all these words must certainly possess some meaning. A different one for each man. There are many answers to my questions. So many that they are almost all devoid of interest. Our lives are full of silly questions and we spend them giving silly answers to silly questions. But then you must fill the void and fill the enormous silence with something."

The master stalked me stealthily, every one of his sentences clinging to me like seaweed. It was time, I thought, to get round to the purpose of my visit.

"What I'am interested in is the girl."

"Oh, the girl... Well, naturally, you're still a young man," he said.

"Where is that girl?"

The master adjusted his cushions behind the small of his back.

"Bella?" he sniggered. "She's right here, sitting beside me."

It would have made little sense to ask how the young woman, whom the master called Bella, had managed to get beside him on the divan. She hadn't entered by the door and the windows of the verandah were all shut. I had to accept that Bella had been there all the while and I only failed to see her because the master had omitted to open my eyes. Oh, the miracles of onirism, I concluded.

"Touch her," the master told me.

Since I refused to do so, clutching my seat with both hands, the master—I couldn't help noticing—was on the point of taking pity on me.

"Kiss her. Her lips or her nipples or wherever you wish. Just to convince yourself she is real even though a mirage, a vision."

"I have not got the nerve," I said.

"Then take her out to dinner."

"No."

"It's as simple as that, though. It's all yours if you can overcome your pusillanimity."

Pusillanimity was then to become a key word in what he had to say. He launched into a lengthy line of reasoning which I seemed to hear in a halfdazed state, and although his train of thought appealed to me, I later forgot every word of his arguments. Only one of his sentences stuck in my memory:

"Adrift in a shambles of a boat between two shores."

I then hurriedly left the house and decided to expunge from my life even the recollection of the man who I was but a reflection of, and who stayed on in the house to remind me as the better and freer half of my self, of freedom with his absence, and to torture me.

"You've only been given a respite," he shouted after me.

I got on a tram before he could have second thoughts and started to give chase. His last words went on echoing in my mind for a long time.

My Miskolc relatives died many years ago, and although awakening was still a long way to come, I soon managed to get the hang of the roles one needs to keep body and soul together. I am happy as the beasts of the field. The outer zone of my existence is encircled by that frightening milieu guarded and watched over by good manners, the laws of the land, and a night squad of policemen.

Translated by László T. András

ENCLOSURE

by SÁNDOR TAR

It is washday at the Csepi's. The older girl's out in the yard hanging up the wash on a line stretched out between two wilting acacias. Her face and shoulders are beaded with sweat, a fairground for flies. The washing machine's in front of the house in the yard; the dirty water lies sprawling over parched clumps of grass. Her father's in the arbour, lying on a clapped out bed. He naps or goes to the pigsty to relieve himself; from time to time he pulls on a shirt with a wide yawn and goes for cheap, home-distilled pálinka sold up on the hill. Then he comes back home and lies down on the clapped out bed again. He is a retired widower who leaves all the work to his daughter. Not that he ever rushes her. If she cooks they eat, if she doesn't, it's bread with pork fat, or nothing. His daughter's not the busy sort anyhow. As she hangs up the wash she stops repeatedly as if in thought, then peers into the adjacent yard where Mrs Zabos sits peeling potatoes on a low stool. The potatoes and a pot lie on the ground in front of her. Its tongue hanging out, the mangy mongrel pants at her feet. Zabos is in the back somewhere, tinkering. He's always at something with his hammer, the yard's crowded with sheds, pens and fences of assorted sizes. Once he had earned his living as a scaffolding-man but fell down and hurt his leg. A handful of hen are lazily pecking at the ground around Mrs Zabos. The air is parched and still, and the dryness with a cracking sound to it, almost. Grapevine, fruit trees and gooseberry shrubs of all shapes and sizes are wilting in the heat.

Mrs Karas is lying on the bed in the summer kitchen, a kind of one-room shack, kitchen and bedroom rolled into one that's reserved for the hot days, with barely a ray of light penetrating the curtained window. It is still unbearably hot, though. Her corpulent frame heaves with wheezy, flatulent sounds. A bottle of pálinka stands on the cluttered table, a plate, a bag of flour, and junk of all sorts. Beside her on the smaller bed a woman (or child?) in her thirties, her hair cropped short, is rocking back and forth with legs crossed in front of her. From time to time she emits a few inarticulate syllables. One hand fumbles at her loins. Wearing nothing but a cropped shirt, she is still too hot, but naked just won't do, she's got breasts and all, like she was normal, even though everyone just calls her the child. Sometimes Mrs Karas feels like they're ringing a shrill bell inside her head. She can't sleep and she can't keep awake. From time to time a bead of sweat starts down her side, itching, the bed a puddle underneath. Stewing in her own juices, she says outloud, then with a groan heaves herself up and reaches for the bottle. She takes a sip or two, hoping it'll help. More sweatridden than ever, at such times her vast, flatulent face is set afire. Out on the makeshift, glassed-in porch something's cooking on the stove. She can just see it through the open door, and when she goes outside, the glass affords her a view of the length of the hillside. She can see the Csepis and the Zaboses in one direction and the Siró bunch in the other, the three of them, now that the older boy's gone into the army, living in a patched-up hole in the wall licked into shape from an old press house. One of them is always gaping over the fence. The younger Siró boy's bought a woman to the house not long since, without so much as a how-dee-do, picked her up someplace in Debrecen, in some tavern. She's much older than he is, too, and a piece missing from her nose. The couple entrenched themselves in the one room, so the old man got stuck out in the kitchen. Her lips curling with condescention, Mrs Karas smiles as she recalls how she'd seen old man Siró, widowed in his prime, beaten black and blue when he tried his tricks with his son's wife once, when they were alone. The old man's as dry and lean as a poker and never washes, and that woman, too, with her crooked mouth and nose with a piece bitten out of it, she's like something my arse wouldn't want nothing to do with neither, Mrs Karas thought, and the boy's no better than he should be, with one eye hooked into the other, sort of, and his pants touching his ass only when he sits. And that Csepi girl, not such a hot item either any more, twenty-eight and not a man for miles around asking her the time of day.

Dumb and loutish, her neck making her look crooked, and her face all pockmarked, a terrain of piss and pimples, she looks a fright, I swear, and that Mrs Zabos, with her breast off two years ago, but she's no match for cancer, and the chemotherapy or whatnot, like a kiss over a dead man. Not that she minds, laughing and giggling and drinking all day, every one of them drinks, around here every blessed soul's got a vineyard and wine that they double in volume with sugar and water, yet never a drop of the stuff sold. They drink it all themselves, pretending they don't, denying it for all they're worth; well, far be it from her to offer them any of her own, she eats and drinks and makes no secret of it, it's her own she's drinking, and if anybody don't like it, they can lick her arse clean. Irén drinks the stuff, too, the child, her sister, the one rocking back and forth on the smaller of the two beds; gimme, gimme, she says in thick accents when she sees the pá-linka or wine jug, and Mrs Karas obliges her. At such times she appears more normal, more relaxed, talking to herself, laughing. She's got no other joy in life anyhow. For the last twenty-five years or thereabouts she gets taken off her bed only when she has to go relieve herself, and even then she's got to be held erect like a straw dummy, she won't sit on a chamber pot or use the outhouse. Mrs Karas hikes up her shirt, come winter pulls down her pants, and they squat by the pigsty, it's the only place she'll do it, and as she sits, she watches the hogs through the planks, and giggles. Ever since their mother passed on nobody can manage the girl except for her sister, Mrs Karas. A sweet child she was, too, as a baby, except she wouldn't stand on her feet when it was time. Come morning, her parents locked her in and went out to the corn, the beet, and could be sure to find Irénke just as they had left her. But after a while there was no getting around it, something was gone wrong with her, her eyes sort of askew, like a Mongol's. They took her to the doctor then, but it was no use, they were told that the child would stay like she was, her place in an institution. She'd be better off with others of her kind. She'd learn to look after herself to a degree and be house-broken, and it wouldn't cost much either. At such times Mrs Karas thinks kindly of her mother for not taking the child to an institution even though her husband was at her about it; but it won't cost us, the state's paying us for her keep almost what we make in a month.

Mrs Karas glanced at the pot outside, where the steam was making the lid dance and the heavy smells came floating in. Heavy, she sat up on her bed. She felt vaguely dizzy. I'll end up with a stroke, she said out loud, that's what that red-faced woman promised in the hospital unless she stops drinking. You drink your share too, honey, it ain't rosewater that's got your cheeks red, she had retorted, infuriated, but the doctor just said, just call me doctor and don't honey me. Incidentally, do as you like. The medical treatment is for free. Incidentally. She'll never forget that word. She smoothed down her sweat-soaked dress and went outside.

Mrs Karas's mother took her time dying. Having grown ugly by then, she lay on her bed by the wall all day in the dimly lit room with the one small window. Mrs Karas had taken the child over to her own place. There was nothing her mother could do for her anyhow. She just made her nervous. There was an unpleasant stale sick smell inside, and the smell of medicine. The urine stank in the pot under the bed until somebody emptied it. The old woman never left the house any more, just took a few unsteady steps in the room or stood by the window or prayed in front of the big, gaudy picture of Christ. She awaited death with resignation, though at times she was furious enough, cursing the Lord for all she was worth, and every living soul with Him. At such times she was like one possessed, ripping the sheet from the bed with the underliner, sweeping the bottles and cups off the shelves, breaking and smashing things around her. Then the ambulance came. Was it two years it took? Or three? They had ordered the coffin twice, at least, but then she'd get better. Mrs Karas couldn't remember it all any more, just the impatience she felt, why couldn't the old woman die, why wouldn't God give her a hand, or the doctor, with an injection? Mrs Karas's father bought a couch so they could sleep apart. The huge, black man had dragged it all the way from Debrecen, fifteen kilometers on foot, then put it down by the fireplace and listened without a word to his wife's cackling, how he won't sleep with her no more, is she that repulsive that she can't be slept next to any more? She never once slept on the couch, and she died one night lying by her husband's side on the narrow bed, everything drenched, only the corpse dry, two bulging eyes between the folds of the quilt. Her husband, Juhos, lay beside her till the morning, drinking wine from the bottle that was always at hand by the bed, staring at the ceiling, from time to time wiping his eyes. Then he got up at the usual hour, laid his wife out on the table, and proceeded to his daughter's, come, your ma's gone, do what's got to be done. Then he went on his way.

Mrs Karas went to the stove, raised the lid, lowered the gas, then from the steps glanced in the direction of the Sirós, then beyond, at the house crouching behind the weed-infested Rehák yard, her father's place. There's a tall sumach standing up front, her husband Géza has tried drenching the roots with gasoline to be rid of it so they could see unobstructed into the yard, see who visits, whom old man Juhos makes friend of, and who he drinks with, because in the hospital Mrs Karas's mother had divulged in a whisper how there were four-hundred-fifty-thousand forints hidden in a box, and she'd better keep an eye on him and not let the old man spend it all on drink. Also, she should see to it that Juhos brings no woman to the house because the fortune's hers, her daughter's, once the old man's gone, but if he gets married again, she can kiss the money good bye. It's all hers, her mother's, Juhos brought nothing into the marriage save for his huge body and insatiable appetite; during their wedding night he had ripped her apart inside, he's got no mercy, that's what had made her sick, yes, and for a while demanded his due from a sick woman, and drank wine as he did it, the wine was always by the bed; not that he wasn't a hard worker, he worked like a dog, but the money, that she'd put aside and nobody else, hoarding and hiding it, otherwise they'd have nothing left now, and she should also take the child Irén in before that pig kills or rapes her.

Mrs Karas moved the insecticide spray further from the table and put the chair back in its place. The place is a mess, she said out loud, but I'll be damned if I'm going to fart, even, in this heat, and the pumpkin, too, drying out under the table, it's been a week I should've cooked it, and the clothes all over the place and on top of the unwashed dishes and foodscraps a swarm of flies, but she'll be damned if she'll look to it before this heat lets up. She leaned against the door for support and looked towards the Csepi yard, where the older Csepi girl was hanging out the wash. She had told her, too, how she'd asked her mother time and again to give her that money. She was looking after her father and the child, wasn't she, cooking and washing for them. She'd give the old man what he needed. But her mother always said, wait. Wait till I feel the end coming. Always this wait. Didn't even say where she'd hidden it. But her father knew, though, of that she was sure, he just didn't know how much of it there was. After the funeral he took the box out and had his daughter count the money. It was just like her mother said, and a few thousand forints in hundred forint bills and change. Mrs Karas grew pale from the counting. She thought how from the money and the price of their house they could buy an apartment someplace where people lived proper lives, where things were in order, everything was clean, and there was a bathroom, a paved road, and they could leave this pisshole of a place behind them for good. But all she said was pa I'm taking this money, it'll be safe with me, I'll take good care of it, from now on I'm cooking and washing for you anyhow, and the child'll be with me too. She said it calmly, sensibly, but the old man snapped her head off, at which she exploded, word followed word, I've got more right to this place than you, she said to the old man, everything's mine after my mother, the money, too, she screamed, beside herself with fury, what do you need it for? Pálinka? Whores? She didn't mention Mrs Szabó yet, though Mrs Karas's mother had also said how well her father and his sister-in-law were getting on, sweet-talking for hours in the arbour while she chewed the quilt from the pain, scorned and neglected, and when her father was telling her to go to the devil, she told him to rot away right where he was along with his precious money, we'll see who's gonna have the last laugh, and she wouldn't so much as look in on him for a time after that, she didn't cook for him either, but what'll people say? That Mrs Zabos, too, said, listen, go take him a bite of food, he's lying drunk in the yard, he'll die because you didn't look to him, others can't be expected to mind how you're at loggerheads. All right, then. For a while she took him food. They didn't speak to each other, though, she just put the dish down and left, and even that, what for?

See what I mean, see for yourself, the door's ajar, anybody that has half a mind to can march right on in, and him lying on the couch, drunk as a sow, though maybe that Mrs Szabó's taken him

under her wings, or maybe the money's gone by now, no, not
maybe, it is gone, the filthy old man would never be the wiser if
somebody went and stole the bed out from under him, not that
there's much left to steal, the good mash barrels, the ladder,
planks, by noon he's stoned out of his skull, and the Sirós, too,
having the run of the yard while she can't even go in now that
they've had that falling out about this and Mrs Szabó. At the time
her father had said get out, I never want to see you again as long as
I live, to her, his own flesh and blood, her husband Géza went
over, though, when he came back from work, let's get this straight,
throwing your own daughter out of her own house, because
everything here is hers, all you've got is the use of the place! And
what have you got, the old man said, you never had nothin' and
never will excepting your prick, that's what your wife had a
hankering for, 'cause she didn't know what to do with herself no
more, everybody's had his way with her but nobody would marry
her, so don't you think you own me! At the time Juhos was still as
strong as an ox, and when Mrs Karas's husband raised his hand to
him the old man grabbed his wrist so it was broken. The Sirós saw
the whole thing over the fence, and later they saw, too, Mrs Karas
take the child out the gate, the two of them tottering labouriously
over to the old man's house. Here, here's the child, she yelled, you
were drunk as a fiddler's bitch when you fucked ma and made her
like this, so now you keep her! The Csepis and the Zaboses saw it,
too; from the fields they saw Mrs Karas let go of the child's hand
and leave her to her fate by the gate. Irén flopped down in the dust,
for a time giggled and talked to herself as if trying to make sense of
things, the time passed, but old man Juhos was not to be seen, at
which Mrs Siró led the child back to the Karas house.

The hillside consisted of four houses lying a few hundred yards
from each other, plus two or three small ramshackle structures,
sheds of sorts once put up by civil servants from Debrecen whose
bit of vineyard had been seen to by Mrs Karas's grandpa, just like
that, for a few kind words. It was nothing compared to his own
five-acre vineyard, while they were grateful, always bringing
things, tobacco, clay pipes, beer, ewecheese. They told him where he
could have a good pair of boots made and fixed the locks; with one
he even came into family relations of sorts. And they brought sul-

phate, too, and fatty sodium carbonate for soap, and everybody called the old man pop. It was like a holiday when they came, sometimes with their families; they ate and drank, talked politics, then filled their baskets with prunes, grapes, walnuts, whatever had just ripened, and whatever was not to be had from the fields and orchards the old man gave them himself, green apples, Jerusalem artichokes, sweet roots. Then the world changed and they stopped coming. The sons and daughters of the former dwellers went elsewhere, some to Debrecen, others to Barcika, to the mines, and to Ózd. They did not visit their parents much; they had problems enough of their own. The deserted barns and wine cellars were overgrown with weed now, the haunt of vermin and mice. Most of the vineyards perished, with only a solitary stake here and there, and the parched, vermin-infested fruit trees reaching barren to the sky. The old settlers along the hillside loved and hated each other in turn. They had ample time on their hands, like gypsies, Juhos said. A stranger among them, he made no friends, but having come from a great ways off, could take more hardship than all of them put together. Blunt, crude, at times even brutal, he was held in awe. All year round a cripple sold home-distilled pálinka up on the hill. Everybody in the neighbourhood went there, and by noon, but especially by the afternoon, staggering figures dotted the dusty road who, once home, washed down what they had drunk with wine, as much as they could handle. The hogs over at the Csepis would sometimes whine for hours, and in the morning the older Chepi girl would sometimes find herself in the yard. At the Zaboses the evenings were much more peaceful. They ate, drank, and slept. If they woke up they resumed eating and drinking. If anybody ran out of money, the cripple would serve them on credit. They always paid him back. Mrs Karas looked her nose down on them, especially the Sirós; they never had any money, and yet they got on, God only knows how, when nobody worked in that family. Still, one's got to make an effort, be friendly with them, and the Csepis, too, and the Zaboses, especially since her father's got this problem, because she's got to get if off her chest, lest she explode. Her husband's away at work all day, then he goes to the cripple, and then there's no more use to be gotten out of him. What do you expect me to do with him, the low-browed, button-eyed man asked the other day about his father-in-law, bash his brains in? After sundown he'd occasionally go to the old man to have a look around and bit by bit move to his own place the stuff the others hadn't taken yet, corn, the cauldron, then the cauldron stand, a small-size barrel, a couple of hens. At such times he generally found everything wide open at the old man's, the keys on the hook nail, his father-in-law lying on the couch stinking drunk, just as he had fallen on it. Once he shook the old man but he didn't come to, and so took the keys from the hook but couldn't find the money anywhere. This made him so furious that he pressed a pillow over the old man's face and bore down on it for some time. The old man didn't stir, then his body jerked, and Géza went on bearing down as long as he could. Well, your pa's gone, he said to his wife back home. They were up all night worrying, then in the morning saw the old man on his bike, riding into town.

Everything would have been fine if only her ma hadn't died. Mrs Karas spooned the meat out of the soup into a bowl, then turned off the gas. It was noon. She drank some pálinka, but it was lukewarm and didn't feel right. But there was no wine in the house; she'd have to go down to the cellar, she thought. Gimme, gimme, Irén grunted on the bed. Hold on, my precious, in a minute, but not from the bottle, you'll gulp it all down that way. She took a small mug from the shelf, poured a little from the bottle, the child drank it with a squelching sound, smiled and laughed, Mrs Karas put her arms around her, kissed her, I'm the only one that loves my precious angel, the only one, she said, can't think what'll become of you once I'm gone. If only the Lord would see that we die together, or burn the house down in our sleep. Your pa's eating now, I reckon, Mrs Szabó cooks for him or takes him something with those deformed legs of hers from the village, more than a mile, and your pa he calls her honey, while he never said nothing to your ma excepting for hey, you, and are you deaf? Mrs Karas wiped herself and the child's face, too; my life's not worth shit neither, she said to no one in particular, I'm not well, my husband can't touch me, you're lucky you're still a child, while that Mrs Szabó, there's nothing the matter with her, though she's as old as the hills. Your ma was a whole lot younger, and she died afore her, can you fathom that, my darling, there's no justice to be had, none, not even in heaven.

It wasn't two weeks after the funeral, she later told anybody willing to listen, people at the market, the Csepis, the Zaboses, anybody, and that woman, that Mrs Szabó was there, she's a widow, ma's sister, looking to things, a real busybody, straightening out the shelves, leaving the village saying how she's going to her plot that's right next to pa's, but she couldn't care shit about the plot, she took food to the old man while what I, his own flesh and blood took, he threw to the dogs. They ate with her in ma's chair while she was still alive, and me with tears in my eyes, that's how it was. I know it's the money she's after, that's what's eating her, and knows where it is, too, provided there's any left, she knows when I, I'm left in the dark, taking from it, too, saying she's buying the old fool things, and he never the wiser, God only knows how much she's taken already when the old man was drunk, and she building a house on her plot from brand new materials, well, where did she get the money, I ask, from her pension? She even had a fence made from real cement poles, there's plenty where that came from, old man Juhos is loaded! When Juliska, that's Mrs Szabó, shows up, the old drunk's up and about in a flash helping her dig up the yard, cut the vine and suchlike, when me he can't help, oh no, his feet ache, he says. Well, why don't they ache him there? And my husband's like my ass, if I'm not there by his side he can't manage, and is gone all day besides, he comes home from the cripple in the evening, or God knows where he goes, maybe to a whore, 'cause the Good Lord himself is a whore around these parts, while they're smiling over there, cooing like turtledoves. I got eyes in my head, sweetheart this and sweetheart that, and I'm supposed to trouble about his child, 'cause he won't so much as look in on her for months, no, what am I saying, it's been over a year since he showed up drunk and even then they had a falling out with Géza.

It had been the child's birthday. Mrs Szabó had found out or maybe Juhos told her, and Mrs Szabó said to him, go see her, it's the least you can do, say happy birthday, and give her some money, too, she's your flesh and blood after all. Drunk as usual,

Juhos was sitting over his cold soup, his hair in his eye, in bad need of a shave. I ain't going, he later said, I ain't going no place. Mrs Szabó was already put out because she had cooked in vain; he wouldn't eat, just sat with his elbow on the table. He was drinking again, with hardly ever a bite to eat. It's no skin off my nose, Mrs Szabó said, but it's the least you could do. Take them ten thousand forints. To hell with the money. Why hoard it when it's going to them anyhow, what do you want it for, and why don't you eat? Juhos dipped his spoon into the soup but then just stirred it around. Eat something, for chrissakes, who do you think I cooked for, the dog? Well, I'd better pour it back, she later said, you'll eat it when you're hungry. And go lie down for a spell, but don't drink any more, then shave and go on over. Don't be a pig. She poured the soup back into the bowl, covered it, cleaned off the table, then picked up her packages. Well, goodbye, she said, I'm off. Don't go, honey, Juhos said, 'cause I'll be all alone again if you do, and then I've got to drink, it's always like that. Mrs Szabó sighed and said there's nothing she can do, if he's not willing to listen to her he should listen to somebody else. He'll end up in the hospital again, is that what he wants? It's what his good-for-nothing son-in-law and daughter want, and him drinking himself to death, and does he really mean to oblige them? Juhos didn't say much; with the tedious concern of drunkenness he rose to see Mrs Szabó out, but she was sadly shuffling along the dirt road by then to her small plot of land.

Mrs Karas and her husband were surprised no end when the old man showed up at their place, his eyes veiled with sleep, his face cut up, still bleeding in spots. He must've shaved while drunk. At first they were at a loss what to do with him, tell him to go away, or ask him to stay, and him too just looking about him stupidly. Well, what is it, Mrs Karas asked after a while. The old man mumbled something about coming to see the child, and how its her birthday, then put ten thousand forints on the table. They talked a little, even offered him wine and pálinka, not that he needed any, then they had a bite to eat. But when he was about to leave he said something like don't you go spending that money on drink now, you hear? Well, that set Géza off. He sprang to his feet, they started yelling, the old man shoved his son-in-law, and he kicked the old man's bad, hurting knee so hard he doubled up with a grunt of agony, but he had it coming, and Mrs Karas shoved the money in his pocket, take it, eat it, is what she said, and get out, I never want to see you again! Géza was so furious he later took off after him saying how he won't leave it at that and they fell on each other in the pitch dark room until the old man found his stick and lashed out with it wildly. He couldn't see anything, but he could hear when it was a hit. He smashed the stove pipe, the mirror, everything, and Karas too got his share of blows, over the head, the shoulder, even his forehead. He looked for something but in vain, and in the end ran out of the house, and all the time the dog barking outside like the devil got into him, pulling madly at his chain. Juhos let him loose, but Karas had gone by then, his retreating figure barely visible by the light in front of his house. Mrs Karas washed the blood from her husband's face. He was shaking with fury. She gave him a drink to calm him down, and some to the child, who had grown agitated, was in convulsions of terror. This is madness, shouted Mrs Karas through her tears, madness, why does the Lord condone it, why?

Something's going to happen, the Csepi girl told Mrs Zabos, and soon. You mark my words. They were sitting in the arbour. The girl's father was at the cripple's and wouldn't be home for some time. But what have they got against the old man, Mrs Zabos asked of no one in particular. They got all they need. Her pa's built a house for them and gave them part of a vineyard, too, sixteen rows, and a corn field, and they get something for the child besides. If any other soul got half as much, she'd kiss her father's arse. Sure, said the Csepi girl, except they're after the money. They want the old man to give them everything he's got and then some, and dance to their tune to boot. They want it all, lock, stock, and barrel, and the old fool dead. They laughed. Here, have some more wine, said the Csepi girl. Much obliged, said Mrs Zabos, but that'll be the last for today. She said the other day, too, the Csepi girl went on, what's the use of getting everything tomorrow when it's today she's hungry, it won't help, feeding her in a month. Well, she don't look like she's hungry to me, said Mrs Zabos, and they had a good laugh over that, too. They're sick, all of them, the Csepi girl then said, but their major problem is drink. They drink like the dickens. What's really ailing her, though, is that Mrs Szabó, Mrs Zabos added cautiously, that's what's afflicting her, she can't stomach having been forced out of there, and she's worried, besides, that Mrs Szabó'll lay her hands on the money, but I better be off now and make something for that good-for-nothing pa of mine so he can go on with his tinkering. He's driving me nuts. If he hasn't knocked ten thousand nails into that damned rotten pigsty, he hasn't knocked in one.

By then everyone was saying, at the market, everywhere, how old man Juhos had beat up his son-in-law, though some would have it that his son-in-law had beat up the old man; and there was talk, too, about how much money Juhos must have stashed away, 'cause where there's so much smoke, there's bound to be fire. Some saw Mrs Karas on the bus turn her back on her father; she stuck her tongue out at him too when she saw him, in front of the whole world, they said. And Mrs Szabó said anybody can go to the bank and check how long she'd been saving for the house, and they can look at the house, too, all twelve square yards of it, not what you'd call a palace, and they can also check and see how much she works, weekdays and Sundays, while some others she'd rather not name sleep or loaf about, 'cause that's how she was taught by her father, and the children, too, when they come out to the vineyard they work instead of milling about in their Sunday best. Old man Juhos helps her, why shouldn't he, but she helps him as much if not more, and cooks for him besides, because he could starve to death for all his daughter cared. And then, too, they're related, him being her brother-in-law. One helps a stranger, too, if he's in a bind. Mrs Szabó was always selling something. Tuesdays and Saturdays she was at the market; apples, pears, vegetables, flowers—she needed little for herself, she could squeeze money out of a turnip. But the vineyard, that was all important, she was born into that vineyard, it meant everything to her; raking and tying it up, spraying, cutting off the tendrils, there was always work to be done, from training the shoot to tubbing. Since her husband passed on she'd sold every drop of the wine. She never drank any of it herself. And she always had good wine. Before the holidays people'd come from as far off as Debrecen, asking her how she did it, but she just laughed, it takes quality grape to make quality wine, she'd say, that's the secret. Healthy, ripe grapes. And clean barrels. She nevertheless managed to clip off a piece of the vineyard for her flowers; petunias, phlox, evening violets, tulips, roses and who knows what else blossomed in profusion in the carefully tended, well-watered soil in front of her small summer cottage. She talked to them, she touched them lovingly, while Juhos laughed at her. Let's do it together, the old man had said once, why bother with the pressing, the spraying, pruning separately? We'll begin at your place and move down to mine. You cook over at my house, why burn wood in two separate stoves? All right, Mrs Szabó said, but they should consult the children, which they did. Mrs Szabó's daughter and son said that it's only logical, and cheaper, too, the old people should've thought of it long ago. Juhos had a word with his daughter, too, who pretended she didn't care, said how it was all right, but if her pa was planning to get married, she'd have a thing or two to say about that. Then she changed her mind, or had somebody change it for her, because one morning she went over to her father and said she didn't like the look of it; once that Mrs Szabó sets foot in there, it'll take the devil to blast her out. But she's not moving in, said old man Juhos, she's not staying here, at night she goes back home. But they could've said anything by then, Mrs Karas yelled and brought up her dead mother into the bargain, and they had an ugly falling out, and that's how it ended.

Mrs Karas's husband went around showing people a ladle he used for mixing slop, saying how he'd bash his father-in-law's brain in with it. He even took it with him when he rode into the village on his bike, showing it off. Since that late-night fight he'd been drunk practically all the time. Some said he was on sick leave, others that he'd been kicked out of the factory for showing up drunk once too often. At home he lounged about, or hurled insults at his father-in-law from the street, except when he had company, then he really got going. Knowing that it terrified her, he started throwing dozens of frogs into Mrs Szabó's garden, though God only knows where he got all those frogs in this draught. At the cripple's he bragged how he'd chop off the old man's head and play ball with it, and chase his whore until her deformed legs wore down to the bone. Mrs Karas's husband was known for a lying man that didn't know what he was saying. Well, Windbag, they used to ask him, what have you come up with this time? He had no friends at the factory either; he told tall-tales, was soon found out and laughed at behind his back. They teased him with his wife, too. How's the wife, Géza, how's the little slut? How do you do it? From the front? The back? The top?

Juhos was up in arms the minute he laid eyes on either of them. I'm going to kill that goddam son of a bitch. Mrs Szabó tried calming him, leave him be, can't you see he's drunk, don't go make trouble. He'll sober up one of these days. There's nothing to be done. Besides, you're stinking drunk yourself. Juhos had promised Mrs Szabó at the start he'd only drink as much as she gave him. He even handed her the key to the cellar so he couldn't get at the wine. But he managed to sneak a barrel out somehow, dragging it from the cellar to the shed. Mrs Szabó was surprised to see that by the time she went to see him, the old man was drunk. She knew that Juhos never spent money on wine or pálinka, he'd rather die of thirst. Besides, he had enough of his own. Then she chanced upon the small barrel. She said nothing at the time, just wept quietly, but the next day put the key on the old man's table. Here, here's your key, you lied to me and don't you deny it! Juhos didn't know what to say, then began to make excuses. It's the only way, can't you see, what they're doing to me is more than a body can take without it; you hear the stuff he's shouting, and when you leave, then too, it's enough to drive a man round the bend. You want me to humble myself? Me?! To go and beg them not to do this to me? Juhos had not been able to lend a hand to Mrs Szabó for a while, but he hobbled over every day, in need of company. He usually stood around her or sat down, thought at times he fell asleep among the vines. Mrs Szabó woke him at supper time. Let him be, she thought, at least he can't drink. He was very frail by then and looked it. The second time the ambulance came for him the doctor said he'd die if he went on drinking. They drew water from his abdomen but not his knees, it's too late, they said. Mrs Szabó couldn't understand how anybody could be so weak-minded when they had got on so well at first. They worked, they talked, they had each other for company. That despicable man wasn't up to his tricks as much either any more, he wasn't shouting filth at them, wasn't throwing frogs, they didn't see him for weeks, in fact. She said to Juhos over and over, leave some over for yourself but give them the money, you got a pension, that should do, and they'll leave you be, it's that money that's vexing them, believe me. But the old man just said, he? to that bunch? after what they'd done to him? to Karas? Not till hell freezes over. He'd rather see the whole lot burn. At such times Mrs Szabó sighed and left the old man after supper to return to her vineyard alone.

The child Irén sat on her bed with her legs crossed in front of her. She wasn't rocking back and forth this time, just sat looking into space in a kind of dull amazement. Then she said mama. She said mama again. Mrs Karas was busy out by the stove when her ear caught the word that send a wave of shock through her body. She went to the child. What did you say, my precious? She raised the child's chin to have a look in her eyes, but she jerked her head away. Mama, mama, she said in thick accents. Mrs Karas looked questioningly at her. What's with this child? She never mentioned her ma before, whatever made her think of it now? Do you need anything my angel, are you hungry? Or thirsty? At such times she had always said gimme, gimme, but now she said nothing. Mrs Karas got the pálinka out, took a swig; well, she asked, would my precious like some? She took out the child's mug, poured some pálinka into it and held it out, but Irén shook her head. Mrs Karas raised it to her lips so the child could smell it, but she thrashed out with her arm so vehemently, she practically knocked the mug out of Mrs Karas's hand. God damn it, Mrs Karas cursed then, did you shit in the bed, is that it? Well?! With a great deal of effort she raised the child and moved her over. You're all filth, she shouted, you hear?! Filth! Shit! Irén said nothing while Mrs Karas hurriedly cleaned her up, washing her backside and changing her shirt, then she carried her over to the other bed. You never had no problem saying kaka and piss-piss before! She took the foam rubber from the bed and replaced it with a new one, covered it with a sheet, then dragged Irén back to her own bed. Irén had grown quite limp. She didn't even try to help, like she used to. So how do you say kaka, piss-piss, there's a good girl. Mrs Karas laughed to cheer her up, but the child remained silent. She sat up, folded her legs under her and groaned a little with open mouth, then the word came bubbling forth: father. Mrs Karas listened, dumbfounded. She knew these words when she was young, but since her mind's been a muddle she had never said them. Mamma, mamma, father, mamma. Irén repeated the words like a ditty, rocking back and forth, working herself into a passion. Mrs Karas tried to restrain her but to no avail; she shook the child by the shoulder and slapped her across the cheek; what's the matter with you, she shouted, what's got into you?! Good God, once she get's going I'm helpless, oh God oh God, but she held the child by the shoulder tight as she could; gimme, gimme, she later heard her say, at which she cautiously released her grip and sighed. Irén sat up, smiling as a thin stream of saliva started down her chin. Mrs Karas poured some more pálinka into the mug, gave it to her, and listened with relief to her slirping gulps. You'll be a good girl now, my precious, won't you, she warbled, who do I love most in the world if not my little angel? She then embraced and kissed her over and over again to calm her, and poured her some more pálinka, taking a swig herself. Then she went out to the glassed-in porch. It was at this point she realized how tired she was, feeling she'd fall over like a sack if she didn't sit herself down. Besides, where's that man, may the devil take him, everything's cooked, the chicken soup, the meat fried, the potatoes gone sour in the cold lard, where the hell is he, she thought. He went to the cripple early on in the day. What's the use, she had asked, there's plenty of pálinka right here, and wine, too, what more do you want, but it's Sunday, he said, you can't expect me to sit home all the time. So don't, don't sit, do something, there's plenty for you to attend to, must I rub your nose in it, and he said he ain't working on Sunday, let the poor folk work, and then, too, he's so strange lately, like when he was in hospital, they told him how he'd better not drink another drop, it's bad for his nerves, and for a time he didn't but he'd been at the bottle again lately. Mrs Karas sighed. He needs a woman, that must be it, God damn this fucking life, what am I supposed to do about it, why can't I be well, and why is the Lord punishing me like this, why? She stood up and went to the door to see if anybody was about. It's more than a body can take, with nobody to talk to for days except the Sirós sometimes, 'cause one of their bunch is always snooping around the fence, or the old Szabó woman waddling over to Juhos and back, 'cause the old man can't go see her much any more, he's nearing the end of the line and all that money to no avail. There was plenty of it to go around except his own child. Well, now he's got neither the money nor his health. The old bastard had it coming. There's somebody's singing. Who the hell is it, for chrissakes? Mrs Karas strained her ears. What the... if that ain't Géza! Just you wait, see what you get! She felt the blood rushing to her head though they told her at the hospital to be careful, her bloodpressure's way up, and her liver's none too healthy either. Come on, you scum, come and try singing in front of me! She saw him toiling down the slope with a shuffling shamble, bearing to one side then the other, with the dogs barking at him. He could hardly pass through the gate and mounted the steps to the summer kitchen only at the second go. So you're back, may the devil take you, Mrs Karas said, do you know what time it is? So what, her husband said, what's that to you? Well, that's all Mrs Karas needed, she let loose about how the Lord is punishing her with such a lazy shithead, a drunken louse, 'cause drinking, that he knows how when he's as dumb as my ass when it comes to doing anything else; she went on and on, slamming down the plates in the meanwhile so the table shook and the soup splashed all over the top as she flung the pot down. Go on pig, eat! Her husband said nothing, just hummed as if he didn't know where he was. Then he said, I ain't hungry. What do you mean you ain't hungry, Mrs Karas asked in a menacing undertone, and waited for the answer. I ate before, her husband said merrily, and resumed his humming, but I could do with some pálinka. Mrs Karas took three deep breaths. So you ate already, she asked, her voice raised above its former pitch, is that why I slave by the stove all day in this heat? She waited a little, then with one swift motion flung the soup out the door and down the steps. Then the meat. And the pickles, plate and all. So then, she said, and exhaled mightily, may my fingers rot to the bone if ever I cook for you again! All ten of them! And you can go eat where you just ate if you're hungry, and live and sleep, too, 'cause I've had it with you, and you can take with you whatever is yours, right now, just get out, I ain't gonna drudge for you, too. Maybe you want me to help you shit like that poor child over there?! Karas said nothing as the flood of words enundated him about how he's a scoundrel, a badmash that they're all laughing at him behind his back, even the Sirós, and they got just about nothing left despite the huge inheritance because his highness got kicked out of the factory, got kicked out of every blessed place because he's yellow, a shit-in-the-pants if ever there was one, letting his father-in-law thrash him for shame like a kid and talk to him like a dog; any other man would have put a stop to it ages ago, while she don't dare show her face for shame any more, with people pointing at her at the market because her precious father's giving away her money with both hands, the money that belongs to her, his own child, and what's left he's meaning to burn. He said to Mrs Zabos how he'd rather burn the money than give it to her, and Mrs Szabó's son, too, he got himself a brand new automobile, and where did he get the money, I ask?... She was still talking when Karas staggered out into the yard and found the insecticide spray. What're you up to again you fool, his wife asked when she saw him fill the tank with all sorts of poison. Wait and see, said Karas, hoisting the tank on his back, I'm gonna finish off them vermin, see if I don't, shouting so the whole neighbourhood resounded. Mrs Karas caught up with him at the gate and jerked the tank off his back, at which Karas gave her a look that made her blood run cold. Standing at the gate she saw, horror-struck, her husband get the slop ladle. Oh, my God, she said, coming to; talk to him, Mancika, stop him, she shouted to Mrs Siró. Mrs Siró passed out the gate and said something to Karas, who slapped her so hard she wheeled against the post. Juliska, my dove, Karas yelled, where are you, my precious, let me give you a stroke or two you won't forget! By then everybody was standing out in the road, the Csepis, the Zaboses, the Sirós. Mrs Szabó heard Karas call her, shouting for all he was worth from a distance. She and the old man were standing by the well. She grabbed her bag and scurried to her cottage with just enough time to lock the door from inside when Karas reached her. Where are you, you filthy whore, don't try and hide, 'cause I'll find you! He banged on the door for a time, then turned back. There was no telling any more what he was yelling. He found Juhos by his gate, heading to protect Mrs Szabó, but he could hardly wobble, even with the help of his stick, he was so stinking drunk. Karas shoved him back inside, the old man lurched against the well, and it was there Karas delivered the first blow with the butt-end of the ladle over the old man's head. The old man staggered back, felt two more blows, then nothing after that, ever.

Mrs Szabó cringed in terror in her tiny house. She peered out the window and when the coast was clear opened the door with trembling hands. She looked around, then leaving everything wide open, snuck back to her village through the fields, using the trees and shrubs for shelter. What happened, people asked, but she just cried and cried, incapable on an answer. It wasn't till the evening that she could finally tell the neighbours how they'd tried to kill her. Then she locked her door and went to bed without even turning on the light. She put a small ax by her bed and didn't bother locking the poultry in for the night or feeding the dog; she took a sleeping pill, but even so lay in a half-stupor, wracked by terrifying visions that lasted till the morning, when she sent a message to Juhos's sister, hurry, something's happened. What happened, Mrs Kovács asked, frightened, when she rolled her bike into the yard. I'm not sure, my dear, Mrs Szabó said, but something terrible's happened to your brother, I fear, and I'm scared to go see for myself.

They reached the Juhos house when the doctor did. The Sirós had notified him, the short, stocky man explained; apparently something happened in there yesterday, and no one's seen the old man come out of the house since. They banged on the door, then the doctor broke the glass, reached inside, and opened it. They found Juhos lying on the floor by the bed emitting a rattling sound and a red, bloody foam oozing from the corner of his mouth. The left side of his face and his head were hideously battered. Jesus Christ, the doctor said, they must've brought him in here and laid him down. They washed his face, there's the bloody water in the basin, see? Mrs Szabó looked horrified, while Mrs Kovács tried fighting back her tears. The doctor barely cast a glance his way; I'll call the ambulance, he said then, he's still alive, though he hasn't regained consciousness. The old man is as good as dead. I'm sorry. Please sign here.

When the police took her husband away, Mrs Karas was lying

on the bed. She couldn't answer any of their questions. I'm not well, she groaned from time to time, her drooping lids fixed on the ceiling. That I can see, said the police inspector; Holy Mother of God, he then said to his partner, just look at that! Irén lay on her bed limp and motionless, her shirt, the sheet, and even the wall smeared with excrement. An empty mug was stuck in between the pillow and the wall by her head, piles of dirty dishes crowded the table. There was a bottle with some leftover pálinka at the bottom and a wine jug, and clothing strewn all over the place. Down on the linoleum floor waterstains, chicken bones. Good Lord, the police inspector said again, find some shoes for this man, we can't take him in handcuffed and no shoes. And this child or whatever she is, we gotta take her away from here, she's drunk like the rest of them. These people must've had some bash here last night. The neighbours say the killer went to some cripple this morning that sells pálinka near by, and he was whistling and singing, the other man added, and he even bragged about how he'd beat his father-in-law to death, he also mentioned some old whore, and how he'll get around to her next. We'll know more once he's sober, the inspector said, and did you find anything? There's a pair of rubber boots, said the other man, that'll have to do for want of anything better. The inspector looked around the room one more time as if trying to imprint the details on his mind's eye, then he shook Mrs Karas. "Why didn't you call a doctor for the old man last night, well?! He might've been saved. Know how much you inherited? Of course not, you were too drunk to attend the inventory next door and haven't stopped drinking since! One-million two-hundred thousand forints plus the property, which pretty much doubles that. From now on you can drink to your heart's content. But for your information, I don't envy you a bit. An ambulance is coming for you and this other, so don't lock the door, understand?"

Mrs Karas heard the car doors being slammed, she heard the sound of the motor, she heard everything, she wasn't so drunk she didn't know her mind, but what could she have said to these men? She rushed to the bed the second she saw them approach. Her husband was sitting in the back of the police car by then, hand-cuffed, brought from the cripple. One-million two-hundred thousand, oh God, where did the old man get so much money when everybody said how he gave everything away, oh my sweet Lord have mercy on me, the old bastard had nothing left to call his own, that's what it looked like, yes; oh Jesus have mercy on me, and the ambulance is on its way, and the child, just look at her; well, she ain't going with them noplace, no, they can't make her, she didn't go last time either; what am I to do now, sweet Lord of charity, how could you have tricked me so?

Slowly, painfully, she heaves herself up, plants both feet on the ground; in her head a throbbing, like the beating of her heart and a chirping sound like a flock of birds; painfully, she searches for a glass, puts it down on the table, gets the wine jug but must hold on to the wall for support; one-million two-hundred thousand and her head about to split from the vicious throbbing, but try as she might she can't calm down, not for a second, while the world has grown so strange and unfamiliar, like a thunderstorm brewing outside the door, then the wine jug slips from her hand, she tries to grab for it, feels a deep, profound silence, then nothing there after, not even that.

Translated by Judith Sollosy

FATHER WINS
by MIHÁLY KORNIS

imagine I'm dead rejoice anarchy may set in and the whole thing
started by me going to the Corvin to buy a cuisinart since I have
said for the longest time that we ought to have a cuisinart and I am
always shushed saying don't talk you don't have the vaguest idea
about it it would be wonderful to be able to dice potatoes and
make coffee in it at the same time and besides I saw one over at
Mrs Zengő it had a red base and it's East German and you will kiss
my hand in gratitude and Mrs Sas said I should go in and not worry I
will have one because she adores me I always tell her that she is an
enchanting slender elegant lady and this makes her swoon and do
anything for me albeit her eyes are hyperthyroid and almost fall out
and I occasionally feel like pushing them back in anyway
   at eleven I told them that if anybody was looking for me I'm
over at number seven since we are watching it that is where I stole
the fur coat that you never wear and you did not want to wear it
now either although it would have been a splendid opportunity
for me to see you in it as long as you have it anyway one can not as-
cend the steps at the Corvin there's some kind of fire ladder
between the floors since the stairs have been temporarily
demolished you can imagine what goes on and those who had
already gone up kick those below them tell me what kind of a
person is that who turns into an animal as soon as he gets on top
and ahead of me there was a woman with a fat ass who farted at me
deary I said control yourself or eat chocolates you could leave these
charming things at home but she goes on just in spite and yells
SHUT UP AND SNIFF so's your mother I thought just let us get to
the top but I could barely squeeze through the floors since these
idiots only cut a small hole for the ladder that was not tailored for my
size and when I got there I was drenched and I had to sit down and
take a nitro but that is no more for my heart that cunt smoke

don't whistle my boy or home you go where the hell do you think you are I'm telling this story for your benefit too in case you haven't noticed you will be old too one day and will remember what your father told you when he died and it's worth six encyclopedias I step up to the counter click my heels and ask where is Mrs Sas SHE IS NOT IN SIR SHE IS OUT OF THE HOUSE SIR would you tell her that Comrade Tábori wishes to speak to her THAT'LL BRING HER RUNNING I SUPPOSE says the little dishevelled cocksucker and in the meantime she drums her fingers on the counter but don't think that I lost my cool I just said goldie watch your language or I will give you a knuckle sandwich perhaps you have an East German cuisinart NO and there won't be one and then she grinned and there was a pimple on her forehead the size of a gherkin and said THERE WON'T BE ONE FOR THE LIKES OF YOU at which I demanded the complaint book and wrote that our workers' state does not bring sweaty and toilsome sacrifices so that an impertinent saleswoman should trifle with the working classes and I told her not to dare and tear out the page and that I would come back anyway next week and I check it and what I will give Mrs Sas she won't want to put in the shopwindow

then I started to climb back down but would you believe there was no separate ladder for the descent and who does not tumble down is an acrobat and at the end I crashed down a whole floor and you know how it goes on such occassions it is impossible to avoid the people below and they were falling down with me what could I do

on the ground they wanted to assault me there was yelling and shouting WHY DO YOU CLIMB WHEN YOU DON'T KNOW HOW IMBECILE IDIOT LET'S TEAR HIM APART I said bug off because when it comes to that I don't heed man or God and started to spin around cutting a circle with my briefcase but I don't know what might have happened if by chance Wakszman had not been there he wanted to beat me too because he did not recognize me although we were old buddies from the forced labour battalion he was famous because his father was hung on a meat hook in front of the Dohány utca synagogue by the Arrow Cross but he did not die and Wakszman's mother took him down at night and

took him home and they survived until the liberation and only
Elsa was gassed in Buchenwald their daughter a splendid little
piece of ass I went skating with her and courted her she had beautiful legs we called her ELSA WAKSZMAN OF THE MARVEL-
OUS LEGS it was always someone else who put the skates on her
feet this Wakszman and I were punished once together in Szent-
királyszabadja by being hog-tied for sneaking out into the village
to make a phone call to let our people know that we were still alive
and when we got back the platoon commander that rascal Garzó
whom I grinned at at his trial gave us each a collossal slap in the
face and said I COULD HAVE YOU SHOT BUT BECAUSE I
AM A GENTLEMAN YOU WILL ONLY BE HOG-TIED FOR
EIGHT HOURS AND WE WILL SEE HOW THE FUCK
YOU'LL MANAGE and when I was hog-tied with Wakszman
we played the city alphabet game and got to "R" when I fainted
and I will forever remember Roma Rimaszombat Rábca Retek
Rigó Rottenbiller and there was not much left and I said Wakszman you ass Retek Rigó Rottenbiller MY DEAREST DADDY
TÁBORI yelled Wakszman and we embraced BEAT IT BEAT
IT FOLKS said Wakszman I FOUND MY BROTHER and
everybody was happy to hear it because even those like to get into
the middle of such an event who have damn little to do with it and
so I got away with it but half of my body started to get numb and
hurt so that Wakszman got a cab and sends his love and will come
to visit next week and he put me in the cab and half way home I
started to choke but the chauffeur thought I was drunk and
stopped I told him I was not going to puke that he could relax that
I was a cardiac patient if he wants to he can smell by breath

  but it was not necessary and when I lurched into the office I
asked the typist whether anyone had looked for me but I could not
finish the sentence since as I stood I fell across the typewriter I
gave a yell and died sh'ma yisroel that's all I needed I thought because during the first few seconds I could not see the whole picture and I was a little scared not knowing how I would get out of
this and in addition the typist was screaming WHAT ARE YOU
DOING WHAT ARE YOU DOING COMRADE TÁBORI
TRY TO GET UP and Palugyai and Mrs Weisz came in with
PISTA WHAT'S THE MATTER PISTA GET UP QUICKLY

YOU CAN DO IT and I said kids this is from hunger it ain't going to work I am not going to get up until Borbíró gets back from lunch then I will furthermore you can talk all you will but the responsibility is mine nothing is too good for the kibitz after all I wasn't born yesterday he will come in nicely and will see what's up and we can negotiate from a common platform and not as you like it YOU ARE SO SMART they said IT'S ABOUT TIME HE FOUND OUT and with this they left and I pulled the phone over to me somehow and called our legal eagle that idiot Bányai to come over for a bit of chit-chat and he came right away but first he knocked twice

for instance that's one reason he's a moron knows exactly what's up but always wants to play the lord HAVE YOU THEN MADE UP YOUR MIND PISTA says he I TAKE OFF MY HAT REALLY DADDY-O FEW WOULD HAVE DARED TO DO THIS WHETHER THEY WILL TAKE OBJECTION OR NOT WHO IS TO KNOW BEFOREHAND BUT I DON'T BELIEVE THAT THERE WILL BE ANY TROUBLE what does it depend on I asked and it turned out that there were two possibilities

they either assume my good intentions or not

if so my case is won since they can kick up a storm all they want both Borbíró and the Federation of Coop Farms they can kiss my ass and let's look at the evidence besides

it happened during working hours

in the middle of the day

no national holiday anywhere in sight

there were two of them in there Palugyai and Mrs Weisz and the typist makes three

but let's not kid ourselves I am not a party member but don't be afraid either because Bányai had said that they could make trouble regardless but they won't not now BECAUSE THEY ARE ALREADY IN DEEP SHIT SINCE RIGHT NOW IT IS IMPOSSIBLE TO SAY AGAIN WHAT WILL HAPPEN

nothing bad can come of this it's a real gas and I began to suspect that I was NAGY and EICHNER but just to be on the safe side I called the ambulance and this was added insurance and I was so right

but this come later since in the meantime Borbíró arrived and immediately called I HEARD ABOUT YOU PISTA YOU

WOULD REALLY OBLIGE ME IF YOU WOULD COME IN
FOR A SECOND IF YOU ARE NOT TOO TIRED THAT IS
Dezső I said you got to be kidding you called and I came running
and you're welcome I went he bade me sit down played the host
offered me coffee and a cigarette and I HEARD ABOUT YOUR
LITTLE ACCIDENT he said WELL IF WE DIE I didn't say
anything of course at which he promptly became lugubrious
LOOK I DON'T WANT TO QUESTION YOU THIS IS YOUR
PRIVATE CONCERN JUST TELL ME IF THERE IS ANY-
THING WE CAN DO FOR YOU OUR COMPANY OUR
UNION IN ANY WAY AND SO FORTH Dezső said I there is
nothing that I need look I have reached my conclusions all I want
is peace that's the only thing I want and thank you very much at
which he started to scream WHO THE HELL DO YOU THINK
YOU ARE QUITTING ON US JUST LIKE THAT LEAVING
EVERYTHING TO FEND FOR ITSELF AND WHAT AM I
SUPPOSED TO TELL DOBROVITS listen to me Dezső I said
with a smile like a marquess to the purple born you don't know
what to tell Dobrovits where is a corner where I can have a good
laugh secondly get it through your head that everything is up in
the air not because I fortuitously had a heart attack which incidentally I wish you would have too you know what and this is really
too much you shoot Irene with your service revolver fine volunteer police help whisk your daughter from church that's your
problem my eyes are blind my ears are deaf but that you should
have the gall what the hell do you think I am damn it furthermore
I will say nothing *about that certain item* to anyone because I can't
and won't and because I am not you relax and with this I left him
to fume because I succeeded where he never will and returned
with utter nonchalance to my own room and there the rescue
squad was waiting for me

    I was king of the roost

    a nice young doctor came and we shook hands well I said no
use examining me my dear fellow my heart's no longer beating
but he wouldn't hear of it and said DON'T DESPAIR OLD FEL-
LOW JUST TAKE YOUR CLOTHES OFF I am not at all in despair I said go ahead and examine me maybe I have made a mistake
it has happened before

he listens with his stethoscope looks into my eyes blows into my mouth

dead as a doornail right I ask at the end

just imagine he did not want to admit it he hemmed and hawed

finally and with great hesitation he admits HE'S GONE a light goes on in my head I rise up if this is true may I please have it in writing my dear fellow

IT IS COMPULSORY said he THE PATIENT DOES NOT HAVE TO ASK AND PLEASE DON'T TALK ANY MORE AND COVER HIM UP WITH NEWSPAPER and in fact he sat down and filled it out and even put a seal on it everything in apple pie order ye these young doctors are quite different much more skilled and as soon as I had the paper in my hand I laid down on the ground and spread a whole bunch of newspapers on top of me aprés moi le deluge I thought and I can rest now don't you think

the rest is of no concern to me

something's bound to happen

but the hours are slipping by everybody has gone home and me still smelling the linoleum

what's happening I ask myself

nobody is coming

I still have to be buried and I really don't know what else there's got to be lots of things to do

and I jump up and curse like all the seven sacraments I am an idiot I forgot that you were on vacation I could have laid there until midnight nothing happens by itself I started to pick up the newspapers so that the cleaning woman shouldn't fuss at me in the morning she does not like it when I leave my junk around she is a nice old bag we like each other I always see her because I'm the first one in what's up old I say can't stand your bed or did your lover throw you out GET ALONG she says OR I STICK THIS DUST MOP UP YOUR ASS we always fool around a lot the poor woman has three sons but not one of them has seen her in ten years or even sent a postcard she will surely miss me

never mind I rushed home to make my dispositions and I wanted to take my clothes off and take a long shower but did you think that I could first the elevator wasn't working well when is the lift working I quarreled with Mrs Stefanik and sent her to her dam when she said

that they were providing MAINTENANCE listen I said don't you
have better things to do than annoy us you sit on your fat ass all year
and come around only at Christmas to collect your tips

this is a real scandal

I can't go up the elevator even when I croak

it's a good thing she did not say that they had turned off the water I would have smashed her head I am mad at her anyway since
she cheated me over the heating costs old money-grubbing whore
I had to climb up but as soon as I entered I stripped my clothes off
and sat at the telephone arranging the funeral first I did not know
how to begin but then I called the temple and talked to a mealy-
mouthed character who started by saying WE COME TO YOUR
MIND ONLY ON SUCH OCCASSIONS kiss my ass I said I pay
my dues you exist only to reach out a helping hand when somebody needs it and anyway what kind of a congregation are you said
I siding with the Arabs and the believers are without support so
then he gave me a telephone number which I called and had myself put on the waiting list thank God I did not have to wait for
many days that's all I would have needed in this miserable heat
and I asked to be cremated but they said that REGRETFULLY
THE CREMATORIUM WAS OUT OF COMMISSION and if I
insist I would have to wait for a week this is just my luck why
should anything go well but then I realized that it was all right and
they could bury me next to my mother they buried her so I guess I
can stand it too I asked how much it would cost they said that had
to be negotiated at the cemetery I must be dressed in my best
clothes and must have a cap on my head otherwise they will not
take me nu what happens if the relatives are away on vacation they
slammed down the receiver what these people think they can get
away with I wanted to call them back but came to my senses in
time just what I need for your mother to go into hysterics and me
feeling like I felt the last time I was floating in amniotic fluid so I
lurched out into the kitchen and gobbled up my diet vitamin salad
I forgot all about it and ate sausage all the time and I will be severely scolded by princess Emerencia Esterházy who is my wife but is
well preserved only the yolk turned to dust in the vinegar and I
slurped it all up and started in on the Blue Light you don't know
what you're missing on TV

it was an extraordinarily likeable murderer who did away with his landlady could not pay his child support stabbed her eighteen times but finally killed her with the floor lamp that he threw at the old woman but found only twenty-nine forints what a cock-up then he wanted to jump out of the window but did not have the guts and chose the death penalty and imagine Géza Hajdú asked him DON'T YOU SEE WHAT A CRUD YOU ARE and the fellow said I SURE DO BUT I NEEDED THE MONEY and his wife bored him that does not surprise me they showed her too she was missing five teeth in front what she had in the back I don't know but I know that if I had the choice I would vote for the noose myself and Géza Hajdú is an idiot that's a fact albeit his hairdo is magnificent his hair shines like the left nut of Salomon and if I had hair like that it's a cinch that even Lollobrigida would piss all over herself from letch what can I do this is the way it is this is the way you've got to like it I lied down and one or two days went by and I felt really swell alone in the apartment

I gobbled down the salad and watched the garbagey programs on the teevee and I did not open the door for the postman it was pure bliss occasionally I thought how surprised you will all be when you come home and discover that I had died and yet took care of everything so efficiently by myself

but for the big day I requested a telephone wake-up call just the same since I was not sure that I would wake up on my own in the morning the telephone made such a racket that I almost fell out of bed and in addition I had to give my name six times since she refused by God to believe that I was awake nobody believes how my voice sags and at the end I said golden flower since we have met like this don't you think it is time we met in person and the young lady said that she is not allowed to do that BUT YET IF if she wanted to see me she should come at noon to Kozma utca 6 and that this was the last opportunity when she hung up I chortled for half an hour she must have thought that I was kidding but she was wrong

then I rampaged around the apartment turned everything upside down you will notice that in the entire apartment there is not a single fucken cap only yours but that does not fit so that I put on my mother's red polka dot scarf and put the hat on top of it and then I trundled out to Rákoskeresztúr you would not believe what goes on on the tram

I couldn't get on till the second one and even then ended up shouting man is not an animal but an intelligent being but nobody gave a goddamn and poked me with their elbows and I had to stand all the way thank God at the Christian part of the cemetery a lot of them got off and so it was just us Jews

not many left

damned Hitler

I could have found a seat but by now I struck up an acquaintanceship with a nice little tart who visits her husband every day this is her *idée fixe* Alfréd Ring died in fifty-one from a myocardial infarct I think I knew him we went to industrial school together but I have not seen him since and I told the little woman she should come and visit me from time to time and she promised but Edith this should not phase you she has a moustache and also the dumpy type is not my style particularly not the sugary ones

but this made the time pass and when I got off my crazy sister was already waiting and a few *goyim* from the office all wearing hats I almost burst out laughing

Olga wouldn't get off my back brought all her girlfriends how she found out I haven't the foggiest she asked WHICH RABBI WILL SPEAK GORDON OR LADOS she knows them by name that's how dumb she is and then I saw this notice on the board saying that it would be my turn in half an hour in the mortuary

and I have made no arrangements yet

like a maniac I ran to the office to show them the paper I had from the ambulance people but I really fucked up because the first question was WHERE IS THE DEATH CERTIFICATE this made me break out in a cold sweat it is simply unthinkable that at the very last moment I should slip on a banana peel but the guy was very nice and we agreed that as an exception they could bring it in later do keep it in mind old girl these folks wouldn't think twice about digging me up again

of course he got some money so that he would keep his mouth shut for a while and I was not quite done yet because Olga said that if I wanted it done well I should give something to the Rabbi and the grave diggers a good thing I put some money into my billfold I would have never believed it of the Rabbi so help me he grabbed it like a goose a grasshopper true he was only an assistant but the grave diggers promised that THEY WOULD NOT SHOVEL ME UNDER TOO DEEP I don't know what that means but it must be important since apparently one can be shoveled under too deep I asked them to please not do that to me and not to disturb my mother and then I went over to the washerwomen and bribed them too they deserve it working with cadavers all the time I would not let them put rouge on me though they wanted to do something extra for me I said it was enough if they bath me and not reach into my drawers well this was a great success I could come back here any time and then they wrapped me up beautifully and wheeled me over to the mortuary there was quite a little mob and I can really be proud the colleagues came in a row to offer their best wishes the Gabos even cried and I said that we were all in His hands my dear Lali and then the Rabbi spoke

it was really moving you don't know what you missed you'd have seen the truth at last because he made no bones about it THIS ISTVÁN TÁBORI LYING HERE BEFORE US LIVED IN DIFFICULT TIMES BUT HE STOOD THE TEST AND ALWAYS KNEW HIS PLACE AND HIS ENTIRE BEING WAS FILLED WITH LOVE OF HIS FELLOW MEN but he particularly emphasized what an exemplary son and outstanding head of the family I had been at least as I understood it this was what he emphasized WHO STOOD IT WHEN HE WAS BE-RATED WHO STOOD IT WHEN HE WAS DEMEANED AND WHO FELT HAPPY ONLY IN THE CIRCLE OF HIS FAMILY this is what I had particularly asked him to mention since this is what I always told you as a joke although it is the bloody truth

and the cantor sang but regrettably only twice since I could not afford more these Jews really know how to sing look at all those opera singers half of them started as cantors though they deny it and this one was particularly gifted just greedy never mind it still suited me very well I almost started to bawl it certainly does not happen often to a man

and the entire congregation was sniffling and then we slowly started outside

the weather was gorgeous the coffin fitted like a glove not a
problem in the world I was just surprised and I thought of you my
son how you were not there and I could not guide your future way
with my parental advice but we can rectify that now I would like
you to be very careful my son
>and be alert and don't let yourself be diddled
>and don't listen to the others if it is the same
>for them don't let it be the same for you
>he who laughs last laughs best for the best
>is yet to come and if you squander
>your strength now what of the future you will tread
>a rocky road paved with regrets but you should
>find the enjoyable and the amusing in all things
>laugh clown laugh and shit
>on the world never mind the rest it will take
>care of itself greet
>everyone politely you can never
>tell what the future will bring and don't
>stuff yourself eat quietly nobody will
>take the plate from you and don't tear
>at your ear like that of you can help it
>no need for you to be nervous just look at me
>am I nervous though I would have reasons aplenty
>oh my what I have gone through and
>yet here I am and I don't tear at my hair
>in other words my sweet child my only request
>is that you don't allow them to fuck
>around with you send those who harm you to hell
>just don't be hasty you have time
>you have the means so don't run after
>women and trams you know that
>there will always be another one the world
>belongs to the wise or as the poet has it be
>efficient create multiply and your country will
>flourish just don't do it haphazardly do it wisely
what are you doing with your mouth I'll swat you one he's
blowing bubbles out of his saliva you come to the cemetery to
blow saliva bubbles son you're standing by my grave you jerk

he's a jackass Edit talk to him I won't stand for it on top of which you encourage him no wonder a weak man and a neurotic woman produce a crippled offspring what have you borne me panther of Nubia and why are you bawling I won't have it the guard will come running you must be quiet here don't sick the guard on me you will leave but I must stay don't you understand I mustn't get on the wrong side of him so many morons in one place nu don't go wait the best is yet to come

as soon as they lowered me down mother knocked and when I went over to her she welcomed me with PISTI DEAR PISTI HOW GOOD THAT YOU HAVE COME I WAS WATCHING THE CLOCK BECAUSE THEY SAID THAT YOU WERE COMING BUT YOU DELAYED EVEN THOUGH THEY HAD NOTIFIED ME A WEEK AGO and she showed me and in fact there it was on the night stand next to her mug the official certificate

in other words this thing was really carefully thought through you can see for yourselves what goes on here and since then I am always with my mother and I help her with everything I wash the dishes and do the dusting and sometimes she sings to me LITTLE LIPÓT LITTLE LIPÓT RÓTH MY LITTLE BOY LIP and I cap it by saying Mother this is not what I had bargained for and we sway with laughter

Translated by Thomas J. DeKornfeld

THE MIRACULOUS LIFE
OF PRINCE BLUEBEARD
by PÉTER ESTERHÁZY

For Helmut Heissenbüttel

Once upon a time, east of sodomy but west of oral copulation, out
where the short-tailed piggy and the kinky-tailed bluebeard rooted, there once lived an East-, or rather East-Central-European
Bluebeard, a *tzentraal-yurop-blaubart*. And he lived happily ever
after until he died. I could say a few things about this.

*

Meat was still rationed, but the rubble had already been cleared
away. The more simple-minded still believed in freedom and in-
dependence, but the Russians were very, very much here, when,
on Pebble Street, in an empty bunker above a deserted lot, Bluebeard, Don Juan and the ill-fated Casanova regularly met. If they
got caught, their mother gave them a whack on the hands. If not,
then everything was great. There isn't much to add to this.

*

Prince Bluebeard, a moderately gifted but (?) eminently diligent,
naturally sweaty piano major, was just practicing *Microcosmos*
when he stumbled upon the terrible secret of Béla Bartók. So now
what? (Let's remember the mood of wartime... The *Arrowcross*
coup hadn't happened yet, but it was already pretty clear that we
weren't going to rise to the occasion like Knights of the Holy
Grail, and even if we had, it wouldn't have been a big deal.) It
seemed most feasible to inform on Bartók to Kodály. Bluebeard
appeared at the professor's–foxy-loxy–saying that he would like
to continue his studies with Kodály.

 —What would be your reason for this, Colleague?—Kodály
frowned suspiciously, while doing his impression of Kodály-the-
fair-man, and rightly so.

— Oh, fuck off, let's cut the crap, you know very well what the score is!

— Get the hell out of here, Sir, and go back where you came from! Which remark could have become—wrongfully, let us admit at the outset—the source of so many altercations, underhanded, ignoble discussions, and ultimate pain, because, as is well known, Prince Bluebeard had come precisely *from* Bartók. In any case, this made the youth realize that it wouldn't be any better with Kodály than it would be later on with women. Well, I could certainly add to this.

*

Bluebeard's classmates began to call him Jewboy. He didn't make a big deal out of it, he took it as if they had called him an idiot, and he even remarked that he wasn't an idiot. But his classmates didn't let up, especially a guy named Kovács. All right, shrugged Bluebeard, so I am a Jew (namely, deep down he was thinking that he had to be something anyway, or rather he had read that somewhere, but who cares).

Then he was dragged off to Mauthausen. He was ninety pounds when he returned, often burst into tears, and on his skin, which had turned a disgusting gray, festering sores would break out, which took a long time to heal. He became taciturn, trusting neither the living nor the dead, nor the stones, nor the Danube. Then in 1945, barely eighteen, he joined the Communist Party because he wanted to break the silence somehow, but this didn't work out either. He also got involved in some shady dealings, was locked up, then around '56 he was let out, and then all was back to the same old tune, one way or the other.

By now he was no longer young. He should have sent little Kovács flying, but then he realized that that wouldn't be a solution, either. There could be more to this story.

*

Following the unspoken but perceptible wishes of the titillatingly exciting biology teacher, well endowed in the T & A department, he succumbed to lepidoctery; first he insisted that it could be done in any room except in that particular one, but we all know how butterflies are, you can talk all you want to—with them, it's out one ear and in the other—meanwhile the butterflies, swish, swoosh, in and out. Later on, he stopped insisting on the business about the room, and anyway, the biology teacher married the coach, a Fascist if ever there was one. There is nothing left to say, really, about this.

*

All his life, Bluebeard cherished a dream—and of this he didn't dare, or never wanted to, or couldn't speak with anyone—that once, on a quiet, melancholy autumn day, when no one would be roused by any desire, yet everyone concerned would become passionate, and would be dressed accordingly, not necessarily elegantly, but naturally, and most of all practically (I'm not going to tackle this for reasons of decency), and after having nibbled on something light, let's say sandwiches of goose-liver paté, washed down with a few splashes of Chablis—come to think of it, there should be a little music, all this not to give an impression of luxury, just completeness, so instead of goose-liver paté, one could have some cheap lunchmeat, and the music wouldn't have to be Bach, or even Vivaldi, a light, entertaining Scott Joplin would do, anyway, on this quiet, melancholy autumn day he would reach the pinnacle of his dreams, burying his head in his mother's lap, and there, amidst merry laughter and good-natured teasing, they would compare whose—shall we say—beard, was—shall we say—bluer. I have nothing to add to this.

*

Scout's honour, the same thing happened as what H. H. mentions in connection with a well-known, most probably German, woman writer, namely, when the Russians came in, Bluebeard, perhaps because of the pain he felt at Bartók's emigration, got hooked on oral whatchamacallit, and could absolutely distinguish by the taste whether these were—shall we say—from the southern flank of the army, those were Nazis, these were progressive Hungarians in hiding, or, *grüss Dich, Helmut!* I could still add to this story.

*

When, in the Jewish hospital named for Martin Heidegger, Prince
Bluebeard—with no mean resourcefulness, humanity and a great
deal of personal courage and perversity, managed to... Oh, what
the hell. Although one could say more about that.

*

Once, on the ferry called Sneezy, Bluebeard ran into a more-beau-
tiful-than-beautiful mermaid of the Danube, whose hair was au-
burn like ebony, with skin dark as alabaster, as plump as a reed,
light and breezy as Beckett, tall and slender as a hawthorn bush or
a dwarf pine. Without any foreplay, the doggone fellow started to
chew on his damsel's mouth, unless that *was* the foreplay.

— Ouch, that prickles, you little hedgehog!—squeaked the dumb
goose, about the beard, then voicing her wish that Bluebeard would
have it cut, or at least dyed, or else she would drop dead.

— So drop dead!—shrugged Bluebeard, but later he cut it off
anyway, and had it dyed to boot. As a matter of fact there's nothing to add to this.

*

— And how is your Mother?
— Thank you very much, terrific! Periodically she even goes on
a fruit diet!—bellowed the man, grinning into his beard. I really
don't have anything to say about this.

*

One of Bluebeard's girlfriends—the one with the big boobs—a
charming, high-spirited woman, would laughingly wake him by
pressing her breasts against his face: each morning the Prince was
almost smothered. Indeed, there is nothing to add to this, except
perhaps that in those days Bluebeard wore printed underwear.
There were different designs on his boxer shorts—a magic Rubik's
cube, a portrait of Bartók, a penis in the shape of a Moebius strip,
and so forth. The girlfriends had to be able to recite the designs by
rote. When he called on one, it was no laughing matter.

*

His girlfriend who time and again mixed up Joseph Roth and Robert Walser ("Come on, sweety pie, this is not Philip, that is not Martin, don't tell me that this makes sense to you...") began whining and giggling like some virtuoso Stradivarius in a high *flautando* until the glass windows, covered by a dubious insurance policy, cracked.

— I know you from way back—why have you kept it a secret that you had this in you?—asked Bluebeard indignantly.

— From way back, what goes around, comes around—answered the woman enigmatically. I really don't have anything to add to this.

Bluebeard exits. On one occasion, Bluebeard married Undine, the restless brook-nymph. As a matter of fact, there is nothing further to add to this.

*

That Prince Bluebeard was gay, impotent, sterile—in fact, a woman,—I shall barely mention, it seems so obvious in today's world ruled by irony and despair. In the morning, in that moment when he staggered back from the turbid undergrowth of dreams, and his still-muddled gaze readjusted to the world above, he immediately remembered that he was gay, impotent, sterile—in fact, a woman. Now will you please transpose this into Hungarian, where not a trace of women's lib can be found, and a man is a man—or so I have heard—if he can fuck a fly in mid-air, pardon my French. (I note parenthetically that precisely because of this way of thinking my days as a young man went to the dogs: I was watching them, that multitude of flies flitting, buzzing, swooning: horseflies, gadflies, and the pesky houseflies; I spied on them, I gawked at them, I marveled at them... and they attracted me and repelled me, but... oh, no... I could not bring myself to do it. All this just to illustrate how tough it is to be Hungarian. And *this* is not going to get any easier, even if, as they promise, the Russians leave...)

Dream's tulle angel still dwelt in Prince Bluebeard's eyes, new day, new adventures, but he stayed the same, gay, impotent, sterile—in fact, a woman, and because of this, this minute invariable, this tedious certainty, this humbling Archimedean fixed point, he was seized by such elation that the Danube froze over, or if it was frozen, it thawed, or if not quite, it became so thin that one could neither skate nor elect a king on it.

The prince ran down to the street and impudently stared into the oncoming faces. He did that every day. Stubbornly systematic, he covered the city from the sloping hills of Buda to the Downtown built for the western tourists, from the solemn gray outskirts to Margaret Island, reminiscent of the *fin-de-siècle,* and thus sizing up the naked faces of the people, by the time the many bells of Pest and Buda struck noon, the whole city was pregnant with joy. (Im Dreivierteltakt: Die Donau so Blaubart, so Blaubart...)

So why all this? Because one of us is gay, impotent, sterile—in fact, a woman. Why, I could still add to this story.

*

Eventually, to be sure, poor Bluebeard got knocked up! For days, he had felt under the weather, he was nauseated, but why should he have been suspicious? Picture yourselves in his place! Such nonsense, eh?! That a man should be pregnant, because, needless to say, Bluebeard was a real man's man.

At first it only seemed as if he had gained weight. He traded his size 33 jeans for a 34, then for a 35, then he bought soft corduroys. After a while he only wore sweats. Six months later, he felt the pinch of the elastic even in those. Granted, we could ask legitimately, why did the prince want to keep the little newcomer, if he was as godless as his reputation, or rather, if he was his own god... My God, this is a contradiction. Such is life, or perhaps not, but I wouldn't want to jump the gun.

Finally, the rugged-looking man had to give in and borrow the worn-out maternity clothes still available on Castle Hill(!)... which was especially gauche because these were obviously out of style. His wives proved to be true companions. In the evenings they sat around together, and one of them always made grapefruit juice, and so forth. There is nothing to add to this.

*

Bluebeard was cuckolded.

— I want to know his name!—he roared.

— I couldn't tell you even if you killed me — shrugged the merry little wife, whereupon the man promptly killed her, upon which the injured party immediately delivered the information, and that's what matters—i.e., that it was only a lie. There is nothing to add to this.

*

It so happened that for a long time he hadn't had anything to do with women or men, and even the beasts had avoided him (including opossums, who are known to be flirtatious) and, as a matter of fact, the tulips had, too. So he was hungry for... you know what I mean... When the prince made the turn toward the Brandenburg Gate, believing that no one was watching, he gave in and grabbed his... you know what. He was wrong, the German people had seen this and, true to their fine custom, were shocked. At that, Bluebeard was incensed, and in the manner of a bold and uncompromising man, risking an *ejaculatio praecox,* he exclaimed:—Everything has its limits!—and united Germany. There is nothing to add to this.

*

Since Bluebeard's mother was crazy about John McEnroe, and his father, Roman jurisprudence, they had divergent yet lofty ambitions for their son. He took everything to heart, nonetheless, and—who knows how—became a writer. He lived in a large castle (there would be more to say about this) with hundreds upon hundreds of rooms, but there was one he was not allowed to enter. It is not that he wasn't allowed, it's more that he couldn't, or rather didn't want to... perhaps, somehow, in the threefold hopelessness of freedom, knowledge and will. With each new book of his, to which he bound his life amidst elaborate nuptial ceremonies, he hoped that it would be the one... the one to clear up the matter of the room... but no, neither that one, nor any other... It was revealed, only, somehow it wasn't that room... or rather it was, but then along came another... and a new wedding... and then once again... forget it, it's too complicated.

He met an enchantingly pleasant man who was also a writer. When conversation turned to topics concerning the profession, modestly but with self-assurance the gentleman declared that, after all, though perhaps somewhat differently, he himself had achieved a thing or two. If I had anything to do with him, namely, if I liked him, Bluebeard thought to himself, I would now surely spit in his face or hug him; finally—so he believed—he understood his fate.

*

Even his father, old Bluebeard, had had shaky hands, and allegedly, so had his father's father. It was a grand old shaky family. (According to the family legend, the hands of one of his ancestors, a fanatical follower of Napoleon, who competed with the great Stendhal for the favours of a Viennese beauty, did more than shake: they undulated all the way down from his elbows.)

Bluebeard was barely thirty, but his hands were shaking so badly that, when he went next door to fix the broken blinds, even the clumsiest neigbour was fired up with pity and wanted to help him, which, to tell the truth, was not in the best interest of the blinds. And when he was offered a drink, he spilled it all over, and his hosts looked away tactfully. He noticed everything.

His habit was that he put his shaky, quivering hand—and now I'm not going to avoid, in a disgusting, obscene way, the word, calling it a dew-covered valley, or the chalice or honey-pot of joy, or Prince Bluebeard's castle—but rather, therefore, that he put it onto or into the cunt and he let it stay there and quiver and quiver and quiver. He suddenly thought of all the fixed blinds, all the spilled drinks, and the tactful sideways glances, and then everything became calm, sad and good like that autumn day that never was. I could say a few things about this.

*

A woman, or rather her baser self, said: I don't know what it is, a cold front or something, but I've been in love with you for days. To this I have absolutely nothing to add.

*

Ultimately... she succeeded in bringing out the Eric Satie in Beethoven,—the Prince sighed into his neighbour's ear. There is nothing to add to this, but there would be to the fact that the season ticket-holder on his other side, his friend's wife, was *called* Judith. Incidentally, the episode happened like this:

Tatyana Nikolayeva, who was more or less born in response to the famous (infamous shot of the cruiser Aurora—young lives on the marh, dilating cervix, Winter Palace—Tatyana Nikolayeva, who at the time of Lenin's death was a piano prodigy in her prime and a blossoming elfin creature, when—out there—we lost Béla Kun, who (not Béla) finished her studies in 1947 in Moscow, as a pupil of Alexander Goldenweiser, this Tatyana Nikolayeva decided to play, over eight evenings, all thirty-two Beethoven piano sonatas in the order of their composition.

Prince Bluebeard, who enjoyed uttering pronouncements about music (such as the *Pathétigue* is like the soundtrack to the four-part Soviet miniseries *Anna Karenina*) and could say a number of things which were bewildering because they sounded true, and in fact they were... on March 1st, 1990, Prince Blubeard once again noticed with delight, after so many years, that the chandeliers of the Music Academy had a delicate phallic shape, when the enthralling woman in her crazy Royal Blue get-up reached the second movement of the Sonata in E flat major, Op. 7, which she instantaneously took apart, as she did everything, not as violently as, shall we say, Gould, bit with no less pluck, and this *Largo con grand'espressione,* which is one of the master's most profound slow movements, fell into a state of constant existential uncertainty—that is, one could never tell whether there would be next note, whether the Blue Lady would strike it or not... then:

*

Danilo Kiš met Prince Bluebeard in the elevator. I have nothing to add to this.

*

A later biography will include that after 1956 the Prince was unable to find work in his profession, in Bluebeardship, and-so-on, as an unskilled worker, he made plastic buckles, and-so-on, *wo soll ich fliehen hin,* he started drinking and-so-on, then he was employed as a stand-in, he was Khrushchev with his shoe in the UN, the passionate Brezhnev, and-so-on, he smooched the world from one end to the other as Gorbachev (may I refer to the mortal kiss planted on Jakes' face in Prague, and-so-on, "sex as the art of the common man," or the scandal at Schönefeld, when he bit out a piece of Honecker's lips, and indeed the GDR collapsed, and-so-on, petting on the bank of the Oder-Neisse, and-so-on-and-so-on); there won't be anything to add to that later biography either. Well, there might be something more to say to this.

*

Bluebeard diary (self-repetition)
MONDAY	Me
TUESDAY	Me
WEDNESDAY	Me
THURSDAY	Me

But I could still add something to this story.

*

Prince Bluebeard, tiring of Judith (mezzosoprano), his previous women (silent roles), in fact, tiring of the eternal struggle of man and woman, of the woman who wants to become one with her beloved by finding out his every secret, tiring of the man too, whom reserve, the binding law of solitude, forces into secrecy (for if he revealed even his innermost, chastely guarded secrets, he would give up his very self) and tiring of the eternally elusive ideal, the one who doesn't want to unearth the secret of secrets, who loves Lohengrin/Bluebeard as is, together with all his secrets, full of blood, pain, tears, and perhaps sin, because we can only love Bluebeard if we accept the torture chambers, the weeping walls of the castle, the bloody-stemmed roses, the blood-drizzling clouds of sorrow (New Opera Guide, Volume 2), picked himself up and went for a walk with his friend along the Danube.

His friend was one of those few who are true believers: he believed in God. Therefore he listened to Bluebeard's pronouncements on the subject of angels and the Lord himself with delicate tact and understanding. These were mostly pompous, but they also contained a measure of pain so necessary, though not always sufficient, to be genuinely convincing. The Danube seemed immense like the sea, multi-storeyed waves rushing back and forth between the two banks, and the setting sun cast a golden bridge over the water.

Bluebeard took his friend by the hand and, like two nursery tots, they walked on together. I have nothing to say.

*

Prince Bluebeard's Hymn (after András Wahorn)

> *Well, love is here again*
> *Well, my palms sweat again*
>
> *What for, what for, what f r, what for*
>
> *Well, she is on my mind again*
> *Well, I want a good one again*
>
> *What for, what for, what for, what for*
>
> *Well, I see her everywhere again*
> *Well, I hear her everywhere again*
>
> *What for, what for, what for, what for*
>
> *Love again love again love again*
> *Love again love again love again*
> *Gotta spit pht gotta spit pht gotta spit pht*
>
> *Well, love is back love is back love is back*
> *Well, my palms sweat my palms sweat my palms sweat*
>
> *What for, what for, what for, what for*

*

When his time had come, Prince Bluebeard died. Now what should I add to this? Perhaps that he buried himself into his beard?

*

When Bluebeard was no more, a void sprang up: it had the prince's shape to the last millimeter. From then on, people called this nothing Bluebeard (because of the blueness of the beard). This I had to add. Hush little Reader... Had Bluebeard had a longer beard, I too would have had a longer tale.

Translated by Paula Balo and Martha Cowan

BIOGRAPHICAL NOTES

ENDRE ADY (1877–1919) One of the great 20th century poets who renewed modern Hungarian poetry with his many volumes of revolutionary verse. Starting out in journalism, he soon turned to writing *feuilletons* and short stories, of which several small volumes were published in his lifetime.

GÉZA BEREMÉNYI (b. 1946) Short story writer, novelist and playwright, his first volume of stories, *A svéd király* (The Swedish King) appeared in 1970. He has also written musicals, filmscripts, and song lyrics satirizing life under socialism.

ÁDÁM BODOR (b. 1936 IN TRANSYLVANIA) Trained as a theologian, he was one of first describe in realistic terms the situation of the Hungarian minority in Romania. His stories are known for their combination of emotional intensity with an epic, descriptive style and elements of allegory and the grotesque. His latest volume of short stories. *Az Eufrátesz Babilonnál* (The Euphrates at Babylon) was published in 1985.

SÁNDOR BRÓDY (1863–1924) Short story writer, novelist and playwright, his consumate artistry as a prose writer influenced many of the young writers who flocked around the avant-garde periodical *Nyugat*. Combining the social concerns of Zola with naturalism, he shocked many by his blunt presentation of sexual desires. Of his numerous novels, perhaps *A nap lovagja* (The Knight of the Sun, 1902) is the best.

GÉZA CSÁTH (1887–1919) Neurologist, gifted music critic and painter, it was under the influence of psychoactive drugs that he wrote his later stories. The first collection of stories, *A varázsló kertje* (The Magician's Garden) was published in 1908. Treating subjects such as matricide and the conclusion that anything worthy of excitement is connected with pain and blood, his focus was nevertheless always on the irrational and the mysterious. Work in English: *The Magician's Garden,* Corvina, 1978, Penguin, 1981

ISTVÁN CSURKA (b. 1934) Short story writer, novelist and playwright, his first volume of short stories, *Tűzugratás* (Leaping Over the Fire), appeared in 1956. Mixing realist tradition with satire, irony, humour and the grotesque, he is a popular portrayer of the conflict between different social groups. His bitter-satirical play, *Házmestersirató* (Lament for the Janitor), played to packed houses for years.

TIBOR DÉRY (1894–1977) Short story writer, novelist, playwright and poet, his first story appeared in 1917 in the avant-garde periodical, *Nyugat.* Among his best known works are the novels *A befejezetlen mondat* (The Unfinished Sentence, 1947) and *Kedves bópeer* (Dear Beaupére, 1979), and the musical, *Képzelt riport egy amerikai popfesztiválról* (Imaginary Report on an American Pop Festival, 1971), which ran for over a decade. Works in English translation: *Niki, the Story of a Dog,* Nelson, London-Edinburgh, 1965; *The Giant, Behind the Brick Wall, Love,* Calder and Boyars, 1966, *The Portuguese Princess and Other Stories,* Calder and Boyars, 1966.

PÉTER ESTERHÁZY (b. 1950) Short story writer and novelist known for his modern experimental prose, Esterházy leans towards the absurd, the grotesque and the ironic by manipulating language itself. Of his many works, one has appeared in English: *Helping Verbs of the Heart,* Grove Weidenfeld, 1991.

ENDRE FEJES (b. 1923.) Short story writer, novelist and playwright known for his portrayal of the social and moral conflicts of post-war Hungary. His novel, *Jó estét nyár, jó estét szerelem* (Good Night, Summer, Good Night, Love) 1969, was made into a highly popular television film and long-running musical. Work in English translation: *Generation of Rust,* McGraw-Hill, 1970.

ERZSÉBET GALGÓCZI (1930–1989) Short story writer, novelist and playwright who explores the lives of peasant families and the changes and challenges they have been faced with in modern-day Hungary. Highly relevant in theme, several of her stories have been adapted to the screen.

ISTVÁN GÁLL (1931–1982) Short story writer, novelist, playwright, editor and critic, he played an important role in promoting the careers of the new generation of writers to emerge in the seventies. His novel, *A ménesgazda* (The Studfarm), was made into a film. His last work, *Életem, műveim* (My Life and Works), was published posthumously in 1984.

ÁRPÁD GÖNCZ (b. 1922) Wheatland Prize winning translator of modern American fiction, dramatist and short story writer, his disciplined and deeply human works, subtle in perception and daring in technique, are a powerful response to the history of post-war Europe. Works in English: *Plays and Other Writings,* Garland, 1990, and *Homecoming and Other Stories,* Corvina, 1991.

LAJOS GRENDEL (b. 1948) Novelist, short story writer and editor-in-chief of the Hungarian-language journal *Kalligram,* published in Bratislava. His first novel, *Hűtlenek* (The Unfaithful) appeared in 1977, his latest, *Einstein harangjai* (The Bells of Einstein) in 1992.

SÁNDOR HUNYADY (1890–1942) Popular short story writer and illegitimate son of writer Sándor Bródy, he showed a deep understanding of characters who leave the safe ground of their natural habitat with the inevitable tragic result. Perhaps his best known story, *Bakaruhában* (Adventure in Uniform), was made into a highly successful film shown throughout the world in 1957.

ENDRE ILLÉS (1902–1986) Short story writer, novelist, playwright and essayist, by the thirties he was a leading literary and drama critic for the *Nyugat.* His writings are characterized by astute intellectual and moral discernment. A pioneer in modern Hungarian social drama, he was also a master of the psychological portrait. His last collected essays, *Mestereim, barátaim, szerelmeim* (My Teachers, Friends and Lovers) appeared in 1979, while his last collection of plays, *Kulisszák nélkül* (Without Backdrops), was published in 1981.

FERENC KARINTHY (1921–1992) Short story writer, novelist and playwright, he was the son of the great writer and humourist, Frigyes Karinthy. His first novel, *Don Juan éjszakája* (The Night of Don Juan), was published in 1943. Novels in English translation: *Spring Comes to Budapest,* Corvina, 1964.

FRIGYES KARINTHY (1887-1938) Prolific novelist, journalist and short story writer who belonged to the avant-garde writers of the *Nyugat*. One of his most original works, *Tanár úr, kérem* (Please, Sir, 1916), in which he brought the world of the schoolboy to life, is a perenial favourite. *Így írtok ti* (The Way You Write, 1912) is a collection of his brilliant parodies of the styles of other writers. As a translator, he is best known for his highly popular rendition of *Winnie the Pooh*. His *A Journey Around My Skull* (1937), which describes his battle with a brain tumour, was published in English by Corvina in 1992.

MIHÁLY KORNIS (b. 1949) Writer and dramatist whose short stories, beginning with the wolume *Végre élsz* (You're Alive at Last, 1980), and his first play *Halleluja* (1979) made him an instant success with audiences. The fascinating blend of autobiographical inspiration, social criticism, a penchant for the grotesque and stylistic innovation set his writings apart from his contemporaries.

DEZSŐ KOSZTOLÁNYI (1885-1936) Novelist, short story writer, poet and translator, his works are characterized by a flair for form, and a combination of precision and psychological insight. Of his prolific prose output, he is perhaps best known for *Édes Anna,* the saga of a poor servant girl driven to kill her employers through humiliation. Works in translation: *Darker Muses: The Poet Nero,* Corvina, 1990, and *Anna Édes,* Corvina, 1991.

GYULA KRÚDY (1878-1939) Novelist, short story writer and journalist who introduced a revolutionary new technique which in many respects was the forerunner of the stream-of-consciousness narrative. The Sindbad stories which he began writing in the 1910s and in which memory is the chief source of his narative material, are favourite reading to this day. His *Szindbád* was turned into an award-winning film in the 1970s, while his *Rezeda Kázmér szép élete* (The Beautiful Life of Kázmér Rezeda, 1944) was made into a play.

JÓZSEF LENGYEL (1896-1975) Poet, short story writer and novelist, his works first appeared in the avant-garde publications of 1916, 1917. A number of Lengyel's works have been translated into English and published by Peter Owen of London: the novel, *Prenn Drifting* and two collections of short stories, *From* *the Beginning to End* and *The Spell,* all in 1966; *The Judge's Chair,* in 1968, *Acta Sanctorum and Other Tales,* in 1970, and *Confrontation,* in 1973. His historical novel, *Bridgebuilders,* was published by Corvina in 1979.

IVÁN MÁNDY (b. 1918) Short story writer, novelist and playwright, he is drawn to the world of out-of-the-way streets, market places, movies and taverns. His style is characterized by a neo-realistic style coupled with rapid changes of scene and an excellent ear for dialogue. His story, *Régi idők mozija* (Movies of the Good Old Days, 1967), was made into a highly successful film. The collection of stories, *On the Balcony* (Corvina), appeared in English in 1988.

MIKLÓS MÉSZÖLY (b. 1921) Short story writer, novelist and playwright, his first volume, *Vadvizek* (Wild Waters), a collection of short stories, appeared in 1948. He was among the first to attempt the renewal of the traditional short story through the use of the grotesque and a narrative technique reliant upon allusions and secondary meanings. His short novel *Forgiveness* appeared in *A Hungarian Quartet* (Corvina) in 1991.

ZSIGMOND MÓRICZ (1879–1942) Novelist, short story writer and playwright, he came to notice in 1908 with his short story *Hét krajcár,* published in *Nyugat* in 1908. The greatest figure of Hungarian realist prose, he looked at society as through a magnifying glass. His *Úri muri* (Gentlemen Make Merry, 1928), which was later made into a film, gives a devestating portrayal of the financial and moral collapse behind the apparent tranquillity of the bourgeoisie. His *Seven Pennies* (Corvina), a collection of short stories, appeared in English in 1988.

PÉTER NÁDAS (b. 1942) Short story writer, novelist and playwright, his first volume of short stories, A *Biblia* (The Bible), appeared in 1967. In his explorations of his youth and the history of his family, he has brought a new style and form to realism by making use of the elements of the grotesque. His major works include the novels *Egy családregény vége* (The End of a Family Novel, 1977), *Emlékiratok könyve* (Book of Memoires, 1986), and *Nézőtér* (Auditorium), three one-act plays published in 1983.

GÉZA OTTLIK (1911–1990) Short story writer and novelist, in his works he concentrated on the possibilities for growth and choice open to the individual. His writing is characterized by rigorous thinking and analysis coupled with an objective, epic style. His best known novel, *Iskola a határon* (1957), was published in English as *School at the Frontier* by Harcourt, Brace and World in 1966.

ISTVÁN ÖRKÉNY (1912–1979) Short story writer, novelist and playwright, his first book, *Tengertánc* (Dance of the Sea), appeared in 1942. He is best known for the grotesque and the absurd of which he was a master, and his drama, *Catsplay* (Macskajáték, 1966), which was also made into a film. Prose works in English translation: *The Toth Family,* a novel, and *The Flower Show,* short stories, both published by New Directions, New York, in 1982.

KÁROLY PAP (1897–1945) Novelist and short story writer who was first published in *Nyugat*. A moralist and a mystic, his chief concern was with the dilemma of Jewish existence. His apocryphal stories, written in plain yet powerful prose, were often inspired by the Talmud. Of his novels, *A kereszt nyolcadik stációja* (The Eighth Station of the Cross, 1933), is the allegorical story of a painter's struggle to create a portrait of Christ.

FERENC SÁNTA (b. 1927) Short story writer and novelist, he is primarily concerned with questions of integrity and morality. His two novels, *Az ötödik pecsét* (The Fifth Seal, 1963) and *Húsz óra* (Twenty Hours, 1964) were made into successful films. A selection of his short stories, *God in the Wagon,* was published by Corvina in 1985.

GYÖRGY SPIRÓ (b. 1946) Short story writer, novelist, playwright and journalist, whose writings have attracted a devoted following since the late seventies. Most of his works have focused on Central European history.

SÁNDOR TAR (b. 1941) Poet and short story writer inspired by the lives of the poor in the Hungarian countryside. His first volume of short stories, *A 6714-es személy* (Passanger Train 6714) was published in 1981.

Dabasi Printing House, Dabas